Half-Life

Half-Life

a novel

Aaron Krach

alyson books
los angeles

For my mom, Mary, with much love.

And for Dick Jefferson,
without whom a dinner under the open sky,
where this book was conceived, would never have taken place.

I am deeply grateful to several people who have supported me and this book in exceptional ways (some massive and others minor yet mysterious): David Bartlem, Dan Cullinane, Jill Dearman, Robert Guinsler, Jim Hubbard, my sister Raquel, Gary Kramer, Michael Liberatore, Jayna Maleri, Ned Rote, Gary Simko, Brian Sloan, Nick Street, Paula Tushbai, Letta Venegas, and Leonara Weiner.

Manufactured in the United States of America.

This trade paperback original is published by Alyson Publications,
P.O. Box 4371, Los Angeles, California 90078-4371.
Distribution in the United Kingdom by Turnaround Publisher Services Ltd.,
Unit 3, Olympia Trading Estate, Coburg Road, Wood Green,
London N22 6TZ England.

First edition: May 2004

04 05 06 07 08 a 10 9 8 7 6 5 4 3 2

ISBN 1-55583-854-5

Credits
- Cover photography by Brand X Pictures (landscape) and Aaron Krach ("Enough #1," courtesy of Paul Sharpe Contemporary Art, New York City).
- Cover design by Matt Sams.
- Author photo by Jason Charles.
- Lyrics to "We Are All Made of Stars" © Richard Hall Music Inc.

"People they come together,
People they fall apart.
No one can stop us now
'Cause we're all made of stars."

—Moby

Star-studded. Desolate. As empty-looking as the desert it was built upon. Incomprehensibly wide—like the Milky Way—rotating around nothing but its own metaphysical force, Los Angeles is centerless, a metropolis pushing forever outward from its own confident sense of entitlement over the surrounding hills and into the valleys and desert plains beyond.

In the center of all this spectacular centerlessness is Angelito, a town very much like the rest of L.A. The sun shines every day, and rain falls only during the winter. Palm trees line faded asphalt streets. There is crime and sadness. There is Little League baseball and love at first sight, fistfights between sixth-grade enemies, and excellent shark fin soup at the Mongolian Palace in the new shopping center on Garfunkle Avenue.

Angelito is called Angelito because late in the afternoon on February 15, 1972, a single mother of three—Mrs. Fernando Velasquez Delouvier—saw the face of an angel in a tortilla she was frying to make tostadas for her family's dinner. No one else saw the face she claimed to see because by the time she realized what she had seen, recovered from the surprise, and pulled the sizzling shell out of the boiling oil, the tortilla had burned to a crisp, and the angel's face had vanished into the darkened corn. But that didn't matter because Mrs. Velasquez Delouvier told her neighbor, and he called his friend who worked at a local television station.

By six o'clock, Mrs. Velasquez Delouvier's celestial sighting was the top story on the evening news, and no one has questioned the veracity of her tale ever since.

"She was beautiful, with a long face and feathered hair…beautiful brushed-back hair, like Farrah Fawcett's," she told the reporter who came to interview her. "But she was more beautiful than any movie star."

Everyone who heard the story either believed Mrs. Velasquez Delouvier completely or never admitted their disbelief, and so her story carried far beyond her kitchen, neighborhood, and surrounding area. The story traveled so far that today, the 9 square miles surrounding her home (or what was Mrs. Velasquez Delouvier's home; the Wongs live there now with their two kids, ages 6 and 9, and beagle named Boris), is officially called Angelito—"Little Angel" in Spanish.

Don't look for Mrs. Velasquez Delouvier in the *Who's Who of 1972*. Don't look for the town of Angelito in the maps put out by Rand McNally or AAA, or on any other map of Southern California. The town does not exist except to those who live within its boundaries. To them, Angelito is 100 percent real, as real as the paper in your hand right now. The citizens of Angelito don't know they are living in a fictional place, a city created by an author looking for the quintessential Southern California locale in which to set his first novel. And I would prefer if you didn't tell them about the situation. At least not yet.

Sunday, June 6, 1999

"I'm hungry," Dart said, more bored than hungry.

"Damn," Adam said, not to Dart sitting across the way, but to the *Los Angeles Times* spread across his lap. "Did you see what that Mahoney idiot—Cardinal of God knows what—said about bombing the shit out of Yugoslavia?"

"I need something to eat."

"He says—quote—'it's part of a just war.'"

"Really?" Dart mumbled as he hopped, unnoticed, from the 4-foot cinder-block wall separating Angelito's biggest 7-Eleven from the Korean barbecue restaurant next door. "Well, I'm so hungry I could eat two small Yugoslavian children and still be hungry."

Adam paid no attention.

"Does he have any frickin' idea what kind of an idiot he sounds like? I mean, fine, think like a selfish idiot, but please, keep those thoughts to yourself. Don't say them out loud. And...don't say them to the *L.A. Times* for all the world to see!"

Now Dart was pissed. It was one thing for Adam to ignore him—Dart was used to that. But for Adam to ignore his attempts at humor was another thing entirely.

"Adam," Dart said, with his right hand on his hip. "They gave us the Yugo. Do you really fucking care?"

Forgive Dart. He isn't a mean person; he doesn't hold the entire

3

ex-country of Yugoslavia in contempt. Dart is just frustrated with Adam and tired of feeling ignored.

Dart and Adam are both 18. They're both healthy, middle-class, intelligent, reasonably attractive young men. Okay, so Adam is a little more conventionally handsome, and Dart has more of a nerdy-cool thing going for him. They've been class-mates since Mrs. Hart's third-grade class ("Like the Valentine," she'd say, "not the organ.") and best friends since the fifth grade, when they both discovered the immaturity of their fellow class-mates, and the exquisite utility of the telephone for sharing their contempt with each other. As they grew older, they developed better strategies than gossip for dealing with the "ridiculousness of humanity," as Dart called it, and the "disappointments of life," as Adam liked to point out. Sarcasm and biting wit became their weapons of choice.

Now, late in the afternoon on a particularly warm early-summer evening, Adam was annoyed. He looked up from his crinkled news-paper and saw Dart's face twisted into a combination of cranky and cute. Adam knew all Dart wanted was to make his trip inside "the Sev" (as they and their friends always called it) a collaboration, a pseudo-mini group effort. Maybe he would get something for Adam. Maybe Adam would suggest the perfect snack. Maybe he would tell him to buy the red coconut Zingers they used to share all the time. And maybe, just maybe, the red dye (or whatever made them taste so good) would now, this afternoon, taste just as good, as weird-good as they did when they were much younger.

Adam could see all of this and more churning around inside Dart's head. He was the poster child for Complicated Ridiculousness, and Adam knew he needed to say something nice to snap Dart out of his funk before it was too late.

"Maybe, Dart, you don't need a snack."

"What?"

"Maybe you shouldn't give Mr. Sevvy any more of your money. Maybe you don't need any more junk food. Maybe you don't need to spoil your dinner, which I'm sure your sweet mother is hard at work preparing as we speak."

Dart was vaguely surprised to learn that Adam had even heard his hungry complaint, but he was not impressed by Adam's pithy response.

Adam continued: "Just think, if you don't waste another dollar inside, you could start saving up and perhaps retire that tired blouse you're wearing someday."

"This?" Dart said, pulling his shirt away from his chest like it was cold and wet. "This is not a blouse."

"What is it then?"

"It is a classic polo."

"Bet you didn't think I was listening to you about your food issue."

"I know you weren't," Dart said.

"Then how'd I know you were hungry?"

"I don't know," Dart looked away, thought to himself, and then continued. "You know what your problem is?"

"No. What?"

"Well, it's only one of your problems—you've got so many problems—but your main problem is that you don't know the difference between classic and camp."

"Oh, God, Dart. Save me the Susan Sontag bullshit you think you learned in humanities last year."

"Adam, my friend, this is vintage Izod. See the alligator? By the size of it—it's bigger—you can tell it's the old logo, the original. The mouth is much larger than it is now. This is the original Izod Lacoste design. And as such, it is a *classic* piece of design. It relates to history, to rich white people playing tennis as much as it relates to preppies who just want to look like rich white people who play tennis."

Dart was on a roll, and all Adam could do was listen.

"Now let's take a look at your wannabe-vintage tiki torch–printed...*thing* you are wearing. Although it is less wild than some of the other secondhand things you have sported this season, it refers, semiotically speaking, only to mai tai–soaked Polynesian-theme

1960s bachelor parties. It is singular where mine is plural. Thus, yours is camp, while mine is classic."

"Dart, I'm afraid you are having a low-blood-sugar moment and may need something to eat after all." Adam lifted his right hand and waved Dart dismissively toward the Sev. "Please go run along and get something, hopefully something with a lot of refined sugar, like Pixie Sticks. Something that can deliver the sugar to your system with the least resistance."

Dart didn't stick around to hear Adam's final words. He left just as Adam raised his hand and entered 7-Eleven's overly illuminated interior alone.

Adam adjusted himself on the cinder-block wall. The sky was turning from blue to purplish gray. It was 7:35 P.M. He thought about going home soon. There was only one more week of regular classes left before final exams—and a year's worth of information to review. Adam also had two more books he needed to finish for his American literature class—*Ethan Frome* and *The Sun Also Rises*—before the week was through. He decided that when Dart returned, he would suggest they head home. They both lived a few blocks away, although in opposite directions.

When they were younger, they rode their bikes to the Sev whenever they could. They played video games and bought candy and messed around for hours. Adam remembered first bonding with Dart over what they later dubbed "endurance candy," like Blow Pops and Now and Laters—candies you have to suck on a very long time before they disintegrate. They competed to see who could keep a mouthful of Atomic FireBalls or Lemonheads in their mouths the longest before choking or having to spit them out.

By the seventh grade, Adam and Dart had moved from video games to magazines, from *Entertainment Weekly* to *People*. Sometimes they'd even buy *The National Enquirer, The Globe,* or *Hello!* but only if some celebrity had been caught doing drugs in a bathroom stall or breaking a heel on a rainy sidewalk. And only if there were good pictures to prove it. They especially liked to read the tabloids when there was a story about a gay celebrity embarrassing himself or herself by flaunting gay love in front of the president, or denying he or she was gay by suing an ex, who claimed to have blown him, for $10 million. Both Dart and Adam were gay, as you might have figured out by now. They never actually admitted this to each other. There was never a *Stand by Me*–style coming-out scene between them. They just both started to assume that each knew about the other, and eventually both of their closet doors were wide open, the hinges removed, and the parts sold for scrap.

From grade school pals to high school confidantes, one thing remained constant. No matter how short or long their stay at the Sev, they always bought Big Gulps—usually filled with Dr. Pepper—and drank them while playing video games, or used them to wash down the chunks of candy stuck in their throats, or simply to pass the time. During the particularly hot summer of 1995, they took a Dr. Pepper hiatus and drank Slurpees. But Adam and Dart tired of their slippery frozenness quickly and returned to Dr. P. before the end of July.

Adam folded the crinkled newspaper back together and checked each side to see whether he had missed anything important. Meanwhile, Dart pushed back through the Sev's glass doors. They shut quickly behind him with a muffled whoosh, trapping the sour scent of microwave hot dogs and stale air conditioning inside.

"Can you believe they want 75 cents for this tiny bag of roasted almonds?"

"You're shitting me!" Adam declared.

Dart stared at Adam with disgust. "Is vulgarity really necessary when discussing the price of almonds?"

Adam ignored him. "What did you get me?"

"Nothing."

"Liar."

Dart tossed Adam a foil bag that matched the one he was complaining about. Adam ripped the bag open with his teeth, poured more than half of its contents into his hand and tossed the nuts into his mouth.

"That was probably 40 cents you just ate in one crude swallow," Dart said.

"Since when did you become a penny-pincher?"

"I am not a penny-pincher. But you, well, you're a pig."

With his mouth half full, Adam suggested they head home.

"Why?"

"I got stuff to do."

"Like?"

"Like reading and stuff. None of which I'm doing any of sitting here."

"No, you ain't," Dart said dismissively.

On the way back to the truck Adam detoured by the front of the store to toss out the newspaper and the shiny wrapper that seconds earlier had held roasted almonds. Bright lights shone on him. Someone was pulling into the empty parking space next to his truck. As he turned, all Adam could see were two automotive supernovas of bright, white light blaring at him like the UFO in *Close Encounters of the Third Kind*. The headlights finally dimmed when the car was turned off. Adam walked to his driver's side door with green spots dancing across his retinas. It was an Angelito police car that had pulled in right next to him. It wasn't black and white like in the old days. It was a converted Ford Taurus, white with baby-blue detailing and the words ANGELITO POLICE DEPARTMENT printed across the side in harmless Helvetica. The car looked like it should be used to deliver clean diapers rather than speeding tickets.

Adam thought it was just the green glowing spots obscuring his vision of reality, but when he looked into the car, he swore he saw the most handsome policeman he had ever seen (on TV or in real life). The officer's jaw swooped gracefully to his cleft chin, which looked gently indented as if by a butter knife. His tanned skin was leathery and tough. He looked like "Man" in the biblical picture books Adam remembered from Sunday school.

The mysteriously hunky officer must have liked what he saw walking past his window; his eyes followed Adam as he stepped inside his truck. Adam and the officer made the kind of intense eye contact that people sing about in country-music songs. Meanwhile, Dart waited impatiently on the other side of the truck for Adam to unlock his door.

"Hello!" Dart hollered across the truck's roof.

Adam's concentration was broken. He slid the key into the hole, turned it, and opened the door. At the same moment, the cop opened his door and out came a huge black boot only slightly scuffed. Adam sat down, pulled his door shut, and reached over to let Dart inside.

"Finally," Dart moaned. "I thought I was going to be left standing there forever."

Not that Adam paid any attention. He was too busy watching a leg, clad in black polyester, follow the boot. Then another leg, just as thick, emerged from the car. On top of both legs rested a belt loaded with gear—a gun, a club, a radio the size of two sticks of dynamite, and a pair of silver handcuffs. Above the arsenal, polyester continued, tightly wrapped around a solid torso, squared off and as wide as any man's chest should be. A line of black buttons ran up the center. Over the heart hung a badge in the shape of a shield with MANFIELD embossed across its shiny surface. Then there were the shoulders, broad enough to stretch any size of uniform shirt. They were connected to muscular arms covered in a light fuzz of blond hair. The arms ended in hands big enough to do whatever they wanted. On top of it all, a slightly grown-out, dirty-blond buzz cut, just shaggy enough to look cool while clean-cut enough to command respect.

Adam tried to take all the information in while the officer walked toward the Sev. He tried to read the name on the officer's badge but couldn't make out more than the first three letters—MAN. Adam was sure he had to be hallucinating. Too much Dr. Pepper combined with the blast of photons from the car's headlights must have warped his brain. This was Angelito, after all—a city not known for producing specimens of manliness, or womanliness, for that matter. He had to be imagining everything. Adam shifted into reverse just as officer MAN-something held the Sev's door open for the female officer who had been driving the car. Before Mr. MAN entered, he looked back at Adam—straight at him—as if he recognized him or something. But then, just as quickly, he turned and went inside.

Adam pulled his steering wheel sharply to the left and made a wide turn until his truck pointed out toward the street.

"Hell...o?" Dart said.

"Yeah, what?"

"Don't yeah-what me, honey. You were cruising that policeman. I saw you."

"I was not."

"You were so." Dart looked out his window as if there was something more important going on outside, even though there wasn't. "I know cruising when I see it, and that was cruising."

"I don't know what you're talking about."

"Your mother doesn't know what you're talking about."

Dart laughed. He knew he was right, and he didn't need to push it. Adam, on the other hand, didn't care that Dart had caught him because he was still reeling from the strange gravitational pull he'd just felt toward a total stranger. He'd been seriously transfixed for a few seconds and wasn't sure how he felt about it.

Dart leaned back confidently and put his feet up on the dashboard. Adam's car was a clunker, so it didn't matter where Dart put his feet.

Although it was officially evening, the temperature still hovered in the low 80s. Dry, warm, comforting wind blew inside the cab through the wide-open windows. Adam dropped Dart off and then drove home. In his room, he finished the last 20 pages of *Ethan Frome* for English class and was surprised by how taken he was with the wintry novel. Although its characters, and their lives, were very different from his own, Adam found the book's ending painfully authentic.

Down the hall, Adam's dad sat at the kitchen table and worked on report cards. Greg was a teacher at Sally Ride Elementary School, only a few blocks away. Greg looked like a teacher—thin and kind, with dark hair that always appeared in need of a trim. Adam and his younger sister, Sandra, had lived with their dad ever since their parents had divorced eight years ago. Their mom, Vivian, left Angelito for Hancock Park to be closer to her job "in the industry." So Adam and Sandra could continue attending the same schools, Greg became "P.U. 1" (parental unit #1). The problem was,

he shouldn't have. Greg was depressed, and his depression preoccupied him.

There were peaceful times—months, even years—when Greg
functioned almost as well as any father. During these times a light
haze blurred his vision—not everything was awful, and everyone
wasn't selfish and self-absorbed. Or if they were, Greg was able to
not notice. During the good times, it was as if he simply couldn't see
as clearly. And without the visual reminders of why he should be
miserable, he wasn't. But most of the time, Greg's vision was too
clear, when everything he couldn't avoid bore down on him...it was
bad, and it affected everyone. There were days when Greg simply
couldn't find the strength to get out of bed. On those days, Adam
would call his dad's school and tell them his dad was "sick" with a
cold or that his "allergies were really acting up" and he wouldn't
make it in today. Greg would stay hidden in his room, praying for a
universe of factors to realign and clear his mind. No prayer ever
helped. Greg's darkened horizon was only ever temporarily clear,
and the knowledge that another low pressure system would follow
each period of calm made even the good times painful to endure. For
Greg, these days were filled with anxious waiting, a dull pain, and
the inability to see goodness right in front of him.

Tonight, the only noise in the dining room where Greg worked
was the sound of his pen moving across paper. He hated noise of any
kind and tried to avoid it whenever possible. As he assigned his students letter grades for their cumulative efforts over the year, Greg's
mind wandered. It wandered to thoughts of sleeping, to scenes of
consoling rest. Greg wondered why it was so painful to finish his
report cards when he knew it meant the year was finally over, that
summer was just around the corner and he wouldn't have to work
for another three months. Why couldn't he find some pleasure in
handing out A's and B's and a few C's to students he had taught over
the course of the year?

Greg knew he had shared knowledge, passed along information, and taught his 31 students something this year. He knew he
should feel good about that, but he didn't. The end of the year

meant summer had arrived. And once summer begins...Greg could only get this far before his mind darkened. Once summer begins...it ends. When it ends, school starts again, and the cycle begins all over again. Making things worse, it was Sunday night, the night when the whole week lay ahead of him.

After exhausting himself trying to stay focused, Greg didn't even close his notebook, stack his folders into a pile, or transfer them to his bag. He just got up and walked to his bedroom. *Tomorrow will be easier*, he told himself. The week would begin, whether he liked it or not, and he would try—really try—to do his best to ride the momentum of time, to take some comfort in the fact that Tuesday followed Monday, and then Wednesday, and so on. He would try to use the forward push of time to his advantage, instead of seeing it as a force beyond his control, an evil churning force in the world that goaded him on, when all he really wanted to do was stay still, hold onto himself, and make sure he was okay. *I will try—really try*, he told himself again as he dropped his pants and crawled under the covers with his underwear and T-shirt still on.

At 1:59 A.M. Eastern Standard Time—10:59 P.M. in Angelito—a sonic boom echoed across central Florida. A second equally loud blast of flattened sound followed moments later. At 2:02 A.M., the Space Shuttle *Discovery* became visible to the handful of Floridians still awake and waiting for it. The shuttle was approaching the runway at Cape Canaveral at 2,500 feet per second. To the naked eye, such speed was an illusion. The shuttle appeared to be floating gracefully, an intergalactic glider easing its way back down to earth. The transition from distant invisibility to landing took less than a minute. At 2:03 A.M., after 230 hours aloft and 153 orbits of planet Earth, *Discovery* touched down smoothly on the specially reinforced tarmac.

Touchdown brought to an end a trip that had included *Discovery*'s first docking with what will someday be the International Space Station. Now it is only the Russian module Zarya connected to an American module called Unity. *Discovery*'s crew of seven astronauts—four men and three women—spent six of their days in space attached to Zarya-Unity. They delivered batteries, water, and hand tools to the station for later visitors to use. Their journey was only the first of 86 trips before the station could be turned into a livable unit of extra-earth housing. In the great expanse of space that held them safely for 9 days and nights, the crew also left behind a 19-inch mirrored satellite called Starshine. Its purpose: to reflect light back to earth so students would be able to track its course in science classes around the country.

No national media outlets carried the space shuttle's landing live as they had done at the beginning of the shuttle's history. Even if some channel had, it was unlikely anyone in Angelito would have watched it. At the exact time *Discovery* touched down, Adam was on the last pages of *Ethan Frome*. Dart was online researching Berkeley, where he'd be moving in the fall. Greg had long since taken a sleeping pill and fallen asleep.

They had all heard sonic booms before—quite often, actually—when the space shuttle landed at Edwards Air Force base north of Los Angeles. During the early days of shuttle flight, they always landed there and sent regular earth-rattling booms across the sky. In the '90s, when NASA began saving money by landing the shuttle closer to its departure point in Florida, Angelito residents were no longer regularly reminded of man's ability to slip through the sky.

Monday, June 7, 1999

Typical Southern California perfect: blue sky, yellow sunshine, and hot: 94 degrees Fahrenheit, no breeze. There hardly ever is in L.A., except during the fall when the Santa Anas blow, or near the beach, where the wind can blow with enough force to compel palm trees to bow humbly down. Everywhere else, the air settles into dense layers: dusty soot around your ankles, just-clean-enough-to-breath for the next 10 feet, then smoggy—gray and greasy—for the next several thousand feet, and finally crisp and clean above that, so the tops of the San Gabriel Mountains are visible. And then, above that, nothing, just pure atmosphere until the universe ends, if it ever actually does.

Under such ordinary conditions—such ordinary but flawed beauty—an ordinary accident unravels in the center of town. A car, a foot on the wrong pedal, a jump over the curb, and a crash. Except isn't every accident—if it is truly an accident, meaning that there is no good reason for it to have occurred—extraordinary? And isn't the same true for the brilliantly sunny days that fill the calendars in Southern California homes. *You live in L.A.? God, it's beautiful there. The weather is perfect.*

Two years and two months before today, on April 7, 1997, Adam Westman turned 16. For a gift, his father bought him a used truck: a dingy white 1989 Mitsubishi Mighty Max that looked like it had belonged to a gardener. Greg thought it was the responsible thing for a father to do. *Give your son wheels,* he thought, *and, well, he might go someplace. Or, at the very least, he'll be able to take care of himself and give his old man a break.* Adam had a different angle on why he was given a car, but he accepted the keys anyway. They weren't wrapped in a misleadingly large package as a surprise. The truck wasn't parked in the driveway early in the morning with a red bow on the roof either. Deciding to buy the car had been exhausting enough for Adam's father, so over dinner the night before Adam's actual birthday, Greg produced the keys from his pocket and set them on the table next to Adam's dinner plate.

"Happy birthday."

"Thank you."

The gift wasn't a surprise. A couple weeks earlier, Adam's mom, Vivian, had tipped him off. Years after the divorce, Vivian still held a grudge against Greg and tried to be cruel to him whenever she had the chance. The bitterness was pure malevolence given the fact that she was the one who had initiated the divorce because of Greg's lethargy, her own growing ambition, and the prospect of finding a younger, more handsome husband to push around.

Regardless of his parents' games—and he knew they were little more than spiteful games—Adam acted grateful for the car. Getting a car for your 16th birthday was a big deal, he knew. But he disagreed with his dad's motives, and he wasn't afraid to share his opinion with his friends.

"It's called guilt. Ever since my mom moved out, he's been trying to look like he gives more than a rat's ass about us. Also, it lets him off the hook. He doesn't have to run Sandra or me around town anymore. I'm sure he's hoping I'll become the Westman taxi service. I'll be doing the shopping, taking Sandra to school, all kinds of shit now."

"Adam!" Dart said.

"What?"

"Do you know how bitter you sound?"

"Bitter? I'm not bitter. I'm being honest. This is the shit, I'm telling you. I see it. I can see what's right in front of me, you know."

"Well, so what?" Dart continued impatiently, "Even if you are right, and it's all just shit, are you going to stare at it forever or are you going to look someplace else for a while? Can't you just forget the shit for five minutes and give us all a break?"

This afternoon, such bitterness was further from Adam's mind than it had ever been since he turned 16. Today was one week and four days before graduation, and Adam was coasting. His view was fixed on a state of independence that appeared right around the corner. Things he used to be so angry about didn't seem to matter anymore: teachers who didn't realize he was the smartest kid in the class, friends who didn't stick by him over the years, parents who took little interest in his daily life. Now there were new things for Adam to worry about, like where to work for the summer and how to pay for school in the fall. Unlike a few of his classmates, Adam wasn't nervous about passing his classes and not graduating.

"You're in way too good of a mood for a Monday," Dart said when he met Adam at his truck after school.

"Well, it's our last real Monday at this godforsaken place." Adam opened his door and left it open, allowing the hot air trapped inside to exit.

"But we do have those little things called finals next week."

"Yeah, but this was our last full day of regular classes," Adam said as he threw the key over the hood so Dart could open his door and let the air out on his side too. "And Dart, if that isn't enough to lighten your mood, then, well, you are in worse shape than I thought."

Seconds passed. *Click, click*. Doors shut. Engine on. They rolled out of the Angelito High School senior parking lot—SENIORS ONLY the sign read—and down the road until a four-way stop sign directed them to halt.

Still disgruntled, Dart reached over and turned on the radio. The music sounded scratchy. It always did in Adam's truck. His stereo was the standard factory-installed unit—AM-FM, no CD—the kind that came right off the assembly line. After a minute, Dart realized what was playing: Adam's newest new thing...oldies. Adam thought they were brilliant. "So chipper, so innocent, so painfully happy sounding," he'd argued. "They're ironic."

"Oh, God," Dart moaned as he reached over and flipped the dial to another station.

"Excuse me, uh-hum."

"Adam. Don't you think your taking this whole retro thing a little too far?"

"Retro thing? Who's got a retro thing? This music is *classic,* which is something I thought you were an expert on."

"Right, and wrong."

"You got something better to listen to?" Adam asked, flipping the dial back to where it began.

"Yeah, I do. Like, um, just about anything else. Except jazz. You know I hate jazz."

It was Adam's car, so he won. Jan and Dean, the original beach bums-turned-pop stars, crackled out of the speakers built into the truck's doors. *"When I get to Surf City I'll be shootin' the curl."* They pulled in front of Dart's house, a big stucco box that looked like it could sleep a dozen, but housed only four: Dart, his mom, dad, and younger brother, Julius. A perfectly fertilized, chartreuse-green lawn ran from the front porch to the sidewalk. Two round shrubs, shaved too close to their trunks, stood symmetrically by the steps leading to the front porch.

"I think you get out here," Adam said.

"You're right."

Since Adam got his truck, he drove Dart to and from school. Dart had a car of his own—a dinky Toyota Tercel his parents gave him for Christmas last year—but he kept riding with Adam. At first, driving to school together was fun. Then, as the years passed and both acquired more responsibilities—and less time to hang out—the minutes spent driving to school and back became "quality time," the only time they were ever really together alone. Neither of them would ever call it quality time. That was way too Oprah for either of them to admit out loud.

"What about later?" Adam asked before Dart shut his door. "You're not still working on that astrology project for Mr. Nichols are you?"

Dart halted his exit, stuck his head back into the car, and looked at Adam like he had two heads. "Adam, you are a relatively smart guy. My mom thinks you're a goddamn genius. Remember when you built a model of the Watts Towers out of sugar cubes in the sixth grade all by yourself, and told the teacher I helped you, which I was supposed to do, but you didn't like the way I glued the pieces together? Anyway, that's beside the point now isn't it?"

"I hope so."

"Well, no matter how smart anyone else thinks you are, you're an idiot. It's astronomy, not astrology."

"And?"

Dart slammed the door and walked away without further comment. Then he turned back. "Pick me up around 10."

Like every Monday afternoon for the last 11 years, Adam's dad emerged from an insignificant door built into the wall of an office building designed to blend in with the condominiums along Ramona Street. Each week, when Greg walked out the very same door, he looked like he'd been to infinity and beyond. And not in a good way. Today, if Greg had left his psychiatrist's office a half-second earlier, he would have seen his son drive down the street in front of the building after dropping Dart off. But he didn't, so Greg walked to his car oblivious to the world around him. He was so burdened by the weight of his session that everything else slipped past him without resistance.

Greg always arrived at his appointments feeling slightly thrilled by the idea that this session might be "the one," the final breakthrough that would push him back from the edge of chronic sadness. Then, about halfway through, he realized the same issues came up again and again without resolution. Why did parenthood seem like such a duty instead of a blessing? Why did living seem so difficult for him but not for others? Why did the world seem to be in a constant state of decay that he was unable to stop or at least slow? These issues were confronted but never overcome, and Greg's relative optimism invariably deserted him by each session's end. It didn't matter how much "progress" they made, as Dr. Myra Erosovic always tried to point out. Greg's same life was always waiting for him outside the peace and calm of her office.

Greg checked his watch to see when he needed to begin steeling himself for the session's end. He did this every week, but today Dr. Erosovic called him on it. "You always look at your watch when we have 15 minutes left."

"I don't want you to charge me for going over."

"But I have never charged you for running over."

"I don't think we've ever run over."

In spite of the sparring, today's session offered Greg a morsel of insight. Because it was in such a weird building, Dr. Erosovic's office had a sliding glass door that led to a pathetically small terrace. The mini patio was only decorative, just big enough for a single chair and a pot of purple impatiens. *A horrible little plant,* Greg thought: over-exposed and genetically warped from decades of inbreeding. This afternoon, Greg focused on the sliding glass door that separated him from the little area of fenced-in nothingness. The air inside was freezing, but outside, the impatiens were wilting under the afternoon sun. Greg's mind grabbed onto the concept of glass, and how mysterious it is. He remembered his old science class. Glass was actually an extremely slow moving liquid, yet solid to the human eye, and able to separate hot from cold, air from water. What a perfect, if pathetic, metaphor for his own head.

"I think sometimes there is a piece of glass in my head," he told the doctor.

"What do you mean?"

"Like there's a barrier that I can feel but can't see or move that stops me from feeling better, even though I want to."

"What do you think that barrier is? Where do you think it is?"

And around they went until the session ended, right on time, and Greg left feeling he had not communicated his idea very clearly, which depressed him even more. He walked out, missed Adam driving by, and headed to the back parking lot where his blue Honda Accord was parked. He opened the door and sat inside. He didn't wait for the heat inside to escape; he just shut the door and didn't roll the window down or reach for the ignition. He sat and began to cry. He cried until his body adjusted to the stifling heat. He cried until he couldn't cry anymore. When his tear ducts were empty, Greg wiped his face with napkins he dug out from the pocket of the car door. Then he started the engine and drove away.

Three blocks west of Dr. Erosovic's office, In-N-Out Burger straddled the corner of Ramona and Fremont. Inside, workers in red-and-white uniforms served burgers, fries, onion rings, milk shakes, and soft drinks—the only items on the menu. Greg drove by In-N-Out on his way to pick up Sandra. He didn't notice the line of cars five deep at the drive-through. He was oblivious to everything, including a woman changing her child's diaper on the trunk of her Nissan Sentra and two police officers sitting at a table outside.

"You know, Jeff..."

"Yeah, Sue..."

"If you don't eat the cheese, you save 110 calories. No mayo is another 100. But I don't think they put mayo on these. So..."

Sue was a no-nonsense cop with almost 10 years experience on the force. She was attractive, almost pretty, in a tightly wound kind of way. She was healthy and physically fit, a condition her form-fitting uniform clearly revealed. Her look wasn't overtly sexual; it was more purely physical, more athletic.

Sitting across the red fiberglass table was Jeff Manfield—equally healthy, about five years older, and judging by the thickness of his chest, quite strong. He stood 6 feet 2 inches and weighed 194 pounds. His sun-bleached buzz cut came down the sides of his face into two evenly trimmed sideburns. He might have been 38 years old, but his perfectly pressed uniform—which was just a tad bit too small for him—made him look younger, like a boy whose parents hadn't replaced his clothes fast enough. It also made him look bigger and stronger, as if when he'd get really pissed off, his muscles would flex and burst through the fabric, like the Incredible Hulk. Personality-wise, Jeff was beyond mellow, especially compared to Sue. Where she was outspoken, he was reticent. Sue would give a speeding ticket to someone going five miles over the legal limit. Jeff was the kind of cop who'd give a warning to Mario Andretti. As a kid, Jeff had been reticent and insecure. When he was 14 he grew five inches in one year and put on 30 pounds. He hit six feet by the age of 16 and realized there wasn't anyone he couldn't beat the hell out of—if he had to. Such a confidence boost, brought on by a purely physiological change, was his turning point, although it didn't completely force him out of his introverted shell.

Sue grew up as daddy's little girl in Beverly Glen, a kind of step-sister of Beverly Hills. She was given anything and everything she ever wanted, which was fine until as a freshman she moved into the dorms at the University of California, Irvine, the cute pseudo-public college in Orange County. It was then that she looked around and saw her life for what it was: easy. She quickly began having panic attacks and developed an anxiety disorder that demanded a prescription for Tofranil, Klonopin, and occasionally Xanax. Her turning point came after college—after she graduated with a degree in sociology. She wanted to do something useful, something physical, and something positive that would also burn off some of her extra energy, so she decided to become a police officer. It worked. Now she was down to a single dose of Zoloft a day and was fine officer of the peace.

Jeff still bugged her, told her she's too "worried about life," which was true. But Sue was also worried about her future, worried about the ground beneath her feet and whether or not it might give way at any minute because of the Big One. But at least she had these fears under some kind of control. Jeff wasn't perfect. He may have developed a healthy level of confidence, but he is still shy at times. Growing up, he could be a real loner. He was happiest keeping to himself, hiding away from a world that seemed always ready to rip everything away from him.

Jeff grew up in Costa Mesa—not far from U.C. Irvine, actually—in an area where orange groves had been replaced by tract houses. One positive aspect of growing up in O.C., as he still called it, was that the beach was nearby. He spent a lot of time there, sometimes with friends, more often alone. And he still did. For as long as Jeff could remember, he hated the suburban banality of Orange Country, so he moved closer to L.A. as soon as he could, which was right after high school. He missed having such easy access to the beach—a place where it's just sand and surf and you. Jeff often thought time spent there was mystically special. He might have even called such moments "spiritual experiences" if he believed in that sort of thing. Now he drove from Angelito to his old haunts—Huntington Beach or Newport Beach—to "catch a few waves" and spend a few hours metaphorically lost at sea. At 38, he wasn't the oldest surfer still riding the waves. He wasn't the youngest either.

"You know, I'm not superstitious or anything," Jeff said after swallowing another high-calorie bite, "but don't you think it kind of feels like earthquake weather?"

"Nah," Sue said. "It feels heavy, a little humid, but it's not hot enough. The air's gotta be hot and heavy and still."

Before Jeff could reply, the police radio attached to the thick leather belt wrapped around his solid, 34-inch waist, crackled with electricity. Sue's squawked too, and they both reached down to adjust the volume simultaneously.

"*Crackle, crackle*"—something about an accident—"*crackle, crackle, crackle*"—at the corner of blah-blah and blah-blah—"*crackle, crackle, crackle.*"

"Damn," Sue said, looking at her half-eaten hamburger, which would now go unfinished.

"Just think of the calories you're saving," Jeff said.

With two flicks of their wrists, they tossed their uneaten food into the garbage. Two steps back and they slipped into their squad car and pulled out of the parking lot with a brief, high-pitched squeal of rubber against steamy pavement. Sue turned on the flashing lights and took off as if they were in hot pursuit of America's Most Wanted. They didn't know that the accident they were heading toward was small, that there were only minor injuries, except for the driver who somehow plowed into an ice-cream shop. There would be little they could do to help. Down Margarita Street, left on Curtis. They passed Eleanor Roosevelt Elementary School, where Greg's Honda Accord was double-parked alongside an entire row of over-size family cars and SUVs. Greg was sitting inside the car, waiting for his daughter to exit the faux-brick schoolhouse at the end of her day. He paid no heed to the flashing lights passing him by.

Although she was only 11 years old, Sandra felt "at least 16" and sometimes acted about 65. More confusing, she didn't look a day over 8, thanks to a growth spurt that had not yet arrived. While all the other girls in Sandra's class were getting their periods and still towering over their male classmates, Sandra felt like she was being held back by something beyond natural explanation. Maybe something like God.

Sandra left Ellie at exactly 3:16 P.M. The final bell rang at 3:15. Everyone called it Ellie because there was a Roosevelt High two towns away and Eleanor Roosevelt was difficult to say quickly, especially for the younger kids. As the other students scurried past like chickens released from their coop, Sandra meandered toward her dad's car. Laid-back compared to other 11-year-olds, Sandra was in her own lit-tle realm of existence, and in there, she was in a constant hurry. Finally, she opened the door to Greg's car, jumped inside, and swung it shut behind her. She slipped the safety belt over her shoulder as Greg pulled away.

"How was your day, honey?"

"Fine," Sandra said with a singsong cheerfulness. Sandra could hum before she spoke her first words. As a toddler, she had sung so often that people stared and wondered whether there was a problem. In kindergarten, Sandra liked singing time so much she would cry when it ended. Now she had grown out of her propensity for emotional outbursts. She was 11, after all, and had long ago realized that no one can sing forever. She sometimes spoke as if she still wanted to sing but wouldn't let herself.

"My day was awful," Greg interrupted. "Two kids got sick and threw up after lunch."

Greg was a fifth grade teacher at the other grade school in Angelito, Jackie Kennedy Onassis Elementary. (Yes, there had been something quite feminist about the school board back in 1978 when Angelito was officially incorporated as a city. All the elementary schools were named after famous women. The junior high schools were all named after local military contractors—Northrop, Boeing, etc.—so the girl-power elementary school names were a good balance. The one high school in town—well, that was named Angelito.)

Sandra was used to listening to her dad complain. Apparently, being a teacher simply sucked. According to Greg, fifth graders were "not cute" and "not grown-up," even though they "thought they were." Then there were his fellow teachers and the principal and the school board: all "without a clue." It wasn't really as bad as he said it was. During the school day, when Greg was in front of the class teaching his students—imparting some piece of knowledge that he knew would help them later on—he forgot about himself. And for those brief moments, he stopped seeing the world as a place of complete hopeless horribleness and felt at peace. The rest of the time he was miserable.

Sandra reached for the car radio and turned it on.

"Oh, no…not today." Greg turned the radio's knob quickly back to the left until there was no sound and then continued his lament. "The air conditioning was out again today too."

As if Sandra cared.

"It must have been 100 degrees in there." Greg's body verified his account of an awful day. His hands fiercely gripped the wheel, his shoulders hunched up toward his neck, and his body bent forward as if he was looking for something important. "It's just too much," he said to himself.

Sandra sank down in her seat, leaned her head back against the upholstery, and watched the tops of the houses whiz by in a stream of diagonals. She followed the rooflines up, down, up, down. She was unaware of the cars around them, each slowly coming to a standstill.

"God, what is with this traffic?" Greg asked no one in particular.

They were still a block away from the cause of the congestion—an accident involving a station wagon that had plowed into the window of a Baskin Robbins. Didn't look like anyone was hurt, just a lot of broken glass. Everywhere the ground twinkled, as if littered with tiny stars. Yellow police tape and burning flares, a fire truck, ambulance, and two police cars surrounded the shop. Officers with blank faces diverted traffic away from the scene, while paramedics extricated a woman from behind the wheel. It was Sue directing traffic from the south while Jeff spoke unintelligibly into his radio on the north side of the street.

"Are you wearing your seat belt?" Greg asked Sandra as officer Sue Williams waved them by.

"Dad…" Sandra said, drawing the word out into a moan. "Why do you always ask me if I'm wearing my seat belt whenever you see the police? I always wear my seat belt."

"Because," he began, but then stopped for moment of silent frustration. "Because I'm the dad and you're the kid, and you have to do what I say."

On the other side of town, slinking through a slow sprawl of traffic along the 405, Vivian sat behind the wheel of her silver 1998 Saab convertible. Ms. Vivian Randall—she had gone back to her maiden name after divorcing Greg—produced low-budget television shows for export. Ever since the Berlin Wall came down, she and her production company had been making big money hawking crap television shows like *Alexandra the Great* and *Operation Dionysus* to the Eastern European masses. All the shows featured female stars with enhanced bosoms wearing skimpy "period" costumes and fighting evil in all its many television-ready forms. No matter the quality of her company's product, Vivian dressed as if she worked for a major studio, which was where she wanted to be. But because she was and forever would be known by insiders as the queen of post-Communist crap, she was destined to create the stuff for as long as there were cable channels eager to carry it. *Might as well make the best of it*, she told herself. *Better to make good money if you're going to be making something this ridiculous.* Not that Vivian was particularly thoughtful about exactly what she was doing; she stayed too busy to think about the pointlessness of her life's work. That's one of the beautiful things about ambition: it can delude people into a dreamy state of "happiness," which is exactly where Vivian's soul thrived.

Vivian's ambition was a major issue during the last years of her marriage with Greg. She had absolutely no problem making schlock for money, though Greg was appalled. When he was younger, he had grand ideas about learning and growing; he thought he was marrying a woman who was going to make movies, create culture. He had fantasies about being part of a couple that made something relevant, that gave something back.

Bling-idi-bling-idi-bling.

"Yeah?" Vivian yelled into her cell phone.

"Hi. It's me," said Marc, her husband, Adam and Sandra's stepfather. Marc was standing silently in his spotless "professional" kitchen. He was home in the afternoon because he was always home. Marc worked from home, in an office at the end of a long hallway. He was a writer of sorts—more of a creator, some would say—who produced miniature inspirational seize-the-day kind of books, the ones that sell for $2.95 by the checkout counter at the drugstore.

"What's wrong?" Vivian barked.

"Nothing. I don't only call you when there's something wrong."

"Oh, yeah?"

Marc decided to avoid confrontation for the moment and continue. "I just wanted to make sure you remembered we're having dinner with the Nortons tonight."

"What time?

"Eight."

"What's wrong with Fidolo?"

"Hunh?"

"I can hear him barking."

Vivian's little chow-chow was yapping at nothing. He was sitting back on his hind legs and staring up at Marc. It wasn't dinnertime; he didn't want to go out.

"Yeah, I don't know, he's been acting snippy all day."

"Well, be nice to him," Vivian said, like she believed Marc was actually being mean. "Anyway, honey, where is dinner?"

"La Limonetta."

"Limonetta, you mean. There is no *La*."

"Whatever," Marc said.

"Okay, fine, I'll be home soon, but there is tons of traffic, so who knows."

"Oh, no," Marc said. He sounded only slightly, if genuinely, concerned.

"Oh, yes."

The kitchen in Adam's house was small and crowded—in automotive terms, a beat-up two-seater compared to his mother's year-old Saab. Adam's entire house could be described as lived in, compared to Vivian's, which looked like no one had ever lived there. Everything happened in the small kitchen in Adam's house. Meals were eaten. Homework was completed. Mail was opened, read, and tossed into the garbage under the sink. Schoolbags were loaded and phone calls were returned. Tonight, Adam and Sandra unpacked take-out pizza and salad from Angelo's, where Greg had stopped on the way home. At the kitchen table, Greg flipped through junk mail while he listened to the local news coming from a small television perched on the kitchen table.

"Today's first-stage smog alert across the Southland surpassed last year's record of 61 alerts by this time. Counting today, we've had 62 days of first-stage alerts, 35 of which also had second-stage alerts. Tomorrow looks to be another day of poor air quality. A second stage alert is not out

of the question, according to meteorologists. Children and the elderly are being cautioned to stay indoors."

"Sandra," Greg said, without turning from the television. "Did you have a smog alert at school today?"

"No."

"What good is it to tell us now?" Greg's hands dropped into his lap. "Our kids played outside all day."

The anchor continued reading (and smiling). *"A double homicide in Arcadia this morning. A cleaning lady found her employers dead when she showed up for work at eight o'clock. Police say there was no sign of forced entry or robbery and that all leads are being investigated."*

"Oh, man," Sandra said, catching a glimpse of a bloody arm dangling from a gurney as the victims were wheeled out of their house. "How gross…"

"Sandra, don't watch that," Greg snapped. "I've told you before."

"It's the news, dad," Adam said.

"She must have bled to death," Sandra said, purposely trying to provoke her father again.

"Sandra!" Greg barked. "Stop."

"Relax," Adam said. "She's just kidding."

Greg got up from the table and threw away his garbage. He couldn't believe his own son scolded him. Greg tried his best to show that he didn't care what his kids did or said, but he did. Greg had primary custody of Adam and Sandra, and he felt that meant he deserved more respect. Problem was: Greg's authority was created by default when Vivian said she only wanted them every other weekend. Her career made it "impossible" to commit any more time than that, she said. Granted, that was during the semiheated divorce, when her first hit show, *Ariel,* was number one in Georgia (the country, not the state). But Adam never forgave either of his parents for their selfishness.

Greg pulled from the fridge a half-gallon of low-fat milk and set it on the table. Adam slid the pizza box into the middle and opened it. He sat across from his dad, as if they were both parents, with Sandra between. With the television turned off, they ate in silence, something Adam always hated and always tried to avoid.

"Great salad, Sandra. You fluffed Angelo's greens perfectly."

"Thanks," Sandra said without looking up from her plate. She knew Adam's style and how to roll with it.

Greg, on the other hand, had been Adam's father for 18 years and still didn't understand his sense of humor. He took 90 percent of everything Adam said the wrong way.

"Adam," Greg began, trying to steer the conversation away from wherever absurd place his kids were about to take it. "Graduation is next week, and I know we haven't planned anything. If you want to do something, well, I don't know, have a party or something, we could—"

"Oh, whatever," Adam said. He hated when his dad tried to be nice. From him, it always felt so forced.

"Don't *whatever* me. If you want to have something, I want you to, but I just don't think I have enough in me right now to do something major. I've got my own school year to finish and report cards to write. This is always a busy time for me."

"Fine. It really doesn't matter," Adam said, unable to keep his annoyance from tipping toward anger.

Greg tried to ignore the chip on Adam's shoulder—a chip much bigger than the large pizza they were eating. He wanted his son to know that he cared, so he continued: "Maybe we could do something small, have a few friends over for pizza. Then later on, in the summer when I have more free time, we could do something bigger."

"Dad, it doesn't matter," Adam said, genuinely wishing the conversation would just end. "It's not a big deal."

"Maybe Dart and your other friends, those girlfriends—what are their names?" Greg looked to Sandra for help. "The one with the earring in her nose and her friend with the, um, very short hair."

"Fran and Veronica," Sandra said, her eyes never rising above the Bermuda Triangle between her mouth, her plate, and the slice of pizza in her hands.

"Yeah, them."

"It's so not necessary. Please forget about it."

"Forget it? Why are you so negative? I'm just trying to…"

Greg's voice trailed off to nothing as he plunged his fork into his salad and stabbed at it until slices of lettuce were stacked an inch thick. Then he slid the fork across the side of his plate until the leaves were all knocked off. What had he done to deserve such an ingrate for a son? Greg was pissed off, but for him, anger turned easily to sadness. "Don't ever say I didn't try," he muttered. "I'm sitting right here right now, trying to throw you something for your graduation, and you are acting like you couldn't care less."

Frustrated and verging on rage at his father's self-pity, Adam was unable to separate his own needs from his father's. "I said I don't care. What part of that don't you understand?"

"Fine," Greg said. And silence crept back over the table, slowly engulfing them like smog.

Four years ago, after the long hot summer of '95, when Adam and Dart traded Dr. P for Slurpees, a new girl named Fran ("the one with the earring in her nose") moved to Angelito and joined Adam's and Dart's eighth grade class. She was from San Francisco and arrived with two moms: her birth mother, Kay, and her "friend," Bailey. Not just because she had two mommies—although that helped—Adam took an instant liking to Fran. He thought she was particularly cool. On her first day, she wore a black sweater vest over a green, long-sleeve shirt, which she left untucked so the shirt-tails hung over her sharply pressed khaki trousers. Adam called them trousers because they looked like the same kind of pants his dad wore. Her look was "way" renegade for Angelito.

Dart didn't take as quickly to Fran, probably because he knew how much Adam liked her and, quite simply, he was jealous. He wasn't keen on sharing his best friend with a new girl, no matter how cool she was. But once he got to know her crude sense of humor, he was quickly won over.

Fran was no dummy. She knew exactly what was going on and quite honestly liked both Adam and Dart. Of all the kids at Northrop Junior High and then at Angelito High School, they were easily the coolest, the most like her friends back in San Fran, as she liked to call it. Before anyone could spell "alliance," Fran was hooked on Big Gulps at the Sev and addicted to Dr. Pepper in a way that would frighten dental experts. Yet to this day, Dart wouldn't shed a tear if Fran moved to Alaska or was exiled to a barrier island off Belize. He would still like to have Adam's friendship all for himself.

Fran worked part time at a trendy restaurant called Limonetta. She was a host; the pay was only decent, but the place had a really cool vibe that kept her there. Fran was a pretty butch. Her hair was cut in a clean mod style, and at the moment she was favoring low-slung pants and heavy-looking shoes. She wore a small silver stud in her nose. While most places in Angelito wouldn't hire her, the hipsters at Limonetta liked Fran's look. "Slightly abrasive," one owner said to the other. "Might give us some edge."

Limonetta was a pioneer in the California cuisine scene back in the early '80s. Then it was "out" through the early '90s. But with a new chef from Thailand via Paris, the place was packed "like in the old days," a critic for the *L.A. Times* wrote. Fran didn't care about the food or the pretentious all-white décor. She liked the staff, who were from all kinds of places other than Angelito. There were a dozen gay actor/model/waiters, two lesbian owners, the Thai-Parisian chef, and a slew of busboys and kitchen guys who thought she was cool as hell because she spoke to them in Spanish.

Vivian and Marc fit perfectly with the pretentiously chic crowd at Limonetta. Their friends, the Nortons, were less perfectly coiffed but still ridiculously put-together. Fran wouldn't have even noticed them if she hadn't known they were related to Adam. They didn't look anything like him, she thought. Vivian was tall—5 foot 10—and slender as an actress. Marc was too tan, too blond, and too buff, Fran thought, especially for a writer who works from home. But what did she know, she decided. At the end of their meal, she delivered a plate of lemon cookies—Limonetta's signature post-dinner freebie—and said hello.

"Oh, hi, Fran," Vivian said, her eyes never rising from the silver tray. All eight eyes focused on the four perfectly round white puffs of lemon pastry. Mrs. Norton looked up at Fran and said "Hello" while everyone else plopped a cookie in their mouth and smiled like only the overly satisfied can.

In the parking lot, "goodbye, goodbye" and "thank you, thank you" came from every mouth—twice—as if repetition implied sincerity. The valet brought the Nortons' car first, and they got inside, slipped the driver a waxy dollar bill, and drove away. Before they were out of sight, Marc smiled and said, "That was nice. I'll call Julie tomorrow and get the name of that new place they stayed in Santa Barbara. It sounded great."

Oblivious to her husband's sauvignon blanc–induced glee, Vivian whipped out her cell phone and dialed her office to leave someone a voice mail. "Terry, it's Viv. Just thinking about tomorrow's meeting with Mr. Pukskili from Tbilisi and wanted you to prepare two more copies of the script before the meeting. I want Elizabeth and Brian in on it."

Marc checked his watch: 9:50 P.M. He would get home in time to catch the news. Marc was obsessed with following the weather; something about knowing the future was elusively seductive to him. He paid little attention to Vivian's conversation, just as she had shown little interest in his comments about dinner or Santa Barbara. Each slid through life dependent on the fact that the other was there, but ignorant of each other at the same time.

For as long as Adam could remember, Greg's bedroom had smelled like hand lotion. More medicinal than flowery, and not medicinal like iodine, but therapeutic—a combination of BenGay-ish mint and dusty homeliness. It all mixed quite sickly with the stuffy, dusty air held hostage by the fact that Greg never opened his windows. With student papers lying in a pile around him on the bed, Greg watched television and marked "check" or "check plus" on each one. Tired and unable to keep his eyes open, Greg hovered between sleep and the distracting dialogue coming from the old television sitting on his dresser. Inside the monitor, men in tight suits and women in tighter dresses spoke in hushed but artificially urgent tones. *Goldfinger* was on.

Down the hall, Sandra read Judy Blume's *Tales of a Fourth Grade Nothing* with her doll, Jacqueline, perched safely beside her in bed. She read by a small lamp intended for much younger children; yellow dolphins and pink ponies were stenciled around the base of the shade. Poor Jacqueline: if only dolls had feelings. Sandra's grandmother had given Sandra the doll when she was very small. It became an instant favorite because at the time Vivian was still an enthusiastic parent and spent time buying extra outfits for Jacqueline. A bond between Sandra and her mother developed, and Jacqueline felt real. The doll didn't feel real; Sandra's feeling for it did. Jacqueline became a symbol of familial loyalty—not that Sandra was completely unaware of the implications of a girl her age feeling so personally attached to a doll. But she did her best to ignore other people's judgments.

In Adam's room, he should have been reading *The Sun Also Rises,* the last book on his senior reading list. Instead, he stared at the clock on his computer screen and waited for it to become 9:55 P.M. He wanted to pick up Dart at 10:05 P.M., which was late for a school night, he knew, but this close to graduation, such considerations didn't seem important. When the numbers finally changed on the clock, Adam made his way through the house. He shut off the light in the kitchen and made sure the back door was locked. He was used to these tasks and did them without thinking. As he walked past his dad's bedroom he could see his dad's eyes were closed. Adam went inside and turned off the television.

"I was watching that," Greg said quietly.

"Yeah? Well, your eyes were closed."

"Doesn't matter. I was listening to it."

"Well…"

"Well, nothing. Turn it back on."

Greg straightened up, brushed the piece of hair that hung down his forehead to the side and turned to his nightstand covered with junk. There was a half-empty bottle of water and a few bottles of pills. Kleenex. A phone. A lamp. An old clock radio with red square lights. A stack of books sat on top of a pile of magazines.

"I could have had an exciting life," Greg said, rummaging through the tabletop support group beside him.

"Like this one is so boring?" Adam asked.

"But I don't think I could've killed anybody," Greg said, pulling out a Kleenex to wipe his nose. "Spies have to be able to do that, you know."

"I'm sure it's only scary the first time," Adam said as he switched the television back on.

"Became a dad instead…and I wouldn't trade that for all the excitement in the world."

Adam wondered whether his dad ever listened to what he actually said. Or was it all just instinctual? *Maybe he's already taken a sleeping pill but not yet fallen asleep,* Adam thought as he turned to leave. He had no time for his dad tonight. Increasingly, he felt like he didn't have any patience for his dad or his problems anymore. At the door he turned back and used a line he knew always hurt his dad's feelings: "I hate to remind you, but we never asked to be born."

Greg ignored Adam's joke, even though it hurt. He'd taken a Xanax after dinner and an Ambien only minutes before, so he didn't care to pick a fight. "Is your sister asleep?" he asked.

"I don't know."

The thought of Sandra pushed Greg briefly back into the land of parental responsibility.

"And where are you going?"

"To meet Dart."

"You…" Greg began, then stopped to push the pile of homework off the bed, "stay up too late. You should sleep more."

"Yeah, dad. See you later."

But Adam didn't leave. Something about the way his dad looked kept him there. Greg seemed to struggle with the smallest tasks, such as pulling up his comforter and switching off the lamp next to his bed. Adam was a little scared. He realized his dad probably looked now like he himself would in 30 years as a very old man. It was sad, a little pathetic, and sent a seasick feeling through Adam, as if he were being pushed through time, a split-second ahead of the rest of the world.

Greg seemed to forget that Adam was still in the room. He moved about as if he were completely alone. He reached over to his table again and picked out one of the burnt-orange prescription bottles. He removed a pill, put it in his mouth, and washed it down with water from the half-empty bottle. When he turned back, he noticed Adam still standing in the doorway. He looked only half surprised. "Don't look at me like that," he said.

Adam held the doorknob in one hand and pushed and pulled the door back and forth across the carpet, making a gentle sweeping sound.

"Look at you like what?" Adam asked.

"I need it to sleep."

"But you were already asleep."

"Don't give me a hard time."

"Whatever," Adam said, and he meant it. Adam let go of the door and walked over to his dad.

"Just let me be," Greg said shrinking back, unsure why Adam was approaching.

"Fine," Adam said. He put one hand on his dad's shoulder, as if trying to hold him still, and leaned over and kissed him on his forehead as a parent kisses his child good night—as if everything was going to be all right, even if it wasn't. Then he turned and left, closing Greg's door behind him with one final sweep against the carpet. As he walked away he couldn't hear Greg shuffling around again on his night table. Adam was unaware of the mess he was making, since Greg had only the light of the television to guide him.

Down the hall, Adam saw light coming from underneath Sandra's closed door. He opened it quietly and stuck his head inside. Sandra heard the door and looked up from her book to see who was coming in.

"You're supposed to be asleep," Adam said.

"So."

"So, nothing. So just keep it down."

"Adam. Do you hear anything?"

Adam stood very still and listened for a moment. "No, I don't."

"Well, then. Don't tell me to keep it down when I'm not making any noise."

"Oh, God, Sandra. Dad's in bed and I'm heading out…just keep it down." Adam closed the door behind him and felt bad about the way he had acted. He'd been rather curt and impatient, he knew, but he wanted to get out of the house and meet his friends. In his room, he grabbed his favorite red jacket off the hook on his closet door. It was a sturdy canvas thing with an elastic waistband like the one James Dean wore in *Rebel Without a Cause*. Wearing it, Adam felt almost as cool.

Jeff sat on the steps of his back porch under the glare of a bright yellow bulb meant to keep mosquitoes away. There had never been a mosquito problem as far as Jeff knew, so maybe something as simple as the yellow lightbulb did keep the insects at bay. It had been there when he moved in, and the only time it burned out, he replaced it with another the previous owner had left in the garage. A few moths congregated near the top of the door—the closest they could get to the light without landing on the burning bulb. Their dusty wings spread out against the screen door, like solar panels on a rooftop.

Twilight was Jeff's favorite time of day. It was cool and sometimes damp, yet not too dark. The sky was blue-gray and still hinted of the shimmering pink that followed the sun's going down. Jeff often spent this time in his backyard reading his mail, playing with Chops, his 5-year-old black lab, maybe smoothing the wax on his surfboard, or just plain sitting and thinking.

Tonight, like so many nights, Jeff came home from a 12-hour shift, peeled off his uniform, and took a shower. Afterward, he pulled on his oldest pair of jeans and one of his oldest, softest T-shirts. No underwear, no socks. After 12 hours covered in shields, security gadgets, and lethal weaponry, he had no tolerance for accessories. He slid his feet into old rubber thongs, the kind people wear on vacation—or if they live in L.A. He'd picked up a burrito on the way home and sat on his back porch to eat it. Not two seconds after taking the last bite, his cell phone rang. Jeff looked to see who was calling. Sue's name and number lit up the screen. Jeff couldn't think of a good-enough reason not to answer her, so he picked up the phone.

A mile and a half away, Sue sat on her own front porch looking sideways into her neighbor's living room, holding her phone right up against her ear. She was a little bored and a little lonely, so she thought up an excuse to call Jeff; she would inquire about Chops and his anxious mood.

"Just calling to see how the old pooch is doing tonight."

"Oh, fine, I guess. Well, sort of the same as last night."

"Yeah?"

"Kind of agitated. Keeps looking at me like I'm not telling him something."

Chops lay at Jeff's feet, on his side with his eyes closed.

"Isn't it times like these you wish you could communicate with him?" Sue asked.

"Well..."

"Not necessarily speaking, but some kind of understanding. I mean, don't you wish you could just ask him what's wrong?"

"Maybe I don't want to know. What if it was something I couldn't do anything about?"

"Oh, God, Jeff, stop it. You are not that sweet."

"You're right."

"Not that you're not sweet," she quickly added. "You're more benevolent than sweet."

"Big word, Sue. What are you trying to say?"

"Oh, stop."

"I know when you start using big words there's something going on. What do you need?"

"Nothing. I'm just trying to say that you are a wonderful guy. Everyone knows it. You're going to be an excellent father someday."

"I'm not planning on it."

"Sh, sh, shh. Don't say that," she said. Sue knew Jeff's story, but she didn't like it. It wasn't that she had a problem with Jeff being gay—just that his being gay kept him unavailable to her. He was so perfect, she thought, and so completely different than any man she'd ever gone out with. "You never know what the future holds."

"You're right about that, but I'm sure my future has nothing to do with kids."

Sue realized the corner into which she'd talked herself and tried to change the subject.

"What are you doing tonight?"

"Oh," he began. He didn't want to hurt her feelings—he also didn't want to spend any more time with her. "Not much. Going to putz around here."

"I was thinking of trying to catch a movie or something."

"Sounds nice."

"Yeah? Maybe you could join me?"

"No thanks. Got an early day tomorrow."

"But we're off tomorrow."

"Sue, don't you think we spend enough time together?"

"I guess so, but we're friends, aren't we? And friends don't ever say, 'Oh, I think we're spending too much time together,' do they?"

"No, not usually. But we're different."

"I know we are, but then again, not really. No, I'm not so sure we're that different."

Jeff knew he needed to wrap up the conversation before it went further. "Yeah, well, I got to get going. Gotta finish up this work before it gets too dark."

"Okay," Sue said, sounding disappointed.

But Jeff couldn't force himself to say anything to make her feel any better. "My ear is burning up. You know I can't spend much time on my cell. Old cells leak radiation and mine's from '96. It's practically radioactive."

"What?"

"Yeah, through the receiver. It's a terrible thing. Read about it in the paper last week. For people with old cellular phones, it's very dangerous. So, um, thanks for calling, and I'll see you tomorrow. Bye."

"Bu…okay, bye," Sue said, both exasperated and annoyed as Jeff disconnected. She let her arm and the phone drop to her lap and allowed herself to become distracted by the glowing blue television visible through her neighbor's window.

After Jeff hung up, he rose quickly and walked inside, flinging the screen door wide open. The moths held on for dear life as the door swung open and slammed shut with a sudden clap. Jeff checked his watch. Too early for bed. Too late for a movie. Too early to read. Too late to…whatever. More restless than anxious, Jeff decided he needed to get out of the house for a while and see people. In his bedroom he traded his flip-flops for sneakers—still no socks—and grabbed his keys before heading out the front door and into the night.

Adam pulled away from his driveway a few minutes behind schedule. *Family can screw up your life in so many big and small ways,* he thought as he dialed Dart on his cell. As soon as Dart answered, Adam said, "I'm turning onto your block right now. Be there in less than 30 seconds."

"Liar."

"Never."

"Adam, shut up…I am standing in front of my house at this very second—because you were supposed to be here 10 minutes ago—and I can see you're not coming down my street."

"Oh, God. Don't be such a stickler. So I'm a block away."

"Where are you, really?"

"Oh, my God. Chill out! I'll be right there."

Adam hung up and slid his phone back into the pocket of his favorite red jacket. He drove down Glyndora Way until he arrived at Dart's house on Third Street.

"Finally," Dart said as he jumped into Adam's truck.

"Chill out, man. I'm like seven minutes late, which is soooo not a big deal."

"Adam. You're right, seven minutes is not a big deal…" Dart looked from Adam to the road ahead and back again. "But lying at your tender age is just lame. You were probably still inside your house when you called me. How am I supposed to believe anything you say when I know you lie sometimes?"

"I do not lie."

"Okay, bend the truth, omit half the story, whatever."

"No, not those either."

"Fine then, you lie. It's simpler. Let's just call it what it is. Didn't anyone ever teach you the story about the boy who cried wolf?"

Adam signaled to Dart that he would be ignoring his further exposition by raising his right hand and showing him his open palm. When the message was conveyed, Adam moved his hand to the stereo and turned up the radio. Stevie Wonder's voice filled the space. "Uptight (Everything's All Right)" from 1966.

"No football hero or smooth Don Juan/...Baby, everything is all right, uptight, ah, ah, ah."

Two more blocks, from Third to Valley to Atlantico, and they were there. Adam turned the wheel and pulled into the parking lot of Angelito's newest strip mall, which wasn't really new—nothing in Angelito was new—it was merely refurbished. On one end sat an enormous Pavilions grocery store so big, so vastly stocked, it should have been called a nutritional department store, except that not everything in it was nutritious. Next door was a Blockbuster Video and next to that a Thai restaurant called Thai-foon. There were a few little shops in between—like Hallelujah, a Christian bookstore; a greeting card shop called Hello; a candle shop ("Disgusting," Adam said, "Who needs that many stinking fat candles?"); and a frozen yogurt store called Taste-E-Treats ("Taste-Less-Treats," according to Dart). At the very south end, right next to Pavilions, was the only nonretail space: Angelito's Bowling, Billiards & Bingo.

The neon sign above the door was 1980s vintage, with too many shades of green and red. The O in bowling was a bowling ball with a pair of angel's wings in white neon. The place had last seen a significant crowd back when Reagan was president, but during the daytime, grannies flocked to the place for team play, so there was a guaranteed amount of income to keep the place open. Bingo? No one knew if it had ever been played there. By night, Angelito's B, B & B was pretty empty, and Adam and Dart found a free pool table easily.

Jeff backed his 1993 white Bronco out of his driveway. He bought it only a year ago—post-O.J., the price reflected its taint—but Jeff didn't care. Tonight he drove with the windows down, letting the wind blow away some of his anxiety. He jabbed his finger at the search button on his radio until he found something he liked. Crackling rock, cheesy pop, talking, talking, talking, and ads on every other station. Finally, Stevie Wonder's silky, soothing voice cut through the static. Jeff stopped and listened. When the last note faded, the DJ came on and said:

"That was "Angel Baby" from 1966, one of Stevie's very first songs. Now we're going to keep the Stevie Wonder-full tunes coming all night long. Next up, a jump ahead 20 years to 1985 with "I Just Called to Say I Love You." This one goes out to Laura in Agoura from Pete in San Pedro. He's thinking about you tonight and wants..."

Before the DJ could finish, Jeff pulled into the parking lot of AK47, the closest gay bar to his house, and turned off the engine. The bar was in Silver Lake, which didn't have a real lake, but no one seemed to worry about such a thing. Calling AK47 a gay bar always seemed a bit of a misnomer to Jeff, since there was nothing at all gay in the happy-gay sense of the word. It was a hole-in-the-wall, narrow and long with a main entrance off the back parking lot. Video monitors hung in the corners playing videos of clean-shaven men working out in tight shorts.

Monday nights were sometimes crowded, and tonight was no exception. Jeff strolled past the bar where a handful of men, some actually young and decent-looking, sat on stools. He went to the back where a pool table was the focus of attention for at least a dozen men. Jeff needed something like a pool table to occupy him so he wouldn't feel like he wasn't simply standing around doing nothing. A tall, handsome black man with white sneakers was beating a smaller guy, about 25 and wearing a T-shirt that said COMPLETELY RARE in green letters. Jeff wrote his name down on the list of players:

David, Andrew, and a smudged Doug. Then he walked back to the front and ordered a beer.

After finishing work, Fran picked up Veronica and met the guys at Angelito's.

"Hey, hey, hey…it's Fran Albert," Fran said, jingling her keys as if she was a grandpa seeing his grandkids for the first time in ages.

"He-ey-ey," answered Dart.

Adam offered a wimpy, "Hey."

"Hey, your mom came into the restaurant tonight."

"Really? Did she spend a lot of money?"

"Yeah, she did, actually."

"Good. I hope you got some."

"Whoa, hello?" said Dart. "When did Mr. Grumpy arrive?"

"I'm not in a bad mood."

"Well, you do seem a bit off," Fran said.

"Maybe because I live with freaks."

"And?" Fran asked. "What else is new?"

By now, Adam was playing Dart and beating him soundly. Dart sucked at pool, and he knew it, but he played anyway and enjoyed it. "Uh, let's see. My dad is passed out in front of Sean Connery and…he told me that he always wanted to be a spy. My sister is hearing things like voices or some shit. My family is fucked up."

"Sean Connery is at your house?" asked Veronica.

As the newest member of their group—and in spite of her lack of "pop-culture awareness," as Dart called it—Veronica was usually quite modest and good-natured, so they let her get away with saying stupid things sometimes.

"No, on TV. My Dad is watching some James Bond shit."

"Shit, man. You like the word shit tonight?" Dart asked.

"Which one?" Fran asked.

"I don't know. I wasn't watching it with him.

"If it was *Dr. No,*" Fran said, "well, that's the best. Ursula Andress is so fucking hot in that."

"Who?" asked Veronica.

Adam tried to ignore them. What the hell were they talking about?

"What about Sandra," Dart asked.

"Don't even get me started on her. She is so weird. She spends every night reading in her bed before going to sleep."

"That's sweet," Veronica said.

"Kids are supposed to hate reading."

"She's an actress," Fran said to Veronica, "a really gorgeous one."

"Sandra?"

"No. Ursula Andress."

"Your family has always been twisted," Dart said as he knocked in one of Adam's striped balls.

"At least she's reading," Fran said.

"Yeah," Dart chimed in. "She could be shoplifting or dealing drugs or something. Kids go down those dark roads so early these days."

"Yeah, it could be so much worse," added Veronica.

"Really, how?" Adam snapped.

"I don't know," she said, taken aback. "But it could always be worse."

Jeff leaned against one of AK47's sticky walls and set his sweaty beer on a ledge lined with empty bottles. He never did like beer the way so many men did, especially his fellow cops. They talked about it, planned their evenings around it, a six-pack here, a case there. Jeff considered drinking beer a way to pass time. Jeff had a friend in college who had timed how long it took to smoke a cigarette—eight minutes—and calculated how much time she wasted smoking a half-dozen cigarettes every day. Jeff could make one beer last half an hour, which was about how long he could hang out at a place like AK47 before he either (a) picked someone up because he was simply horny, (b) let someone pick him up because he was horny, or (c) got so bored that he went home empty-handed. Sometimes Jeff jerked off when he got home, but other times he just crawled into bed and called Chops up to sleep near his feet.

Tonight was still early. Under the dingy light, Jeff stood and waited his turn. His cool masculinity caught the eye of many admirers, but his plain face did not reveal any hint of emotion. Interested parties remained bystanders intimidated by Jeff's unintentional stoicism. Not that Jeff was cold, but he'd grown up during '80s, when the first he'd learned about gay men was that they had or were going to get AIDS. By the '90s, when he should have been spending his late 20s screwing his way through the Southern California dating pool, Jeff was unable to shake his fear of the virus. At first he was so paranoid he rarely went home with anyone; he settled for quick get-offs at the gym. Becoming a police officer took up a lot of Jeff's time and energy and he didn't really mind his situation. But once he settled into his job and had some time to think—and police officers have plenty of time to think—he realized he needed to make some changes and grow up. He came out to his parents, who had since traded Orange County for Santa Barbara. And he turned 35. It was 1997, and instead of getting depressed at the sign of another year passing, Jeff finally realized he was more than okay. He was healthy and enjoyed his job. He recognized that whatever he'd been doing—safely—would keep him from getting infected. Slowly, Jeff started to hang out more socially in gay places. He went on a few dates, few of which were any good, but at least they were dates. Eventually he worked up to going out with a man for a few weeks.

Which is not to say that all was right in the world. Jeff mainly transferred his anxiety about HIV to paranoia about love and all of its potential for complicated but somehow rewarding human entanglements.

Jeff finished off his beer before his turn came up. He got tired of waiting, and since there wasn't anyone at AK47 he cared enough about to approach, he decided to leave. All he'd wanted was a break from his life, from his house, from Sue, and he got it.

"Let's go outside," Adam said to Dart, while Fran and Sandra set up the next match.

"Why?"

"It smells like shit in here."

"It does?"

"Whatever, man. I wanna get some air."

"Shit, man. What is up with you tonight?"

Adam went first, pushed open the door and walked out into the parking lot with Dart trailing behind. They found Adam's truck parked right in front. To the right, they could see the automated doors at Pavilions sliding open and shut as customers approached and entered. *Neeerrrww.* The sliding doors squeaked as they slid out of the way for each customer.

"I don't think I'm jealous of Fran," Dart said. "Veronica really isn't my type."

Adam didn't laugh.

"What's up with you?" Dart asked. "Earth to Adam…Come in, Adam."

"I don't know." Pavilions doors opened and shut. "Yes, I do. It's my dad."

"What now?"

"He's such a fucking mess."

"And?"

"Well, he's…"

"But he's always a mess."

"Yeah, but he's so fucking depressed these days. No matter what is happening in the world. I am so over it."

"What can you do? He's your dad."

"That's the problem. It's not like I can tell him to snap out of it. It's not like I can tell him that his shrink obviously sucks and that he needs serious help."

"Is it really that bad? I mean, are you sure you're not exaggerating?"

"Dart, why would I exaggerate about this?"

"Don't you think you can stick it out for a couple more months until you go away to school?"

"I don't know," Adam said. "But it really sucks right now."

The discouragement in Adam's voice was as clear as the glass doors sliding open to release shoppers pushing carts loaded with Stovetop stuffing, Tropicana orange juice, blueberry muffins, and strip steaks. *Neeerrrw. Neeerrrw.*

"Once we move out, go away to school, it's going to be okay. You won't have to take care of him anymore. Once we blow this town, who gives a flying fuck what happens?"

"Yeah, but, who do you think is going to take care of him?"

"Maybe he'll finally realize that nobody is going to take care of him, and he'll have to learn to take care of himself."

The men, the smoke, and the video boys left Jeff slightly unwound but still feeling unsatisfied. He pulled into a Tommy Burgers thinking it was his stomach, but quickly changed his mind when he heard Sue's voice in the back of his head counting calories. He drove down Glyndora and turned left on Atlantico toward home. Then Jeff saw it: the big, purple sign, all 15 feet of it. Pavilions. Tonight it shined like a beacon on the dark streets of Angelito. He continued his approach. Surely he could find something healthy to satisfy his cravings. Not that Jeff would ever admit that Sue's nutritional obsession was rubbing off on him. But it was. His new favorite food was crunchy granola in a bowl of cold milk, preferably late at night. In the morning, it tasted like cereal. At night, the crunchy nutty bits mixed so well with milk that Jeff thought he might have invented a new dessert. He reached down and pulled his jeans up slightly to give his crotch a little extra space. Then he hit the gas pedal. Nothing like having a goal, he thought, to give your life a new purpose.

Jeff pulled into the lot, parked the Bronco, jumped out, clicked his alarm on—*bleep, bleep*—and headed straight for the automatic doorway. He flipped his ring of keys around his forefinger, let the soles of his sneakers scuff the cement in soft, evenly spaced shuffles. Jeff's police-trained eyes scanned the scene out of habit: store, doorway, walkway, parking lot, street, and city beyond. Then back again, store, doorway, sidewalk, parking lot—stop. There were two guys, young, different, perhaps cute, sitting on the hood of a truck parked just beyond the door.

In between his complaining to Dart, Adam heard a whoosh and a clang, a little slap of something small and metallic hitting a callused palm. He looked up and across the quiet parking lot. There was a man, alone, walking toward Pavilions and swinging a set of car keys around in his hand—*whoosh...clang*. He was very tall and very handsome, wearing faded jeans that stretched around his thighs to accommodate serious leg muscles. On top he wore a plain T-shirt, untucked and loosely hanging over his waist, but tight under the arms, accentuating the round, broad shoulders that made the man look like a human letter T. While Dart tried to convince Adam that his life wasn't so bad, and Adam tried to convince Dart that it really was bad. Adam continued to evaluate the MMO (moving masculine object) in his view. Above the T-shirt, there was a face, striking but not intimidating. He looked for the eyes. Who was this guy? If he could only find the eyes, make contact, maybe he could figure something out.

Jeff strode toward the light like he was trapped in the scene from *Reservoir Dogs*—the one where the men walk down the street looking badder than badass in their black-and-white suits, moving in super-slow motion while the music drives full speed ahead. As he moved closer, Jeff's eyes settled on the kid with the darker hair in the red jacket. He looked familiar. He wore jeans that ended in a casual rumple, blue and green sneakers that were half-fashionable, half-utilitarian. *Who is this guy, and how do I know him?* Jeff wondered. But Mr. James Dean Wannabe was deep in conversation, so Jeff's investigation was thwarted. He glanced to the door, six more steps, probably. Six more seconds for this guy to look up and make eye contact before Jeff would be inside Pavilions.

Four, three...two...one...The planets slowed their orbits to accommodate Adam and Jeff's connection. Everything was drawing to a standstill, yet Adam remained in control of his conversation with

Dart, and Jeff was walking one foot in front of the other.

"That only means that Sandra is stuck with him when I leave."

"She's a big girl. She's very mature for her age. Maybe you don't have to worry about her."

Touchdown. Their eyes connected. Jeff saw a young man with eyes shaped by innocence and cynicism. Adam saw the opposite: slightly worn eyes surrounded by wrinkles of optimism. For a second, the planets stopped, everything stopped, except for the waves of light that bounced off the two men and reached their retinas allowing them to see the shape, size, color, and depth of each other's forms.

Jeff reached the door, stepped on the motion-sensitive mat, the door swung open, and he was ushered inside. Adam, as taken as he was by the vision of manliness before him, continued his conversation. It wasn't the first and surely wouldn't be the last time he was swept away by the sight of an extremely hot guy. Adam was at a point in his life when every third guy seemed like the hottest guy in the world, and he knew it.

Hit by a flood of fluorescent light and a soundtrack of jazzy Muzak: Jeff was thrown off balance inside Pavilions. The image of the guy on the hood of the car hovered in front of him. Their momentary connection registered mysteriously on Jeff's consciousness. The memory was joined in Jeff's mind by images of every hot guy he'd ever seen on a hood of a car—a shirtless fireman in a calendar, the blond who got fucked on the hood of his red Mustang in the Falcon video he first watched 10 years ago, the man who washed cars at the police station in cutoff fatigues that revealed his muscular calves. *Cereal, cereal,* he told himself. *Find the cereal aisle.*

Down he walked through the space between the cash registers and the 24—yes, 24!—aisles of food, household products, international selections, and produce that made Pavilions a "superstore!" The abundance wasn't distracting enough. More men entered Jeff's mind.

There was the neighbor in college who liked to wash his Jeep wearing only running shorts. Jeff remembered the hair running down from his chest into the elastic waistband of his shorts. The scene was all soapy water, shiny metal, and sweat-covered skin. And the bodybuilder in his neighborhood; he was too big for Jeff, but he paraded his incredibly developed but shaved-smooth chest for all to see in his convertible Miata. *Shop, just shop,* Jeff thought. Baked goods: sugar, powdered sugar, cocoa, flour, wheat flour, no-wheat flour, cake frosting in plastic tubs with labels showing their contents—colors from bubble gum pink to chocolate. Next aisle: pastas, cereal, and "international grains" (which meant tabouli and couscous). Oh, yeah, and *him,* the guy on the video he'd just seen at AK47: a dirty-blond model with a goatee filmed driving through some Sedona-like desert until he arrived at a piece of knocked-over split-rail fencing. He hopped out of his truck and lifted up the poles with a smile. The camera zoomed in on biceps covered by beautifully tanned skin. Then there was the magazine spread he'd seen only once, but now remembered as if it had been his all-time favorite: a flannel shirt-wearing, hairy-bear type jerking off in an auto repair shop, stroking himself next to all the greasy equipment until he shot his load. *Granola, find the granola!*

Pavilions smelled like Windex and freezer burn, but Jeff could only smell the scent of his childhood garage—a combination of old boxes of God-knows-what, rat poison and rat piss, plain old dirt, and rusting patio furniture. He remembered finding his dad's old *Playboy* magazines. There weren't as many men in them as in *Penthouse,* but sometimes in the cartoons he'd find a man with his cock rendered in simple lines. By the time Jeff located the Nature's Choice Almond and Cranberry Granola, he remembered how intense it felt to look at those two-dimensional drawings of naked men and shoot his teenage load on the cement floor of the garage. Afterward, he always rubbed it into the dirt with his size 6 K-Swiss sneakers until the evidence of his erotic life became nothing more than another layer of dust on the floor.

Jeff picked up the cereal and headed for the dairy section of Pavilions, where milk (of every possible fat content) and milk by-products of every imaginable type were stocked. He grabbed a gallon of two percent, turned down the very next aisle—canned vegetables, fruit juices, soda, and water—none of which Jeff noticed because inside he was still watching the slide show of hot guys in parking lots and garages playing in his head, all leading back to one question: Who was that guy outside, and why did he look so good? Young, handsome guys were a dime a dozen. So…?

"Parents are fucked up," Adam said, breaking a peaceful lull in his conversation with Dart.

"No argument there, except that a lot of kids are fucked up too."

"So is this conversation. You ready to get out of here?"

With that, they got up and went back inside. Dart headed straight for the table and told the girls they were leaving. Adam hit the bathroom to take a leak. They met the girls again to say good night. They were ready to leave too, and everyone walked out together. "See you tomorrow," "Bye-bye," "Later, later," they said. Fran and Veronica walked to Fran's car and Adam and Dart went to Adam's truck. While Adam slid the key into his door, he took one last look over at Pavilions' sliding doors. Just then, the man in the bright white T-shirt was coming out. *Neewr, neewr,* and there he was, as if it were orchestrated by some cosmic force. Jeff walked out with a bag in one hand and his keys starting to twirl around his finger in the other. He looked toward Adam's truck and saw Adam and Dart crawling inside. He found Adam's eyes again and was momentarily thrilled to catch his attention. Jeff smiled the smallest, least committal, slightly shy smile he could. Adam squinted one eye—just enough to show he'd noticed the smile—and then ducked inside his truck.

Fran drove Veronica home, and Adam dropped off Dart. Jeff found his way home to his quiet house and to Chops. Neither Adam nor Jeff spoke out loud about what they'd seen, but each man wondered about the other. Was that briefest of flirtations a moment that would pass unrepeated, like so many connections in

Southern California? Were they like two drivers who smile at each other across lanes of sluggish traffic, share a brief moment, and then move on, loosing each other in the flow? Not that fleeting connections like these were unimportant, not that they weren't crucial to survival in Los Angeles. After all, without them, what would be left? Adam and Jeff each wondered—hoped, maybe, but would never admit—if they wanted more. To admit that was to set oneself up for disappointment, and that was something neither of them thought they could handle.

TUESDAY, JUNE 8, 1999

Breakfast in the Westman house was cold cereal from a plastic bag inside a cardboard box. The last time anyone had combined food with heat to make breakfast was St. Patrick's Day, 1989, when Adam was 8 years old. That day, his dad hadn't yet given up on mornings entirely; it would be another couple of years before Greg saw the time before noon as merely a price to pay to get to the afternoon when his mood naturally elevated. On March 17, 1989, Adam woke up to the sounds of his dad in the kitchen and went straight in to see what was going on. In the frying pan, there were green eggs and ham—"Like the book," Greg said. Adam stared wide-eyed and half-asleep as the eggs shimmered like magic in the oily pan. *How did he do it?* Adam wondered. But then he noticed little tubes of food coloring on the side of the stove and his enthusiasm deflated.

Ten years and a few months after the green-eggs-and-ham incident, Adam entered the kitchen to find Sandra hypnotized by the side of a Kix box ("With six whole grains inside each bite!"). She was alone at the table and muttered "Hi" under her breath. Adam followed his usual routine. He scooped coffee grounds into the top of the coffeemaker and then poured himself a bowl of cereal. He sat down across from Sandra and started eating. Usually, around this time, Greg would wander out, pour a cup of coffee from the unfinished pot, and return to his room without speaking. Today, there was no sign of him.

After Adam finished his cereal, he was swept by a rare feeling of benevolence. He stood up, poured a cup of coffee for his dad and brought it to him. He pushed his father's bedroom door open and heard the clock radio playing beside the bed. *"Beautiful morning this morning. We've got 71 degrees already at 7:35, and it's going to be a hot one today. Should be going up to the low 90s by three o'clock this afternoon. Looks like a pretty good commute so far. We've got only one Sig Alert on the 210 near the racetrack but..."*

But nothing. Adam quieted the perky voice with a flick of his finger on the wake-set-off button. "Come on, Dad, get up."

"Uh. I don't feel so well," Greg said, half to Adam, half to his pillow.

"Oh, well, here's some coffee."

Greg didn't respond or even pretend to. He turned like a child about to be forced by his parents to get out of bed. Adam shoved aside some junk on the bedside table and put down the mug.

"Oh, I see," Adam said sarcastically. "You must be exhausted after staying out all night partying. What you need is some light."

Adam yanked the nylon string on the blinds, sending them up inside themselves. The sun streamed in brightly, violently, revealing the billions of dust particles flurrying frantically through the air.

"Maybe you're a closet alcoholic...maybe you're just hung over? You know what really works for my hangovers...a very hot shower. Why don't I start one for you?"

Adam was shooting for funny and hitting passive-aggressive. He was entertaining no one but himself. And he wasn't exactly cracking himself up. Adam wanted his father to get up and get on with the day. For once, Adam wished his dad would be the adult. Couldn't his dad show—for once—how to simply get up and face the day? What else is there? What else can you do? You can't stay in bed feeling shitty and watching *Rosie* forever.

Adam continued his routine until it morphed from ineffective to pathetic. He went into his dad's bathroom thinking, *What's the point? Why do I care what he does, anyway? Why not let him sleep all day if that's what he really wants?* But no, something drove Adam to keep on keepin' on. He turned on the shower. It sputtered, cleared its copper-piped throat with a rumble, and shook itself awake before beginning to spray.

From under his pillow, Greg sounded like he was actually feeling something...something like anger. "Adam," he demanded. "You are wasting water. Really. Turn it off."

Adam ignored his plea and left the room saying, "You'll have to turn it off yourself."

On his way to his own room, Adam poked his head into the bathroom he shared with Sandra. She was brushing her teeth. She was standing on the yellow plastic footstool she was given before she was tall enough to reach the sink but now didn't need.

"I'll be ready in a couple minutes," he said. "So just wait up because I'm going to drive you to school today."

Greg's snooze button expired, and the momentary quiet since Adam left the room was interrupted by headlines. *"Wrangling over the state budget continues today. Chief among the sticking points is the cost of increased law enforcement and where the money for statewide Y2K preparation should come from. Also, a new report out this morning says that publicly held financial institutions are the most prepared for Y2K, compared to other businesses and state and local governments."*

Greg reached an arm from under his covers and hit the snooze button, again. Financial institutions? Are those for the financially insane, or the very rich but insane? This little joke hopped around inside Greg's head and entertained him for about half a second, which was just long enough to distract him from his lethargy and get him out of bed. Or maybe it wasn't the joke. It could have been the sound of running water being wasted that made him anxious, inspired him to, at the very least, get up and turn it off. Southern California, as usual, was in a drought.

Inside his small bathroom, Greg left the shower running and sat down on the toilet to take a leak; he couldn't be bothered to stand up. He watched the steam rise up over the top of the shower curtain, push cooler air down, and fog up the mirror above the sink. He found it fascinating to ponder the fact that the same immense forces that controlled the weather outside were miniaturized inside his bathroom. Amid the microcosmic hurricane, the door began to open. Greg pulled his pajama pants up above his knees, but made no move to actually get off the pot.

"Dad?" Sandra asked, her face slowly peeking through the crack in the door. "Adam is taking me to school."

"Okay, honey."

"Okay?" she asked, annoyed by her father's linguistic minimalism.

"Yes, okay. I'll pick you up after school."

Jeff fed Chops first thing in the morning; he filled his bowl with dried food shaped like brown Goldfish crackers and orange Cheese Doodles. Chops gobbled it down as if it was his last meal on earth, while Jeff went back to his room to get dressed. Today he traded his boxers for swimming trunks, slipped on the same T-shirt he'd worn the night before, and brushed his teeth. It was his day off. He threw his surfboard into the back of his Bronco and drove toward the beach. The McDonald's near his house was never crowded on weekday mornings, so he drove through and picked up a Sausage McMuffin with egg and a coffee—440 Sue-free calories, not counting the cream in the coffee. He drove to the beach and spent three hours riding the waves. While metaphorically out at sea, Jeff didn't think about work, Sue, or his parents, who were growing older and starting to complain—a lot—that he didn't visit them enough.

The world Adam and Sandra passed through—from the warm interior of their home to the creaky, clamoring metal of Adam's truck—was basically calm. No breeze had yet stirred the morning air. The sky was pink and blue, not yet hazy. Out of the driveway and down the street, Adam turned left, then right, and then pulled into the left lane on Engleverd Boulevard, Angelito's main street. They passed the stores and businesses that marked Angelito as a city barely able to keep pace with the past. A fabric store filled with bolts of fabric no one wanted hovered next to an Italian deli whose most popular item was the Galaga video game inside the front door. A post office shared a parking lot with a bank that had nine automated teller machines built into its façade.

Before turning, Adam drove by the Sev and the enormous Arco station next to it. Between the gas station and the street, a small piece of lawn was surrounded by clumps of marigolds, begonias, and salvia. Sprinklers poked their little black heads out of the lawn and sprayed water over the miniature garden, preparing it for a day of looking fresh. Cars and their drivers flowed steadily through the station, filling up, paying, and heading out. Behind the cashier's cinder-block office, near the car wash in the back, a line of immigrants from countries between San Diego and Antarctica waited for other men—mostly white, but not exclusively—to pick them up and put them to work on their renovations, landscaping, or construction jobs. The men stood anxiously holding paper cups of coffee from the gas station, ready to be picked like avocados on a neighbor's tree, the extra ones you didn't have to ask permission to take.

Adam dropped Sandra off in front of Eleanor Roosevelt Elementary School and drove away past Ellie's playground, where oversize sprinklers soaked the turf before the day's abuse. *Chink-chink-chink* went the old-fashioned two-part sprinklers. Water shot out one end while a swinging metal arm sprang back and forth against the jet, dispersing an arc of spray...again and again...again and again.

Jeff returned home before noon. He picked up a burrito for lunch at his favorite drive-through. On his way inside, he noticed a group of seriously parched hydrangea bushes alongside his house. He retrieved the back hose and dragged it around the corner to water them. Jeff didn't care for their poofy blue flowers, yet he couldn't bear to get rid of them either. They were overgrown and healthy and had been in place before he moved in. Jeff felt they deserved some sort of botanic respect, and so they remained and flourished under his care.

Jeff's cell phone began ringing inside his back pocket. He dropped the hose onto the ground underneath the bush and flipped open his little metal communication device.

"Hello?" he said, knowing it was Sue.

"Hi. It's me."

"Really?"

"Yeah, I'm fine, thanks," Sue said, not getting his joke. "How are you?"

"Great. It's a beautiful day." Jeff tried to keep his delivery as unemotional as possible until he figured out what Sue was calling for. "I'm currently watering some dehydrated hydrangeas."

"Now? Oh, my God. You're supposed to water later in the day. Right now, during the sunniest part of the day, you can really burn the leaves."

"I'm not watering the leaves, I'm soaking the ground, which is the right way to water any time of the day. Anyway, it was a plant emergency…it definitely couldn't wait."

"What are you doing later?" Sue changed the subject quickly, trying to catch Jeff off-guard. "Because I know a couple friends who are meeting to play some basketball around four, and I thought you might want to join us."

"But I hate basketball."

"I know, but we need a few extra bodies."

"Is that all I am to you? A body?" Jeff knew his teasing would flatter her even though it bored him. He looked around his yard and appreciated it. It wasn't perfect, but it was pretty nice, in a single-man-with-free-time kind of way. And most important, it was his, and his efforts kept it in shape.

"Jeff, you're 6 foot 2. There's no one else playing taller than 5 foot 10. You could really help us out." Sue pleaded. "So what if I am only asking you to play for completely selfish reasons."

Sue thought her exaggerated honesty might charm Jeff into playing, but she was wrong. Their conversation ended with an

"Okay, later" and Jeff went back to his rapidly rehydrating hydrangeas.

From outside, Jeff's life appeared quiet—a little lonely, perhaps—but it wasn't. Today, he will putter around the house, do some laundry, and clean up the recycling that has piled up over the last week. Later, he'll head back outside to wash his Bronco—not because it is particularly dirty, just dusty, which in L.A. is just as bad. Afterward, he'll drive over to Angelito's excuse for an art-house movie theater and watch *eXistenZ,* something he's not that interested in, but having read so many rave reviews, feels he needs to see. When it's over, he will think it was interesting, creatively conceived, but ultimately a bit rudderless—none of which will particularly matter because the afternoon is Jeff's favorite time to see a movie and the experience will have been pleasurable. Hot outside, the lobby will feel cool and inviting. When the movie ends before the sun goes down, Jeff will find it fantastic how time seems to stand still outside while whole lives are lived inside on-screen.

Nothing as magical ever happened at Angelito High School, from which Adam and his friends were about to graduate after four sequential, consequential, but not exactly thrilling years. By 2:30 P.M., the classrooms were empty and the parking lot was filled with students searching for their cars, their rides home or to after-school jobs, to trouble, to anywhere.

"I can't fucking believe that asshole gave me a B on my last— my last!—essay," Dart declared with righteous indignation.

"Like it matters?" Fran asked as she moved her shoulder bag into a more comfortable position across her chest.

"Yes, it matters. What the hell did you get?"

"A-minus."

"But you didn't even read the book!"

"You know that old queen Mr. Dryden always liked me more. Maybe you should have been a little more out to him about your ho-mo-sex-u-ality," Fran said, dragging out the word like it was a species of tropical fern. "Maybe then he might have found it in his fey little heart to be more generous."

"Mr. Dryden knows I'm gay!" Dart said.

"How do you know? Have you ever mentioned it to him or even joked about it with him?"

"No, but...hello...isn't it obvious?"

"Yes, but...he's old—and old school, so you can't assume anything," Fran said conclusively and dismissively.

Adam met them mid-argument by the side of his truck. "Greetings, comrades."

"What did you get?" Dart snapped.

"B-plus," Adam said.

"Oh, my fucking God, even you got a higher grade than me. I hate that queen. I hate fucking Jane Austen. She can take her pride and her prejudice and keep 'em."

Fran turned to Adam, and spoke in her best, I'm-the-narrator-of-our-own-19th-century-novel voice: "His already-weak spirit was crushed, simply crushed under the weight of a B, a tragic, lowly B, which stands for below an A, and will forever blight his record."

Once Dart was cut back down to size, Fran took off. "Later days, dudes," she said as she headed toward her little orange Beemer, Veronica trailing silently behind her.

Adam and Dart hopped inside Adam's truck and drove off. Later, when the parking lot was completely empty, it became nothing more than a black square with little yellow lines, each painted exactly six feet apart.

Seeing his dad's car already in the driveway, Adam pulled his truck in as far as he could. Adam grabbed his bag from the floor and headed inside. He picked up an old *PennySaver* lying on the porch. Adam remembered seeing it there at least a week ago and had to stop himself from asking why rotting newspaper bothered no one else in his family. All was quiet inside the house. Adam walked through the living room, the dining room—no sign of his dad or Sandra—and into the kitchen. He threw the paper out under the sink.

"Hello? Anybody home?"

"Yeah."

Sandra's voice came from somewhere near her bedroom.

"Is dad home?"

"Yeah," Sandra repeated.

Then Adam saw him. His dad was sitting in the backyard, alone, on top of the picnic table with his feet resting on the bench below.

"Hey," Adam said as he swung open the back door.

"Hey, what?"

"Hey...nothing."

Greg's keys were on the table next to him. The day's mail sat unopened in a pile as if he'd just arrived. "Look at this shitty lawn you never mow."

"Oh, God," Adam said, like he'd swallowed a Valley Girl. "It's just very healthy."

Making a joke was Adam's favorite defense mechanism against arguments he knew no other way of winning. But joking about lawn mowing wasn't easy. Mowing the lawn every week was not such a big deal, he knew, but it sure felt like a waste of time. Adam had hated mowing the lawn ever since he turned 13, when his dad gave him instructions on how to start the mower for his birthday. From then on, it was his responsibility. And of all the responsibilities life had handed him without asking, Adam thought this had to be the biggest waste of time. Shitty? Is that what his dad was calling it? Now he was pissed. Overgrown, maybe. But shitty?

"It's not that bad...dad. Have you ever seen the Strumpet's yard next door?"

"I don't live at the Strumpet's, Adam."

"Too bad," Adam whispered, just loud enough for his dad to hear.

"All I'm trying to say is..." Greg paused, looked from the

scrubby but lush lawn to his son's questioning face. "I just think it could look a lot better."

"Yeah, well, we never come back here anyway. So who cares?"

"That doesn't matter."

While Adam decided there was nothing else to say, Greg got up to go inside. "Well," he began, "you'll at least try to cut it this weekend, right?"

"Yeah, fine, whatever."

"Are you home for dinner?"

"Why? It's not even 4:30."

"Because I picked something up for your sister. I didn't think you would be..."

"Don't worry," Adam interrupted, "I can fend for myself."

"Sometimes—" his dad muttered as the backdoor swung shut behind him.

Adam stayed outside and tried to remember whether he'd ever had a "normal" dad—one whose primary tool for dealing with life wasn't sarcasm. He looked at the yard again and noticed the various shades of green turn deeper as afternoon became evening. *It's not all that overgrown,* Adam thought. There were some bushes that needed trimming, but the lawn didn't really need to be mowed right that minute. It wasn't exactly a specimen of prize-winning landscape design; never had been. It was just a simple fucking yard in the middle of goddamn suburbia—a square of grass, a couple of shrubs, and a lime tree that made more limes than a single family could ever eat. *It's fine,* Adam thought. *Why wasn't that enough?*

Night fell and the sky turned into deeper shades of gray. In Angelito, the night sky was never black—only smudgy, charcoal gray, like a conservative suit. The lights from the city were too bright to allow darkness to ever fully take hold of the sky. Across the city's loose pattern of streets, people ate dinner and watched television. Homework was finished. Books were read. Computers sent e-mail, and people chatted online in hopes of finding sex and/or romance. In houses across Southern California, telephones rang, friends and family checked in on each other, or perhaps argued about something that seemed dire today but would be irrelevant tomorrow. These activities continued until it was late enough to turn out the lights and go to bed. Across Angelito, a few lights were left on in certain houses, in places where people bent the hands of time to fit their own needs. Reading lamps remained lit by the bedsides of insomniacs. Bathroom night-lights made of colored plastic stayed lit to guide sleepwalkers and individuals with weak bladders. Some living room lamps were left shining to deter burglars. And other sources of light were left illuminated for reasons only their owners could understand.

In Greg's bedroom, the television cast a cool, fluttering pall across the cluttered room. When Adam came in to turn off the mumbling television, Greg didn't move. He was deep asleep…looking almost content. TV off. *Click.* Hall light down. *Flip.* Adam returned to his room and found his bed cool and the crispy sheets comforting. He'd just finished *The Sun Also Rises,* the last book on his list, and was glad to have it behind him. Unbothered by immediate concerns, he slipped easily into a restful state of preliminary sleep. Thoughts of Brett and Jake stayed in his head. As he lay in bed, he hoped the book would be on his English final next week. The idea of writing about impotence as a force in modern literature seemed too perfect. How would he frame it: Man against Nature or Man against Self? Adam thought he'd do well because he genuinely liked the book, empathized with the characters. He could imagine meeting them, hanging out and drinking cheap red wine together. His bedroom became a train station, central station in Madrid. Trains were coming from all directions, entering and then leaving again toward an infinite number of destinations; each train an opportunity for arrival or departure.

Adam slid deeper toward sleep and the trains kept coming, going, and passing each other in the night. Each became quieter than the last, until they moved along their tracks in total silence, and Adam joined millions of others in the Pacific Time Zone in deep sleep.

Yet the trains continued to run. Adam's bedroom was the waiting room and also his bedroom. The situation was strange and yet made perfect sense. Through his bedroom window, beyond the glass, was sun, not night. It was afternoon in Madrid. Hotter than hell and bright as noontime on a summer day. Brett stood just a few yards away on a platform waiting for a train. She looked beautiful and sad; her face revealed the high cost of knowledge, recognition, and the pain of knowing what life might have been.

"Hey..." Adam said futilely. His window was shut and the sound of his voice ended at the pane of glass. He wanted to tell her how pretty she was, and always had been—always would be. Then he saw Jake off to the left. He was so strong. His shirt wrapped tightly around his shoulders. His pushed-up sleeves revealed sunburned forearms. His mustache was bristly and black.

Clankity, clankity, clankity, clankity, fthpt, fthpt, fthpt. Adam turned away from the window to see travelers dragging suitcases across his bedroom floor, which was the station's floor—big marble slabs as far as he could see. Children were dropping their toys as their parents dragged them toward trains filled with passengers eager to depart. His bedroom ceiling disappeared. The roof was raised, creating a cavernous space. Open skylights and windows let in light along with families of pigeons the color of storm clouds. Across the lobby stood his bedroom wall and his door. Adam walked across the station's marble floor to open it. There he found his hallway leading down to the living room—no children, no luggage—but the sounds of the station continued. Adam followed the noise; he hoped it might lead to a way outside, a way to the platforms where he could find Brett and Jake.

Adam walked down his hallway. The clamor of the station became clearer as he approached his father's bedroom. Some light shined through the crack at the bottom of his father's closed door. Maybe that was the way out, Adam wondered. He heard Spanish track announcements, women scolding their children, and men arguing about things he couldn't understand. He heard hard shoes *clip-clip-clipping* across the floor. Adam pushed through his father's door, hoping it would lead him outside. He wanted desperately to find Brett and Jake and tell them what he knew how their story would end. Adam wanted to warn them. He wanted to help them to avoid their own sad ending.

Adam pushed his father's bedroom door open. The room was empty. Greg's bed was empty, too, the covers pushed back. It was dark, except for a light in his father's bathroom that spilled across the carpeting. It was quiet too, except for some muffled sounds coming from inside the bathroom. Adam went further inside and found his father rustling through his medicine cabinet. A razor, a bottle of Tylenol, a can of shaving cream: various toiletries lay haphazardly atop the counter.

"What are you doing?" Adam asked.

"Looking for something."

"What?"

"The white ones. They're small."

"Small white whats?"

"The really small ones." Greg stopped, looked at Adam, said nothing, gave no hint of his emotional state and turned back. "They're tablets."

The sounds of Spain were still audible, but growing fainter by the second. Adam's dad opened another bottle of pills and poured the contents into his hand. These were blue. Greg separated one from the pile and scooped the rest back into the bottle. He put the pill in his mouth, kicked his head back, and swallowed it without water. With his right hand he put the bottle on the counter, and with his left he went back to the medicine chest, which could have been a ticket window at the station. The bottles and jars stood tall, like bars protecting the salesperson from theft. Four shelves were fully stocked; jar next to bottle next to jar like a pharmacist's well-stocked shelf. Each row held dozens of small, burnt-orange plastic containers topped with little white caps. There must have been dozens of different bottles. Each was covered with little pink and yellow stickers that said what to expect after ingesting; whether you could drive afterward, if you should expect diarrhea, drowsiness, or blurred vision; whether you can take it on an empty stomach, or if you need to take it with a meal.

Adam was used to seeing his dad's medication, but he rarely paid attention to it. As long as he could remember, his dad was always taking one thing or another. Over the last few years, the number of different medications had increased as he switched prescriptions or tried new ones that were supposed to work better. Each new drug had a new side effect, and for each side effect there was a new drug. Once you're taking two or three different pills a day—why worry about taking six or seven, eight or nine? They seemed to be working lately, so why should Adam care? Greg's disposition wasn't great—he wasn't exactly chipper—but at least it was stable.

Adam cared because all of his dad's energy went to making himself feel better, except that he *never* felt better. Greg had settled for simply being able to function. And because of this, during all of Adam's life, he never felt he could depend on his dad for anything, ask him for anything. Each request—for time, money, a ride someplace—seemed to Adam like an imposition. And this was before he even knew what an "imposition" was.

Greg opened another bottle, emptied its contents into his hand, pinched one between his lips, and poured the rest back into the container.

Adam wasn't used to watching his dad take his medication. He was a little embarrassed seeing him so focused on it. Of course, he had generally tried not to pay attention. Who wants to watch his parent become so dependent on something, especially something as incomprehensible as the magic inside little colored pills? It was his dad, for Christ's sake! No matter how much anger he felt toward him for being a fuck-up, he loved him. Adam didn't want him to suffer.

But Adam couldn't get his dad's attention. It was like the window that separated him from Brett and Jake was now separating Adam from his dad. He would have to speak louder.

"That was a blue one!" Adam yelled.

Greg stopped, looked Adam straight in the eyes, and said calmly,

"Quiet, Adam. There's no need to yell. I'm standing right here."

"Then why aren't you listening? It was blue."

Greg turned away. "I know. Where did I put the white ones? They should've been by the bed, but they weren't. Can you turn the light on?"

"Dad," Adam said, his voice rising again. "The light *is* on."

In a zone of artificially illuminated midnight, the fluorescent light inside the medicine chest hummed ever so softly. Greg's actions appeared robotic; his arms moved smoothly and methodically, like they were programmed. He reached for a bottle, looked at it, and put it down on the counter. Or he opened it, looked inside, liked what he saw, and popped one into his mouth. Then he reached for another bottle, poured its contents into his hand, squeezed one between the crinkles of his palm, and shifted the rest back into the bottle. Again. Bottle to hand. Hand to mouth. Head tossed back. Sometimes twice from the same bottle.

What the fuck was going on? Why was this happening? What *was* happening? Adam wanted to go back to his room, back to bed, back to sleep. He wanted to leave, wanted to catch a train before they all departed for the night.

"Maybe this is it," Greg said to no one in particular.

"Yeah?"

"I'm not sure."

Greg sounded unsure, but he took the pill anyway.

"Why are you taking it if you don't know for sure?" Adam asked

"Just in case."

"Dad, you've taken enough. You'll never wake up for school tomorrow. Let's go back to bed."

Adam sounded bitterly patronizing. He grabbed his father's arm, as an angry parent would grab a child about to walk out into the street. Greg looked over but was so distracted that the pain from his arm never made it to his brain. He looked Adam up and down and asked, "Why aren't you dressed?"

"I was sleeping. It's the middle of the fucking night!"

Greg paid no attention. He pulled his arm loose, reached for a dirty glass on the counter, and filled it with water. He drank from it and washed down another pill in the process. Greg opened a bottle of white pills—small and oval, like tiny eggs. "Oh," he said, with something that sounded like excitement. He poured them into his hand too quickly, and they overflowed in a rush, spilling over onto the counter. Some fell onto the floor, onto the shiny marble in Madrid's Central Station. Loose pills danced on the cool stone until gravity reclaimed them.

Adam reached out and tried futilely to catch some as they fell. "Damn it, dad! What the hell are you doing?"

"I want to make sure I get the right ones. These are the ones I've been looking for. They've been working very well lately. Don't you think?"

"Fine," Adam said, completely frustrated and filled with rage. This whole encounter was going on too long. He'd surely miss the train now. Once again, his dad was going to get in the way of him getting where he wanted to go. Who knew how many experiences, ideas, adventures, and opportunities his dad's depression had cost him?

"Goddamn it," Adam said, leaning down to pick up some of the pills. "You're making a total fucking mess."

He handed the pills back to his dad and walked away. *I am so fucking out of here,* he thought to himself. Through the doorway and back into his dad's bedroom he walked. *Crash.* Broken glass. Unable to get the dirty glass of water to his lips, Greg had dropped it into the sink. It had shattered into a half-dozen jagged pieces and millions of smaller ones.

"Fuck!" Adam screamed, when he saw what his dad had done.

"Fuck what?" Greg asked. "Fuck what? What are you fucking?"

"Shut up! You're making such a mess. Why do you always have to turn everything into a fucking disaster?"

"Fuck, fuck, fuck," Greg said, like he was learning a new word.

"Okay," Adam said, more calmly now. He was deadly serious and ready to take control. "You've taken enough to sleep for a few fucking days. So go to bed!"

Adam grabbed Greg's arm again, even harder this time, and led him back to his bed. Only steps into his bedroom, Greg resisted and pulled away with a powerful jerk.

"I can take care of myself," he slurred. "I need time off. Let me be. I need rest. I just need to sleep."

"Yeah? Then…whatever! Do whatever the hell you want. Sleep as long as you want, at least that way you can't fuck anything else up."

"I want to sleep. I'm down. Really down. Been so down these days."

"Well, you're going to be down for a while, that's for sure. And you're going to sleep for a long time," Adam yelled.

"Good," Greg shouted back. "I'd like that."

"Good? Then why don't we call your principal now and tell him you won't be in tomorrow. Hell, you can take a few more and sleep all week. Why settle for only one day off? Take the whole fucking rest of the school year. It's almost over anyway."

"Yeah," Greg said as he turned and shuffled back into the bathroom, now agreeing with everything Adam said. He grabbed another bottle. No matter how many he took out of the cabinet another seemed to appear. It was a constantly refilling bottomless pit of pharmaceutical quicksand. He opened, released, picked, swallowed, and moved on.

"No. Not just one," Adam urged. "Take two, maybe three…"

Adam grabbed the next bottle and opened it for him. Greg was getting messy. Like a drunk, he needed help. Adam twisted open the caps and handed dusty pills to his dad one by one, two by two. Helping made Adam less angry, less embarrassed for his dad. Helping, yeah, he was helping.

"Here, take these. They're white too."

Greg did. And anger, hate, and pity rolled through Adam like invisible pounding waves of sound from the ocean. Adam knew what he was doing, or at least what he wasn't doing. And he didn't fucking care. Adam just wanted it all over and done with.

Greg swallowed another pill and moved away from the counter, away from the mess of colorful pills and broken glass. "Maybe I don't want this anymore. It's too much trouble. Too much work. I've just got too much to do. You understand, don't you, honey?"

"Of course I do, Dad. Your life sucks. Always has and always will. Who needs it? Here, take another."

And he did.

Greg stumbled back to his bed and fussed with bottles of pills in the drawer of his nightstand. It looked like he was just checking to see what was available, what would be close at hand. "I'm so tired of all this mess. I'm tired of this house. I wish it would all just disappear." Then he started opening the bottles one by one.

Greg's voice sounded disconnected from his body. He was angry, furious even, but the pills were slowing him down considerably. He continued to rant, only stopping for moments of silence as he picked, popped, and swallowed another pill. Adam walked over to his dad, stood next to him, and watched as he knocked over a huge pile of shit from his nightstand. Books, magazines, and a cheap cardboard box of Kleenex tumbled quietly to the floor. Adam stood still, resigned, watching the debris fall onto the carpet, some onto the bed. Anywhere the shit wanted to go, it did. Artifacts of Greg's life went anywhere they goddamn well pleased.

"Oh, God, Dad. What the fuck? Sit down," Adam said. "Before you make an even bigger mess...let me help you. You're missing a whole fucking bunch of stuff over here."

Adam crawled around the table and picked up a handful of bottles from the floor.

"Yeah, why not," Greg growled like an angry, drowsy bear about to go into hibernation.

"Take a couple of these. I don't think you've had any of them yet."

Shake, pick, swallow.

"I think you missed these too."

"Yeah?"

Pick, swallow.

"And these."

Adam kept finding more, pushing on the childproof caps and releasing the pills from their confinement. Maybe he was releasing his dad from confinement. Maybe fucking life was confinement, and everyone was just fucking stupid to not recognize the fact that all we're doing is waiting out the clock. What's the big fucking deal about taking your hand and pushing the hands around the clock, pushing time forward? What's the big fucking deal? *Doesn't seem like a fucking problem to me,* Adam thought. Seems like a useful fucking trick and why don't more people use it?

"You're a good son," Greg said, sitting on the side of his bed, as if he was waiting for something, maybe a train or a car or a stretcher. His bare feet touched the carpeted floor. His toes curled under in a knot of anxiety. "You always helped. I hated my dad, but you knew that—you know that."

And on it went.

"You don't need me. You can take care of yourself. Go live with your mom. She's got all the money anyway. I don't have to worry, you'll be fine."

"No, dad," Adam said. "No worries. No fucking worries." Adam stood straight up, almost at attention except that a force beyond his control pushed him forward at an angle that made him look as if he was about to jump on his dad. "Of course," he continued. "We'll be fine. Always have been. Always will. Take one of these, they're adorable…little blue and green ones. Here's some water. Don't want you to choke. This way I, we, whoever, don't have to worry about you either."

"You were always my favorite, my favorite son."

"I'm your only fucking son."

"I know, I know. Nobody worries about me. Nobody will care. You always helped. I always appreciated that."

"Yeah, right."

"I did, I did—always told you that. Remember? I always said, 'Thank you, thank you, love you, love you.'"

Standing over his father, Adam watched the drugs catch up with and overcome Greg's desire to ingest more. Adam watched his dad slide inside his bed, shrug the covers up, and slip inside himself.

"No, missed that," Adam said, mostly to himself. "You must have been dreaming."

"No, I said that. I did, I did."

Greg's head sank into the pillow; he looked like he'd never stop falling into the bed's comforting arms. Adam, right next to and almost on top of him, could see the hint of a smile turn the corners of Greg's mouth for the first time in years.

Wednesday, June 9, 1999

During the summer, morning arrives in Angelito with little warning. The sun sneaks above the mountains to the east and goes from dawn's-early-light to full-blazing in just a few minutes. The heat, though rarely unbearable—"It's a dry heat," they say, and "they" are right, whoever "they" are—goes from warm to warmer as soon as the sun hits the prickly stucco-covered houses that dot the land. Most citizens of Angelito aren't aware of the weather at all. They slip from temperature-regulated homes to air-conditioned cars, offices, classrooms, shops, and studios where the atmosphere is kept at a stable 68 degrees Fahrenheit, the temperature least likely to distract one from oneself. Sixty-eight degrees is the temperature that feels most like there is no difference between you and the outside world.

Vivian stood inside her pristine bathroom, allowing the halogen bulbs to shine hot, white light upon her bare shoulders. With a fluffy white towel wrapped tightly around her torso, she proceeded step-by-step through a series of tubes and bottles, squeezing the contents into her palm, applying the substance onto her face and then removing it until she was cleansed, astringed, moisturized, sealed, and concealed.

Beyond the closed bathroom door Vivian heard Marc getting up. She didn't care. Like yesterday and the day before, he got up after her and never interrupted her routine. This was her quiet time: No music, no news, no telephone calls were allowed to interrupt her method of easing into the day. It was tricky, though, Vivian had to concentrate on nothingness or else thoughts from the nether regions of her consciousness came to the fore. Thoughts like how much of a failure she felt like for having been married twice, for not being a good mother, for not realizing that she'd married a mental case the first time around. In retrospect, she could see that Greg had been unstable from the beginning. She'd concentrated on the man she thought he could have been, instead of the man he really was. She was smarter now, she told herself.

Vivian and Marc had been together for almost eight years, which Vivian felt good about. She felt good about her job too. So what if she wasn't a great mother? She was good at other things. And her kids weren't disasters—just slightly weird. Why did every woman have to be a fantastic mother? What was so wrong with settling for okay? Everyone's kids are a little weird, aren't they?

Downstairs, Marc made coffee. He always made the coffee. While the boiling water traveled through the grinds picking up bits of color and flavor, he opened the front door and brought in the newspaper. Sometimes, depending on his mood, he'd empty the dishwasher, or just sit and wait until the last drop of coffee had dripped. Today, like every day, when the coffee was finished, he filled two spotless white cups and took one up to Vivian. He opened the bathroom door without knocking and set the mug down on the counter. He then proceeded to his studio-office to begin his day. Delivering the coffee was something he did for Vivian every morning; it was something he didn't have to think about.

In the very beginning of their relationship, Vivian would stop whatever she was doing, coo "Thank you," and give Marc a little kiss. Then it became a peck on the cheek, then a smile, and now it was rarely so much as a silent nod amid the din of the running bathroom sink.

Behind Angelito's huge Arco station, a crowd of day laborers waited to be picked up. Across the street, Bollywood Bakery & Bagel Shoppe exuded a yellow and orange version of homey warmth—"homey" if you lived in a jaundiced land of buttery yellowness. Bolly's, as everyone called it, had a drive-through along the side of its A-frame building. Wrapped around the lot was a line of cars with drivers waiting to pick up a doughnut or a bagel and an oversize cup of cheap coffee. Bolly's coffee came in cups too big to fit inside the tiny built-in cup holders in all the new cars, so drivers snuggled the Styrofoam cups between their legs as they drove away.

Fran refused to drink the coffee from Bolly's. Last summer, her father took her to Europe for vacation. He was trying to compete with his ex-wife—and her new wife—who he knew were much more hip than he was. So he took Fran to Paris, Berlin, and Rome all in one week: introduced her to red wine, "real coffee"—as he called it—and fresh-squeezed orange juice from Spanish oranges. "The best in the world," he declared. When Fran returned from her European vacation, she vowed to never drink "American coffee" again. After tasting café au lait in Paris and cappuccino in Rome—in Berlin, they decided, the coffee was nothing special—Fran returned to L.A. convinced that Europeans drank coffee and Americans drank...something else, something weak and pathetic, uncultured and brown, a liquid of unspecified provenance. And that was that.

This morning, like every morning for the last nine months since returning from Europe and buying her own espresso machine, Fran swiveled the miniature stainless steel pitcher—filled halfway with milk—up, down, and around against the steamer as it blew hot air, made bubbles, whirred, whizzed, and sounded just like the machine in the café next to Campo de Fiori. That was where Fran had her first "real" cappuccino and where, for the first time, she first felt less like her father's daughter than a woman dealing with a man, who just happened to be her dad.

"Sunshine, my only sunshine. You make me happy..." The voice sounded human but was purely digital. The high-pitched song came from inside Sandra's super-pink, free-form alarm clock that looked like a melted-down Hello Kitty without any recognizable

feline features. The blob with a clock on its face was Sandra's first alarm clock. Greg had given it to her as a gift before her first day of kindergarten. "It's for your first day at 'big girl' school," he said.

"Dad, it's kindergarten," Sandra said. "I think 'big girl' school starts in first grade."

Seven years later the clock still worked, and Sandra still didn't feel like she was in "big girl" school. She considered most of her classmates to be immature and underdeveloped. Sandra reached her 12-year-old hand out from under her blanket and hit the big blue "Sweet Dreams!" button in the middle of the clock. The voice stopped, and she slipped under sleep's wing for exactly 10 more minutes until—

"You'll never know dear," it started again, exactly where it left off. *"How much I love you ... "*

Again, she hit "Sweet Dreams!" with her tiny fist, but this time she couldn't fall back asleep. She tossed, turned, and thought about getting up. She knew that after two "Sweet Dreams!" the lullaby wouldn't return. The third time brought the real get-out-of-bed alarm. She thought about getting up; she thought about breakfast, and about summer starting in less than two weeks and how then she wouldn't have to use the alarm to wake up—*bzzzzz. Bzzzzz. Bzzzzz. Bzzzzzzzzz.*

The otherwise harmless looking blob became a menace after two "Sweet Dreams!" A dry, electric sound screeched monotonously, as if little elves were playing Operation—the Milton Bradley game—and were purposely hitting the metal side of the organ holes to make that horrible sound the game made when you "couldn't keep a steady hand."

It was 7:15 A.M. What a rude awakening. Sandra stumbled out of her room, a slight scowl across her face, and went straight into the bathroom, shutting the door behind her with a bit of a slam.

The sound of the bathroom door closing woke Adam. He was on the couch only a short distance away, uncomfortably balled up inside a web of blue, green, and black yarn—the afghan his grand-mother had knit years earlier while watching countless episodes of

Wheel of Fortune. Adam kicked his feet out and stretched his legs. They didn't feel like they'd slept at all; they were achy and tight and cold. For the tiniest, most precious second, he didn't remember what had happened. Then, just as quickly, that moment passed.

Muffled sounds of traffic and weather "every ten minutes" came from the radio in Greg's room. A flush of the toilet could be heard from behind door number two—Sandra in their shared bathroom. Adam stared up at the cracked ceiling and listened to the sounds of his house. Adam heard water running and pictured Sandra washing her hands. The radio in his dad's room kept relaying information about sunny skies and high temperatures. Adam knew he needed to go in and turn it off himself.

Sandra opened the bathroom door and walked into the kitchen. Adam stayed horizontal on the couch—he didn't want to have to explain anything to her—and she didn't notice him. Once she was past, he got up and went into his dad's room. It was stuffy as usual. The windows were shut, keeping the outside out and the inside in. He walked past the bed and around to the cluttered table and found the alarm-set-off button. He looked at his dad. His eyes were closed. His mouth was open slightly, like when you're all stuffed-up and can't breathe through your nose. His fingers were wrapped around the top sheet like he was cold.

Alone at the kitchen table, with a single bowl of cereal in front of her, Sandra looked up to find her brother standing in his printed boxer shorts, the bottoms still hiked up slightly, revealing more of his thighs.

"What's wrong?" she asked.

"Nothing. Overslept. Dad's not going to school today. Can you get a ride from Mrs. Brown?"

Adam grabbed a bowl of his own from the cupboard, a spoon from the silverware drawer, and sat down across the table from Sandra.

"Why can't you take me?"

"Does it look like I'm going to be ready anytime soon?"

Sandra didn't answer. She stood up and grabbed the phone off the wall and dialed a number penciled onto a sticker on the inside of the phone. "Important Numbers" it read across the top.

"Hi. Tricia? It's Sandra. Do you think your mom could give me a ride to school? Yeah, he's sick. Okay. Thank you."

Sandra returned to the table, annoyed, and finished her breakfast in silence. She put her dish in the sink without saying a word and left to pack up her bag. When Adam finished, he cleared the table, washed and perched the dishes carefully on the drying rack. On his way back to his room, he saw Sandra reaching for their dad's bedroom door.

"Quiet," he said, with more urgency than he wanted. "I told you already, he doesn't feel well. He isn't going to school today."

Sandra ignored her brother. She knew how to open the door quietly, like a sneaky private investigator. She knew she could say goodbye without waking her dad up.

Sandra turned the knob and held it in position so she could push the door open quietly. The only sound was the *whthphph* of the wooden door against the carpet. She peeked inside and saw that her dad didn't move an inch. He faced away from her toward the closed windows. Her heart sank just a bit. Sandra wanted to at least whisper a goodbye—but what was the point? He wouldn't hear her. She pulled the door back again against the pile in the carpet. *Whthphph.* She held the knob turned so the latch was tucked inside itself until the door was completely shut, and left without saying a word.

Back in her room, she grabbed her schoolbag, stuck Jacqueline inside and stopped by Adam's room. He wasn't really doing anything, she would remember later. If he was late, shouldn't he have been rushing?

"Bye," she said. Her voice sounded hopeful, not hopeful for anything in particular, just hopeful. It caught Adam's attention, and he stopped staring at a pile of dirty clothes on his floor.

"Okay. If dad's not up later to pick you up, I will."

"Okay."

In Dart's bedroom, hidden behind the furniture and under the rug, completely out of sight, lay the necessary hardware for an extravagant electronics system to rival the imaginings of Bill Gates, had he not half a trillion dollars more than Dart to spend. Dart's cell phone, laptop, mp3-only stereo, and television were all wired together in a maze of cords and plugs. To wake up, he programmed his computer to turn on his stereo at a given time and play a certain song. The volume was programmed to increase over a few minutes in order to force him to get up. Dart thought this was much more sophisticated than a snooze button. This morning, he woke up to TLC's greatest song, at least according to Dart: "Waterfalls."

"A lonely mother gazing out of her window / Staring at a son that she just can't touch..."

His eyes still closed, Dart listened. *"Don't go chasing waterfalls... blah-blah-blah."* Dart had no idea what the rest of the words actually were, but he liked the song anyway. He'd been waking up to it for three weeks now and was convinced that he'd slowly unravel all the song's secrets. He particularly liked the video because there was a little man-on-man action. Okay, so it portrayed a bisexual guy getting HIV—but, oh well, nobody's perfect. Dart lowered the volume and got up. He showered, shaved (something he did once or twice a week max; he wasn't exactly hairy) and dressed. Today he put on a pair of light-blue jeans, a white T-shirt, and a short-sleeve green button-down left carefully untucked. Dart checked his e-mail while waiting for Adam to honk outside. Then the phone rang. Dart hit "pick up" and spoke into the air. He'd long since hooked up a hands-free cell phone designed for a car in his bedroom.

"Hello?"

"Hi, it's Adam."

"I know, Adam. I've had caller I.D. for three years. Remember?"

"No, Dart. I don't actually remember when you purchased each individual piece of shit in your room. Do you?"

"Oh, snappy, snappy. What is up with you?"

"I don't think I can give you a ride to school today."

"Okay. Okay, that's no reason to get nasty."

"So, you'll have to drive yourself."

"Fine. But why?"

"There's something wrong with my dad."

"What?"

"I'm not sure."

"What do you mean you're not sure? You just said there was something wrong."

"Are you on your speaker phone?"

"Yeah."

"Well, who else can hear me?"

"Um, no one. Everyone's gone. It's just you, me, and my cell phone service provider who can listen to anything they want, but I don't think they can legally use any information they might gain from our vital conversation since they haven't informed us of their intention to record anything."

"Well, I think it's going to be one of those days when he goes back to the hospital."

"Oh." Silence. "Really?" Dart's tone changed. "What can I do?"

"I don't think anything."

"Well, how serious is it?"

"He's not waking up."

"Oh."

"I think he might be—"

"Oh, come on."

"No, really."

"Really?"

"What should I do?"

"I don't know."

"Well, I don't either."

"Call 911."

"Yeah, but, it might not really be an emergency...anymore. He might already be—"

"Doesn't matter. I think you should still call 911."

"I gotta go."

"Call me later."

"Okay."

"Bye."

Adam didn't put the phone down. He hit "flash" and "3" to speed dial his mom. It rang and rang until Vivian's voice mail picked up. *"Hi, you've reached..." Click.* He hung up and dialed again. Vivian was ignoring her phone while speeding along the shoulder trying to get the upper hand against a clogged off-ramp. She had things to do, a desk to sit at, and people to accept reports from. And by the end of the day she'd have a few decisions to make and instructions to give before leaving to start the cycle all over again tomorrow. Not until she had fully exited the freeway and stopped at a red light did Vivian reach inside her bag to find her phone still ringing. She flipped it open and said "Hello" with a level of exasperation only someone who's just survived a mini battle with L.A. traffic is justified to express.

"Mom, it's me."

"Oh, hi. What's going on?"

"You got a second?"

"Yeah, a second. What's up?"

"It's dad."

"Oh, God, what now? Is it money again? What does he want?"

Ignoring her routine whine, Adam continued, "I think he's not doing too well."

The light turned green, and Vivian sped onward toward her destination.

"What do you mean 'not too well'?"

"I think he's...well, I think he might be dead."

What he couldn't say earlier now slipped easily from his tongue. With his mother, Adam instinctively knew he needed to cut to the chase in order to get her attention. Vivian pulled into her office parking lot, found her assigned space, and shut off the engine.

"Are you sure?"

"I think so."

"How do you know?"

"Mom, I don't know. But he's not moving."

"Maybe he took an extra sleeping pill or something. He always liked those, you know."

"Mom. I don't think he's breathing."

"Oh."

From inside her car, a clean place where the world was cut into nice, neat squares by the shape of the windows, the idea of death was more than foreign. It was otherworldly. Beyond belief. Adam's voice on her phone butted up against the shiny perfection of her surroundings. A hedge of abundantly blooming oleanders separated the parking lot from her building. The creamy pink blossoms screamed abundance and health. Bees buzzed, and a few small, white butterflies fluttered from flower to flower. A dozen questions rose from deep inside her, and Vivian knew right away that she didn't have answers to any of them. This frightened her. This lack of information—of control—upset her. She suddenly realized a vast segment of her life had become a big question mark.

"Sandra got a ride from Mrs. Brown," Adam said.

"Good, very good."

"I didn't tell her anything."

"Okay. Okay."

"So, I guess I need to call someone."

"Yeah. I think so."

Vivian was at a loss for words. Convincing a Polish television executive to buy her programming—no problem. Dealing with a flesh-and-blood family crisis—forget it. Human crises were so…human and messy, and their solutions were so unclear. Vivian sat straight up in her seat and slid into her executive mode, into the person who could speak her way out of any jam, convince anyone of anything.

"What do you want me to do?" she asked with an impatient clip.

"I don't know," Adam said with growing frustration. Why the hell did he call her? She was never any help. Why did he think she would be today? "What do I need to do?" he asked.

"I don't know, Adam."

"Should I call the police or 911?"

"I think they come together if you call 911."

Silence, again. They both fell quietly into a pathetic (Adam thought) familial time warp, the kind in his family that tested the limits of humanity to the extreme. Adam realized he was in a situation where no family member or friend could help him. He could see his life splitting off, taking another trajectory into uncharted territory. Behind him was his previous life as a typical son in a typically dysfunctional family. Now he was a son without a father, and a son with a mother he could barely talk to. He imagined a radar screen on which the blipping green light of his life had been floating in one direction—in a relatively straight line with no sign of danger in its path. Now it was veering toward the opposite side of the black screen, heading off into the unknown. Standing in his bedroom with the phone in hand, he knew that from this moment on everything would be different.

"Do you want me to come over?" Vivian asked, sounding almost genuinely concerned and willing to get involved. She also sounded like she wanted to get off the phone. "I could send Marc over. I'm sure he's free."

"That's cool. I think I can take care of it."

"Okay. I guess you don't have to go to school today. Call me in two hours and let me know what's happening."

From 25,000 feet up, about the height of a 747 approaching Los Angeles International Airport, LAX—"X" like it's sexy, like there's something hard-core under the miles and miles of concrete and asphalt—Angelito is hard to spot. Approaching from the east, homes start to line up side-by-side about an hour's flight time away from landing. Similarly sized homes stand side-by-side; a dozen fill a block. Then another dozen fill another block. And then another. At first, there are differences. A few blocks have holes in them, spots of underdevelopment. Some are imperfectly shaped, yet they all flow together. Each is painted the same few color combinations—sand with brown trim, creamy beige with off-white trim, bright white on white with red Spanish-tile roofs, moldy green with colonial gray trim—so they can almost hide against the desert floor on which they have been built. Closer to "the city," lawns begin to appear larger and darker green; their owners exercise what they believe is their god-given right to as much water as they please. Swimming pools begin to appear—three or four, even five on a block—marking areas of greater affluence. Farther on, even more pools and swing sets—not rusted a monochrome brown, but brightly painted steel or richly varnished redwood from California's state tree.

Just before the plane reaches downtown L.A., where the city's skyscrapers loom in a clump, a stretch of land lies below unnoticeable because of its ordinariness. For only a few dozen blocks there is little more than two- and three-bedroom homes. Very few bright pools dot the monotonous pattern of porches and patios attached to houses connected by driveways to blackish streets that connect all the homes to each other in a pattern not unlike the surface of a microchip. This is Angelito.

Passengers approaching LAX this morning would have been unable to see Sandra walking from Mrs. Brown's dented van toward the front door of Eleanor Roosevelt Elementary School. At four-and-a-half feet—"And a sniff," her doctor said last time she had a physical—Sandra was too small to separate from the crowd of kids going to school. A keen-eyed passenger may have been able to see bigger things, like the ambulance rolling down Adam's street from the south, or the black-and-white police car approaching from the north, each moving slowly like they were in no rush to reach their destination.

The ambulance arrived first and backed into Adam's driveway as if it was making a delivery. *"Beep, beep, beep"* bleeped the vehicle warning to pedestrians—if there had been any—to move aside and avoid being run over. The police car pulled up in front of the house and parked on the street, as if a friend or relative were stopping by to say hello. Adam watched from his living room window. He saw the police officers put their paper coffee cups back into their car's built-in holders. He saw two stocky EMTs tumble out of the ambulance and approach first, dragging behind them a gurney-type contraption. Actually, Adam knew, it wasn't a gurney-type anything. It was a gurney.

One of them rang the doorbell, a seemingly unnecessary courtesy considering the situation. Adam, of course, was waiting for them and opened the door as the bell rang its synthetic chime. *Bdring, bdreeng, bdrong.*

"Good morning..."

"Hi."

"We got the call about..."

"Yeah," Adam interrupted. "It's the second door on the left."

Adam hoped for no small talk as he backpedaled out of the way, pointing halfheartedly down the hall to his dad's bedroom. The men in navy blue cargo pants shifted their safety-orange tackle boxes and followed his pointing finger without question or comment. Adam looked back at the front door, still open, to find two police officers waiting to be let in. Adam nodded. The female officer entered first. Her hat was already at her side, revealing dark hair pulled back tightly into a knot. Adam thought she looked tougher than necessary, and he felt himself tighten up.

"Hi. I'm Officer Williams," she said with her right arm outstretched.

It was calorie-conscious Sue Williams—but Adam didn't know that. He shook her hand. Her grip was softer than he expected, but he kept his guard up. The light streaming through the open front door dimmed as the male officer entered. Adam looked up to see Officer Man-something walk through the door—the same guy from the Sev and from Pavilions the other night. Adam thought he looked even better up close, more like what Adam had imagined him to be. His uniform was perfectly pressed, unwrinkled from a day not yet spent crumpled inside a police car. His eyes were bright, open, and searching.

"Officer Manfield," Jeff said. "Good morning."

Adam met Jeff's outreached hand with his own. While their shake lasted only a fraction of a second, Adam tried to look him over without being obvious about it. Upon release, Jeff moved farther inside the living room.

From his short-sleeve, light-blue police shirt (*Light-blue for day-*

time? Adam wondered.) to his shiny, black boots, Jeff was ridiculously hot and unbelievably handsome in a fantasy-of-a-policeman kind of way—like "Pull over, get out, and show me what you've got, and maybe I'll forget about your speeding ticket." He was big, but not too big. His body wasn't man-made by hours spent at the gym. He was big as if he'd been born that way: strong and perfectly proportioned, with each muscle defined enough to be diagrammed in Adam's physiology class.

Although Jeff and Adam recognized each other, neither made any mention of it.

"My dad's room is right there," Adam said.

"Good," Jeff said, before walking away.

Sue followed behind, disappeared with Jeff inside Greg's bedroom, but then returned immediately. Her look was all business, as it had been when she walked in the door. *No one gets a break,* Adam thought. *Not even when your dad dies.*

"Are you alone?" she asked, adjusting her belt until she could settle her left elbow on her radio as if it was an armrest.

"Yes."

"What about your mom?"

"She's at work."

"Did you call her?"

"Yeah."

Adam couldn't decide what emotion to show. Exasperation? Sadness? Hopelessness? Terror? Boredom? So he showed none. He walked over to the couch and fell onto it, sighing as if he knew it was going to be the longest day of his life, and so he might as well get comfortable. Sue swung her belt around again, this time so she could fit in the chair across from Adam. She pulled out a small pad with light-green paper and red, thin lines across each page.

"Is your mom coming home?"

"No," he answered, continuing to find his place in the couch.

"Why not?"

"They're divorced. She doesn't live here."

Sue looked down and scribbled something on her pad much

longer than Adam's answer. Adam wasn't trying to sound rude. It just came out that way. To him, the questions seemed unbearably stupid and therefore deserved equally stupid answers. Why should he make this woman's job any easier? He didn't know her. Adam dug his finger into a button-size hole on the arm of the couch. He wanted to know what was going on in his dad's room.

"Okay," Sue said with a deep breath, trying to signal to Adam that she wouldn't be intimidated by his orneriness.

"My mom called my stepdad, and he's coming over."

"Siblings?"

"Yes." Adam waited a few seconds to see whether she would ask the next obvious question: How many? Then, just when her lips started to move, he continued: "A sister. Younger."

Sue wrote something in her notebook that Adam couldn't see.

"Where is she now?"

"She's at school."

"And what does she know?"

"Nothing. I told her to go to school before I was sure what was happening. I didn't and don't know what's going on anyway."

"What school?"

"Eleanor Roosevelt."

Crackling sounds came from Sue's radio at her side. She reached down to adjust the volume quickly, like she didn't want to disturb the artificial calm that had settled over their conversation.

"Okay," she said. "I should call Sandra's school. Is there a phone I can use?"

"Yeah. In the kitchen."

Sue left and Adam was alone again, except for the muffled sounds coming from his dad's bedroom; objects bumping into each other; cases being opened and shut; talking in the plainest of tones. From the kitchen came the beeps of Sue dialing the phone—each beep signifying a number punched; each meaningless without the beep that followed. Adam listened to the soft buzz of wheels on asphalt as a car passed and the rubbery brushing of his shoes nervously rubbing against each other. None of these sounds were new, yet they competed for Adam's attention in fierce little battles.

Adam didn't know what to think. He was nervous, unsure how the unfolding events would play out. What kind of questions would he be asked? What expectations for him would there be? Would the cops, paramedics, detectives—whoever—want to ask him very personal questions? He didn't want them to. He hoped they wouldn't. Can't they just see the guy OD'd and take it from there?

Adam sat still on the couch, as if everything around him was separate, as if he had nothing to do with any of the activity in his house. Being alone in the living room should have been a peaceful respite. Being alone had always been Adam's refuge. He enjoyed being away from everything and everybody he couldn't stand. Now that sense of refuge was gone, and he didn't want to be alone. For some unclear reason, he felt an urge to go into the kitchen and be with Sue while she called Sandra. He wondered whether he could go into his dad's room and help with whatever it was they were doing in there. Maybe he should make some phone calls, do something.

Then he saw Jeff walking slowly, confidently from the bedroom, down the hall, and toward him in the living room. He looked like the law of the land, but instead of clomping his boots on sunbaked dust at high noon, Jeff pushed down old carpeting, and the black leather of his boots almost gleamed under the filtered interior light. From the couch, Adam thought Jeff looked about eight feet tall, like John Wayne without the angles. The same easygoing sort of half-smile that looked so effortless and disarming outside Pavilions had returned. *Smiling?* Adam wondered. Maybe Jeff was glad to see him but didn't want to show it. Or Jeff realized how strange it would look under the circumstances to be smiling and stopped himself. Having been a policeman for 15 years, Jeff had seen all kinds of shit—nasty murders, angry assailants, furious victims of assault, terrible strung-out addicts—yet today, in this three-bedroom one-story house in the center of a town no one cared about, he didn't know how to think or behave. Luckily, his insecurity-driven sense of humor kicked in when he needed it.

"Don't mind her," Jeff said. "They've only recently started sensitivity training in Angelito and they are only on N." Jeff pointed to his badge. "See, Manfield, I've had it. She's Williams. Not even close."

"Yeah? I noticed."

"She just looks tough…Sue is actually quite harmless."

Jeff didn't sit down or lean or anything. He just stood in the center of the room, straight and tall like he couldn't imagine needing anything or anyone for support. *Is he nervous*, Adam wondered, *or just so unbearably masculine that chairs are of no interest to him?*

"They're going to be taking your dad out in a minute. If you don't want to see…"

"I'm cool," Adam interjected.

"Okay."

But Adam stood up as soon as he heard them coming down the hall. Suddenly, he didn't want to watch, but there they were, and there was no place to turn. Adam watched what looked like a blanket-covered go-cart move steadily through the living room and out the front door. *That's not the way it's supposed to be*, he thought. Wasn't it supposed to be more serious? How about a moment of silence? Some reverence, some wailing, some incense…a candle? Before he could put his confusion into words, ask a question—say something—it was over. The cart was out the door. It was unreal. The two men led the lumpy go-cart down the walkway to the driveway and into the ambulance. Then they shut the doors and drove away—without even turning to see whether they'd forgotten something or to wave goodbye.

Adam felt nauseated, indecisive, confused. His head felt like a million degrees. Should he be crying, hiding, wailing, numb with shock? The layers of confusion felt like dirt piling up on his shoulders, and he tried to shake them off by going into the kitchen. He wanted to feel clean again but didn't know how. He opened the refrigerator and stared into the glowing coolness.

"Anybody want a Dr. Pepper or something?" he asked no one in particular.

Sue hung up the phone and said, "No thank you."

"Me neither," Jeff added from the front room. Two more offi-cers had arrived, one in a suit with his badge hanging out of his coat pocket, and the other in jeans and a windbreaker, like the FBI guys in *Silence of the Lambs*. Jeff led them into the kitchen to meet Adam. "This is Detective Stone and Officer Michaels," Jeff said. Then he stopped. He looked at Adam standing still, holding a can of Dr. Pepper. He couldn't tell how Adam was handling the situa-tion. "We need to finish up some stuff in your dad's bedroom," Jeff said. "Excuse us."

The new guys said "Good morning" and "Hello," and then dis-appeared with Jeff into Greg's bedroom, leaving Adam alone again with Sue.

"Your sister needs to be picked up," Sue said. "She still doesn't know. They didn't want to tell her at school and, well, what could I say?" With this, Sue began to sound remarkably more human. "Nobody ever wants to be the bearer of bad news. It's like we're all so afraid of hurting somebody's feelings, yet all we seem to do is hurt each other's feelings. Sometimes I think about how many people I'm upset with at any given moment, and that really begins to upset me."

Does she get what she's saying? Adam wondered. Her conviction was genuine, but was this really the time and place for a discussion like this?

In the bedroom, Jeff showed the other men around. Officer Michaels collected the medicine bottles and all the pills that had spilled onto the floor. He put them into large Ziploc bags that looked as if they were intended for some other, less official use, like holding cookies or carrot sticks. Detective Stone dusted the bathroom for fingerprints. Each man wore rubber gloves, as if Greg's bedroom was contaminated. Together, they looked at everything, touched everything, bagged and inspected everything. Someone threw Greg's comforter across the bed, making the bed look half-made. On top of that the officers piled their notebooks and specimen bags, each containing a piece of evidence, proof that Greg indeed had existed.

Alone in the kitchen with each other, Sue tried to get the process back on track. "I need to ask you some more questions," she said. "You want to sit down?"

"Sure."

They both took seats at the table. Sue pulled her chair right back under the table and placed her notebook in front of her. Adam stayed back as if he really wasn't going to cooperate.

"What time did you find the body?"

"You mean my dad?"

"Yes. What time did you find your father?"

"Around 7:30 this morning when his alarm kept going off. Usually, he hits snooze a few thousand times, and it goes on and off for a while, but...this morning it just kept playing."

"You called us around 8:30. What happened until then?"

"Nothing."

"Nothing? What do you mean?"

"I don't know. Nothing. I was trying to figure out what to do, who to call. Sandra was getting ready for school and getting another ride." The look on Sue's face made Adam feel like his answers weren't the ones she was looking for. Something in him snapped: "It's not like every day your dad dies."

"I realize that." She put her pen down and tried to look sympathetic. "Please understand these are questions I have to ask. I'll try to go through them quickly."

"Okay."

"Who was home last night?"

"All of us...all three of us."

"No one else? No visitors?"

"No."

"Were you all three home all night?"

"Yes."

"Is there a significant other, a girlfriend or something?"

Adam started to laugh and then caught himself. "No. I don't

think he's had a date in years." Sue looked puzzled. "Let's just say that wasn't a priority for him."

"How had he been feeling lately?"

"I don't know. The same."

"What's the same?"

"Depressed. Like usual. It's nothing unusual."

"He didn't complain about special problems recently? Any other health issues or problems at work?"

"No."

"Did you see him go to bed?"

"Not really. I saw him in bed around 11 or so before I went to bed."

"Did you hear anything from his room after that?"

"Nothing but the TV. He always went to bed watching TV."

Adam noticed Jeff come back into the room. He put one hand up against the wall behind Sue, like a cowboy holding up an awning over the saloon.

"How long had your dad been taking all that medication?" Jeff asked. "There's quite a bit in there."

"I don't know exactly. It's not like he had a drug problem."

"I understand that—I'm not implying that."

Adam didn't respond. He wanted to let Jeff feel guilty for a few seconds.

"Did he ever need help—I mean, assistance with them all? Did he ever want anyone to help him keep them all straight, organize them?"

"No. That was his business." Then Adam's annoyance got the best of him: "He could take care of himself, you know."

Jeff did his best to move the interview forward. "I heard you say you didn't hear anything after you went to bed."

"Yeah."

"Well," Jeff said, "there's some broken glass in there, and it probably made some noise."

"Probably, but I didn't hear it." Adam said.

Vivian called Marc before she got out of her car and asked him in her nicest voice to go over and check on Adam and Sandra. She had a "big, big meeting" and wouldn't be available until the afternoon so, "Would you be so nice as to go over and check on things until I can get away?"

Marc said yes, of course, and drove over. On the way, he couldn't help considering the contorted familial geometry that forced his early-morning trip. He was going to visit the children of his wife in the house of her ex-husband who might be dead. It was L.A., and it was 1999, but even so, the whole scene felt scripted within an inch of its life. Not that Marc didn't like Adam and Sandra; he genuinely loved them—sometimes felt like they were his own children. They were older, though, and Marc hadn't known them their whole lives. Someday, that fact wouldn't matter, but until then...

Marc parked across the street from Adam's house. As he marched up the steps, his $400 soft-leather Tod's made gentle padding sounds on the cement.

"Who's that?" Sue asked, sounding one part condescending and another part genuinely concerned.

"Marc, my stepfather."

"An evil stepfather?" Jeff asked. "Should we bar the door?"

Adam was thrown off by Jeff's joke and took a second to recover. "No. He's not that special. And he's probably here instead of my mother."

"Where is she?" Jeff asked.

"At work."

"I see.

Marc walked right through the already open door. "Hi, Adam," he said. "Is everything all right?"

"No, not really."

"So I understand."

Marc looked at the police officers and wondered why they were watching him so closely. Were his khakis pleated or something? He disregarded their stares, walked over, and hugged Adam in a vaguely paternal way. No one spoke.

Jeff took advantage of the awkward moment to excuse himself. "I'm going to pack up the stuff in the bedroom so we can get out of your way."

Sue turned to Marc. "Sandra's school has been notified, but she needs to be picked up."

"She's just around the corner, isn't she? I can get her and be back in no time." Marc looked at Adam for approval.

"Yeah," he said.

"I guess, I suppose—" Marc sputtered, trying to find the right words, "that you'll be staying with us...so...can you pack up some stuff for Sandra too?"

"Yeah, okay."

Jeff strode down the hallway, and Marc left through the still-open front door, leaving Adam and Sue together again.

"I'll go pack," Adam said, getting up.

Adam passed by his dad's bedroom on the way to his own and saw Jeff and the other men loading plastic bags into rubber bins. Jeff looked up from his organizing in time to catch Adam's eye, but Adam didn't stop; he kept moving toward his bedroom. Adam didn't want to be involved with anything going on in that room. Any questions he could avoid—about his dad, his dad's medication, or his dad's life—he would.

In his room, Adam looked at his unmade bed, the sheets cast aside from when he got up in the middle of the night. He pulled at the covers haphazardly. Focus on now, right now, he told himself. What would he need for tomorrow? No further. He was going to his mom's, but how long would he be gone? Would he need all his school stuff? Shorts or jeans? Socks, underwear? He decided he didn't need much. He wasn't going very far; his mom only lived 20 minutes away. This conclusion—that he didn't need much at a time when something so large had already been lost—felt overwhelmingly sad.

"Great movie."

A deep, steady voice came from beyond the room's perimeter.

Adam turned to the doorway where Jeff stood looking at a poster for Clint Eastwood's *A Perfect World* that hung in the middle of his bedroom wall.

"Yep," Adam said. "Too bad America wasn't ready for Kevin Costner as a killer. It pretty much flopped."

"Well, I saw it twice."

"I don't know how many times I've seen it, especially since I got the DVD."

A nervous pause insinuated itself into the room.

"The whole thing was kind of bizarre," Jeff finally said, "especially since people usually love anything Clint Eastwood touches."

"You're right," was all Adam could think to say. Where did this conversation come from and where was it going? Adam wanted to know.

"It was only the year before that everyone went crazy over *Unforgiven,*" Jeff continued.

"Right...and—" *Cool down,* Adam told himself. *This is a very normal conversation. Relax, just talk*—"*Unforgiven* was a good movie," he said. "I'm glad people liked it, but then they go and miss something cool like *A Perfect World.* And let's not even talk about *Bridges of Madison County.*"

"You liked it?"

"The movie, not the book."

"Me too," Jeff said, with intimidating calm. "It was totally unappreciated."

Totally? Adam wondered. Are men in positions of authority—with guns at their side—allowed to use the word "totally" in conversation?

Jeff went on: "I was weary because of the book being so popular...I usually stay away from anything that popular."

"Popular success in America," Adam said, "is nine times out of ten a good reason to avoid anything."

"Exactly."

Nervous, quiet pause number two. Jeff undetectably shifted his weight from one side to the other. Adam looked down at the bag he was packing, pushed the last few things inside, and zipped it up.

He was keenly aware that Jeff had not moved from the doorway. He wanted him to…no, he didn't. Okay, he really didn't know what he wanted.

"So," Jeff began, then stopped.

Adam looked up.

Jeff took Adam's open expression as a sign he could continue. He was more relieved at not being rejected than he would ever admit. "You hang outside of Pavilions often?"

Adam put a hand on the back of his desk chair and leaned against it—for moral as much as physical support.

"Well, it *is* open 24 hours."

"You're right about that."

"But it's really not the hot spot it used to be," Adam said.

Strange, but kind of nice, Jeff thought. *This guy—Adam—has a sense of humor that's sarcastic without being vindictive.* He tried to hide a smile from crawling across his face. "But it's only a year old," Jeff suggested, then was instantly ashamed to have said it. That whole notion of how long something has to be around before it's "over" is such an easy way to look old and out of touch. But Adam didn't seem to notice.

"My friends and I play pool next door," Adam said.

"Oh, at the bowling alley."

"Yep."

For Jeff, the conversation continued on two tracks. One was automatic, driven by instinct and curiosity about a handsome young man standing 15 feet away, a man who only the night before had flashed before his eyes so vividly. The other was forced: This was the scene of an incident he was investigating; it was his job to ask questions. Jeff was supposed to be on his way out to the car with a box of evidence from Greg's bedroom. He held the plastic box between his left hand and his hip.

Adam glanced at the box and told himself it was nothing important, but the yellow tape sealing it shut could not be ignored. It made him nervous. Having this man holding this box in his bedroom made him nervous. What was going on? Was this guy cruising him or being nice? Was he some kind of lecherous old man, or just one of those unnecessarily sympathetic adults who can be so creepy? Or was he being a detective? Was all this friendliness just a cover for trying to extract more information?

Jeff noticed Adam looking him over, trying to figure him out. He could tell he was making Adam nervous, and wondered whether his attempt at conversation had been a mistake. "I guess I'll go and put this in the car," he said.

Adam looked straight at Jeff and then at the box.

"Don't worry about this," Jeff said, tapping the bin with the palm of his hand. "We take it in, run it through the system, and after a day or two, we'll call you and you can come in and pick it up…depending on what you want."

"I doubt there's anything I need, let alone want."

"It's up to you."

It sure was easier to talk about movies, they both thought. As Jeff walked away, he was glad he'd spoken to Adam—and more intrigued than ever—but completely confused about how, or if, he would ever be able to talk to him again. Jeff walked down the hall and out the front door, down the walk and back to the car. He loaded the box into the trunk and locked it. Adam watched Jeff through his bedroom window until he realized what he was doing and turned away. He left his room and went into the bathroom. He grabbed his toothbrush from the sink, wrapped it in a Kleenex to keep it almost clean, and returned to slip it into his bag.

"He's back."

Adam turned to see who was talking to him. It was Jeff, back in his bedroom's doorway.

"Who?" Adam asked.

"Evil stepfather."

"Oh."

"He's got your sister."

Pregnant pause number three. Adam and Jeff simply stared— stood still and stared. They were looking for answers to questions they had barely begun to articulate.

What Jeff did know was that he understood something about the way Adam looked and the way he spoke. Jeff imagined they might share something important, some experience, but he didn't know what it was. He looked at Adam and tried to memorize everything about him: the hair pushed back on one side from sleeping, the clothes slightly rumpled, the sneakers very clean yet not at all new. Jeff stood still like a 5-year-old boy at his first show-and-tell. He nervously fingered a business card hiding deep inside his pocket. Back and forth, back and forth, again and again he flipped the edge of the paper between his fingertips. In his head he tried to make a decision. He wanted to make a move, extend a hand, try to keep a door open between them—but when and how?

Finally, he pulled the card out of his pocket and handed it to Adam. "If you need anything or have any questions…" Adam took the card, looked down at the way it fit inside his hand. JEFF MANFIELD it read in bold letters. Underneath, ANGELITO POLICE DEPARTMENT, and an address, telephone, and fax number. *What does this mean?* Adam wondered. It was definitely an official card, but was Jeff's intention professional or personal? *If you need anything, or have any questions*—Adam replayed Jeff's comment in his head. It sounded professional.

Jeff interrupted Adam's analysis: "My cell phone number is on the back."

Adam flipped over the card and looked: 10 digits were hand-written in blue ink. What did that mean? A cell phone is definitely personal, but…Adam looked up to say something, anything, but Jeff had already turned to leave. Adam swallowed nervously and found himself at a loss for words. He looked at Jeff's back and noticed the solidity of it, the ridiculously straight posture. Then Jeff stopped and turned around.

"Thanks, Officer Manfield," Adam said before Jeff could speak.

"You're welcome. But call me Jeff."

When Vivian moved out of the house in Angelito, she first bought a small two-bedroom cottage in Pasadena. The place may have been smaller, but the address was better. When Vivian met Marc, and after they had dated for about six months, she upgraded to a four-bedroom, three-bath near Hancock Park, one of the more chic areas in L.A. All the houses were from the '40s, or at least they all looked like they were.

Sandra and Adam never quite moved into any of Vivian's new homes. They had bedrooms assigned to them—like at boarding school—and each kept a drawer full of clothes. But the rooms looked more like guest rooms for out-of-town visitors than rooms for Vivian's flesh-and-blood children. Then again, Vivian never cared for all that flesh-and-blood thicker-than-water talk. *Too visceral*, she thought.

Adam's "room" held little more than a TV and a sofa that turned into a bed, which he liked because the sofa was more than long enough for him to lie down across comfortably. There was also a phone and a cable jack so he could hang out, talk, and watch TV all in private.

The detectives left first, then Jeff and Sue. Marc asked Sandra if she was ready to go but didn't wait for an answer. She looked at Adam, confused, and then went out to Marc's car. Adam followed shortly behind them. When he locked the front door there was no one left inside. He drove alone behind Marc, barely able to see Sandra's head above the passenger's seat headrest. Marc drove through El Pollo Loco and ordered a family-style meal for lunch. He thought that was better than forcing Sandra and Adam to have to make a decision about what to eat. Back at the house, the rest of the day passed in a blur of grilled chicken and reruns on television shows. Adam surfed through all 300 digital stations. There was something fascinating on the Korean station that Adam believed was some kind of pan-Asian *Who Wants to Be a Millionaire?* The ubiquity of wanting to be a millionaire seemed to Adam, at least at the moment, to be hilarious and incredibly sad.

Vivian came home around 8 P.M. and found Adam lying on the sofa in his room, watching television. On any other day, he would have slipped his feet off the couch quickly, but after the day he'd just been through, he didn't bother. *My sneaker-clad feet,* he told himself, *on this goddamn couch are the least of the world's problems.* Vivian noticed the dirty rubber soles on the beige chenille and cringed slightly, but found the will to bite her tongue: *Of all the days to worry about shoes on a couch, today isn't one of them.* She asked a few basic questions, which Adam answered in equally basic terms. Marc joined Vivian in the doorway. He held a pile of white sheets so clean the faint smell of bleach preceded them.

"These are for you," he said. "I don't think the ones on there have been changed in a while."

Marc's voice sounded so kind and ordinary, it almost hurt Adam to hear it.

"Thanks," Adam said. He sat up, took the sheets, and put them down on the couch next to him.

Sandra heard everyone talking and came across the hall from her room to see what was going on. She peeked through the space in the doorway between Marc and Vivian.

"Hi," she said.

Marc reached down and instinctively put his hand on Sandra's head. He rubbed her hair absentmindedly. "We made Sandra's bed already," he said.

Sandra didn't say anything. She just turned her mouth in a feeble, tight-lipped smile.

So many people in such a small space made Vivian uncomfortable. "Well then, it looks like everyone has everything they need," she said.

Nobody knew how to respond to the comment—least of all Vivian, who had made it. So she squeezed between Sandra and the door to escape.

"You gonna be warm enough?" Marc asked, not expecting an answer. "You know your mom likes to keep the air on just above freezing. Let me get you guys an extra blanket."

Suddenly, Sandra and Adam were alone again. Sandra sat down on the couch next to Adam. Not too close—a good two feet remained between them.

"It's hard to understand," Sandra said without looking at Adam.

He looked over at her, watched the television's blue light flicker across her face. "I know."

"He wasn't sick yesterday."

"I know."

"So what happened."

"I don't know, Sandra. Sometimes things happen quickly." Adam knew his answers were bullshit. "I don't know. We'll find out eventually after they do some tests."

"But people don't just die like this..." Sandra said, then stopped. Tears slid slowly down the centers of her cheeks. Sad tears, without a trace of anger, and she made no effort to wipe them away. The tears just came out, ran down her cheeks, and dropped off onto her T-shirt, where they quickly disappeared into the pink cotton.

Adam didn't know what else to say. He'd spent the whole day wondering how his dad's death would affect him; he'd hardly thought about Sandra. Her life would be changed forever too, and he tried to assess how responsible he should feel—for getting her into this situation, or for moving forward, or for helping her deal with it. Adam scooted closer to Sandra on the couch, then reached out and pulled her toward him until they met somewhere in the middle. Adam put his arm around Sandra and settled his hand on the part of her arm where her T-shirt sleeve ended. *She's so small,* he thought. She fit beneath his arm so easily. Sandra leaned into and against Adam, found a place for her head between his arm and his chest. Adam squeezed gently and held her beside him.

Whether Adam and Sandra should stay home from school was never discussed. Everyone assumed they would. There were bigger questions: How was everyone supposed to act? Where in the stages of grief were they supposed to be? Adam, especially, wondered how he was supposed to feel. He lay in bed for a while staring into space, trying to figure out exactly what he was and who he was supposed to be.

Getting dressed but not for school—just some shorts and a T-shirt, no brushing her hair or putting on shoes and socks—made Sandra wonder whether she should feel sick, like she had the flu or something. She'd always believed you needed to be really sick if you were going to miss school. Not getting ready for school but not feeling sick was disorienting.

Vivian went to work as usual, but left feeling distracted by all the activity in her house. Should she stay? *Oh, God, can't stay…too much drama…Marc can handle it,* she assumed. As she rushed out, Vivian told everyone she would try to work "only half a day" so "we can spend some time together this evening."

Marc didn't follow his routine. He didn't go to his office with his own coffee and spend the morning in his own little world. He woke up feeling like making breakfast. In a perverse way he was enlivened by the situation at hand. It felt a little creepy, he had to admit, for someone's death to light a little fire beneath him. But apparently that was the case. Or maybe it was the new people in the house—new responsibilities, and new routines.

"I'm making breakfast," Marc announced. "Real breakfast, so watch out."

Adam and Sandra came into the kitchen to watch. Sandra almost smiled at Marc's sense of adventure; Adam was more circumspect. They watched closely as Marc put together an impressive spread of eggs, bacon, pancakes, and sliced pink cantaloupe.

The phone started ringing right after breakfast. It ceased for short breaks throughout the day only to be interrupted by the doorbell. Friends and family called and dropped by with condolences and questions and horrible looks of sympathy. The casseroles and hugs Adam didn't mind as much as the pained expressions on the faces of the well-wishers.

Between disturbingly unpredictable moments of apathy and rage, Adam made calls himself. The one call he wanted to make was to his Aunt Patricia, his dad's only sister, who lived in San Francisco and was probably a lesbian. She had long since moved north to create her own life. The news of Greg's death didn't surprise her, which Adam found reassuring. It made him feel like he hadn't been imagining how miserable his dad had been all these years.

Vivian had said she would call Greg's principal on her way to work, and she must have kept her word. By early afternoon, Greg's fellow teachers all started calling to find out whether the facts were as they had been told

"Yes, it's true. Okay, okay," said Adam. "Yeah, yeah. He is. Yeah, yeah. Thank you." And on and on it went.

The day disappeared in a haze of sandwiches and glasses of "sun tea, Diet Coke, or water." Those were the options Marc constantly repeated. Conversations—whether on the phone or in person—flowed like sewage in old plumbing: all stops and starts, sometimes gushing and other times slowing to a painfully silent halt. So many questions. So many answers repeated again and again. "Oh, how are you? Oh, you poor thing. Oh, you must be devastated." And on and on it went.

Every Thursday Jeff and Sue worked half a day in the field and the other half indoors at the Angelito PDHQ (police department head-quarters). By late afternoon, they were deep into the rhythm of fill-ing out forms, replying to inquiries, and doing whatever else need-ed to be done with pens, paper, and hundreds of staples bent into their final, folded shape with a quick shot of the fist.

"Do you have any idea how many trees we waste?" Sue asked. They sat at adjoining steel desks, each stacked ridiculously high with paperwork that no one wanted to claim as their own. "And not only here, but think of the bigger picture. We probably waste more paper than any other organization in the city. Thousands of trees are sacrificed to keep track of every ticket, summons, warn-ing, complaint, and arrest."

"I suppose you'd rather we stopped keeping track?" Jeff asked, not looking up from his work.

"I'm serious. Think of what we—you, I, and everyone else in this building right now—use every week. What are there, 27 Angelito officers and at least as many support staff? Then think L.A. County, Corrections, INS and ATF, FBI...E-T-C." She spelled out the abbreviation and considered herself quite clever, for a moment. "You've got enough government paperwork to deforest a small country every year. It's a crisis!"

Jeff could not have cared less. There was only one thing on his mind: Adam Westman. Ever since they had officially met 36 hours ago, Jeff had let Sue's tirades float past him like exhaust on the high-way. He was too busy to listen. He was too busy trying to figure out how an 18-year-old man—someone almost 20 years younger than he—had been able to crawl inside his head and refuse to leave.

On the television left playing inaudibly in a corner of the living room, the evening news became *Entertainment Tonight* and the number of visitors slowed to a trickle. Vivian was still not home from work. She'd called several times throughout the early evening to say she was on her way, "I'm leaving the office right now...really." But she never arrived. After seven she called again and Sandra answered. After hanging up, Sandra reported, "Mom's on her way home with Chinese food."

Adam could have sworn he noticed Sandra rolling her eyes as she spoke, but he had no energy to comment on it.

"And she said 'not to worry,'" Sandra added.

Nobody was worrying. Nobody was doing anything but talking and sitting around. When Vivian finally arrived home, she barreled through the front door with two big shopping bags at the end of each arm. Inside, white boxes clipped shut were stacked on top of each other: mixed vegetables and chicken, white rice, broccoli and beef, chow-fun noodles, double-fried pork, and scallion pancakes. Death delivers strange bounty: an abundance of hollow words, stiff upper lips, and food. In a flurry of arms and hands and chopsticks unsheathed from red paper wrappers, dinner unfolded with little discussion. Everyone was tired of talking.

"Do you want to go back to school tomorrow?" Vivian asked.

"Yes," Sandra said. This staying at home thing was not working for her. She looked to Adam for affirmation.

"I don't know about 'want,' but I guess I 'should,'" Adam said.

"It's Friday, so if you want to skip until Monday—that's fine with me," Vivian said.

"Whatever," Adam said. "Tomorrow is the last day before finals, I guess I should probably go."

"Well, I'm definitely going," Sandra said, her mind made up. But that was tomorrow. For the moment, her goal was to find the fortune cookies she knew had tumbled out of the bags along with the napkins and soy sauce. She began her hunt by rifling through the debris left over. Marc watched bags and wrappings fly, and thought about what a mess they had on their hands. *Thank God it's all disposable,* he thought. Sandra found the fortune cookies inside a handful of small wax-paper bags, along with packets of sweet plum and mustard sauce and individual moist towelettes. She passed the prophetic cookies around the table as the phone began to ring again. With cookie in hand, she jumped up to answer the phone.

"Nice to see everyone so hard at work, not wasting any time talking about environmental issues or other irrelevant topics."

Sue looked up first. They knew whose voice it was: Sgt. William H. Winbridge. What they didn't know was when he'd come into the room.

Technically, he was their boss, although some wise-ass "management consultants" had recently swept through the department and taken away everyone's hierarchical titles, which were supposed to be passé. Winbridge still acted like he was the boss. His brutish demeanor and close-cropped flat-top (the same haircut he'd had since he was 5 years old) endeared him to no one. Nonetheless, he was the asshole everyone had to deal with.

"Good afternoon," Jeff said respectfully.

"Hello," was all Sue could muster. She hated the guy.

"Whose case is yesterday's OD?" Winbridge barked.

"His." Sue pointed across the desk to Jeff, only lifting her head high enough to see Jeff's eyes.

"Okay, then," Winbridge said as he lumbered a little closer. He dropped a skinny file on Jeff's desk. "Manfield," Winbridge began, "This looks like a straight-up OD, but the kid's got his dirty little prints all over his old man's shit. We've got both of their mits on just about everything we dusted. Get him in here and lean on him a bit. Probably nothing there, usually isn't, but just in case…do your best to be a real cop. That's what we pay you for. Then you can check off the empty boxes on all the appropriate forms so our bases are covered and our asses are protected. What you've got to do is make sure there are no dead fish swept under the rug because it smells like a sardine can in there."

Winbridge didn't wait two seconds for Jeff to unravel his mixed metaphors, which he mixed on purpose because he thought he was hilarious. He walked out of the room without saying another word.

"A laugh riot," Sue said with a lip-twisting snarl that Jeff completely missed. He was already inside the file searching for signs of Adam.

"Yeah, a real wordsmith," Jeff mumbled back. He didn't want Sue to know he was secretly thrilled to have been handed the

Westman case. He was annoyed with Winbridge for suggesting there might be more to the story, especially if it involved Adam. Jeff had been there, after all. Shouldn't he be the one who's suspicious, if anyone is going to be suspicious? *What a fucking idiot with that fish-under-the-rug crap,* Jeff thought. But he did now have a professional excuse to call Adam, which was a good thing.

"On that chipper note, I'm outta here," Sue said. "Want to walk out together?"

"No, let me get this file opened…so I can get it closed again as soon as the kid comes in."

"Sure?"

"Yeah, you go ahead. This'll only take a minute."

Sue left Jeff alone, sitting up straighter than he had all day. He slid his finger along the side of the file labeled GWESTM6/99. It was thin and deceptively simple-looking. There were only five sheets of paper: a death certificate, a list of drugs found in Greg's system, the notes Sue took the day before, a sheet with fingerprints and their identifications, and an uncompleted close-out sheet waiting for the appropriate signatures.

Jeff focused on the fingerprint sheet. The two sets of prints looked so similar—obviously from two people who were closely related. The only difference he could find was a distinctive turn on the sides of Adam's thumbs. Otherwise, they were exactly the same. Each had been found on the medicine bottles, the countertop, and the pieces of broken glass. The only place Adam's prints were missing was on the water bottle beside the bed. Jeff tried to imagine a series of events that might lead to these results, but couldn't see the steps in any logical order. How could anyone force someone to OD one pill at a time? Maybe Adam didn't touch everything that night? Or maybe he'd tried to clean up before calling 911?

Jeff knew he needed to call Adam and ask more questions. He'd probably get a few simple explanations and be able to sign off on all the appropriate paperwork. Jeff was nervous about calling Adam—about what he might find out—until he remembered that he was in control of this situation. If he found something strange, he didn't have to report it. Recognizing this power relaxed him, calmed him down a little. Jeff flipped the file back to the opening page and found the phone number for Adam's mom's house. He quickly dialed before he could change his mind. A young girl answered the phone.

Dart rode shotgun in Fran's beat-up two-door orange BMW 2002. As she sped along, he rifled through piles of accumulated debris on the floor, in the glove compartment, and in the pockets of the door. He sifted through a collection of old-fashioned cassette tapes looking for something to listen to while Fran drove them to Vivian's house to visit Adam.

"You have the absolute worst collection of music in the whole world," Dart said. "Sheryl Crow? What's that...proto-lesbian music?"

"Shut up. That is from my pop phase. Everyone has a pop phase."

"*Annnnhhh,*" Dart screeched, trying to mimic the sound of a penalty buzzer on a game show. "Wrong."

"Oh, fuck you. Any time you want to buy me some new music— even if it's for your own selfish reasons—so you'll have something satisfactory to listen to while I'm driving—go ahead."

"Hunh," Dart exhaled. "Finally." He'd found an Alanis Morissette CD he approved of. "My God, it's filthy. And I gave this to you for your birthday." Dart blew on the CD as if he'd just dug it up from the backyard. "And this is how you treat it?"

Fran grabbed the CD from him, pulled a napkin printed with Arby's Roast Beef from the pocket in her door, and wiped it off.

"Is she gay?" Dart asked.

"I don't think so."

"Just because you haven't slept with her doesn't mean she isn't a lesbian."

Fran slipped the CD in, and the music began mid song. "Please," she said, making a right turn more quickly than was necessary. "You *know* she's not a dyke. Her best song is about giving head to her boyfriend."

"Oh, yeah. No wonder I like her."

"You are so fucking gross."

"Anyway…how fucked up do you think Adam is going to be?" Dart asked.

"Oh, I don't know," Fran said. "I don't think he'll be too bad. He's pretty sturdy."

"No, he's not," Dart said, looking out the window. "He's a mess."

"I don't think so," Fran said. "Well, at least not usually."

"Adam?" Dart said. "Please. He just acts all cool on the outside. Inside, you know he's a mess."

"Adam," Sandra yelled from the kitchen. "It's for you."

Adam wondered whether it was another excruciating condolence, or if it might be one of his friends—finally—calling to rescue him from exile in Hancock Park.

"Who is it, honey?" Vivian asked Sandra as she sat back down.

"Don't know. Office of…or officer something."

Vivian looked across the table at Marc, as if he knew who was calling. He looked back at her with a face that asked, *What are you looking at me for?* They both sat still in order to listen in on Adam's conversation. Sandra watched their behavior closely and was sure they were out of their minds.

"Hello. Yes. Yeah? Okay," Adam said, leaning against the kitchen counter. "Of course. Sure, that's fine. Okay, see you then…Bye. Okay. Bye."

Vivian and Marc shook off their frozen postures as Adam walked back to the table. He could tell they were eager for an explanation, but he wasn't about to make it easy for them. With his chopsticks, Adam picked up a single cashew from the white box of kung pao chicken and put it in his mouth. "Where's mine?" he asked Sandra.

She grabbed a fortune cookie half-hidden under the white paper wing of an open box and handed it to Adam. He opened it—*crinkle, crinkle*—cracked open the shell—*crack, snap*—and popped a piece into his mouth while he unfolded the paper.

"It is very possible that you will achieve greatness in your life-time," he read before he tossed the rest of the cookie into his mouth. "In my lifetime would be a lot better than after my lifetime, don't you think?"

No one laughed. They still wanted to hear about the phone call.

"Too much about the future," Sandra declared. "I like 'em when they're closer to today. Did you hear mine?" she asked Adam.

"No."

Sandra read her fortune out loud: "Your demeanor hides a gen-tle interior."

"Oh," Adam said, leaving the vowel sound to wander around the room.

"Bor-ing," Sandra whined. "Can I have yours?" she asked Vivian.

"Of course, honey," Vivian said as she passed another crinkly plastic pouch over to her daughter. "So, Adam," she began, unable to wait any longer. "What was that call about?"

Adam knew he would tell them eventually; he just hated to be pushed. And he didn't want to sound like he was nervous about visiting a police station, which he was.

"Just that policeman," he finally said.

"Which one?" Marc asked.

"The one from the house. He wants me to stop by the station tomorrow."

"Why?" Vivian asked, her focus on Adam unwavering.

"Something about picking up dad's stuff and signing some papers," Adam said. He was trying to act cool but came off as aloof. "I don't know, really."

"You want Marc to go with you?" Vivian asked without even looking at Marc for approval.

"No. Of course not," Adam said as he slid his plate away from him.

"Sure?" Marc asked.

"Yeah, I'm sure. It's totally no big deal."

The knot in Jeff's stomach unwound as soon as he hung up the phone. He tried desperately to push the corners of his mouth down so it wouldn't look like he was the least bit satisfied, which he was. He put the Westman file away and packed up his bag. Jeff felt embarrassed to be so excited to see Adam tomorrow, and he drove home sitting a little higher up in his seat than usual. He rolled down the windows to let the still-warm evening air blow around him. At a four-way stop—the kind where everyone has to wait even longer than usual as they decide who got there first—Jeff let a little orange Beemer with Alanis Morissette playing inside go before him.

Dart and Fran walked halfway up Vivian's driveway before taking a shortcut across the grass. The dew-covered blades of hardy St. Augustine crunched quietly beneath their feet.

"Knocker or bell?" Dart asked.

"Bell," Fran answered. "Knockers scare me."

"Bullshit. You're a dyke! Knockers are what it's all about." He pushed the button on the side of the door. *Dingngngngg, dong*. The bell sounded like a recording of an ancient Mongolian gong, but it came from somewhere inside a quaint little 1940s bungalow—and almost made sense.

Vivian pushed her chair back and walked toward the door, unlatched the lock, and saw two people she recognized but whose names she couldn't remember. "Hi," she said, raising her pitch toward the end like a question.

"Hi, Mrs. Randall, it's Dart."

Fran interjected: "And Fran. We're Adam's friends."

"Yes, of course, come in."

"Is he home?" Fran asked. She carefully wiped her boots on the mat while Dart just walked right in.

"Place looks the same," Dart said, trying to make conversation. "Same as the last time I was here, I mean."

Adam recognized his friends' voices and hurried in from the dining room to greet them. "Hey," he said, so glad to see them.

"Hey," Fran said.

"Hey, hey," added Dart. "How are you?"

"I'm fine," Adam said.

Everyone, including Vivian, looked to see whether Adam was telling the truth about how he really felt. Vivian watched their conversation like an anthropologist observing an unknown tribe of indigenous people for the very first time. Except Vivian wasn't really interested in learning anything about her son's friends or his life. She was just tired and confused and inexperienced with 18-year-olds in her foyer.

In the dining room, Marc opened his fortune cookie and read the fortune out loud: "Your ameliorative façade masks a forthright agenda."

"What does 'ameliorative' mean?" Sandra asked.

"Being nice," Marc said.

Fran felt the tension between Adam and his mom. "So—" she said to Adam, "we're wondering if you might, um, want to go to the Sev and grab a Big Gulp or something."

"Yeah, of course." Adam looked to his mom, who stood woodenly, like a guard unsure of what exactly she was supposed to be protecting. "I'm going to go out for a few minutes," he said.

"Sure, sure. Of course," Vivian said. She was visibly relieved that a course of action had been decided.

Adam turned back to his friends and opened his eyes wide to signal that he knew this was an awkward situation and his mother was crazy. "Let me just grab my Birks," he said.

In the car, Adam took Dart's place in the passenger seat. Dart sat in the back but perched himself between the front seats like a kid who wanted to be near his parents.

"How are you, man? I mean, really?"

Before Adam could answer, Fran added, "Yeah, we were really worried about you."

"God. I don't think I've ever been so glad to see you guys."

"Oh, thanks," Dart and Fran said simultaneously.

"Seriously, I am so glad to be away from that house." Adam

slipped his feet out of his sandals and put them up on the dash, pulling his knees to his chest for comfort.

"Your mom is a little stiff," Dart said.

"Oh, she's not so bad," Fran added.

"That's because you like mothers," Dart snapped.

"Whatever…"

"You do have two of them," Adam said.

Above the staccato *chig-a, chig-a, chig-a* of Fran's old car, their voices overlapped in a pattern of comments, understandings, and quips that were comforting to all of them, but especially to Adam. Normal life, he realized, or at least what passed for it two days ago— was still out there. He just had to find his way back to it.

"I guess I'm okay. Although I'm not so sure."

"The word is out at school," Dart said. "But not in a bad way. Nobody's saying anything stupid. Everyone just feels really bad."

"That's cool. I guess I won't have to tell anyone then."

Fran pulled into a different 7-Eleven than they were used to— one just outside Hancock Park. Adam's friends prided themselves on knowing the exact location of every 7-Eleven in Los Angeles, so Fran drove straight into the parking lot without pause. She pulled right in front of the door, allowing the store's light to fill the inside of her car like it was the middle of the afternoon.

"You fly, I buy," said Dart as he handed Fran a $10 bill. It was bribery, yes, but Dart wanted a few minutes alone with his best friend.

"The usual?" Fran asked.

"Dr. P., please" Adam said.

"Me too," said Dart.

Fran left and Adam turned around in his seat. He put his back to the dashboard and folded his legs Indian style.

"You will never believe what you missed today," Dart said.

"What?"

"The most amazing substitute for Señora Cardenas. He must have been like 25, six feet tall, and built like Vin Diesel."

"Sounds like just your type."

"Totally. His Spanish was pathetic. I don't think he even knew any. He was probably some football jock who injured himself and didn't know what he was going to do with his life and decided to become a teacher."

"Did he tell you that?"

"No."

"Well then, I'm sure it's true."

"What do I care," Dart said, hunching his shoulders up around his ears. "He's hot as hell, and I had an hour of eye candy."

"How nice for you."

"Basically we had study hall, except that I didn't get any studying done because he was so fucking hot."

Fran returned carrying three huge cups. She passed them through her open window, and Adam took them one at a time.

"Is he still talking about Señor Douglas?" Fran asked. "That's how he introduced himself. 'Hello, my name is Señor Douglas.' Doo-glass. And Doo-glass was his first name. He really was a total idiot."

"Okay, okay," Dart said. "We've established that fact. He was only a sub. Can we cut him some slack?"

"What are you drinking?" Adam asked Fran. She wasn't holding a Big Gulp, but instead a Slurpee cup with electric-orange ice forming a peak above the paper rim.

"They have orange-pineapple," she said defensively. "It's my favorite."

"Gross," said Dart. "Sugar and water and some chemical that keeps the individual ice granules from sticking together."

"Gross? Let me tell you what's gross," she snapped. "Dr. Pepper is made with prune juice, and you know what prune juice does to you."

"Whatever. That is so not even true. I looked it up online. Dr. Pepper is made from 13 different fruits, and nary a prune in the mix. And it's been around longer than Coca-Cola, and way longer than the sugar-color-ice-Slurpee thing that you're drinking."

"So, does everyone know how he died?"

There: Adam said it. Asked it. Just threw it out there and let it hang.

"Oh, God, Adam," Fran said. "I'm sorry. But I think so."

"Mr. Williams told us in first period that it was kind of adverse reaction to medication," Dart said.

"Sort of," Adam said.

"What do you mean?" Fran asked.

"Well, he'd been taking the same medications for years and never had an 'adverse reaction' before."

"What do you mean?" Dart echoed.

"That he probably took more than he was supposed to."

"You mean, like, an overdose?" asked Dart.

"Yeah."

It was quiet for a moment as they let Adam's words settle in their ears. Dart took a sip from his Big Gulp. Fran looked at Adam empathetically, wondered what she could possibly say at a time like this, and came up with a quiet, muttered "Damn."

Completely unsure how to react, Dart asked, "But you don't know that for sure, do you?"

"It's my dad, idiot. Why would I say it if I wasn't sure?"

"Well, how do you know?"

"I just know." He looked straight at Dart, who looked like he was waiting for Adam to change his mind or at least explain more. "The doctors said stuff, and there were bottles left out and other junk."

"Adam," Fran said. "It's cool. It really makes no difference."

Dart was lost. "I don't know of anyone who's ever killed himself before."

Now it was Adam's turn to stare at Dart and want more—more patience, more understanding.

Dart leaned away from them and against the backseat of Fran's car. "Well, at least not until now," he said.

"You know," Fran said calmly, "last fall, when Veronica's parents found out about her and me, and started giving her a lot of shit?"

"Yeah," Adam said.

"Well, you know how she got mono and missed school for a couple weeks?"

"Yeah," Dart said, leaning forward.

"She tried to kill herself and was in a hospital."

"Damn," Adam said. "I had no idea."

"I know," Fran said. "But shit was out of control, and she didn't know how to handle it. Thank God she screwed up, and it didn't work. But anyway…my point is that I understand it a little more, or at least I think I understand the idea of it more."

"Whoa," Dart said. "I just went from not knowing any people who have tried or succeeded in killing themselves to knowing one person who tried and another who succeeded."

"Oh, shut up, Dart!" Adam said. "This is not about you."

"Nah, it's cool," Fran said.

Dart took that as an okay to continue asking questions. "How did she…"

"Dart!" Adam snapped, just shy of losing his temper.

"No, really, it's okay," Fran said. "She tried the old running-the-car-in-the-garage method because she thought she would just fall asleep and not feel anything. She did fall asleep, but then her dad came home from work early and opened the garage door and found her before it was too late.

"Why didn't you tell us earlier?" Adam asked, his anger giving way to sympathy.

"It's Veronica's story, and I never felt like there was a right time to tell you. Also, it's not really something very easy to bring up."

"Does she know you're telling us this?" Dart asked.

"No. And I expect this conversation to stay in this car and not leave it. If she ever tells you on her own, cool. But you didn't hear it from me."

"Of course," Dart and Adam both said.

They talked a little bit longer, segueing from death to school and other stuff until they decided to head home. Fran dropped Adam off at his mom's house first. Adam told Dart to remember to drive himself to school tomorrow, since picking him up would be way out of his way. In between comments, Adam imagined how different his life would have been had he lived with his mom, in this fancier neighborhood, and not in Angelito. He would have gone to a different high school. He wouldn't have the friendships he had with Dart and Fran. And he would have been someone else entirely.

The last day of regular class at Angelito High School was almost a complete waste of time. Most teachers spent the day prepping their students for next week's finals. Some reviewed the points they'd been trying to make all year, while others dropped not very subtle hints regarding the topics that would be on their final exam. No teacher wants their students to fail; it would reflect poorly on the teaching. And other teachers, who had fallen far behind in their planned educational trajectories, spent the last day cramming in as much as possible. History teachers who only made it up to the 1960s desperately tried to fill their eager pupils' minds with at least a passing knowledge of everything from Vietnam to the Gulf War, Watergate to Whitewater. It was pointless for the students to try to learn so much in only one final hour, but the teachers felt better knowing they had made the effort.

Adam was in fine shape, academically at least. Being an overachiever was something he could do to show his parents—and himself—*Hey! I'm okay in spite of everything.* But, after the last few days, Adam wasn't exactly enjoying himself. In between classes, instead of getting his friends to sign his yearbook, he received condolences and smiled back appreciatively. Adam's day was spent in wordless conversation, and no one seemed to mind.

The constant sympathy meant that Adam couldn't stop thinking about his dad. He'd gone to school hoping for distraction, but instead he couldn't get the recent events out of his head. Where was his dad's body? he wondered. In a freezer? Being touched by strangers, or painted with thick, pasty makeup?

Sandra found more comfort in the rhythm of fourth grade. By first recess, she had fallen under the spell of a hot summer day in a classroom with weak air conditioning. The teacher talked, the chalkboard held words, and kids asked questions. She was able to forget about life outside of long division, the history of California, and the differences between sedimentary and igneous layers of earth.

Reality reappeared during lunch, when Sandra grabbed her brown bag and took her place at the fiberglass lunch tables with the other fourth graders. She opened her bag and found contents very different from what her dad used to buy for her. Marc made Sandra a tuna sandwich with tiny pieces of chopped celery. A piece of green lettuce lay neatly between the mound of cold fish and the bread. *It is so complicated*, she thought. Also, inside the bag, rested a little plastic baggie with exactly four cookies inside—all lined up like well-behaved children—and a shiny red apple loosely cradled in a paper towel. This must be someone else's, she thought. She must have grabbed the wrong bag out of the closet. She turned the bag around, looking for the name, and there it was, in blue permanent marker. She was the only Sandra in her class. It had to be hers.

For the rest of the day, Sandra was unable to find refuge in the world of fourth grade. Things were different; life felt so unstable. When the last bell rang, she exited Ellie and walked toward the line of cars holding parents waiting for their children. She wondered who would be there for her. She thought maybe her dad would be there—maybe it had all been a mistake. Then she saw Marc. He'd stepped outside of his car and leaned against the passenger's side, so she could see him. She was relieved and disappointed.

"Hello, Sandra," Marc said. He opened her door and held it open like he was a chauffeur. "Right this way, please."

Sandra looked up at him and wondered, *Is this guy for real?* She got in cautiously. Marc shut the door and went around to his side.

The air was cool inside—Marc had left the air on—and there was music: soft, sweet singing. A woman's voice filled the car.

"How was school today?" Marc asked as he pulled away from the curb.

Did he really care, or was he just playing the role of the perfect parent he'd learned about watching television? "It was fine," Sandra said as evenly as possible.

"That's good," Marc said.

Sandra weighed the difference between "fine" and "good" in her mind for a moment. "I guess good is definitely better than not fine."

Marc kept driving. "You're right about that," he finally said. "And sometimes better than not fine is all we can hope for."

By the end of his day, Adam had gone from obsessing over his dad to obsessing over his rapidly approaching meeting with Officer Manfield. The situation was starting to worry him. Two days ago, he was quietly thrilled to have Jeff's phone number—a connection to a man he could call and talk to in ways he hadn't even imagined. But now Jeff had called him first. That meant it probably wasn't personal. Adam knew there were plenty of unasked questions about the night his dad died. There was the broken glass in his dad's bathroom, which Adam denied hearing. *Why did I say that?* he wondered now. No one had pushed him to answer that way; Adam had made his own decision to tell that story, and now he wasn't sure it had been the right decision. He wasn't even sure what had happened that night...was he? Lucky for Adam, before he could work himself into a purely neurotic frenzy, he saw Dart approaching his locker.

"Dude. We are so close to being done with this...hole. I can't even believe it."

"Dart," Adam said, looking him up and down. "Talking about holes...Through what hole in your brain did you lose my instructions never to wear that shirt again?"

"Well, hello to you too," Dart said. He was wearing an oversize rugby shirt with a big orange stripe across the chest. The orange matched his reddish hair—it did look a little weird, like he was trying too hard. "No, I didn't get that memo. But anyway, what the fuck is wrong with this shirt? I love this shirt."

"It's so...jockish. And you are *so* not a jock."

"Puh-lease," Dart responded. "It's a rugby shirt; it's Australian. No one in the continental United States plays rugby. It's totally a fashion statement—and even better—I'm not someone who makes fashion statements, so it's 110 percent ironic."

"Whatever. Your sense of irony is ironic." Adam shut his locker. "B-T-W"—he spelled it out—"You know I can't give you a ride home today, right?"

"Hello, you told me that yesterday, remember? I drove myself." Walking toward the parking lot, Dart thought about how much stress Adam was under...but really, did he have to be such a prick about everything? "It's cool, though," Dart continued. "I gotta run my science project presentation by Mr. Nichols one more time before tomorrow's fair."

"That's another reason not to wear that shirt, Rugby Man. You are science fair, not soccer fan."

"Give it a rest," Dart said. "What're you doing now?"

"Got an appointment."

"Where?"

"The police station, actually."

"Oh. Why?"

"Questions, questions. You got a lot of questions today Mister Science Fair."

"Oh, whatever," Dart said, his patience running thin.

And Adam knew it. "It's nothing," he said. "I gotta pick up some of my dad's stuff and sign some papers."

"Already?"

"Yeah, apparently in this town nobody wastes any time once you're dead."

Angelito's police station was built in the '70s but had been designed by a 60-something architect who was still, intellectually, in the 1950s: The station was a perfect two-story box made of cinder blocks and painted pure white. In front, there was a screen of square cast-cement cubes stacked together from ground to roof about four feet away from the actual façade. Between the façade and the large windows of the main building grew a grove of bamboo, spindly and pale from the lack of direct sunlight. A baby-blue, kidney-shaped pool with lounge chairs alongside would have looked perfect in the back. Instead, there was a parking lot filled with half a dozen police cars.

Inside, Adam found a waiting room filled with seven or eight random people, young and old. He thought the place was awfully busy for a Friday afternoon. He noticed there were no cool junkies shaking in the corners; no crooks wearing Army-surplus, like on *Law & Order*. The front desk was only a window cut out of an otherwise blank wall. Adam thought it looked just like the receptionist's desk in his dentist's office.

"I'm here to see Officer Manfield."

"Your name?" asked a frumpy man in an ill-fitting uniform.

"Adam. Adam Westman."

"Have a seat."

Adam didn't move. He needed more information, didn't he? Mr. Frumpy noticed and continued speaking without looking up from his desk: "We'll call you when we're ready for you. Please have a seat."

Adam turned to face the waiting room. Every chair was different. The magazine selection was as pitiful as at his dentist's office. Growing up, he'd had too much time to read magazines at the dentist's office; when one Westman went to the dentist, the whole Westman family went to the dentist. It was never just Adam's appointment or Sandra's. It was an hour-and-a-half stretch of dad, mom (when she was still around), and the kids, one right after the next.

Today, he scanned the rack: year-old *Highlights* for kids; *Time, Newsweek* and *U.S. News and World Report* for adults. Adam thought it was a particularly stupid idea to keep old newsmagazines around because the news in them was continually less relevant as each day passed. Then, just as Adam began to thumb through a two-month old copy of *Entertainment Weekly*, Mr.

Frumpy yelled out the window. "Mr. Westman? Officer Manfield is ready for you."

Adam looked up to see a kind of secret door—a piece of the wall without a handle—open to reveal Jeff. He was holding a clipboard and looking very professional, slightly intimidating, actually. He seemed taller than Adam had remembered, his arms thicker. A wave of embarrassed, nervous nausea passed over Adam as he forced the magazine back into the overstuffed rack. Anxiety and attraction mixed uncomfortably inside him as he tried to force his horny fantasies and his fear of invasive questioning to the back of his mind. This was a fucking police station after all! This was about his dad, wasn't it? And Jeff, after all, hadn't exactly come on to him in any sort of blatantly flirtatious way. Maybe he'd imagined the whole thing. Maybe Jeff wasn't even gay. *Yes, I know there are gay cops,* Adam told himself. *But are they absolutely hot, hot, hot?* Jeff was not only hot—he was straight out of some charity calendar. Real gay cops, at least the ones Adam had seen on newsmagazine shows, were so nerdy.

"Want to come on in?" Jeff asked.

His deep voice sounded so friendly, as if he was inviting Adam over to watch a football game or something. *Weird, really weird,* Adam thought. "Well, I don't want to stay out here."

"Me neither, so…"

Adam walked through the doorway and started down a greenish hallway that smelled like ammonia mixed with dust. Jeff walked right next to him, leading him from hallway to hallway until Adam was completely disoriented. How could all these hallways be inside such a small building? By the time they arrived at the small office where Jeff and Sue worked, Adam was sure he'd never be able to find his way out again.

"Grab a seat," Jeff said, pointing to a metal chair next to his desk.

"Nice office," Adam said

"Thanks. They offered us a corner upstairs with a view, but we turned it down. This one just felt right."

Two points for Jeff, Adam thought. *Sarcasm at a time like this?*

Impressive. "I didn't know cops were allowed to have a sense of humor."

"Oh, you'd be surprised what we're allowed to get away with," Jeff continued matter-of-factly.

Adam slipped his backpack under the chair and fidgeted with the seam on his jeans while Jeff sat at his desk, leaned back a little, and looked straight into Adam's eyes. Jeff had consciously avoided eye contact so far, but now he gave in. "So. How are you?"

"Fine."

"Staying at your mom's?"

"Yes."

Their eyes may have connected, but their conversation was going nowhere. Adam was weary of Jeff's formulaic kindness, and Jeff was too. Jeff wondered whether he was being too nice, too soon. He didn't want to show any personal emotion until after he'd asked the questions he needed to ask. He looked away and shuffled through a pile of papers until he found the sheets he wanted.

"Here's the medical examiner's report. Your father definitely died of an overdose. The death certificate has been signed and sent over to the mortuary. They'll give it to you there. I can give you a copy of it if you'd like."

"Oh, great."

"I'm sorry," Jeff said, looking up from his papers toward Adam. "I'm sure this is not easy."

"No, it's fine," Adam said defensively, angling his eyebrows down into a bit of a scowl. "I'm fine."

Jeff reached down to the floor and lifted an oversized Ziploc bag out of a box. It was filled with pill bottles, an empty water bottle, his dad's watch, and pieces of broken glass. And that was only what Adam could recognize immediately. "Here is your dad's stuff," he said.

Adam didn't make a move for it.

"Of course, you actually don't have to take it. His watch is in here, though. You might want that."

"Okay" was all Adam could think to say. He took the bag and put it into his backpack without looking at it.

Jeff didn't like the tension in the room any more than Adam did. He tried to be as officious as possible. *Move on, move on,* he told himself.

"If it's okay, I need to ask you a few questions."

"Okay."

"There was quite a mess in the bathroom that day," Jeff began, "and I need to ask you about that."

"Yeah," said Adam, not twisting in his chair or looking around the room nervously.

"Well, with everything spilled all over the floor, including a broken glass, it seems unlikely that you wouldn't have heard anything."

"Yeah, I guess it does."

"Let me put it this way. In police work, when something doesn't make sense, we like to ask questions about it until it starts to make sense."

"Sounds logical."

"Okay." Jeff took a breath. "Can you tell me why you think you didn't hear anything?"

"I don't know. I'm a sound sleeper. I'd been studying a lot and I'd been out late the night before." He emphasized the latter to remind Jeff that *he* had seen him out late the night before; he wasn't making anything up.

"Okay. So let's assume that you didn't hear anything."

"No...I didn't hear anything."

"Okay, so you didn't hear anything. Not the broken glass or the spilling bottles of pills."

"It's not like his bathroom is next to my room," Adam said with an insistent tone.

Jeff felt bad. Something in Adam's eyes revealed a deeper level of hurt than he'd previously noticed—a hurt that appeared to transcend, or precede, Greg's death. Jeff tried to adjust his tone again, to find a balance between his professional needs and his personal sympathy. He took another breath before continuing.

"Okay. About the fingerprints…it looks like all the fingerprints we took that day were either from your dad or you. Yours were on just about everything we checked."

Jeff looked to Adam for a response. None was forthcoming. "Did you often handle his medicines?"

"No. Well, sometimes."

"What do you mean?"

"Well, sometimes I picked them up for him. He'd call them in or his doctor would, I guess, and I'd pick them up at the pharmacy."

Jeff stayed quiet, to let Adam continue. He wanted to see whether he would give anything away.

"He wasn't exactly the neatest person either, as you saw. I did a lot of cleaning up."

"So you'd say you did a lot of work around the house? You guys didn't have a cleaning person or anything?"

"No. No maid, no gardener, no nothing…just us."

Jeff flipped through his papers, trying to remember what else to ask. He realized he was going nowhere fast.

"So, is there anything else you think we should know before closing out the file on your Dad?"

"I don't think so," Adam said, even though he knew there was so much more—too much more—that he couldn't even begin to explain.

"Okay. Well, you know, we have to ask these questions—cover all the bases, as they say." Jeff scribbled something on the top piece of paper and handed it to Adam. "If you sign this saying that you've picked up your dad's stuff, we're finished."

Adam signed the paper without reading a word on it.

Jeff thought Adam looked so helpless sitting alone in a chair scribbling his name on a document he didn't read. He looked smaller, like the world was getting bigger and messier around him by the second. Jeff was torn. What kind of a cop was he to let other issues—romance, lust, infatuation—get in the way of a simple Q&A?

Adam handed back the paperwork and the pen.

"That's it," Jeff said, sounding defeated. Finally confirming—

somewhat—that Adam had no more to do with Greg's passing than he already knew, didn't make Jeff feel any better.

"Okay."

Adam picked his bag up but didn't move. He stayed in his seat and looked around the office. He felt like he didn't know how to get up, and he needed to wait until he remembered.

"When is the funeral?"

Jeff's simple question snapped Adam back to attention.

"Tomorrow."

"Sounds soon."

"Yeah, but there isn't much reason to put it off."

"Guess not."

"There must be a lot to do before then."

"Not really. My dad wasn't exactly Mr. Popular. And my mom is helping out a lot."

"That's very nice of her."

"I guess so."

"How's your sister?"

"She's okay."

Adam looked at Jeff. He looked like the old Jeff again, the friendlier one. "She's lucky. She's young enough to not really understand what's going on."

"I guess that makes her lucky."

"No?"

"Well, someday she might wish she had more memories."

"Maybe."

Jeff and Adam were both glad to have the conversation settle into a more casual pattern. Adam wondered whether Jeff might actually understand where he was coming from, or was he just a really good actor? Jeff sat, slightly slouched, and looked just empathetic enough. He was calm. He didn't look nervous. Adam liked all of these things and Jeff could tell, and that made him feel good, like he was useful. *It's amazing*, Jeff thought, *how good feeling needed can feel.*

"Your sister might want you to tell her more details later on. That's something you can do for her."

"I hope she finds someone better than me to fill her in on the details," Adam said with wide eyes, like he was trying to make a joke. "I mean, it's just...he wasn't exactly the greatest dad, you know. I might not remember only good things."

"So few dads are 'great.'"

"No, it's, I mean, people don't realize, and I don't know if I would even tell my sister about it someday, but he wasn't exactly there for us."

"You mean after the divorce?"

"No, I mean, because of being sick. He was out of it so much he might as well have not been around. In a way he really wasn't around."

Jeff wanted to find a few perfect words to explain the bitter complexities of life to the handsome young man sitting across from him, but he couldn't find them. "Well, you don't have to decide what to tell her until later."

Adam heard what Jeff said, but he was still following his own train of thought. "It's hard to miss someone who wasn't always there."

Jeff didn't respond right away, and Adam took his silence the wrong way—convinced he'd gone too far, shared too much, and shown how much of a spoiled brat he really was. Adam thought he'd better leave before he revealed any more. *So much for impressing this guy,* he thought. Adam stood up, reached out to shake Jeff's hand, and then pulled it back. He felt so deeply sad that he couldn't find the strength to keep his arm out. He desperately didn't want to cry in front of Jeff. He wanted to get out of there quickly, but he needed Jeff to help him find his way out, so he remained calm.

"I'll walk you out," Jeff said.

Adam didn't say anything. He slid his bag over his shoulder and followed Jeff quietly. They walked in silence from hallway to hallway until Adam was convinced he was in some sort of video game maze. He wished it were all a bad dream. Why couldn't he just fucking wake up?

At last, they reached the secret door, still solid white but more obviously a door from the inside.

"Good luck tomorrow," Jeff said. He reached out to shake Adam's hand.

"Yeah, okay." Adam shook Jeff's hand quickly, then pulled away to reach for the door.

"Maybe I'll see you around," Jeff said, wanting to leave some part of their meeting open-ended.

"Yeah. Maybe."

Most people who call Los Angeles beautiful do so because of the dry and mild weather, the combination of tropical and desert plants, the sandy beaches between sheer cliffs and the deep blue sea, and/or the mountains that stand just beyond the hills. During the summer the mountains are blue-green and gray. In the winter, they're topped with white caps of snow that touch the bluest sky.

Others who consider L.A. beautiful, find mystery in the city at night, when neon signs glow from every block and lamps run along avenues and streets farther than the eye can see. Enormous billboards feature half-naked men, fabulously dressed women, or picture-perfect vistas of Hawaii. Ads for blockbuster movies loom even larger when the backdrop is night and huge halogen bulbs light up the stars.

If pressed, Adam would side with the city of night. He would do so because of one street on the edge of Angelito that he thinks is out of this world. The street runs up and over a hill. At the peak, the road levels out—almost too quickly—and the horizon pops up between the light-speckled landscape and the dark sky above. Adam loves this street because for a fleeting moment, as his truck hovers between ascent and descent. The whole city—hell, the whole universe—spreads out before him like a blanket of flickering lights— white, yellow, orange, and in between—with a few streaks of red along the highways.

A second-story balcony ran along the entire back of Dart's house, connecting his bedroom to his parents' room. But since they never used it, he felt like it was his. Dart had a very expensive telescope that he purchased with his own money on the occasion of his 12th birthday. He only brought it outside on very clear nights, and tonight was one of them. Dart could usually see quite a few stars clearly and even a planet or two from his personal outpost. Finding Saturn, as he did tonight, always thrilled him. The rings looked exactly as they did in books. So much so that he had to remind himself that they were real.

Dart sat outside on a metal folding chair while he gazed up at the sky through his telescope. Venus hung above the horizon like a single piece of glitter. Dart should have been making last minute preparations for the science fair, but he didn't really need to. He'd done the work, and it was ready to be presented.

Dart had no problem spending a Friday night at home alone. He was a bit of a nerd, and he knew it, especially if a nerd is someone who excels in science and math and doesn't quantitatively have a lot of friends. But Dart was much more than a nerd. In the last year, he began to develop into a relatively handsome young man. In the last 12 months, the man Dart would become had begun to appear. He was no longer as terribly awkward and clumsy as he had been through puberty. In a way, he was returning to a time before his awkward adolescence when he was confident, in complete control of his hands and feet. Way back when, Dart actually had been athletic. He played Little League baseball beginning when he was 5 years old and enjoyed it.

"You have such good eye-hand coordination," his mom always told him after he hit a home run or two during each game.

But when Dart turned 11, he quit baseball. No matter what his mom said, Dart felt less and less like he fit in among his old friends. The whole guys-on-a-team thing became unappealing when he didn't like any of the guys on the team. Dart always knew he was gay, so that was not the problem. The problem was that when his friends and teammates realized they were straight—and their hormones turned them into hyperactive idiots—Dart couldn't stand spending time with them.

When he was 14, Dart had his first *real* sexual experience—not counting the times he messed around with curious childhood friends. It happened at summer camp in the San Bernardino Mountains, and it happened because Dart loved to swim. His parents didn't have a pool at home, so when he was at sleep-away camp every summer, swimming was the highlight of each day. Dart was always the first one in the pool and always he last one out.

"Get your butt out of the pool, Mr. Dart, or we are lockin' the gate with you inside," the counselors would threaten.

During his sixth and final year at camp, more than just his love of the water kept Dart in the pool until the very last second. His name was Brad—the camp's swimming instructor-lifeguard. The last kid out of the pool was also the last out of the showers. The last *adult* out of the pool—and the showers—was Brad.

Dart had felt something for Brad, a kind of invisible force like gravity, since he was 5 years old, when Brad taught him how to swim. He would put his hand underneath Dart's belly to keep him afloat while Dart learned to rotate his arms like two propellers. The whole experience was magical in Dart's mind. The combination of self-propelled movement and the warm support of a man's hand beneath him combined to form an integral part of Dart's fantasy life for years to come.

Unfortunately, each summer Dart moved another year further away from swimming lessons, and from Brad. Dart had to settle for grabbing onto Brad during water polo games or chicken fights, which weren't allowed, but sometimes Brad let them slide. Dart could watch Brad teach the new kids how to swim from a distance, but that was often painful to watch without being able to participate. So he settled for observing Brad as a lifeguard, studied Brad's body as he paced around the pool making sure no one drowned. And Dart plotted how he could maybe, someday, have muscles just like Brad's. During water polo or in-the-pool volleyball games, Dart took any opportunity he could find to bump into Brad— preferably underwater—and learn more about his body. Dart was painfully aware that Brad never pushed him away during these not-so-accidental collisions, and that Brad, in general, did not ignore Dart's attention. Then, finally, *it* happened.

It happened exactly halfway through Dart's final week of camp—in the middle of a very dry August—during the otherwise uneventful summer of 1995. For three straight days, Dart was the last one out of the pool so he could share the locker room with Brad and catch a glimpse of him changing. Then Brad changed everything. Instead of walking to the showers with a towel tied properly around his waist, he strolled slowly—and nakedly—into the showers. Brad went into a different stall than usual—he picked the one right across the narrow hallway from Dart—and didn't even try to pull the mildew-covered plastic curtain between them.

"Hey," Brad said. "Has anyone told you your chest is really starting to develop?"

Zzzzip. Dart's penis shot halfway to attention before he could mumble, "Um, no."

"Well, it is."

Dart turned his water quickly to hot, hot, hot. *Maybe I can burn my hard-on away,* he thought. But then Brad started talking again. "You should try this brush I got," he said across the tile divide. "It's great."

"Yeah?" Dart said, his brain so cluttered he couldn't think.

"Here, I'll show you."

And with that, Brad left his shower, walked across the sticky tile floor, and entered Dart's steamy cubicle. "Damn, you like it hot," he said. "Mind if I turn this down?"

What was Dart supposed to say? No!? He said nothing, and Brad turned the temperature back down to simply hot.

"Turn around," he instructed. And Dart obeyed. Brad ran his gently scratchy brush over Dart's shoulders and back, his arms and "developing chest." Somehow, Dart found the courage to look up at Brad's face and found him smiling. This only made Dart dizzier, so he quickly looked away.

"Cool?" Brad asked. But before Dart could answer, he continued: "Here, do my arms." And he handed the brush to Dart.

Brad turned around showing Dart his broad back. He pushed his arms back, flexing his triceps. Dart started scrubbing with a boiling sense of excitement he didn't know what to do with. At one point, he looked down at Brad's butt and swooned as he'd only done once before when he stood at the top of the Sears Tower in Chicago with his family years ago during an extended layover.

"Thanks, man," Brad said, looking over his shoulder. "That's great." He looked down and found Dart's 14-year-old boner and smiled. Brad took hold of it in his big wet hand and for a few exhilarating seconds, became a roller coaster—the most exciting, scariest one Dart had ever been tall enough to ride. When it was over, Brad said, "Thanks, man."

Thanks, man? Dart thought. *Thank you!* But he didn't say anything. Dart just wiggled the muscles in his face back to life and smiled at Brad. And Brad smiled back. For a second, everything was absolutely right in the world.

Dart wasn't thinking about Brad tonight on his balcony looking at Saturn. He'd long since replaced him with other objects of admiration and obsession. When he was 16, his driver's education teacher, Mr. Trettin, put his hand on Dart's leg every time it was necessary to slow down—and left it there until Dart accelerated again. Mr. Trettin provided Dart with three months of fantasy material. Last year, Dart had fallen into a deep obsession with a man he met at the computer store where he frequently shopped. This guy gave Dart steep discounts and even came over once to help him set up some new equipment, but surprisingly—at least to Dart— nothing happened.

Brrrrrring, brrrrrring. Brrng, brrrng, rang the phone inside Dart's bedroom. He let the answering machine pick up.

"This is Dart's mean, green message machine. After the beep, well, you know." Pause. *Beeeeep.*

"Hey, it's me. Pick up the phone. I know you're home 'cause you're a loser..."

Hearing Adam's voice through the tiny speaker on his machine, Dart came inside to pick up the phone.

"And where else would a loser like you be tonight but home? So pick up—"

"It takes one to know one," Dart interrupted. "You are a loser if you're home on a Friday night calling someone you believe to be a loser."

"Oh, please. How are you?"

"Fine, thank you," Dart said, laying down on his bedroom floor to get comfortable. "And you?"

"Fine."

"Is this your one phone call from prison?"

"Please. You think I'd waste my one call on you?"

"Like anyone else would take your call?"

"Yes," Adam said.

"No," Dart replied.

"What are you doing?"

"Nothing. Why?"

"Then we are both losers," Adam said. "Because it is our last Friday night as high school students, and we're sitting at home. My whole family is trying to watch a movie together. My mom, Marc, Sandra, and me—*together*—like in the same room."

"What could they possibly be thinking?" Dart exclaimed.

"I have no idea."

"Well, what are you watching?"

"*Parenthood,*" Adam said from his room at his mom's house. He'd escaped family time and was now sprawled across his couch dramatically, one leg over the arm and the other onto the floor.

"Oh, God," Dart said, his fingers still inside the pages of his dog-eared copy of *Guide to the Stars.*

"Marc suggested it. He said it was one of his favorite 'dramedies.'"

This cracked Dart up. "Gu-ross," was all he could say.

"This movie is so old-school it's almost new-school," Adam said, pleased to have made Dart laugh. "I think they must have planned it, like 'Okay, let's watch a movie about families who are more fucked up than ours and we won't feel so bad about our own fucked-up situation.'"

"I've heard worse plots by parents less intelligent than yours," Dart said.

Adam reached above his head and fingered the shade on the lamp unlit above him. Then he walked his fingers down to the base, found the switch and began flipping it on and off, again and again. "I don't even think they noticed me get up and leave the room."

"That's a surprise?" Dart asked. "What did you want them to do—pause and wait while you went and called me?"

"Excuse me?"

"What happened at the police station?" Dart asked.

"Not much. Signed some papers and shit."

"Oh," Dart said, letting go of his book and reaching for the remote control. "Sounds okay." Dart turned on the television but kept the sound off. He flipped through dozens of channels barely noticing what was on.

"Yeah, but a little weird," Adam said. "They gave me back all my dad's medicine, and all the stuff they took from his room."

"Oh, God."

"I know, like I want it?"

"That is creepy."

"It was the same cop, though, as before," Adam said. And as he spoke, he let go of the light. He left it off and let his arm drop down to the floor. The carpet was not as soft as he remembered.

"Which cop?" Dart asked, halting his channel-surfing for a moment to concentrate on Adam.

"From the house, the one I told you about, the one who was trying to be nice."

"What do you mean *nice?*"

"Nice. Friendly-nice. You know who I'm talking about. We saw him together, outside Pavilions and at the Sev."

"I don't remember that," Dart said.

"Oh, God."

"He's nice?" Dart rolled over onto his back. "Like *gay* nice?"

"Yeah, I think so."

"A gay cop?"

"Can you believe it? We're everywhere."

"How do you know he's gay?'

"I don't know for sure. It's not like he told me about his boyfriend or if he's a top or a bottom. But he seems gay."

"And you think he's cool?"

"Yeah."

"Hmmm," Dart muttered into the phone like a skeptical teacher. "Point him out next time, and I'll tell you if he's cool."

Adam could tell Dart was getting weird—as in jealous weird—so he changed the subject. "What are you doing?"

"I was just about to go over some last-minute science-fair shit. You know...make sure I have everything." Dart looked across his bedroom. Of course he had everything. He'd been ready for days. It was all packed up and ready to go right by his door. He looked over at his perfect packing and thought, *Jeez...I am a loser and a geek.*

"Oh, yeah," Adam said. "I completely forgot. How's it going?"

"Fine, fine...I've got all my pushpins, Scotch tape and number 2 pencils—all that really scientific stuff together."

"I'm sure you're more than prepared."

Lame topic, Dart thought. He rolled over on his side away from the door. "How are the funeral arrangements going?"

"Well, we need a lot more than pushpins and Scotch tape," Adam said, aggressively pulling puffs of lint out of the carpet. "And a lot less. I guess we're ready." Each puff of wooly nothing he extracted from the floor, he then shoved under the couch. "Nothing else to do but show up and cry."

"I can't believe I can't make it because of this goddamn science fair."

"Whatever. It's no big deal."

"Adam, you're my best friend. I'm supposed to be there to hold you when you break down crying."

"Don't worry about it, Dart," Adam said, "I don't plan on collapsing. When have I ever been so dramatic?"

"When have you ever gone to your dad's funeral before?"

"Oh, whatever."

"Fran's going, right?"

"Yeah," Adam said, like it didn't matter.

"Well, I'm going to talk with her tonight and make sure she's prepared to be very nice to you, maybe even hold your hand."

"That is so unnecessary."

"We'll see," Dart said.

"So…I guess I won't see you until Sunday, after you're done with the fair?"

"Guess not. So let's hook up Sunday night after the fair?" Dart asked.

"Yeah, cool," Adam said.

"Maybe we can cruise Pavilions and look for Mr. Coppy," Dart said, still jealous but not even close to admitting it. "Since apparently I didn't notice this incredibly 'nice' man last time we were there."

"Oh, God, would you drop it?"

"Fine, fine," Dart said, then continued in a much more friendly tone, "Good luck tomorrow…at the funeral and all."

"Thanks. I'm sure it's going to be a total blast."

"Can't possibly be more fun than the science fair."

"Okay. Later."

"Yeah, later."

Adam hung up the phone, got up off the couch, and walked back toward the living room. The movie was still playing, and everyone was still in the exact same position they were in when he left 15 minutes earlier. No one appeared to have so much as shifted in his or her seat while he'd been gone. Adam slipped back into the chair he'd been sitting in earlier, and no one looked up.

SATURDAY, JUNE 12, 1999

The funeral was short. Or maybe it just felt that way to Adam. He sat with his mom, Marc, and Sandra in the very front row, which was set aside for just them. The whole thing made Adam feel like he was trapped inside a bad segment on *60 Minutes*—all earnestness and tinkly music with a wise old man's voice narrating the story.

The church was smallish and bright-red brick on the outside, blond wood and plain white Protestant restraint on the inside. The only objects for wandering eyes to settle on were the cut-out felt banners illustrating various proverbs. Adam couldn't remember the last time he'd been inside this church. But he'd been often enough as a young child to make the current experience uncomfortably new and old.

Greg had grown up as a member of this simple church in the center of Angelito. He and Vivian were married in front of the blocky, wooden altar, which looked like a coffin crossed with a Dumpster—boldly minimal or downright ugly. Adam and Sandra had been baptized as infants by the same clean-shaven pastor who officiated today. Their baptism had satisfied Greg's parents' need to have their grandchildren "saved," and since then the Westman family had steadily reduced their attendance until it was negligible.

Vivian had only cared because Greg did. She had been brought up without any relationship to a church—and she turned out just fine, she thought. In the beginning, when she still took Greg's feelings into account, she acted concerned about getting everyone in the pews for Christmas and Easter. But apart from those two holy days, the family slid out of God's house willingly. And it did not go unnoticed by any of the Westmans that lightning had failed to strike them for their wandering.

Sandra took the aisle seat. Adam, Vivian, and Marc filled in the rest of the church's front pew. They looked like an artist's rendering of a family: a mom and dad, girl and boy. Adam found himself pondering the theory that dead people like to stick around and watch what goes on after they leave. If that was true, what must his dad be thinking now? What would he think of the pastor rambling on about fretful lilies and walking through the valley of death? There were no lilies in Angelito except in pots at Easter, and Greg hadn't walked into the valley of death.

If Adam's father had bothered to stick around in some kind of ghostly/spiritual sense—which didn't make much logical sense to Adam—he imagined his dad probably felt vindicated by the turn of events. He probably thought he really was irrelevant—look how perfectly Adam and Sandra fit into the quaint little shape of a family with Vivian and Marc.

Anger. Not sadness or hurt, but anger. Adam felt slow, burning anger as he imagined his dad watching the funeral and feeling anything but remorse. He was angry because Adam knew how wrong his dad always was about these things, and how wrong he was today. He and Sandra were not better off with Vivian and Marc. Adam felt himself getting steadily angrier until he knew he had to stop himself or fly into a rage right there in the front row. Adam had to find a way to push his feelings back down—deep into their painful little caves of bitterness—so he wouldn't explode. Adam did this by telling himself that maybe none of this was true—maybe it was all in his own imagination. Maybe, when you die, all the bad feelings just float away, like little fluffy clouds. Maybe his dad was no longer bitter or depressed at all. Maybe he was just hanging out in the church somewhere watching the scene because what's the point of anger once you're dead? Maybe, just maybe—death was it.

There was no hovering-around bullshit. Dead was dead.

Two ancient men with comb-overs took turns with the pastor at the lectern. They read passages from the Bible and led prayers that everyone but Adam's family seemed to know by heart. During the course of their ultimately pointless ritual, Adam came to another conclusion. His dad was really gone.

As the last hymn began, four overweight men and two old bald guys pushed Greg's casket down the center aisle. *What is up with this place?* Adam thought. *You're either hugely overweight or a step away from the grave.* A young boy who should have been outside playing on a Saturday afternoon led the procession in a white robe. He carried a large brass cross and kicked his too-long robe out in front of him with every step. The clean-shaven pastor walked behind the boy and sang from an open hymnal. He stopped in front of Adam's pew and motioned for his family to rise and walk with him down the aisle. Everyone quickly grabbed their belongings and followed Pastor Clean-Shaven's bright white robe and flat voice. Adam looked up only once when he walked. He saw Fran and Veronica standing against the back wall. They were ever-so-slightly dressed up and held a hymnal between them, but weren't singing. Fran gave Adam her plainest face, like she wasn't going to feel sorry for him, like she knew he could handle it. It almost worked. Adam felt an initial boost of confidence, then he looked down. He didn't want to think this much, at least not yet.

Sandra looked around, and so did Vivian. Adam's mom smiled like it was a networking event, and she wanted to make as many people as possible know she was on hand. Marc appeared present, but his mind was elsewhere. He had shifted into party-planner mode. His newfound, nurturing side had planned a post-burial lunch at their home. While he was walking down the aisle, Marc began to count the number of people in attendance. He hadn't planned for this many, and he wondered whether he had ordered enough food from the caterers. And since it was so warm, he wasn't sure he had ordered enough ice.

At the door, Pastor Clean-Shaven stopped and instructed the

family to stand beside him in a receiving line. While they stopped, the casket continued through the door, across the church's cement entryway, down a few steps, and into the parking lot. The men kept walking and pushing until Greg's coffin was up against the back door of a charcoal-gray hearse.

Adam stationed himself on the outside of the reception line. As soon as the first guests distracted the pastor and Vivian, he ducked away and sneaked out a side door. He walked past a hedge of dusty camellias and around to the front of the church, where he waited under a towering pin oak until it was time to leave for the cemetery. Fran and Veronica found him hiding and came over to say goodbye.

"Not the worst service," Fran said.

"No, I suppose not," Adam replied.

"You look good in a suit," Veronica said, searching for a compliment.

"Thanks," Adam said, unable to find a creative response.

"Well, we're ready to take off," Fran said.

"Take me with you," Adam pleaded, with more earnestness than he intended.

"Oh, please, Adam. You are fine."

Adam definitely didn't feel fine.

"I'm sorry we can't spend the rest of the day together," Fran said. "I switched shifts and now I have to work dinner."

"And I've got to seriously study before I fail geometry," Veronica added.

"It's *so* not a big deal," Adam said, regaining his cool. "Thanks for coming at all."

Adam made his way back to his family when he saw the rented black Lincoln pull up in front to pick them up and take them to the cemetery. Marc took the front seat. Vivian and Adam sat in the back with Sandra between them. Adam looked at the back of the driver's head. His crinkly white hair was flattened and shiny. *Oh, God,* Adam thought, *Another old fart two steps away from his own funeral.* Morbid thoughts and stifling heat sent Adam reaching for the button to make his window roll down. *Flip-flip...flip, flip, flip.* Nothing moved. He flipped the button back and forth to no avail. The sound of Adam's struggle with the button was barely audible, but Grandpa-behind-the-wheel heard Adam's plight.

"Easy does it back there, bud. Got the AC on high. Just give it a sec to kick in."

Bud? Bud! Beads of sweat formed on the back of Adam's neck. He had to lean back, take deep a breath, and tell himself this would all be over soon.

From the parking lot to the street, the boulevard to the highway, the 110 (L.A.'s senior freeway, at a mere 60 years old) to the 10, they drove east for the burial. The cemetery was in Covina, a piece of civilization—if you must call it that—defined by nothingness; dirt and houses and people doing what they're told. The drive should have taken half an hour, and it may have. Nobody spoke except for Marc, who made a call on his cell phone to the caterer to tell him to make sure to bring extra ice. The air conditioning never "kicked in" enough to cool Adam down. His skin remained damp with sweat. Each mile they drove seemed like a dozen. Where the hell were they going? Some place farther than anywhere—someplace past beyond?

Adam thought about the chapter in his world history textbook about the Dobe !Kung—the bushmen in Botswana who click their tongues between words, which is what the "!" means. They still live like hunter-gatherers, although it's 1999 in Botswana too. Somehow, eons ago, the !Kung found a way to stop the forward push of evolution and remain content in their Stone Age lives, at least until very recently, when contact with "the West" began to unbalance their equilibrium.

Trapped in a car on the way to Covina, Adam remembered a diagram in his history book that mapped out a traditional !Kung village, which was circular and divided into rings. The main residences were all in the center. Then each layer outward was designated for other activities. Cooking was allowed in the next ring, followed by cleaning and the butchering of animals. Beyond that was a ring for defecation and waste. And beyond that, in the furthest ring, was an area for burial of the dead.

The freeway climbed a hill and curved to the left. To the right was dry brush the color of brown rice. The border of the freeway was purple, covered completely in blooming ice plant. At the top was a huge sign that read FOREST LAWN in huge, white letters with very Romanesque serifs. Above the lettering stood three enormous reproductions of classic and neoclassic sculptures: Michelangelo's *David* (*If he's 20 feet tall,* Adam thought, *then his wanker must be...*), the *Venus de Milo* (broken limbs and all), and a single female figure copied from the Erecthium (but separated from her sisters and not holding anything up but the sky).

Forest Lawn was the most imperfectly named cemetery in the whole world. There was no forest, no forest's lawn of fallen pine needles and small but sturdy undergrowth. At this outer ring of civilization there was only a perfectly sheared, lime-green expanse of fine grass that spread for miles in every direction. A few trees dotted the headstone-studded landscape like refugees from a real forest. The driver followed sign after sign until he delivered them to the right spot—a section labeled Sheep's Meadow on the map. Again, no sheep, no meadow, nothing but a small, white-on-green sign that read: FOREST LAWN SHEEP'S MEADOW SOUTHEAST BB in three lines of the signature Romanesque type.

Already at the gravesite was a small crowd of familiar faces. Mr. and Mrs. Tostado, who lived down the block, were there with all three kids. Aunt Patricia was there, already chatting with whomever stood nearest to her. She'd flown in "just this morning" and was "taking the last flight back home" tonight because Southwest had a sale on same-day flights. The grizzled pallbearers were there too. They'd found some shade under the nearest tree. Adam scanned the crowd as the Lincoln glided to a stop. He recognized a few teachers from Greg's school but didn't notice that the pastor wasn't there yet. *Clean-Shaven so lacks a personality,* Adam thought, *he'd be hard to notice even if he was standing right in front of you.*

More cars followed, and people got out as if they had made this trip before. Adam wondered why everyone looked so peaceful. They were all walking around so slowly, floating like stoners and zombies across the grass, kissing and hugging—all very gently—and not saying much. Greg's casket sat on an aluminum contraption next to a big hole in the ground. On the other side of the hole, a mound of dirt hid under a bright AstroTurf rug. In front, there were a few rows of plastic folding chairs, the same kind used for weddings and outdoor luncheons.

Aunt Patricia found Adam and silently put a fleshy arm around him. As much as he liked her, Adam counted the seconds until she let go. He was saved from conversation by a discrete "a-hem" from one of the pallbearers. Everyone turned to hear what the old codger had to say. "Just got a call from Pastor Songenberg," he said. "He's stuck in a tiny bit of traffic. Says he's only a couple miles away and should be here in 15 minutes or so."

Women wearing high heels took the delay as an opportunity to sit down on the party chairs. Adam ducked away from his aunt and started back toward the car. Even with the scary driver inside, a few minutes away seemed essential to his sanity. Their car was no longer the last in line; it was just one of many that stretched down the gravel road. The farther Adam walked, the quieter it became. The voices around the gravesite slipped away, and he could concentrate on the task of taking one step after another.

The *cli-clunk* of a car door opening caught Adam's attention. He looked up from his shuffling feet and down the road. Standing outside the door of his police car was Jeff, his badge glimmering in the sun like a pocket mirror sending a message in Morse code.

Oh, man... What the hell am I doing here? Jeff asked himself. *Have I lost my mind...given up all concern for professional discretion?* These were serious questions, which Jeff was genuinely concerned about. But he was already walking toward Adam; it was too late to change his mind. Jeff nervously pushed his police hat back on his head and waved hello.

"What's going on?" Adam asked, pleasantly surprised but not about to show it.

"I got a thing for cemeteries," Jeff said.

Adam kept down the grin brimming up inside of him. "Does your boss know about this—your thing for cemeteries?"

"Not yet. So, I'd appreciate it if you kept it between us. Higher-ups don't appreciate such—individuality in members of the force."

"The *force?*"

"Yeah, man…the force."

Jeff pointed back toward the car. Adam's eyes followed. He spotted Sue sitting inside. She waved like a parent trying to act cool about something that totally puzzled her.

"Come on," Jeff said, finally cracking a smile. "We were in the neighborhood and—"

"So you and Miss Friendly just decided to swing by? Angelito is a half-hour away…"

"Well…"

"And say hello, or something."

"Well, not exactly. We had a short day today, so I made up some bogus errand way out here. Thank God Sue is naïve enough to let me drive her out here…and yet smart enough to not ask too many questions."

"So you're deceitful, and you have a cemetery fetish?"

"Mister…I was actually just trying to stop by and—" Jeff paused. He wondered if this was all just a huge mistake about to backfire and embarrass him royally. But he found the courage to continue. "I was just wondering how everything was going."

"Hmm," Adam mumbled. "Thoughtful."

"Yeah, it's a bad habit. I'm working on it. Really, I am." Jeff tried to play his hard-to-explain visit for laughs; his strategy was only partly working.

"The cemetery fetish was a lot more interesting, edgy even. Thoughtfulness, well, that's so early-to-mid '90s, so first-term Clinton."

"Okay, then let's go with the cemetery fetish. Everyone needs a hobby, right?"

"Guess so," Adam said.

Jeff looked away from Adam toward the small crowd. "Everything looks to be coming together. Quite a few people are here."

"Everyone but the pastor. He just called to say he would be late because he was stuck in traffic. Whatever. Don't know what freeway he's on. Did you see any traffic?"

Jeff shifted his weight from one muscular leg to the other, squinted his eyes, dug a hand into one of his pants pockets, and jingled some loose change. He fidgeted like anyone would in the hot sun in the middle of June. But somehow, to Adam, it all seemed painfully charming.

"You staying for the service?" Adam asked, to save Jeff from having to say something.

"No, no. I just wanted to stop by and say hi."

"Hi?"

"Yeah, hi."

Adam pushed his hands into the back pockets of his suit pants. His chest stuck out like he was showing how strong he could be. "If you were here to stay—well, at least half the people here haven't spoken to my dad in years. So I'm sure he'd have no problem with you joining in. The more the merrier, right?"

Jeff sensed an opening. Adam was sharing something personal through his complaint. This had to mean that he was comfortable with him—that he didn't mind that Jeff had stopped by for a visit.

"I'm glad I won't be around for my own funeral," Jeff said. "God knows what I'd say to most of the people there."

"That's an upside to dying," Adam said agreeably. "You don't have to deal with anyone you really don't want to anymore."

Adam leaned comfortably against the side of the car parked closest to them and exhaled. He reached up and loosened his tie just a bit. Jeff relaxed too. He leaned against the trunk of the same car, removed his cap, and wiped his brow.

"How's the weird stepdad?" Jeff asked.

"He's okay, I guess. Now that my dad's gone, it's so different. Marc seems calm about everything...I don't know, maybe he feels, at least subconsciously, that there's no more competition. He can be whatever kind of father he wants to be."

The sound of gravel being crushed by a speeding driver inter-rupted their conversation. *Cli-clunk*, and the pastor jumped out of his squat family car. He scrambled unnecessarily toward the gravesite. It was like he was trying to appear repentant for his tar-diness, but instead he drew attention to his false sense of alarm.

"Guess you better get going," Jeff said. "Looks like the show's about to begin."

"Oh, I doubt it. I'm sure they'll find something else still missing. Like a shovel." Adam swallowed the last of his words when he saw Vivian approaching with an overly concerned look on her face.

"Mom," Adam said, interrupting the internal dialogue he could see running through her head. "This is Officer Manfield. He's one of the officers who came by the house the other day."

"Oh, how do you do? I'm Ms. Randall."

Ooh...how Adam hated the way his mom used *Ms.* as if she were some kind of liberated woman.

"Nice to meet you, Ms. Randall. I'm very sorry for your loss."

"Thank you. My husband, whom you must have met at the house, said everyone who came by that day was very helpful. We appreciate that."

A painful pause was about to begin; Adam could feel it. He decided to nip it in the bud. "Looks like everyone's here," he said, looking toward the grave.

Vivian turned to confirm her son's report. "Yes, we should get started," she said. But before she left she turned to Jeff and said, "You know, we're having a big lunch back at our house in about an hour and a half. You...and your partner," Vivian craned her neck to get a better look at Sue still sitting comfortably inside the air-conditioned police car, "are both welcome to join us."

"Oh, I don't know," Jeff said, looking down at his uniform. "I'm not exactly dressed for it."

"Neither are most of them," Adam said, cocking his head toward the people milling about in suits and dresses they never wore except to weddings and...

"Well, it's up to you," Vivian said. "Adam can give you the

address. Stop by if you can. Now, if you'll excuse me." She looked at Adam. "We should get going." Without waiting for Jeff to respond or Adam to follow her, she walked away. Adam stayed back, caught off-guard by his mother's invitation. He turned to Jeff and shrugged his shoulders like a child facing the owner of a house whose window he'd just thrown a ball through. He wanted to say, "Thanks for stopping by and showing interest in my life"…but he didn't. Adam didn't know whether it was cool to show that much appreciation. Instead, he pulled the funeral program from his suit pocket and handed it to Jeff.

"The address is printed inside. My mom lives near Hancock Park. So, if you've got absolutely nothing better to do this afternoon…"

"You sure? I mean, I'd only stop by if it's cool with you."

Adam momentarily panicked. Jeff was asking for way too much commitment.

"I can't say," Adam said. "What if you have a terrible time, get food poisoning or something. I'd feel totally responsible."

"And you hate responsibility?"

"Well…"

"Okay. I'll take the address and play it by ear."

"Okay."

"That way, if I show up, it's 100 percent my choice."

"Sounds good to me."

"Cool," Jeff said, purposely giving no hint of his intentions.

Adam dug his shoe into the soft grass for no good reason. It felt slippery and moist from being watered too much. "Are cops allowed to say the word 'cool'?"

With his hat firmly in hand, ready to be put back on his head, Jeff answered: "Only when there aren't any other cops around."

Adam turned and walked away, a little excited and a little scared. By the time he reached the grave, two women from the church choir were singing. Their voices hid the sound of Jeff getting back in his car.

"Hey," Sue said sympathetically after Jeff shut his door. Never before had they driven to a funeral for any victim, in any case. She wasn't clear on the details, but she knew enough to not ask any questions. Yet.

"Hey, hey," Jeff said back.

Staring at Jeff for a moment, Sue ran through the situation in her mind. Then she decided to run through it out loud. She always thought better out loud. "This family, you know, is weird in the most ordinary way. There's a highly successful mom with a new and slightly younger husband of indeterminate occupation, two sort of screwed-up kids who never really knew what it was like to live with two parents. Do you think that matters anymore?"

Jeff didn't want to get into a long discussion about parenting, and his silence let Sue know it. So she let it drop. This was something Jeff always liked about Sue. She was, deep down, a very thoughtful person, empathetic and aware of other people's concerns, no matter how different they were from her own. She started the car and pulled away from the curb.

Not until they were back on the freeway did Sue speak again. "We're off in half an hour," she began, "and you know how hungry all this driving around makes me."

Jeff heard her, but he was distracted by his conversation with Adam. Sue continued, filling the air with words. "You know that's why there are so many fat police officers. It's a real problem. Sitting around actually burns off calories, just not very many. It's, like, 216 per hour for a 190-pound person. I read that in *Men's Health* last month."

"What were you doing reading *Men's Health*?"

"I read it at the gym. You know, there isn't exactly a magazine called *Women's Health* that takes fitness seriously. That *Self* thing is too girly. I don't follow all the stuff in it. There is a difference between men and women, you know."

Jeff had lost complete track of Sue back at "216 calories per hour." He could only think about one thing: *Should he or shouldn't he show up at Adam's later on?*

"If I'm hungry, you must be hungry," Sue continued. "We should get something to eat. I'm feeling like something healthy, maybe Chinese. It can be good for you, if you order carefully. All those vegetables and tofu and stuff are great. Steamed chicken is wonderful. Unless you order something fried, or duck, or something like kung pao chicken, which has like hundreds of calories a serving because of all the peanuts and oil in it, you're fine. Chinese food can have very little fat. There's loads of fat in nuts, though. Just don't order anything with nuts in it, and you'll be fine. The double-fried pork isn't very good either. Any time you see fried, it's bad, but double-fried, that's just wrong. Forget about it. Stick to anything steamed, anything veggie. And oh, yeah, brown rice is so much better than white. I know, it can be a little rough and chewy, but white rice is like pure carbs."

Sue wasn't born a chatterbox, and food wasn't always her obsession. Both were defense mechanisms she had adopted as an adult— efforts to protect her ego against a selfish and uninterested world. Jeff didn't always like listening to what Sue had to say, but in times like this, he appreciated her neurosis. It filled the time-space void left by his zoning out. Sue ran out of things to say after she worked out the relative merits of baby corn and bamboo shoots. By the time they pulled into the Angelito Police Department's parking lot, all was silence again.

"I'm going to have to decline your invitation for lunch," Jeff said as they entered the station.

"What?" she asked. "Why not?"

Jeff kept walking. He turned to the left and headed toward the men's locker room. "I'm not eating today," he said. Then, just as he opened the door emblazoned MEN, he said, "I'm fasting for Lent."

Sue, left standing in the crossroads between entrance and exit, men's and women's, morning and afternoon, said to no one in particular, maybe to herself: "But it's not Lent."

The graveside service was shorter than Jeff and Sue's drive back to Angelito. A prayer, a song, an invocation, a few tossed handfuls of dirt, and it was over. Adam watched as everyone went through the motions like they'd been practicing for weeks. Everyone seemed to know what to do: when to sniffle, sing, and when to toss a handful of dirt—an exercise in vapidity that Adam thought might be quaint if it weren't so premodern. Toss some fucking dirt? Adam felt like throwing some dirt right at the coffin—like a fastball inside...*Strike!* He wanted to roll some wet dirt from the top of the pile into a ball of hard mud and swing it at his dad's coffin. Lucky for the shiny coffin, the service ended quickly and Adam followed the rules. Once it was over, the crowd scampered like roaches back to the dark interiors of their cars, away from the bright afternoon sun.

By the time everyone reconvened at Vivian's for lunch, the hottest part of the day had ended, and the exquisitely landscaped backyard was beginning to recover from the wilting heat. The petunias were almost vertical again after a few hours spent cowering thirstily from the sun. Equally regimented in design as the flower beds was the buffet table. Along the back of the house, there were two tables covered with white tablecloths. They held enormous platters of food arranged in large Spirograph designs. On the largest tray, meats spun out from a center of prosciutto and spears of cantaloupe, to salami and ham, then turkey and roast beef, mortadella and pimento loaf with pieces of red pepper spread unevenly throughout. Another platter, the size of a medium pizza, held thinly sliced cheese—white, yellow, Swiss, Muenster, and everything in between. Wicker baskets lined with blue linen napkins cradled assorted slices of bread, braided rolls, focaccia and ciabatta, croissants, and slivers of spindly baguette.

Among the perfect circles on the tables were points of well-intentioned imperfection. Visitors brought salads and bowls of personal favorites, which Marc set generously along the table. Aunt Patricia brought "from all the way up North" her special macaroni salad: "just chopped black olives, a small onion, and salt and pepper to taste." Every time someone complimented her, she recited the recipe like a mantra.

Adam listened again today as his aunt explained her secret to macaroni-salad success. He'd found a small table where he could sit with her and eat. He understood why his dad liked her best of all his family. She was genuinely cuckoo and not a bit embarrassed about it. She reveled in it, actually. Adam knew that most people were afraid of her, so by sitting with her, he avoided having to chat with people he knew were only there for free lunch.

They sat near the back of the garden, next to an "appetizer station," as the caterers called it. As Aunt Patricia prattled on, Adam watched Sandra and her cousin Beth holding court with the chips and dip. The two girls took turns nibbling asparagus spears, "home-made" tortilla chips, and dates rolled in sugar—their pits replaced with clean white almonds.

"I know how to make guacamole," Beth said as she plopped a tortilla chip, heavy with green mush, into her mouth.

"So do I," Sandra said. "It's not hard."

"My mom taught me the secret to make it stay green and not go brown. You gotta keep the seed in it."

"That's not a secret. Everyone knows that," Sandra said.

Beth's mom approached and interrupted the girls' conversation. "I think we've had enough chips for today. Why don't we go have a sandwich?"

As Beth's mom put a hand on her daughter's shoulder to lead her away, Sandra dipped another chip in the guacamole and shoved it into her mouth with a smile.

While he undressed, showered, and dressed again, and even during his ride to Vivian's, Jeff moved in silence—no TV, and no CD or radio in the car. There was more than enough noise inside his head, thanks to second (and third and fourth) thoughts about what he was doing and where he was going.

What in the name of God—any god—oh, yeah, he didn't believe in God, but maybe he should—was he doing, driving over to the mother's house of a guy—barely a man, not a boy—he hardly knew for lunch after the guy had just buried his father? *There is a completely plausible, professional explanation for what I'm doing,* Jeff told himself. I'm going to get to know everyone better so I can make sure there isn't anything more to the case.

Who was he kidding? Jeff was only going because something deep inside him, something somewhere between his heart and his groin, was making him do things he knew he shouldn't. Did he even really care about the case? That was a question he couldn't answer. Officially, he'd already signed the papers and closed the file. All he had left to do was hand them in.

Jeff had to park several houses away because he arrived late. He straightened his casual-but-nice shirt, tucked it into the front of his pants, and adjusted them until they rested perfectly on his hips. *Shit,* Jeff thought while he walked. *I'm trying…trying to look nice. Trying means something. And meaning something is bad.*

At the end of the driveway was a large gate that was latched electronically, and Jeff couldn't open it. He looked for a buzzer, and found it. It must have rung inside because Jeff couldn't hear it work.

"Hello…"

First came the voice, and then Vivian, around the corner. She looked at Jeff over the gate and made no movement toward opening it. "Can I help you?" she asked.

"Yeah, I'm Officer Manfield, Jeff, from…"

"Oh, my God." Vivian laughed out loud at some joke only she could hear. "Of course. Come on in. I didn't recognize you without your—"

"Uniform?"

"Yes, exactly."

"I try not to wear it off duty."

"Come on in. Lunch is in full swing."

She unlatched the gate and swung open the door. "Heaven knows we've got enough food. It's like somebody…" she stopped. "Well, you know."

This time she didn't laugh, not even a chuckle—just kept talking as she closed the gate behind them. "Everyone's around back. My husband oversees all this gardening. He does a beautiful job, doesn't he?"

They turned the corner and the backyard came into full view; Jeff spotted Adam right away. He was sitting next to an older

woman who watched Adam lift his arm to signal a silent hello. Jeff
did the same and for a split second: they were the Indian and the
Pilgrim meeting for the first time at Plymouth Rock.

Vivian led Jeff to the buffet table and slid one hand gently
behind his arm to guide him. Adam excused himself from Aunt
Patricia to go meet Jeff, but his mom was giving Jeff a tour of the
buffet like she was auditioning for Hostess of the Year. So Adam
decided to meet Jeff at the end and avoid dealing with his mom and
Jeff at the same time.

Adam was both surprised and unsurprised that Jeff actually
showed up. *I guess if someone drives all the way out to Forest Lawn to
"check on things," he'll show up anywhere,* he thought. Adam studied
Jeff as he filled his plate under the chattering guidance of Vivian,
Super Hostess. *He is so handsome,* Adam thought. It's amazing what
a clean pair of khakis and a new-looking shirt can do. The shirt's
light-blue color made Jeff's hair look blonder, and the sleeves were
snug enough to make his arms look even bigger. When Jeff breathed,
Adam noticed his nipples pressed up against the fabric just enough
to show through.

Adam greeted Jeff at the end of the table with a fork and knife
rolled up inside a white napkin—dozens of them poked out of a
wicker cornucopia at the end of the buffet.

"Oh, Adam," Vivian said. "Officer Manfield is here."

"Hello, officer."

Adam handed Jeff the napkin-bundled utensils.

"Thank you," Jeff said.

"Okay, then," Vivian added after an uncertain moment. "Adam,
why don't you find somewhere for Officer Manfield to sit?"

Confident that her hosting duties were over, she walked away
without waiting to see whether Adam followed her instructions. But
he did. Adam pointed to an empty table near the back of the yard.

After taking one step, Jeff said, "Please, call me Jeff."

"Okay, Officer Jeff."

"No, just Jeff. No officer, no Manfield, just Jeff."

"Kidding, kidding…"

They arrived at an empty card table near the garage. "This was the kids table," Adam said, "but they've eaten and moved on, so we can take it without a fight."

"Good. I hate fighting kids. Adults are one thing, kids are another."

"Glad you know the difference. It's a tough one for some people. They look so much alike these days."

Jeff and Adam sat across from each other at the rickety table. Adam leaned way back as if he was uninterested. Jeff sat up straight, uncomfortable in the small chair. Adam thought Jeff was nervous, and Jeff thought Adam wanted to flee. They were both a little right.

"Looks good," Jeff said, poking his plastic fork at a mound of shiny whiteness.

"It's okay, but I'd skip that potato salad. It's store-bought and, well, you gotta be careful with potato salad. The macaroni salad, that's fine. It's my Aunt Patricia's, so we know it's okay. Actually, it's pretty good."

"Thanks for the warning. Anything else I should know about before traversing this minefield?"

"Ouch," Adam said.

"Metaphorically speaking of course."

Adam's and Jeff's knees both reached the underneath of the table, but didn't touch each other.

"How old are you?"

"What?"

Adam knew it was the wrong question at the wrong time, but he couldn't find a way to control the malfunctioning connection between his mind and his mouth. It just came out.

"And how did you get here?"

Jeff put his fork down quickly and assessed the situation. First, he looked into Adam's eyes to see whether there were any ulterior motives behind such pointed questioning. What he saw was a state of confusion he could easily understand. He recognized the combination of cynicism and innocence that he'd noticed in Adam when they'd first seen each other at the Sev.

"I drove."

Adam kept still, quietly trying to force Jeff to continue.

"And I'm 38...39 next month, to be exact."

Jeff was secretly proud of himself for being completely honest. He went back to his plate, lifted his sandwich to his mouth, and took a confident bite. For a second, he thought of Sue and wondered what she was eating and where.

"I'm glad you drove," Adam said. "People might have talked if they saw you walking."

"Anything else you want to know about me? Food allergies? Boxers or briefs? Stationary bike or treadmill?"

Jeff spoke with enough of a smile to let Adam know he wasn't bothered by the questions and was, just maybe, enjoying the attention.

"Not at the moment," Adam said, "but maybe later. Am I allowed to revisit discovery later, your honor?"

"As long as you never call me 'your honor' again, discovery can remain open indefinitely."

"Indefinitely? That's a long time. Try the macaroni salad."

"All right, all right." Jeff scooped up a forkful of Aunt Patricia's specialty, but on its way to Jeff's mouth it became smaller and smaller as little noodles tumbled easily from the plastic fork. "It's great," Jeff said. "Best I've ever had. But I wish I had a spoon."

"Told you it was good."

"So, I think it's my turn to ask a few questions," Jeff said.

"Okay, but remember, you're a cop. Don't go asking me if I've ever smoked pot or anything. I might have to plead the Fifth...or even lie."

"Don't worry. I'm off duty."

"Didn't think that mattered."

"It doesn't. But between you and me, let's pretend it does."

"Okay."

Jeff paused for a second to take another bite. Adam leaned back in his chair until the front two legs were off the ground. He tried to make sense of his burgeoning happiness at this very moment, of the knot in his belly, of his excitement. But there was no sense to be made out of any of it, and he knew it.

"Have you been back to your dad's house?"

"Once, to pick up some stuff."

"Must have been strange."

"Not really. The place didn't feel that different actually. In fact, it was so not different that I'm thinking about moving back."

"Really?"

"As you can hopefully see, this is so not my house," Adam said with a cock of his head toward the house, "let alone my style."

The youngest kids, long since finished with their sandwiches, chased each other around the table. The adults sat in their chairs, barely moving and hardly aware of anyone they weren't speaking directly to.

"Would you stay there by yourself?"

"I think so. It wouldn't be for long. I'm graduating next week."

"Congratulations," Jeff said confidently.

"Thank you. And in two months I'm going away to school. So, it'd only be for a couple of months really."

"What's your mom think?"

"Don't know yet. I haven't actually talked to her about it, but I don't think she'll care, might even secretly support it. Sometimes she surprises me."

"That's pretty open-minded of her."

"You think?"

"Yeah, I think most parents prefer to keep their kids under their own roof as long as possible, sometimes even longer than they should."

"You don't know my mother."

"No..."

"Hey," Adam said, getting up from the table and trying to change the subject. "You want something to drink?" He walked a few steps over to an ice chest filled with canned and bottled drinks. "Soda, water, beer...Country Time Lemonade. Damn, who knew they even made that shit anymore?"

"Water is fine."

Adam grabbed two bottles and returned.

"Let's talk about you. Who is Officer Jeff Manfield? Or, since the officer isn't here at the moment, who is Jeff Manfield?

"What do you mean?"

"Well, let's review what we've learned. He's 38—almost 39—apparently prefers roast beef over all other cold cuts, drinks horrible coffee from the Sev, shops at Pavilions, and is an Angelito police officer, but only sometimes."

"That's about it."

"And he's got a thing for cemeteries."

"Now, that's really it. That's about all I know about him too."

"Somehow I doubt that. I hear you two are very close. And anyway, what I see today, all cleaned up..." Adam stopped, he could feel a revealing smile creeping across his face, and he wanted to hold it back. "What I see today is quite different from the guy—man?—or guy?"

"Guy."

"From the guy I swear I saw putting Sweet'N Low in his coffee at the Sev."

"That's Sue's fault. She recruited me into her anti-sugar cult."

"You guys have a twisted relationship."

"What do you know?"

"Not much. It's just a hunch."

"She's not so bad. Yeah, she's the only partner I've ever had—but I've seen my share of bad ones."

"Tell me something I don't know."

"I have a dog, a black lab named Chops."

"And?"

"When I'm not hanging out at cemeteries or backyard buffets with relative strangers, I surf."

"Now that's interesting."

"Oh, you never met a 38-year-old surfer?" Jeff asked.

"You've got a bit of an issue with your age, don't you?"

"No, I don't think so."

"Then why did you ask if I think you're too old to surf? I didn't say anything to suggest that."

"'Interesting' means different things to different people," Jeff declared.

"You're right."

Adam reached his hands up and back behind his head like he was about to do a sit-up. He leaned back into the stretch, unaware that he was loosening up. But Jeff noticed. "You don't care for the beach?" he asked.

"No, actually, I do like the beach a lot. It's just that I don't get there very often. It's not all that close to Angelito."

"Tell me about it. Where I like to go is an hour away."

Throughout their conversation, Adam kept an eye on the crowd. He didn't want his talking with Jeff to draw any extra attention, which he knew was more likely as the crowd thinned out. There were fewer people outside, and Jeff had finished his sandwich, so Adam made a suggestion.

"You wanna get out of here?" he asked.

"Why?"

"You always answer questions with another question?"

"Sometimes," Jeff said stubbornly.

"Well?"

"Sure."

"Great. Follow me." Adam stood up. "We're going to walk in the house through the back door so it looks like I'm showing you something inside the house. Then we're going to walk right out the front door, and nobody will even notice we're gone."

And no one did. They were out on the front sidewalk before another word was spoken.

"Sorry about the rush, but those people are dangerous," Adam said, breaking the silence.

"Yeah? A couple of the older ones did look ready to pounce."

"Most of them have never been in the same room together. Then, someone they all know dies and…Boom! Everyone pretends to have known and liked each other all along. It's total bullshit.

Tomorrow, actually tonight, they'll all go back to their own pathetic little lives and forget about everyone else until another mutual
acquaintance dies."

Apparently, Adam needed to vent, and Jeff let him. When he saw
an opening, he interjected, "Want to drive somewhere?"

"No," Adam said decisively. "We're walking."

"Okay."

Jeff wasn't used to walking, but hell, today was all about new
things. So he followed Adam down the sidewalk and didn't give it a
second thought. They wandered south to where domesticity eventually bumped into commercial traffic along San Vicente Boulevard.
You could either turn right or left. If you went straight, you'd run
smack into lanes of traffic. On the right, a pedestrian bridge spiraled
up and over the busy boulevard—all six lanes of traffic and a medi-
an of old plantings. It was a bridge used by almost no one anymore.
Pedestrians were a long-extinct species in this neighborhood.
Sometimes kids walked across it, instructed by their parents that it
was the only safe way to get to the other side. In the early morning,
grannies could be spotted power-walking over the expanse, using the
incline as a hill to raise their heart rate. But late on a Saturday afternoon, the bridge was empty.

Adam and Jeff walked up and halfway over. They stopped in the
very middle. Through the chain-link fence, the western sky turned
yellow, orange, and almost pink as the sun began to set.

"This is cool," Jeff said, looking down at the rivers of red and
white lights running to the horizon and beyond. "Up here is so different from down there...and I spend so much time, down there."

"At least you're always going somewhere," Adam said.

"Not always."

"Maybe you don't always have a specific destination, but you're
moving."

"Yeah, but you know how traffic can get. Forward motion is
never guaranteed in this town; it can take forever to go a mile. I
spend a lot of time standing still. Waiting."

Adam turned around to face east. The sky was blue turning to steel gray. "Well, when you're not moving, when the traffic is stopped, at least you know you'll be moving again eventually," Adam said. "You never stand still forever."

"You're right," Jeff said.

Adam sat where the fence and walkway met, facing west. Jeff noticed how the pink sky reflected off of Adam's face. He sat next to Adam on the small ledge. "You're moving too," he said, "just in different and sometimes imperceptible ways."

"Not so sure about that."

The whirring drone of the traffic separated Adam and Jeff from the rest of the world. They only heard each other above the din. It felt like they were the last two people in the whole universe.

"What are you doing after graduation?"

"Not so sure about that either."

"You're not going to college?"

"No, I am. I don't know what I'm doing before that. This summer, I need a job of some kind. But realistically, I'll probably get a lame job somewhere, hang out with my friends—you know, all that proto-adulthood-bonding stuff, we'll do a lot of that—and then we'll all move away in August and change into people we don't like, let alone recognize, and so by the time we come back for Christmas, we'll try and be friends again but quickly realize we have nothing in common anymore."

"That's really optimistic," Jeff said, leaning back against the fence. He kicked his legs out and placed one over the other, making himself comfortable. Adam found this rather cool. He thought it showed Jeff didn't care about his fancy pants getting dirty or scuffed.

"What is there to be optimistic about? I think I do a decent job remaining realistic and not pessimistic."

"Where are you going to school?"

"Stanford."

"Pricey."

"Yeah, but my mother is paying for it."

"That's nice."

"I guess...It's the least she could do."

"You're angry."

Adam looked over at Jeff. Who did he think he was to be making all these pronouncements?

"Forget it, forget it," Jeff said, trying to escape Adam's confused glare. "What do I know?"

"You seem to think you know a lot."

Adam turned back toward the setting sun, releasing Jeff from his gaze.

"So, do you know what you want to study?"

"Sort of."

"Well?"

"Probably psychology. I hear you get a lot of free therapy out of it."

"You don't look the part."

"Oh, yeah?"

"No. Psych majors, at least when I went to college, were much stranger, more homely, and way less hip."

"Are you saying I'm not strange or homely…that I'm hip?"

"Yeah."

"Are you flirting with me?" Adam asked quickly.

"No way, man."

"Kidding, kidding…" Adam half-smiled to reassure Jeff—and himself—that he really was kidding, even though he wasn't. Adam knew what was going on; it was just too early to name it. "I'm not studying psychology. I'm thinking about English Lit or something. I think I want to write."

"You shouldn't have a problem finding material."

"That's for sure."

Adam pulled his eyes away from the streams of traffic below and turned to Jeff. He looked at how Jeff's profile cut a shape out of the sky. Who exactly was this man sitting next to him with a voice so calm and reassuring. When he spoke he sounded kind, as if he didn't need anything from anyone else in the world. This was exciting. This was where Adam wanted to be: independent, at a stage in life where he didn't need anyone else. He wanted to be healthy, strong, and confident, a man who spoke as if he truly believed life was every man for himself, but that you could make it better by wishing, truly wishing, people well along the way.

Jeff knew Adam was looking at him, and he savored the feeling of Adam's eyes on his skin. Jeff's pleasure at being watched was mixed with apprehension. Jeff was afraid of how good it felt to think someone he admired might like him. Jeff turned to Adam, to see the eyes he felt looking at him. Adam moved. He leaned forward, right toward Jeff, closer, and kissed him on the mouth.

Two mouths, four eyes, all closed. Gentle pressure, then release. As they disconnected, Adam opened his eyes first and saw Jeff's eyes still closed. *How long his lashes are,* Adam thought. They looked much shorter from farther away, but now Adam knew why: The tips were sun-bleached and almost invisible. Jeff opened his eyes to find Adam looking right at him, maybe right through him. The six inches of space between them felt like everything and nothing. *What happened? What's happening? What does this mean? Can we do it again? When? Now?* Both men ran though millions of questions inside their heads and found few answers. Jeff leaned in first this time. Adam followed. They met again in the middle of space, connected, kissed. Pressure applied, held—a few seconds longer this time—their closed mouths, their lips touching. Contact. Pressure. Release.

"Hmm," Adam said as he leaned away.

"Hmm?" Jeff mumbled back, his lips so numb from excitement that words were difficult to form.

"Yeah. Hmm."

Both of them turned away and looked out toward the cars again. The sun was completely gone, yet the sky seemed brighter. From horizon to horizon, streaks of purple and pink gave way to dull blue and then dark gray and then dark night. An entire day's story filled the arc of the sky above.

Jeff reached over, found Adam's knee and squeezed. Adam liked this feeling; it said so much—too much, maybe. He couldn't take it all in. There was something paternal and gentle in the gesture. Adam's dad never touched his knee—or shoulder or head or any-where else. Maybe it was something kids, or humans, were born needing—squeezes and touches—but never received enough of. Maybe that's all that really draws people together—the need to be touched—because it reminds you that you're not alone.

Adam hopped up on one knee, bent the other beneath him, and faced Jeff. Without pause he reached over and put a hand on the side of Jeff's head. He pulled Jeff's face to him and kissed him. Jeff showed no signs of resistance. He put his hand on the back of Adam's head and pulled it toward his own. Their mouths opened and closed together. Adam inhaled some of Jeff's breath and found it was warm, moist, and alive. They kissed gently, trading breath, then more. They reached their tongues out to find each other. They tasted each other, again and again, and liked it more each time. Cars whizzed by, but they couldn't hear them anymore. The only sounds they could hear came from each other.

This time, Adam pulled away first. He fidgeted nervously with his shirt. He pulled the collar up to his mouth and bit it like a child. It looked to Jeff like he was having second thoughts.

"Thinking about something?" Jeff asked quietly.

"Yeah, I guess so."

"Well?"

"I guess I'm thinking about getting back…just in case they have noticed I'm gone and are discussing whether or not to call 911."

"Oh…" Jeff said, trying to hide his disappointment.

"Little do they know I'm already with the police."

Adam laughed nervously at his own joke. Jeff did not. He wanted to kiss Adam again but was afraid to come across as too aggressive.

"Then we better go," Jeff said, slightly confused by Adam's quick change of heart. Jeff forced a smile, though, and looked right at Adam. He wanted to let him know how he felt without having to try and put his feelings into words.

He stood up and so did Adam. They walked back down the bridge and back to Vivian's house in silence. When they arrived at Jeff's Bronco—four houses away from Vivian's—they stopped.

"Here I am," Jeff said.

"Yes, here you are, and so is your truck."

Awkwardness prevailed as they both fought the desire to lean against each other, to hug, maybe even kiss again, and taste each other once more before saying goodbye. They wanted to feel more of each other. After all, they'd only just begun.

"Well," Jeff dug his hands deep into his pockets like a little boy looking for his favorite secret. "Do you still have my card?"

"Yes. I do."

"Well," Jeff shifted his weight, "Will you be holding onto it?"

"Yeah, I think so."

In the kitchen, Marc dealt with the leftovers, washed the last of the serving trays, and cleaned every counter until all evidence of the day's events was removed. Vivian sat in the dining room with a few straggling guests including Aunt Patricia, who was waiting for the Super Shuttle to take her back to the airport.

"Where were you?" Vivian asked as Adam walked through the front door.

"Nowhere," Adam said plainly.

Vivian was powerless over him and she knew it. "Well, next time you might let us know that you're going to 'nowhere' so we don't have to wonder."

Adam walked past and into the kitchen.

"Hi," he said to Marc.

"Hi," Marc replied, without looking up from the sink.

Adam thought he was hungry, maybe thirsty, but he really wasn't. He left the kitchen through the side door to avoid his mom and reach the den. Sandra wasn't home. She'd gone over to Beth's house to sleep. Alone, Adam flipped on the television and cruised through a hundred stations before he heard the Super Shuttle honk outside. He flipped off the TV and joined everyone outside to say goodbye to Aunt Patricia. The other stragglers took her departure as a reason to leave, so there was a brief flurry of goodbyes. Adam knew this was probably the last time he'd see his aunt. She was part of his dad's family, and with his dad gone, there would be little reason for them to see each other again. It didn't make a lot of sense, but it was true.

"Thank you for coming down," Adam said.

"Don't thank me, honey. That won't do me a lick of good. You know that."

What was she saying? Why did she have to be so direct? Can't she just say goodbye and be done with it? Yet her...forthrightness...was exactly what Adam, and his dad, liked about Aunt Patricia most. "I know. But, I love you," Adam said, just loud enough that only she could hear.

Aunt Patricia reached over and kissed the same lips that had kissed Jeff's only minutes earlier. It felt good, almost better than a kiss from your aunt is supposed to feel. While she held Adam's head, Aunt Patricia whispered in his ear with her best movie-star Southern accent, "Now you just go and grow up right. Outdo your daddy— who tried his best, I know, and someday, I hope you know too— and make your aunt proud."

Adam wanted to cry, to burst out with real tears and unleash a reservoir of emotion he'd kept inside all day. He'd said too many goodbyes, participated in too many heart-to-heart conversations. He'd simply had too much real life for one day, and he couldn't take it anymore. And it must have shown on his face.

"Don't worry," she said, letting go of Adam's head. "You're going to be just fine. I'm already proud of you."

Then she turned and crawled into the blue van. She didn't wait for Adam's response. It didn't matter. She'd said what she had to say and anything else, well, it didn't matter. Adam watched as she slid across the van's bench, waved a last goodbye to Vivian and Marc, and then turned to face forward, her handbag safely on her lap.

The driver slid the van's door shut with a sliding *whoosh cah-buh-clang.* Then he hopped around, jumped inside, and drove away. When he turned the corner, the street became quiet again. Adam turned to find his mom and Marc already halfway up the driveway.

The soles of Adam's feet felt glued to the sidewalk. The air around his head swirled silently, aggressively, the molecules spinning and crashing and going about their elemental business without concern for Adam's place in the world.

"Fuck," he said out loud. Or maybe not. He didn't feel his lips move. He only felt his heart pound. It wanted out of his body, to run after Aunt Patricia and the goddamn Super Shuttle with her in it. Adam's eyes welled up with tears and overflowed before he could do anything about them. The pain rose above his carefully reinforced façade of calm and overwhelmed him. No one could hear him. No one could see him or the tears that spilled over the banks of his eyelids and rolled gently down his cheeks. Adam thought that no one could begin to understand his terror, his feeling of being so alone at this moment. And if no one did—if no one saw him feeling, crying, or breaking down, then maybe no one would ever be able to help him, or to understand.

It may have been seconds—it felt like an hour—before Adam's reservoir of fear was empty. His head rocked with a slight pounding, yet he felt lighter, if only because he was empty. By the time Adam made it inside, Marc was in the kitchen again and Vivian was pacing the hallway with her phone against her ear, checking for messages. Adam went back to the empty living room and grabbed the remote. The second hundred channels weren't half as interesting, so he went through them faster, creating a slide-show effect. Vivian carried the phone with her into the living room and sat down in the chair next to Adam. She kept dialing and listening and dialing again, while he stared at the flickering screen. Finally, she stopped, hung up the phone, and set it down in her lap.

"Oh, God, Adam, pick something!" Vivian snapped. "Can't you just pick something?"

Instead, Adam turned the television off.

"Mom. Can we talk?"

"Of course..." she began, but Adam cut her off.

"Well, I want to say that I really appreciate today and all you guys did."

"You don't have to appreciate anything, Adam. We're glad to do it. That's the way it's supposed to be."

"Well, I don't know if this is the way things were 'supposed to be'," Adam said mostly to himself, "but it is the way things are now, that's for sure." Vivian had nothing to say, so Adam continued. "What's going to happen to dad's house?"

"I don't know, haven't really thought about it yet."

"Well, what are the options?"

"Well, it's all up to you and Sandra. Neither of you really need a house yet, so I think we should probably, well, eventually put it up for sale." Vivian looked to Adam to see whether she was saying the right thing. "But I don't really know."

"I have an idea. I would like to live there for the rest of the summer."

"What do you mean?"

"I mean, well, I mean that I know you guys are doing all you can, and that me and Sandra can stay here as long as we want, but…"

"Adam, it's not a question of what you want or what we want. You should think of this place as your house too."

"But it's not, you know, and it never has been. And that's fine. It's okay."

"But?"

"You know how you always wanted us to be independent? Well, why don't we think of it as a bit of a test? Moving back in would be a test of my own self-reliance. I could live there on my own until I go away to school?"

Vivian's tone changed. "I'm not sure I understand what's wrong with staying here. Why would you want to live there, alone, when you can stay with us?"

"There's nothing wrong with this place. It's just that it's not my home."

Marc heard the conversation in the kitchen. He moved toward the door to listen. Bright kitchen light washed over his shoulders.

"Oh, Adam," Marc said, "you should stay here with us. You have always been welcome to stay here as long as you wanted. Your mom is right. You should think of this as your place."

Adam ignored Marc's well-intentioned plea and continued

working on his mom. He knew it was only her opinion that mattered anyway. "Graduation is a week away, and then it's summer. I'll probably get a job in Angelito, so it'll be a lot more convenient too."

Vivian mulled the issue around in her mind and couldn't come up with a fair reason to say no. She knew it wasn't a question of money; Greg's mortgage wasn't much and there was no rush to sell the house. It would likely sit empty, she thought, which was never a good idea.

"You might be uncomfortable there, considering what happened," Vivian said.

"I've thought about that, and it might be true, but I would at least like to give it a try." Adam could feel the tide turning in his favor.

"Okay," Vivian said, "but only on a trial basis."

Any other day, under any other circumstances, Vivian's words would have felt like a vote of confidence. But it was barely 10 P.M. and Adam was exhausted. Between the services, the party, Jeff…they felt like a reprieve.

"Thanks," Adam said.

SUNDAY, JUNE 13, 1999

At 8:55 A.M., Dart sped away from his house in Angelito along
Interstate 5, going north into the San Fernando Valley. He passed
Toyotas and Mazdas with single men or women driving them. He
zipped around Pontiacs, Fords, and Mitsubishis too, with couples
inside, two men, two women, old, young, straight, gay, parent, child,
friends. The morning air that streamed through his open window
was exactly 70 degrees, almost cool.

Dart saw the cars around him as little self-contained worlds that
he could see but never know very much about, separate units moving in basically the same forward direction yet never coming into
contact with each other. Contact was bad. Contact meant an accident
and damage and injury. Each car sped up, fell behind, passed side to
side, weaving together invisible threads to create nothing more than
a few blank stares, maybe a searching glance.

Dart was on his way to North Hollywood High School, another perfectly named Southern California locale because it is north of
Hollywood, yes, but isn't actually connected to Hollywood in any
way, geographically or conceptually. Dart pulled into the NHHS
parking lot at 9:40 A.M., almost early. All he had to do before the
fair opened was make sure his foam core display boards were still
standing. This was the fourth and final year of science fairs for
Dart. His brightest science-fair moment had come during his
freshman year. He'd won Honorable Mention for a project dis-

playing the effects of phototropism on bean plants. Dart was only 14 when he decided to enter a project in the fair. For his first foray into scientific research, he put a handful of beans between wet paper towels that he then put between two clear sheets of Plexiglas. All of which was correct, except that he did this weeks before it was necessary.

Dart rotated his Plexiglas garden every four days and, as expected, the young beanstalks spiraled outward toward the light. By the time the fair arrived, his beans' tentacle-like arms reached well beyond the edges of the Plexiglas and burst into leafy abandon. The result of Dart's miscalculation was a veritable plant sculpture of twirling stalks growing from a tangle of twirling roots as impressive as it was cautionary—a story about the power of life to exceed expectations. The project's sheer botanical lusciousness impressed the judges, so despite its unrevolutionary scientific value, they awarded Dart a Special Honorable Mention for "Vibrancy of Presentation," or what Dart called, "third-and-a-half place."

During his sophomore and junior years, Dart won ordinary Honorable Mention, or "fourth place," as he liked to call it. This year, he hoped, was going to be different. The turning point had been New Year's Eve 1998. Dart was in the backyard of a so-called friend's house at a party where straight boys took advantage of midnight to kiss as many girls as possible. Maybe it was the aggravating display of heterosexuality, or maybe it was the forward thrust of time—it was becoming 1999, the beginning of the end of the millennium—but Dart felt an anxious rush to take action, to get his shit together in case the world really did end in exactly one year.

So, in January, Dart came out to his parents. They weren't surprised. His mom asked him to go to therapy to make sure he was sure, but no one ever made the appointment. And in February, Dart signed and returned his acceptance letter to Berkeley the day it arrived in the mail. By March, he relaxed into an even more comfortable groove with Adam and Fran, and eventually Veronica, when she joined the group. Together they were the queer amigos of Angelito High—at least to each other; 80 percent of the school didn't have a clue. (What does all this have to do with the science fair? Hold on.)

With his premillennium ambition at an all-time high, Dart decided to screw biology—the science-fair subject he'd explored every year because it was the one everyone said would look best on his college applications—and chose astronomy, a topic he truly loved. As a back-porch astronomer, he'd long been annoyed by light pollution, the excess light created by cities that clouds the sky and blocked out his clear view of the stars. Dart decided to try to figure out whether light pollution had an effect on people's daily lives, or whether it was merely an aesthetic problem for stargazers like himself. There were plenty of studies already completed that showed how excess light made detailed planetary observations impossible from anywhere but distant tropical islands with observatories built atop their volcanic peaks. Dart wanted to push the topic further. Through Angelito's physiology teacher and science-fair adviser, Mr. Nichols, Dart teamed up with the National Center for Sleep Disorder Research at the University of Southern California. There he obtained data regarding the number of reported sleep disorders in Los Angeles County. They had data broken down by the number of reported cases per city, which wasn't ideal because many cities varied in size and population. But for Dart's high school science-fair project, it was good enough.

First Dart took the numbers and mapped them out. Then he visited each city by night and took several light readings at various spots in each town over a month to get an average reading of the ambient light in each city. Often he dragged Adam along on his late-night adventures in light-reading. They each took turns driving while the other navigated through a dog-eared *Thomas Guide* to figure out just where each city ended and the next began—something almost impossible to deduce in Los Angeles, where city boundaries are about as apparent as the horizon on a smoggy day.

Sometimes Fran would tag along, and they'd make an evening out of the excursion. They'd look up coffeehouses in *LA Weekly* and stop there for an espresso, a brittle scone, or a muffin the size of a grapefruit. Once they were completely wired on caffeine—and on the possibility of life beyond Angelito's elusive borders—they hopped back into the car and cruised around the city taking light readings from the car window.

One night, they all went together to measure the light on the roof of the Bonaventure Hotel downtown. Dart had called the general manager of the hotel, who must have been gay and realized Dart was gay, because he not only allowed them roof access but escorted them up to the roof himself. Adam could see the guy's obvious interest, but Dart was so excited by the access, he didn't notice how much he was disappointing this man by ignoring him. As soon as they overcame how beautiful L.A. looked from above—"Almost like New York," Adam said—they took the measurements Dart needed. Then, just when they were about finished, Fran broke the reverent mood by yelling, "My God! We are *soooo* fucking *Ghostbusters.*"

Everyone laughed, except Dart. Even Bill, the gay manager, chuckled a bellowing chuckle that sounded like it came from somewhere deep inside his soul. Dart was hurt. He had assumed everyone was happy to be working on his project and was taking it as seriously as he was. Adam pulled Dart aside later to remind him that it was funny to be driving around measuring light in the so-called dark of night. And when it came to Fran, a joke meant she was having a good time. Even so, Dart was glad when Fran met Veronica a few weeks later and started spending all her free time with her. After that, he had Adam to himself for his midnight light-reading expeditions.

After a month of late-night drives across L.A.'s overly-illuminated cityscape, Dart compared the average levels of light during the night in each city to the number of reported sleep disorders in each city. He found only a small correlation between the two numbers, but a correlation, nonetheless. The cities with the highest levels of ambient brightness contained more residents who had visited USC for treatment. In the beginning of May, about a month before the fair, Dart gave Mr. Nichols a progress report.

Yikes! Dart thought when he got his report back covered in red ink. What happened to Mr. Nice-Guy Nichols? He'd ripped Dart's project to shreds, mostly by suggesting that his conclusions were "meaningless." Mr. Nichols thought a direct correlation between light levels and sleep disorders was severely inconsequential. Dart made an appointment to get Mr. Nichol's explanation in person, and it turned out to be not as bad as Dart had thought. Mr. Nichols basically explained that there were a multitude of other factors that could have caused the sleep disorders in each city, apart from the level of darkness in each neighborhood. Maybe the brighter areas were more densely populated, congested, noisier, or the residents had less stable income—all things that could increase stress and cause people to have trouble sleeping. Maybe it was as simple as the residents in these areas had to work longer hours for less pay and thus had very good reasons for not sleeping soundly. Dart listened and understood.

Mr. Nichols was a garrulous man, about six feet tall, and a science geek from way back. He'd always liked Dart, thought he was a bright young man, so the intensity of his criticism was well-intended, and Dart knew it. It didn't make it any easier for him to hear, but he took the criticism to heart. Ultimately, Mr. Nichols suggested that Dart change his experiment to report its failings as much as its successes—its limitations as much as its revelations. Initially, Dart did not understand. He couldn't comprehend the benefit of disproving his own hypothesis, especially when his data supported it, however slightly. But he trusted Mr. Nichols and followed his advice.

Eventually—after a few of days of whining about his "disaster" of a project—Dart came around to see the benefit of revealing both sides, and how that actually made his piece more complex. There was something genuine and honest and humbling about the exercise—surprisingly appropriate to where Dart felt he was in his life as he faced other people's expectations for him and made decisions about his future.

Thus, going into the competition, Dart believed in the value of his project more strongly than any of his previous ones. He knew it wasn't sexy enough to win a prize, but he was proud of it on a personal level. Instead of hovering nervously around his booth and overexplaining his project to anyone who would listen, Dart let the project speak for itself. He'd spent yesterday—"Judgment Day," he liked to call it—wandering the halls and checking out the competition. Dart had to admit, at least to himself, that he enjoyed watching the nerdy freshmen swim in their oversize button-down shirts and neckties. He took pleasure in seeing the bags under the eyes of the juniors who'd worked too many all-nighters in a row. Dart also had to admit that he and his fellow seniors—the few who actually completed projects—were enjoyably aloof about the whole thing.

Because the judging was over, Sunday was much more relaxed than Saturday. The public was allowed to visit and see how their kiddies measured up to the competition. Dart's own parents stopped coming after his sophomore year, so for him, there wasn't much to do but hang out and wait for the award ceremony after lunch. By noon he'd walked by every booth twice and talked with everyone he wanted to. Still, there were two more hours until the awards would be handed out.

Dart wandered off campus to find something to eat. Across the street from the school was a sandwich shop filled with science-fair students. They all seemed to know each other, so Dart assumed they were from North Hollywood, but he wasn't sure, especially since there were science geeks from Ventura to Irvine present for the fair. The shop was called Lovebirds Café, and inside, two enormous green-and-red lovebirds were painted on the wall. The birds were six feet tall—*Absolutely killer lovebirds,* Dart thought.

A year ago, Dart would have turned and left a place like this, inhibited by so many unknown but cool-looking people. This year, however, the new and improved millennial-edition Dart walked right in, ordered a turkey, Swiss, and avocado sandwich on a croissant, and settled into his own table near the front window. He analyzed the group of students while he ate. They were definitely science-fair kids—button-down shirts and name tags gave them away—but they were much cooler than the Angelito science-fair kids. At one point, a group of five guys went outside to smoke cigarettes. One of them, the shortest (and cutest) of the pack caught Dart's eye. His disheveled hair was blond and his eyes were blue. He wore light-tan cords and a bright-white button-down shirt with the sleeves rolled above his elbows, revealing forearms that looked strong.

Dart thought this guy was hotter than hot. He liked the way he stood—like he wasn't even trying to be cool. He was so casual, like he wasn't trying to be anything other than himself. Mr. Casual, also, was not smoking, a definite plus in Dart's hygienic mind. He was just hanging out. Dart desired and hated him for being so cool.

Remembering that it would all be over soon—every last bit of high school bullshit—Dart felt instantly more comfortable. He sat up in his chair, concentrated on his sandwich, and tried to ignore the guys outside. After all, hadn't he survived pretty well? He'd never been beaten up. Never went postal against the kids who'd teased him over the years. He'd even managed to have a good time, here and there. So who gave a fuck about a few cool kids in some clique from some school he didn't even attend? But there was that cute short one with the blue eyes. But whatever…he was too cute, Dart assumed, to be interested in him.

The cool clique was long gone by the time Dart finished eating, except for Mr. Casual. He and his blond hair and cords the color of tanned skin sat alone on a bench across the street reading a book. He was also wearing a tie, Dart could see—baby blue, very pale, just like his eyes. The tie was skinny in a sort of early '80s art-rock kind of way. But Dart knew this guy had to be too young to know anything about early '80s art-rock firsthand, so either he was a fashion victim or incredibly hip. Was that more or less cool? Did that make him more or less attractive? Who knew?

Dart exited the café and realized he had to walk right by Mr. Baby Blue. Was he waiting for him? Had he planted himself on the one bench Dart would have to pass? Or was this whole scenario of Baby Blue waiting around to meet Dart all a figment of Dart's imagination?

Dart approached steadily, prepared to keep walking in case Baby Blue made no other sign of interest. Then Baby Blue looked up. Dart panicked, but before he could choke on his words, Baby Blue spoke.

"Want one?" he asked, pulling a pack of cigarettes out of his shirt pocket.

"No thanks."

"Don't smoke?"

"No, actually."

"Me neither," said Baby Blue. "I just carry them around in case I decide to start."

"That makes sense."

"You think? Seems kind of stupid to me. Don't know why I do it."

Baby Blue slipped the full pack back inside the back pocket of his cords. He was even more adorable up close. Dart scolded himself for not wearing something more cool—instead of his standard science-fair dress pants, white shirt, and silverish gray tie. Dart wondered whether he should sit down or keep on walking. Was this the beginning of a conversation or not? In a rare burst of risk-taking, Dart took a chance and sat down on the painted bench next to Baby Blue, but left plenty of room between them.

"You here for the fair?" Dart asked.

"Yeah. Shit is so lame this year, no?

"Yeah, at least it's my last year, so I don't really have to care."

"Me too. I'm a senior at John Marshall, in L.A. proper…which is nowhere near here. You?"

"Angelito," Dart said, twisting the science-fair program he'd been reading during lunch into a cylinder. He rolled it inside itself until he couldn't roll it any further and pointed south toward Angelito. "Do I look like I could be from around here…from the Valley?"

Baby Blue smiled. "Not really."

Smiling worried Dart. Was Baby Blue a smiler, one of those dumb guys who had no idea how cruel the world was and just smiled all the time? *Jee-sus,* Dart said to himself. *You don't have to try, convict, and hang the guy before you even know his name. Conversation. Conversation. Make conversation.*

"My parents thought I was going to get a huge scholarship out of all this shit," Dart finally said. "Boy, were they wrong."

"Mine too. All I've ever won was $100—and only once, three years ago."

"Let me guess, Honorable Mention?"

"Yep," said Baby Blue.

"I've won Honorable Mention—or 'Honorable Almost' as my friend Adam calls it—three years in a row. My cumulative winnings are a whopping $300."

"Whoo-hoo," said Baby Blue, lifting a fist like he was cheering.

Dart noticed that when Baby Blue smiled a dimple formed on only one cheek. How fucking adorable! "Three years ago, I won a Special Honorable Almost."

"Yeah?"

"You must have been there."

"Three years ago? I definitely was."

"I did the big bean plant display that took up a whole table."

"Oh, my God. I remember your project. I did a stupid crystal-growing thing just down the aisle from you. I got Honorable Mention for growing salt crystals large enough to conduct electricity. Don't know if you know this, but the prize money for Honorable Almost is the same as for Special Honorable Almost."

"Yeah, yeah. I know. My dad complained about it for weeks." Dart lowered his voice to imitate his dad. "If they're going to go to all the trouble of calling it 'special,' they ought to put some extra cash behind it to make it special."

While he was talking, Dart wondered how different Baby Blue must have looked three years ago. He was also glad Baby Blue didn't remember what he looked like then. Baby Blue was so good-looking, Dart was sure he must have always been cute; he was probably born cute.

"What did you do with your money?" Dart asked.

"I have no fucking idea."

"Me neither."

They both laughed, both genuinely enjoyed the simple pleasure of sharing a common experience. Yet Dart began to panic again anyway. He started obsessing about how cute Baby Blue was and how he most definitely couldn't be finding anything of interest in Dart. So he quickly decided he should cut his losses and go back inside before he really started liking this guy and had to deal with disappointment when nothing happened. But what if he was wrong? While Dart debated the pros and cons of fleeing a situation like this, he asked Baby Blue what his project was this year.

"Oh, God. Do we have to talk about that? It is so boring."

"No, of course not," Dart said, slightly embarrassed.

"It's some boring chemistry shit about the wasted chemical reactions taking place in catalytic converters, blah, blah, blah."

Okay, time to go, Dart decided. *I'm overstaying my welcome.* "Staying for the awards?" he asked as he stood up.

"Don't think I've got much of a chance this year, but yeah, I've got nothing better to do."

Dart rubbed his sweaty palms nervously down his pants. "Well, I guess I should go check on my booth and make sure it hasn't fallen over again. I got the cheapest foam-core this year. And let me tell you, there's a reason why it's so cheap. It's shit."

Baby Blue laughed because he didn't know what else to say. He wanted to say something more. He wanted Dart to stay and hang out and talk, but apparently Dart wasn't that interested. Baby Blue thought Dart was funny, unique, and his own person. He just couldn't find the words.

"I'll look for you in the front row?" Dart asked before walking away.

"Nah. I'm more of a back-row kind of guy...if you know what I mean."

"Okay, I'll look for you among the potted plants in the back of the auditorium."

"Exactly."

And off Dart went. Confident that he'd left before he really embarrassed himself, but afraid that he was leaving prematurely. Two steps farther he stopped, turned around, and looked back at

Baby Blue on the painted bench. He wanted to make sure there
really was a cute guy back there with blue eyes and a blue tie, and
that he had indeed been talking to him.

"Hey," Baby Blue said when he noticed Dart turn around.

"Yeah?"

"What's your name?"

"Dart."

"Like the board?"

"Yeah."

"And yours?"

"James."

"Like Jesse James?"

"Yep."

On his drive back to his dad's house, Adam didn't notice any of the
cars sharing the road with him. He didn't notice any pedestrians,
red lights, or men selling oranges by the 10-pound bag at major
intersections. He was completely zoned out. After yesterday's funeral activities, his exciting walk with Jeff over the bridge, and his conversation with his mom about moving back home, Adam slept more
deeply than he had any night since his dad died.

He woke up early. The sun came blazing through the window—
he'd forgotten to shut the blinds. Adam ate breakfast with his mom
and Marc—cereal from thick white bowls and coffee from freshly
ground beans in matching white mugs. Sandra was still at Beth's and
wouldn't return until Adam was already gone. He wondered how
she would take the news of his moving back home. Maybe she
wouldn't care.

Vivian followed Adam in her Saab. It felt like the right thing to
do. At "home," Adam pulled into the driveway and Vivian parked
on the street. Adam walked to the front door with his backpack
slung over one shoulder and a shopping bag in his left hand. He slid
his key into the lock as he had a million times before. Vivian stayed
a few steps behind as they went inside. The house was quiet and still;
it held its secrets well. Adam dropped his stuff on the kitchen table,

while Vivian went straight for the sliding glass door. She slid the sheet of glass along its track to let in some fresh air. It made a nice, smooth, *zzzzszssfffthhh* sound as it glided open.

Everything was exactly as it was when Adam left Wednesday morning. A few glasses sat in the sink. The countertops were clear. Vivian walked back to the front door and scooped up a pile of mail from the floor. Adam walked down the hallway toward his room. When he passed his dad's bedroom, he looked inside. The bed was stripped and the mattress looked naked, wearing only a dingy, quilted pad. Adam's room looked the same as before, but felt different, like it belonged to someone else. The posters on the walls, the bulletin board, the old iMac—everything looked like it belonged to someone else, some other guy whose tastes were similar yet different.

"You should probably throw a bunch of this stuff out," Vivian called from the other end of the house. Adam heard her yelling and went back to the kitchen to find out what was wrong.

"Yeah, yeah. I can go out later and get some new stuff," he said.

"Good idea," she said, standing up quickly and letting the refrigerator door swing shut. Adam could tell that his decision to buy everything new was a relief to his mom. It made her feel like a problem had been solved. Vivian reached into her pocketbook and pulled out a wallet with her initials engraved on the gold clasp. She handed a $100 bill to Adam. "Honey, just pick up whatever you need."

Adam took the money and wondered whether this was no-strings-attached generosity or whether he was being paid off. He looked up at his mom's troubled face and tried to figure out how to say thank you without sounding fake. He settled on a smile, something he was lately learning to value above words.

"Adam, will you give me a call later?" Vivian asked, saving herself and Adam from the awkward pause engulfing them. "I'm going to take off now."

And she did, leaving Adam alone in his old-new home. It was unbearably quiet when she shut the door behind her. Adam went straight for the television and turned it on. He walked away before seeing what station it was turned to. It didn't matter. The noise immediately made him feel better.

Parents took up most of the space in the back of North Hollywood High's auditorium. Overdressed underclassmen filled the seats. A few seniors who'd finished projects hung out in the back, pretending it was standing room only and they couldn't have found a seat if they tried. After years of sitting up close, losing, and being left with an up-close-and-personal view of the winner, why go through it again?

Dart looked everywhere for James. When he couldn't find him, he hated how disappointed he felt. He found space against the back wall and settled in. Five minutes later, "James Mackenzie from John Marshall High School in Los Angeles," was announced as the Second Place winner in the chemistry division. Dart quickly stuck his program in his pocket and joined the applause. When he realized he was clapping louder than the people around him, he toned it down. James walked up to the stage, shook hands with North Hollywood High's principal and some suit from a pharmaceutical firm who was sponsoring the contest, and gave the audience a quick nod of his head. Dart tracked James as he left the stage and walked to the back of the room. Dart slithered through the crowd of parents to offer congratulations.

"Hey!" Dart exclaimed as quietly as he could, in a sort of loud whisper.

"Hi."

James sounded happy to see him, Dart thought.

"Congratulations."

"Thanks. I'm pretty surprised."

"This explains why I didn't know your project. I don't have a lot of friends in chemistry."

"Well, now you do," James whispered while the announcer moved on to other winners.

"What?"

"Now you do," James repeated with a one-dimpled smile.

And Dart turned to mush. *Who cares about this flipping award ceremony?* he thought. *The prize I want is right here, and if I stay much longer whispering, I'll surely say something terrible and blow it.* Although James showed no signs of losing interest, Dart's insecurities were relentless. He reached into his pocket and pulled out a piece of paper to hand to Baby Blue.

"What's this?"

"I'm outta here. My awards were already announced, and I didn't even get an Honorable Almost this year."

"I heard. Sorry."

"No big deal. Three years is a good run," Dart said, balling his hand into a fist and lifting it like he was cheering for himself.

James unfolded the paper.

"It's my e-mail," Dart said too quickly.

"Yes it is. Is this so I can e-mail you?"

"If you want."

"Cool. I will."

It took Adam less than half-an-hour to fully unpack, straighten up a few things, and begin to feel like himself again. The house still felt terribly strange, but he figured that was going to be the case for a while. He picked up the phone and invited Dart and Fran and Veronica to come over. Dart wasn't back from the fair yet, so Adam left him a message.

"Yo, Dart. I'm back home. Call me. Come over. Calling Fran and Veronica next."

The "lay-dees," as Adam sometimes called them, weren't doing anything so they zoomed right over. They all hung out in Adam's room and listened to Lauryn Hill's *Miseducation of Lauryn Hill* CD for the umpteenth time. Fran knew all the words by heart and sung-spoke-rapped along with Ms. Hill. Adam flipped through new magazines that had piled up while he was gone. Veronica thumbed through Adam's DVD collection until she found one of her favorites.

"Oh, my God. I haven't watched this in, like, forever."

"What?" Fran asked.

"*Ferris Bueller's Day Off.* I love this movie. Can we watch it? Please?"

Not a bad idea, Adam had to admit. He hadn't seen it in years, and it would cut Fran off from her singing, which was getting old fast.

"How can you say no to a dame like that?" Fran asked.

They moved out to the living room and settled into the couch together.

"My mother hates this movie," Veronica said while the credits began to roll.

"Why?" Adam asked.

"You know she's a teacher, right?"

"No, I didn't."

"Yeah, she teaches seventh grade over at Mother T."

"I didn't know she was Catholic."

"She's not, but my mom says they have good benefits, and you know what a total hypochondriac she is."

"Does that mean she has to teach all that Catholic bullshit?"

"She says it's not so bad once you get used to it. I think she skips over a lot of things."

"And they don't care?"

"I don't know. Anyway, can I finish my story?"

"Yes, yes, honey," Fran said supportively.

"Well, she hates this movie because she thinks it shows teachers in a very bad light, as bumbling idiots mostly."

"They are bumbling idiots," Adam said.

"I know, but..."

"Your mom should start an antidefamation league for teachers," Fran said. "That or a support group. They could call it Catholic Hypocrites Anonymous."

"Or Catholic Hypochondriac Hypocrites," Adam suggested.

Veronica looked seriously insulted.

"Oh, God, baby. We're kidding. I don't know about Adam, but you know I'm kidding."

"I'm kidding too," Adam said.

"Doesn't she understand that is half the point of the movie?" Fran asked. "Teachers are stupid, and so are parents most of the time. The film is a fantasy about one guy—and his two best friends—who spend a single day away from both parents and teachers. They visit art museums and eat in fancy restaurants. And it's not all perfect. Insecurities creep in and people get hurt; there are very sad moments. But ultimately, Matthew Broderick joins the parade and sings 'Shake it Up Baby,' and for a few brief, shining moments it's all okay."

Fran was on a roll.

"And sometimes that's all we can or should hope for, a few brief shining moments." Fran liked to play the part of the anti-intellectual tomboy most of the time. But every once in a while, she'd give herself away as a brain. This was one of those times when, against her better judgment, she spoke concisely and with clarity.

"Right on," Adam said. "But what must your mother think of our generation's movies. I mean, *Ferris Bueller* is a classic. How does she handle shit like *Cruel Intentions*? She must think it's the devil's work or something."

"She doesn't watch many movies anymore," Veronica said, both insulted and disappointed. All she had wanted to do was share a funny story about her mom and now her friends were judging her mother as totally lame. She was pretty lame, but Veronica wanted to be the one who pointed that out. By the time Veronica's favorite scene came on—the part where Ferris and his friends are cruising the Art Center of Chicago and "Please Please Please Let Me Get What I Want" is playing—all was forgiven. And when the final credits began to roll, Dart rang the doorbell.

"Ho, ho, ho and Merry...Housewarming!" he yelled as he opened the unlocked front door.

Adam walked to the door to meet him.

"Doesn't quite have the same ring to it, does it?"

"No, not really."

Dart handed Adam a brown paper shopping bag.

"Oh, you shouldn't have. You're just too generous."

"I know."

Adam looked inside.

"An ice-cold six-pack of Dr. P," Adam announced. "And without a single one missing. Dart, really, you shouldn't have."

"I know," Dart said before he flopped down on the couch in Adam's space between Fran and Veronica. He gave them big, sloppy hugs. Veronica giggled, and Adam thought that was particularly cool.

"Well," Adam interrupted, "glad you could make it because we were all about to go outside and wash my car. It's absolutely filthy."

"Mine's disgusting too," Fran said. "Can we simulwash?"

"Of course, we can't let such strong workers as Veronica and Dart go to waste."

Fran pulled her Beemer up into the driveway and parked it right next to Adam's truck. Veronica hosed both of them down while Adam filled buckets with soap and sponges. He pulled out Windex and a pile of old newspapers—the best things to wash windows with, something about the acid in the ink makes everything evaporate more quickly—and Armor All, of course, for the tires, dashboards, and vinyl interiors.

Fran was the first to notice Adam missing, just as they finished his car.

"Where the fuck is Adam?" she asked.

"Adam?" Dart sort of yelled.

There was no answer.

"He is such a loser," Dart said.

"He could of at least stuck around until we were finished," Veronica said, stating the obvious.

They heard the front door open and looked up. There he was in his wrinkled black polyester cap and gown.

"Oh, no," Fran said.

"Oh, yes," Dart said. "It's you, so you."

"Who," Adam began, "I mean, really, who designed these things?"

"They're like some sort of dark-ages leftover," Fran said, "an identity-blurring symbol of conformity."

The intellectual streak that had taken flight during *Ferris Bueller's Day Off* was apparently still alive. Dart, Adam, and even Veronica turned to see whether it was the real Fran speaking and not some lesbian-feminist graduate student who had taken over her body. To display such verbal dexterity once in a day was special. Two examples in one afternoon—absolutely unheard-of.

"I can tell you one thing," she continued. "Graduation may be the last time any of you will see me in what can only be described as a dress." Then Fran doubled over in laughter. She could really crack herself up, and usually it was over something that no one else found funny.

"Girl, calm yourself!" Dart snapped.

"Oh, puh-lease," Adam said. He turned to Dart to try to change the subject. "Darling, how was the science fair?"

"Same as last year."

"What does that mean?" asked Veronica, who hadn't been part of the group last year.

"That he probably won Honorable Mention again," Fran said, with tears of laughter still in her eyes.

"Very funny," Dart muttered, then turned to Veronica to explain. "It means there were projects, students, and freaky parents all inside a gymnasium stinking of body odor and floor wax. And it all came to a furious conclusion with an awards ceremony where I usually win Honorable Mention." Dart raised his hand for emphasis: "But no, this year was different. I didn't win shit."

"Oh, my God," Adam said, hiking his gown up to his waist so he could sit down on the driveway without ruining its precious "satin" finish. "Your streak of three straight Honorable Almosts has come to an end? I am so sorry."

"I know. Can you believe they wouldn't just give it to me for consistency's sake?"

"Shit, man," Fran said. "I did so much work on that thing."

"You did?" Dart quipped.

But he didn't sound as depressed about it as he usually would have, Adam thought. Losing is something that should have ruined Dart's mood for a week. Something else had to be going on, Adam thought. He just didn't know what.

"It's kind of comforting, actually. I was getting sick of feeling like a real loser every year for being so close, yet so far, from a 'real' prize." Dart made little rabbit ears with his fingers around the word "real." "Now, I can accept I had no chance and can reasonably conclude that the judges this year must have all been morons."

"That actually sounds like one of your better rationalizations," Adam said.

"I'm just glad to hear you're not letting such an insignificant quirk in the judging ruin your—and our—whole day," Fran said. "Although, with all the work I put into that damn project, I am a little pissed off myself."

"Well..." Dart began, and then stopped.

"Well, what?" Adam asked.

"Oh, God. There's more to this story," Fran said. "There's a reason you are not devastated by the loss. It was only days ago that a B-plus sent you into major depression.

"Puh-lease," Dart said, showing Fran the palm of his hand."

"Oh, God, Dart," Adam said. "Break it down. Spill it."

Dart looked at Adam. "Okay, well, I met someone."

"And?"

"His name is James. James Mackenzie. He's from John Marshall."

"Ooh, fancy," Fran said.

"I know," Dart said, slightly embarrassed to agree.

"And?" Adam asked, unimpressed. "Are we supposed to know him by name? And what kind of 'met someone' are you talking about?"

"Met, met."

"Oh, my God," Veronica said. "Is he cute?"

"No. He's butt-ugly," Dart said.

Adam rolled his eyes at Fran as if she was responsible for Veronica's questions.

"Of course he is. What do you think I am, totally desperate?"

"Well, you're not known for your taste in men," Adam said. "Must I remind you of your momentary crush on the Robocop guy?"

"Hello. I was 7!"

"Whoa, back on track," Fran yelled from inside her car, where she sat wiping down the dash. "Cut to the chase, please. Who is he, and did you get his number?"

"Don't be getting all Nancy Drew on me," Dart yelled back.

"Well, did you?" Veronica asked.

"Better. I got his e-mail."

"Thank God," Fran said. "There is hope for you yet. We may not have to listen to you prepare to lose your virginity forever."

"Hello, it's called taste. I have discerning taste. I don't go after every idiot who goes after me."

"You got a thing with the word 'idiot' today," Adam said. "And I wasn't aware of all the men you've been turning away because they weren't up to your standards. Please, remind me who they were."

"Ignore him," Fran said. "What was his project? Nothing too geeky, I hope."

"Not sure exactly, it was in the chemistry section—where I never like to venture. Have you ever seen the chemistry people? Anyway, it didn't sound so bad, something about catalysts or catalytic converters."

"Oh," Fran said. "Sounds butch. Cars and shit."

"Sounds like you showed a real interest in his work," Adam said.

"I showed interest in many parts of him," Dart said defensively.

Finding her brother not only gone but without plans to return sent Sandra into a minor fit of anxiety, confusion, and disappointment. In fact, she didn't know where one feeling ended and the other began.

"Honey, he has not moved away," Vivian said. "He is just going to stay there this summer because it's probably closer to wherever he's going to work."

Sandra wasn't buying it; her face remained on the verge of anger. Vivian kept trying. "He's going to be around a lot. I promise. Now go put your things away. It's time to eat."

Sandra walked to her room, dropped her bag, and picked up the phone. In her other hand, she held Jacqueline, not even aware she was holding her. Sandra dialed her old phone number. She wanted to ask Adam why he was leaving her too.

When the phone rang at her dad's house, Adam was outside with his friends and didn't hear it ring. The answering machine picked up and Sandra heard her dad's voice. *"You've reached..."* She hung up immediately and walked to the kitchen. Marc heard her coming and turned to greet her with a bit of a smile.

"You're just in time," he said.

Sandra tried to analyze Marc's smile, to figure out whether it was real.

"You didn't eat, did you?" he asked, searching her blank gaze for information.

"No, not yet."

Adam and his friends ordered pizza: fresh tomato and mushrooms on one side—because Veronica was a vegetarian, of course—and sausage and mushrooms on the other.

"Did I mention Jeff showed up at the funeral?" Adam said to no one in particular. He timed the revelation perfectly so the words came out while everyone's mouths were full and a quick bitchy retort would be impossible.

"No," Dart said, putting his slice down on his plate, "You didn't."

"Who's Jeff?" asked Veronica.

"Yeah, who *is* Jeff? repeated Dart.

"He's the cop from the other day," Adam said, as if it were no big deal.

"No, I don't think we know him," Dart said, his sarcasm barely hidden.

"What 'other day' cop, who?" Fran asked.

"And since when is he just 'Jeff'?" Dart asked, without looking at Adam.

"How do you know a cop?" Fran asked, shoving the last bit of crust into her mouth. "Cops can be so hot, can't they? Not all that power macho bullshit—that's bogus. But those shiny black uniforms, black leather boots, motorcycles and shit. H-O-T—hot."

"You think cop uniforms are hot?" Veronica asked as if Fran had just admitted enjoying the taste of Rocky Mountain oysters. She was particularly caught off-guard by Fran's declaration of an erotic fantasy that didn't include her in any way.

"He's the one who came by the house when my dad passed away," Adam said.

"We weren't exactly there with you," Fran reminded him.

"Dart knows him," Adam said, dismissively.

"I do?"

"Yeah, you've seen him around town. At least once at the Sev and another time at Pavilions."

"Huh?" Fran asked Adam. "So, a cop you recognize at the Sev— Who even knew you were paying attention to the cops at the Sev? But that's another story—shows up at your house and now you're 'friends'?"

"Fran, wait…" Veronica said. She was still too hung up on learning about Fran's cop fetish to concentrate on Adam's love life.

"Yeah, I guess so. Then he showed up at the funeral, and my mom invited him over for lunch. I know…sounds crazy. But, oh well."

"Wait?" Fran asked Veronica. "Wait for what, honey? It's a look I like—the tight black shirts and pants, the way a bulletproof vest squishes your tits. Don't worry. It's nothing serious."

"I never knew you liked that stuff."

Fran reached over and put her hand on Veronica's arm. "Baby, I can't tell you everything right away. There would be no mystery."

"Puh-lease," Dart interjected. "In private, please. Can't you two have this conversation *sans nous*?"

"Well, I think he's nice," Adam said, continuing as if there had been no interruption in his train of thought. It was all Jeff, all the time in Adam's head. He'd been thinking about him all day and couldn't keep it to himself any longer. He barely noticed the tension Fran's uniform fetish was causing, or Dart's simmering jealousy.

"Why would he stop by the funeral?" Dart asked, his slice still on his plate, waiting for him.

"I don't know. Just being nice, I guess."

"Just being *nice?*" Dart asked. "God, I hate that word."

"Said he wanted to see how everything was going."

"What exactly did he say?"

"Hi. How's it going?" Adam said without inflection.

"Puh-lease. There must have been more."

"Not really."

Fran, sensing an opening, asked, "Do you think you like him…in *that* way?"

Sometimes Fran could sound like such a little girl. And this was one of those times. She was picking up on Adam's vibe, could tell what he was trying to say even though he himself didn't know what or how to say what he really wanted to say. "Sounds cool to me," Fran declared as if the subject was over.

"Cool?" Dart asked.

"Yeah, why not?" Fran wondered

"He is cool," Adam said. "And kind of hot. Even out of his uniform."

Adam smiled at Fran like she'd become his accomplice.

"You've seen him out of it?" Dart asked, wide-eyed.

"Well, he didn't wear it to lunch at my mom's."

"And was he still hot?" Fran asked.

Adam paused. "Yeah, in a completely different way, but yeah, I'd say he was hot."

"Oh, God," Dart said. "Now tell us again. Why the hell did your mom invite him over for lunch?"

"I don't know, Dart. Maybe she was trying to be nice."

"Doubt it," Dart declared. "That woman has never been *nice* a day in her life."

"Since when do you hate my mother?" Adam asked.

"I don't," Dart had to admit. "But since when do you *not*?" Then Dart realized he'd maybe gone to far. He wiggled in his chair before confessing. "I'm just mad because you've had lunch with Jeff before I've even had the chance to call James."

"You just met him today," Adam said.

"So?"

Dart took a breath, realized he was sounding like a jerk, and tried to turn back the clock to before his jealousy got the best of him. "And anyway," he said, "you know, life is a competition, and I like to be in the lead."

"Anyway..." Fran said with a roll of her eyes so wide she could've permanently damaged her optic muscles. "So, Adam, what's up with you and this...cop?"

"Nothing, yet," Adam said, unable to keep from grinning.

"You had lunch and that's all?"

Dart's calm didn't last: "He came over. You guys had lunch. He left and now you call him...this policeman...cute *and* nice, and you say that's nothing?"

Fran wanted to show Dart two things: She was on his side, and this was not a big deal. "Don't hold out on us, man," she began. "If you've got a connection to policewomen and you're holding back, well, that goes against Friend Rule Number 14. Thou shall hook up friends whenever possible, especially if the prospective hook-ups work in—or even just own—tight black uniforms."

"Fran!" Veronica said, hot, bothered, and confused.

"Relax, baby. It's a joke."

Fran reached out and put a hand on Veronica's arm, like a mother calming her child. Fran was half-kidding, but only half. She was happy with Veronica, enjoying for the first time having a girlfriend. (Don't ever ask her about Samira, the Iranian girl she lusted after last year. Di-sas-ter.) But Veronica was two years younger, and Fran knew their relationship was a limited engagement because of that. Veronica would still be in high school next year while Fran would be in college; she was going to UC Santa Barbara. Not that this made their relationship any less meaningful. But for Fran, it was halfway over before it ever began.

Sandra sat down with Marc and her mother to a quiet dinner. To accompany the roasted chicken, salads left over from the reception were brought out. The green salads were wilted. The fruit ambrosia was just beginning to turn, but the marshmallows still squished pleasantly in Sandra's mouth. And there was just enough of Aunt Patricia's macaroni salad with celery and black olives for each of them to have one last scoop.

After the last stray mushroom was picked off the cardboard box, Fran and Veronica left for the night. Adam piled the paper plates and napkins inside the empty box and carried the whole mess out to the garbage. When he returned, he found Dart still sitting at the table, looking confused. Adam jumped up on the counter nearby. He remembered how his dad always yelled at him to get down off the counter. "It's not built for people," Greg would say.

"Did you...with Jeff?" Dart asked.

"Did I what?"

"You know...anything."

Dart wanted details.

"No, not really."

"Not really? Are you even sure he's gay."

"Yeah, he's gay. I'm pretty sure of that."

"Why?"

"I could tell."

"How."

"You want details, don't you?"

"Yeah, and?"

"When I walked him out to his car, we were talking and..."

"And?"

"And he sort of kissed me."

"Kissed you goodbye?"

"Sort of."

"He 'sort of' kissed you? I just asked you if anything happened, and you said no."

"Well…"

"This policeman, this Jeff, put the moves on you on the very same day that your father was buried? Isn't that a little weird?"

"It's not like I just stood there and let him. I guess we sort of kissed each other."

Monday, June 14, 1999

The sound of air—of hydrogen, oxygen, carbon, and nitrogen crash-ing into each other in clamoring, disorienting silence—woke Adam up. He opened his eyes and looked around. Yes, it was his bedroom, in his house filled with the same stuff. And he was the same Adam he had been yesterday.

Last night, after Dart had finally left, Adam spent the rest of the evening reviewing the ins and outs of Washington, D.C.—a city Adam felt was as foreign as Paris or Pyongyang—but which he needed to know about for his American government final today. Adam devoted most of his reviewing to the 20-something amendments to the U.S. Constitution. He was sure they would be the subject of at least one of the two essay questions. He knew this because his teacher, Mr. White, had all but told his class exactly what to study.

Adam understood them by concept—Equal Protection Clause, Women Get the Vote, Prohibition, and Prohibition Repealed— but he had trouble remembering them by number and year rati-fied. He had tried arguing many times before, in government and in various history classes, that dates were unimportant compared to the big picture, but always lost the argument with his teachers. *So old-school*, he believed.

Around midnight, Adam gave up, clicked off the TV with the remote, and went to bed. His sheets felt the same as they always did.

His pillow smelled the same, too—human, a little dusty—and he fell asleep easily.

But now it was morning, and Adam stood in the kitchen listening to a deafening silence. Without the sound of water running while Sandra brushed her teeth, without the chattering of alarm clocks, or the coffeemaker gurgling in the kitchen, morning was weird; it was different; it was kind of frightening. The small piece of pure sadness that lived deep inside Adam—the one he was born with, not the one created by his dad's passing—began to grow, fed by the lonely quiet of unused appliances and empty bedrooms. Adam's sadness grew larger and joined melancholy, intersected with self-pity, and dropped him off at a fork in the road. He could freeze up and crawl back into bed until the pain passed, or he could burn the energy—use the anxious sadness like it was fuel—and keep moving, leave the house, head to school, whatever. Ultimately, it was fear of what lay waiting for Adam in his now-cold bed that pushed him to choose action over inaction. He went back to his room, but only to get dressed. He grabbed his backpack with only a cursory check of what was inside and took off.

With more than an hour before the first bell at Angelito High School, Adam stopped at Bollywood to pass some time before picking up Dart. He bought a dozen doughnuts and a large coffee with milk—no sugar. He sat down at one of the three small yellow tables off to the side and ate an apple fritter while watching the customers come and go.

"Oh, Buttercup," Dart said as he shut the door to Adam's truck. "You shouldn't have."

"Oh, Butter-head, I didn't get them for you."

As Adam pulled away from the curb in front of Dart's house, his best friend opened the waxy bag. "You even remembered that I love the sprinkled ones."

Finals week at Angelito High School was two periods each day instead of six, although they were twice as long so teachers could extract maximum discomfort. Lunch was extended to an hour and a half to allow students to study, panic, or just waste time. In slight consolation, the day ended two hours earlier. Teachers said they needed the extra time to grade the exams. Students said they needed the extra time to study. In reality, everyone was glad for the reduced schedule, no matter what they ended up doing with the time.

"So, kiddos," began Mr. Edward M. White, Angelito's very proper teacher of American government for the last 30 years. "I've decided I don't want to read hundreds of essays over the next three days, so I've changed the final to 100 multiple choice questions..." A cloud of relief passed over the class. "And only one essay question."

"Ooh," the class communally exhaled. A few nervous students giggled at their good fortune.

"But the essay will be worth 50 percent of your final grade, so don't think it doesn't matter. If you do the math—which I realize is not a strong suit for many of you—it matters more than ever that you write me something that is not only lucid enough for me to read but also shows me that you've gained at least a minor understanding of the way our government works and affects our lives."

Mr. White pulled a pile of papers from his briefcase and began distributing them.

"You have the next two hours to finish the exam. I suggest you use the time wisely. "

Communal "oohing" turned to "unhhing."

"Oh, quit whining."

Adam breezed through the multiple-choice section. Every once in a while, the none-of-the-above-option threw him for a loop, but not often enough to seriously matter. For his essay, Adam chose a question he was prepared for: "Do you think the Equal Rights Amendment would be ratified by the states if Congress were to pass it today?" Adam argued that it probably would not pass because in its original form it focused primarily on women. Adam argued that such a law might be considered exclusionary to people of color, immigrants, non-English speakers, and gays, lesbians, and trans-gendered people, all of whom had fought their own battles for equal rights since the ERA sank in 1979. Near the end of his pages-long epistle, Adam decided to get personal. Maybe it was the rush he got from knowing he was doing well—who knows?—but he decided to write himself into the story.

"As a gay man living at the end of the 20th century, I personally would argue against supporting the Equal Rights Amendment in its original form."

In the classroom, Adam had never strayed so far out of the closet. But he liked Mr. White, often wondered whether he was playing on Adam's team, and decided he had nothing to lose at this point. It was the third-to-last day of school. It was basically impossible at this point for Adam to fail the class. So why not?

After arguing that the Equal Rights Amendment was not likely to pass today, he changed tacks and said that it should be passed for the very reason that it probably wouldn't; that discrimination is still so pervasive—if mostly sublimated—that an Equal Rights Amendment should be introduced as an all-inclusive nondiscrimination law that would constitutionalize equal rights for all citizens regardless of *any* perceived or real distinctions. Adam then mentioned the fact that because he was gay he "personally understood the discrimination homosexuals, or those perceived to be homosexual, faced in America." Adam left out the fact that as a good-looking white kid in the middle of a middle-class neighborhood in the middle of one of America's most liberal cities, he had not actually faced anything more than a halfhearted heckle in his short gay life, yet he finished the exam and felt like he'd made a strong case. And he'd outed himself to Mr. White in the process.

"Okay. Time's up," Mr. White announced. "Pass your papers up and have a good life. And please...remember to vote."

Adam's crew met at their usual lunchtime spot along The Wall between the administration building and Cheryl Tiegs Auditorium. (Ms. Tiegs was a graduate of Angelito High School, and back when she was a proto-supermodel she had donated some money toward renovating the auditorium and thus guaranteed her name in lights forever—at least in Angelito.) What The Wall *was,* was not as important as what The Wall was not. It was not the cafeteria where the truly uncool people ate, nor was it the picnic tables by the vending machines where the jocks and their social club-belonging, superpink lip gloss-wearing girlfriends ate. The Wall was a wall, wide enough to contain a few different groups of misfits and outsiders yet narrow enough to keep out the truly groupless.

Toward the south end hung the musically outrageous kids, the kind who said they liked punk rock, even though they'd only heard it downloaded on Napster. On the other end, a handful of fashion victims—always very put together, way too put together—hung out looking like the members of an experimental theater troupe. A few of Dart's nerdy science friends hung at The Wall too, when they weren't kissing a teacher's ass by studying through lunch or running off to an internship at NASA. The Wall was where Fran met Veronica, in an area occupied by a group of girls who could have been labeled lesbians-in-training, if high school students weren't so clueless about lesbians. Adam and his friends resided literally and physically between cliques, in an amorphous area between cool and not cool, disasters-waiting-to-happen and geniuses-in-training.

"Are we eating here or is somebody driving us to get something decent to eat?" Dart asked Fran and Adam.

"Eat these," Adam said, pulling the bag of doughnuts he'd bought that morning from his backpack.

"My geometry final totally sucked," Veronica said to no one in particular.

Dart grabbed the bag from Adam and took out a buttermilk twist. Then he turned to Veronica and said, "You think geometry is hard? Girl, just wait till you grow up and take big-girl math. Try calculus. Calculus really sucks. Geometry is a fucking walk in the park." Dart took a bite of his doughnut and kept talking with his mouth full. "And if you make it to calculus, just hope you don't get Mrs. Hsu. She is the suckiest."

"I'll take sprinkled," said Fran

"There's only a jelly-filled and two French crullers left," Dart said, looking inside the bag.

"You know a dyke cannot eat a cruller," Fran said. "Those are for old ladies and fags. Only you, as a card-carrying fag, would even buy them, Adam."

"What crawled up your pussy and died?" Dart asked.

"Nice..." Adam said. "Real nice."

"Veronica's new rabbit-shaped vibrator, that's what," Fran said, taking a bite of jelly-filled and sending white powder sprinkling down her shirt.

"Oh, great, getting nicer," Adam continued.

"I warned you not to use it so much," Veronica said nonchalantly. She was getting the hang of Fran's friends' sarcasm. "If you used up all the batteries, then you're buying the next ones."

"Girls!" Adam said with a huff. "Maybe my dad was right."

"Huh?" Fran asked, arching her eyebrows.

"I mean, maybe my dad was right about women."

"Oh, God. Where is this going?" Dart asked.

"After my parents' divorce, and before I pointed out to my father I was gay, he used to complain about women to me. 'Be careful,' he'd say. 'They're very needy.'"

"Your dad was quite the little feminist wasn't he?" Veronica said.

Everyone looked at Veronica, shocked by her boldness. Was she consciously criticizing Adam's dead father?

"Yeah," Adam said. *Oh, shit,* he thought. *The next thing I'm about to say is in the past tense.* Adam's voice quieted just slightly as he finished: "Wasn't he?"

"Well," Fran said, trying to bring the conversation back up to easygoing, "with idiotic stories like that, you are starting to sound like your old self again. Glad to see you're feeling better."

The slight panic at speaking of his dad in the past tense was only momentary. "Who'd have thunk," Adam said, trying to make a joke, "that one week after my dad kicks the bucket—and kicks it himself, I might add—I would be back here sitting with y'all and having such intellectual conversations?"

"Puh-lease," Dart whined, glad to see Adam joking, but not completely. "It's called denial. You're sitting here shooting the shit because your subconscious still hasn't dealt with the gravity of the situation. It's normal. It's part of the grieving process."

"Can't you wait until you've at least graduated from high school before opening your own psychiatric practice?" Adam said.

"It's not like I'm charging you."

"Whatever. I'm outta here," Adam said, standing up. "Gotta visit Ms. Gary before our Spanish final. I need to see if she's letting me out of my Algebra 2 final. I calculated that I'm getting a B no matter how I do on the final. So why bother, right?" Adam threw the almost-empty doughnut bag in the garbage and slung his backpack over his shoulders. "Why should she have to grade an extra exam?"

"Always thinking of others, Adam," Dart said. "That is one of your most admirable qualities."

"Whatever, man," Adam said.

Jeff's days off were often Sunday, Monday, and Tuesday. It gave him a four-day workweek, but Jeff had to put in 12-hour days to get those three days off. Jeff didn't think much of it after so many years. He was used to the policeman's life and had long ago given up on having any so-called weekends. He had no patience for people who always went grocery shopping on Saturday and always ate brunch on Sunday. That kind of life seemed too regimented, caused him stress to even imagine. Jeff's days off came when they came, and there wasn't anything he could do about it. Jeff's schedule fit his personality. He couldn't make very many plans with other people too far in advance because he was never sure what his schedule was going to be. In a way, it kept him safely single too.

This morning, Jeff skipped the beach and occupied himself with errands—shopping for dog food, picking up a card for Father's Day—but mostly Jeff spent the day thinking about Adam. He played the imaginary tape from yesterday again and again in his head. Throughout the day, Jeff's feelings jumped back and forth from excited to nervous until he wasn't sure where his heart was. Part of him wanted to walk away from what he saw as an exciting, but scary mess. Another part of Jeff wanted to park across the street from Angelito High School and wait for Adam to come out. He wanted to see him again soon. And yet another part wanted to quash the nagging suspicion that there was more to the story of how Adam's dad had died.

"He's fine," Fran said after Adam was gone.

"How can you say he's fine?" asked Dart. "Even if he's acting fine, with everything that's happened? Maybe it's just a big show?"

Dart and Fran collected their bags and began walking to their Spanish final. Veronica said goodbye, gave Fran a little kiss on the cheek, and scampered off to her American lit final.

"What are his options?" Fran asked. "Mope around forever?"

"Oh, God, Fran. Must you always be so fucking practical?"

"Huh?"

"Don't you think Adam should be upset for a few more days, at least?" They turned the corner and dodged students walking in every possible direction. "He should mope around a bit. Would that be so bad?" Dart said, stepping out of the way of a runaway underclassman apparently late for something very important.

"Well..." Fran said

But Dart interrupted her. "Fran," he said. "I know it's hard for you to imagine that anyone else in the world would see life differently than you do, but maybe, just maybe, in Adam's world—as it would be in mine—losing your father is really hard-core."

"I'm not saying it isn't," she said, slowing down to emphasize her point. "I'm just saying that there are levels of sucking. Like maybe it's devastating at first, but then you realize that life is going to go on whether you want it to or not—whether you're feeling like shit or not. And maybe realizing that makes things start to change, and that could be a good thing."

"How can you even think that change is good when we're talking about Adam's dad dying—dead—gone? Adios forever."

"I'm not saying that the situation changes," Fran argued. "What I'm sayir   :hat your feelings change. I think the way you're affected by certain events—no matter how awful—changes. And over time, then your feelings change."

During lunchtime, Jeff took his Bronco in for a smog check he needed in order to renew his registration. He skipped the garage's lemony-scented waiting room and went to the mini-mall next door to get something to eat. The only place open served wraps. Jeff didn't care for wraps—*What was wrong with the sandwich?* he always asked himself—but that was the only option, so he went with it. Afterward, he walked back next door and watched the men finish running the test on his car. The attendant pressed buttons on a computer attached to a hose, which was attached to his car's muffler. Any thoughts of the link—or lack of a link—between what was going on in front of him and the sky above, the balance of chemistry in the air, the changes in the weather, did not enter his mind. On any other day, it might have. But today Jeff's mind was elsewhere. What looked like a big receipt printed out of the computer. The attendant stapled it to another form, traded it with Jeff for some money, and went on to the next car in line.

By the time Señora Cardenas passed out her final exam, Dart and Fran had called a temporary truce and settled into their seats. Adam flew in at the very last minute and had to take an empty seat in the front row. The first half of the exam was written; the second half, oral. Señora Cardenas had each student come up to her desk in the corner of the classroom and sit next to her for a short *conversación*. In a low voice she asked generic questions about high school, the future, and books they had tried to read this year. Fran, whose Spanish was better than Dart's or Adam's because she practiced at work, breezed through and went back to her seat quickly. Dart's interview was a little more halting, but he would eventually earn an A, anyway. With Adam, Señora Cardenas lost the will to quiz. She asked a few introductory questions—"What's your name?" "How old are you?" "Where do you live?"—but then switched to English. "I'm very sorry about your father," she said.

"Thanks," Adam said in English. His heart sunk to the seat of his plastic chair. He hoped she wasn't going to get into anything serious now, not while they were within earshot of half the class. Senora Cardenas crossed her leg, straightened her skirt subconsciously, and started telling a long story about when her own father passed away years ago. Adam listened as politely as possible and then went back to his seat when she was finished.

When class was over, Fran, Dart, and Adam met outside.

"Fine, fine, fine," Fran declared, almost happy.

"That's because you like that oral shit," Dart said, unaware of his good grade yet. "Thank god it's over—that's what I've got to say."

Adam, still annoyed by Señora Cardenas's unnecessary story, didn't speak.

"Oh, well, going to find Veronica. Later." Fran said before walking off.

"Bye," Adam said.

"What are you doing tonight?" Dart asked, wiggling his backpack over both shoulders.

Adam had nothing planned. His last final was English tomorrow, and there was nothing he could do to prepare. It's not like he was going to read all the books again. But he wasn't feeling like hanging out. Not that he felt like going home either. He didn't know what he wanted.

"Well," Dart said. "No biggie. Can you at least give me a ride home?"

"Yeah," Adam said. Then he looked at Dart and wondered how long he'd been standing in the same position. "Of course. Sorry."

Frozen macaroni and cheese. After dropping Dart off, Adam began craving the super–thick and salty macaroni and cheese that came frozen and had to be heated up in the microwave. His dad used to make the cheaper kind in the box, the one with the really bright orange coloring. Adam didn't like that kind as much—too skinny were the noodles and too inconsistent the sauce. The frozen stuff was always exactly the same creamy thickness, and the noodles were fat and soft. "Too expensive," Greg would say. "We can eat two boxes of Kraft for the price of one of the other kind."

This craving came to Adam between Dart's house and home. At first, it was an unspecific craving for something warm that urged Adam toward Pavilions. By the time he pulled into the parking lot, he'd figured out exactly what he wanted.

"Adam?" said a man somewhere behind Adam as he reached into the freezer. Adam turned around—mac and cheese in hand—to see Mr. White, his teacher ask, "How are you?"

"I'm fine," Adam said. He looked inside Mr. White's basket to see what he was buying. There were only a few items: a quart of milk, a couple of unidentifiable cans, and some meat wrapped tightly in plastic wrap.

"How did you feel about the final exam?"

"Oh, uhm, okay…I guess." Adam put the macaroni and cheese into his handbasket. He'd never seen Mr. White off campus. Seeing him now, in an aisle of frozen food, felt strange. It made Adam feel older, more equal to Mr. White, and this disturbed him slightly.

Mr. White could tell Adam was uncomfortable. "I'm sure you did well," Mr. White said, looking down at his basket as if he was ready to move on.

"I hope so," Adam said.

"I'll let you get back to your shopping," Mr. White said, walking away. "Have a good evening."

Adam watched Mr. White head down the aisle. "Thank you," Adam said, just loud enough for Mr. White to hear.

Mr. White turned back, lifted up his arm, and waived silently.

Sandra joined her classmates on their annual end-of-the-year field trip to Griffith Park. A tour guide named William met the group after the planetarium show, the kind that explained the entire history of the universe in 45 minutes. Sandra and her 28 classmates, four adult chaperones, and one teacher, exited the dome-shaped theater and entered the brightly lit Great Hall. The children rubbed their eyes and twisted and stretched their necks, sore from the backward tilt of the seats and headrests. They resembled a gaggle of baby birds just out of their protective, but confining, shells.

"Isn't that the point of life? Or maybe not *the* point of life, but at least one of the most important points—*the* thing you need to know in order to get by in this fucked-up world?" Dart said. "You have to understand that no one else can see the world in exactly the same way you do."

"You've got a point," Fran said, standing by a table at Angelito's after school, shifting her weight back and forth on the pivot of her cue stick. "I'm with you on the whole empathizing-with-others thing. It's crucial. But, my question is about the next step. Even if you recognize the fact that others see the world differently, how do you make yourself care when you know everyone else is seeing things the wrong way? I mean, look around this room. All you see are people who are so damn wrong about so many things. What good is it to recognize that fact if you can't do anything about it? It just depresses me."

It was almost dinnertime, but Dart and Fran had been going at each other over the meaning of life since after their last final hours earlier. Their English teacher threw them a curveball essay question: "What book that we have read this year has had the most impact on your daily life? And second, what book do you think will have the greatest impact on you later in life?"

Arguments began immediately afterward. As shoes scuffed down the rickety stairs and through the asphalt walkways between buildings, Fran and Dart started arguing. Their discussion continued well into the group's finals-are-over celebration at Angelito's.

Adam thought Mr. Dryden' question was completely vain: They were books, and this was only high school. Wasn't it a bit premature to think about lifelong influence? "Mr. Dryden just wants validation that what he has been doing all his life is important," Adam said. "Reading books and talking about them, probably the same books every year since he began teaching—that's all he knows."

"Yeah," Dart said, "but can you blame him? I mean, I wake up every day wondering what the fuck I'm doing, and I'm not even 18! I can only imagine how lost I might be when I'm 50-something."

"You, Dart," Fran said, "are going to be scarier than hell when you're 50. I can only hope I survive to see the day."

Adam's focus on the argument had strayed long before they made it to Angelito's to play pool. Dart and Fran, undistracted by a parent's death, a new romance, or a police investigation, continued with glee.

"This conversation is becoming so stupid it's scary," Adam said to Dart. "Stupid-funny scary, like when you told us you believed in *The Blair Witch Project*."

"Anyway," Dart said, glaring at Adam. "Stupid-funny scary is how random and *meaningless* your comment is. Back in the real world, we're…"

"Oh, yeah," Fran interrupted. "This is so *The Real World*. I hope you mean the MTV version."

"Hello! Can I finish?" Dart snapped, his hands thrown down at his side. "We are surrounded by idiots who don't think. Just look around the room at the way these people dress. Flat-front khakis have been around for-basically-ever and yet thousands of men—and some women—continue to wear pleats! What good are people if they don't think about their actions?"

"Oh, God, Dart," Adam pleaded

"Okay, okay. It's a bad example, but work with me. My point is that people are stupid, or they're blind, they don't see what's right in front of them." Dart continued: "I don't think the people who wear pleated khakis know that they really make themselves look fat and sloppy. I don't think they know that because they don't really look at themselves. If they did, if they saw themselves the way others see them, then they would give, well, they'd give 'em all away to the Salvation Army."

"Forget it," Fran said, shaking her head. "You're totally losing it."

"No, wait. Don't give up and just walk away and let the stupid people stay stupid." Dart was really worked up. His heart was racing. "They are only going to get in our way. Don't you see? That's the problem. We have to figure out a way to help them so at the very least they don't drag us down by continuing to create a world of pathetic mediocrity."

"Pathetic mediocrity?" Adam asked. "Are you on crack?"

"Pathetic mediocrity…pleated khakis, so you don't like my vocabulary," Dart's voice rose with each passing word. "Oh!" he exclaimed. "Fuck all of you!"

And with that, Dart stormed off. He didn't stay away for long; he just went to the bathroom. While he was gone, Adam and Fran looked at each other, waited for someone to make sense of Dart's little explosion of angst—to say something understanding.

"Do you think Dart's okay?" Veronica asked.

"He's fine!" Adam and Fran answered simultaneously, and then cracked up. Finally, when they couldn't laugh any longer without their cheeks aching, they just smiled and breathed deeply, gazing at each other with a deep sense of understanding.

Dart returned and walked straight up to the table. He put both his hands down on the edge and announced that he was unwilling to continue the discussion. "Perhaps, at a later date when at least one of you has seen the light, I'll have the strength to speak on this issue again," Dart announced, "but for now it's over." Then he turned around and planted himself on a stool to watch Fran take a shot.

"So, Adam, have you heard from your policeman friend?" Fran asked after the balls stopped rolling.

"Not since the weekend, no."

Adam had thought about him, though. He'd spent much of the last two days trying to decide how long he was supposed to wait before he could call Jeff without looking too interested. Between Jeff's job and—yes, his age—Adam wasn't even sure he should call at all. So he'd convinced himself to wait for Jeff to call him in order to confirm Jeff's interest in him first.

"Don't you have his number?" Dart asked.

"Yeah."

"Then why don't you call him?"

"It's too soon, and, well, I don't know." Adam tried to shrug off any insecurity Dart's question caused him. "I got a feeling he'll call or I'll run into him or something."

"Well, don't wait too long," Fran said. "Uniform pants have no pleats, which puts him squarely on the side of good."

Dart glared at Fran, and was equally annoyed by Adam's confidence, although he tried his best not to show it. Dart had followed no rules himself and had sent James—Mr. Blue Eyes—an e-mail this afternoon: *"Hi. It's Dart (Mr. Light Pollution). Nice to meet you this wknd. If you want to get together for a movie or something, let me know. And just in case you wanna go old school: here's my #..."* It wasn't anything too deep or special, but at least he'd done it. He'd taken the initiative and that made Dart feel infinitely better, at least until Adam came along with his stories.

"Fran, would you mind if we forget about your uniform fetish for a little while?" Adam asked.

"Why?"

Pointing toward the door, Adam said, "Because that's Jeff walking right toward us...out of uniform."

"And he's coming this way," Dart said with a gleam in his eye so bright you'd think it was the man of his dreams sauntering over.

Sauntering is the only way to describe how Jeff propelled himself forward, one leg in front of the other, his arms swinging gently from side to side until he was almost at their table. Adam waved hello, and Jeff waved back. Then Jeff slipped his hands nervously into the pockets of his jeans.

"Hi," Adam said, trying not to sound surprised.

"Hi," Jeff replied, his voice as deep and soothing as ever.

For a second, everyone just stood still, staring at each other, taking in the scene. "Hi—you must be Jeff," Dart interjected.

"Yes, I am. And you must be Dart."

"The one and only."

"Jeff, this is Fran," Adam said, speaking up, "and this is Veronica."

Each of them approached and shook Jeff's hand like he was a visiting dignitary from some faraway land. Jeff offered his hand in as relaxed a way as possible, but couldn't help worrying that his palms felt old and callused against the young women's smooth skin. Call it generational obliviousness, or something, but to Adam's friends the difference went unnoticed.

"So. You must know a lot of policewomen," Fran said.

"Oh, Fran," Veronica said, embarrassed.

"I'm kidding. I'm kidding," Fran said, putting her arm around Veronica's shoulder like a big sister. "You know you're the only woman in or out of uniform I want."

"She has a thing for uniforms," Adam said.

"Oh, well, we should talk sometime," Jeff replied gamely. "I work with a lot of people in uniforms." Then, trying to make conversation, he said to Dart, "Great name."

"It's from Dartagnan," Dart said.

"Something about his parents watching *The Three Musketeers* the night he was conceived," Adam said. "Don't ask. It's very strange."

"You told me they just liked the sound of it," Fran said.

"So," Dart began, trying to ignore his friends. "You're a real police officer, eh?"

"I prefer officer of the peace. It sounds better, don't you think?"

"Sounds more serious," Dart said.

"Police work is very serious. But I'm off duty, so call me Jeff, please."

"Oh," Fran said, disappointed.

"Yeah. See? No gun." Jeff lifted his blue polo shirt away from his side and revealed the waist of his jeans. They were old 501s and hung from his hips without a belt. While everyone else focused on the absence of a weapon, Adam noticed the pink skin and the hint of an elastic-waistband that peeked above his jeans.

"I was just about to win this game," Adam said, trying to keep the conversation flowing. He took a few steps over to the table and hit a quick bank shot that sank the eight ball right into the corner pocket with a final winning thud. "Okay," he said to Dart. "That means you go get more quarters."

"Try not to judge poor Adam by how he treats us," Dart said. "We're only his best friends."

"Save it, loser," Adam said, trying to cut Dart off before he said something really embarrassing. Dart took the hint and walked over to get more quarters. Fran and Veronica settled back on their stools, giving Adam and Jeff a semblance of being alone.

"Dart is very charming," Jeff said.

"He tries."

"I hope you don't mind my stopping by."

"Oh, no," Adam said quickly, but then caught himself and added more nonchalantly: "It's cool."

"I was in the neighborhood, saw your truck and..."

"Am I under surveillance?"

"I'm sorry. That's classified."

"Oh."

"Don't worry, it's an unofficial classified kind of thing."

"Surveilling us—if that's even a word—would be a pretty boring assignment," Adam said. "We're either here, at the Sev, or at home. And sometimes at school."

"The school part is the most challenging," Jeff said. "We're not very good at going undercover in high schools. Plus, they get all crazy about us bringing guns on campus."

"Understandably so," Adam said.

Jeff noticed Adam roll his eyes ever so slightly. He felt like he'd seen him do it a million times, even though it was the first. "Anyway, I was thinking," Jeff said.

"Thinking is good."

"No, I'm serious."

"Oh, okay." Adam sat up straight on the stool he was resting on.

"Not that serious," Jeff said.

"Okay, okay. Go ahead."

"I was thinking about the other night."

"And what were you thinking about the other night?" Adam said, half-jokingly, but only half because he began wondering whether Jeff was about to say something bad.

"No, it's not bad—"

Adam interrupted Jeff by raising his hand. He didn't believe him and wanted to get some complimentary remarks in before Jeff let him down. Adam quickly decided this was Jeff's blow-off appearance. And how crazy was that? "I was thinking too," Adam said. "I was thinking that it was cool of you to stop by. Thanks."

"You're welcome," Jeff said, relieved to hear Adam was thinking about him. It made it easier for him to say what he'd wanted to say. "Well, I wanted to apologize for what happened on the bridge. I'm afraid I might have been a bit too forward."

"Well, I don't think you should take all the responsibility for that."

"No?"

"There were two people up there, remember?"

"I know. But, well, I'm very, um, glad to have met you and don't want something like that to get in the way of our, um, burgeoning friendship." Jeff exhaled. He was halfway there. "So, what I was thinking was that maybe we could start over and pretend it never happened."

"I guess we could," Adam offered. "But only if you promise not to use 'burgeoning' again in a sentence."

Jeff smiled, but before he could continue, Dart returned and started talking while he put more quarters into the table. "Boy, you should see what I had to go through to get these. That guy..." then Dart stopped. Neither Adam nor Jeff, although they were only a step away, were paying attention to him. So Dart continued in a louder voice. "Gone for a minute and look how quickly one becomes a third wheel. I guess I'll have to go and steal some frozen chickens from Pavilions..." But still no response. "Oh, forget it," he said.

Adam ignored Dart because he wanted to know what else Jeff had to say. Jeff didn't even hear Dart because he was so focused on what he was trying to say. Yet Dart's interjection had disrupted the flow, and Adam tried to get it back.

"He really is nice," Adam said. "And you were saying..."

Jeff inhaled, wiggled a bit on his stool, and found the words he was looking for. "So would you like to go to dinner with me some-time?"

"I don't know."

Not exactly the answer Jeff was expecting. He looked to Adam for a sign of his intentions.

"I don't know," Adam repeated. "I barely know you. You could be a psychopath...or, what is it, a sociopath?"

Damn, Jeff thought. It had been a very long time since a man—a guy, whatever—had been able to make his stomach turn to nervous mush. *But so what?* he thought. *I can play this game.*

"It's never been officially diagnosed."

"You've been tested?" Adam asked.

"No, not officially. I've been called both before, but not by trained professionals."

"That doesn't count," Adam said. "But I don't think so."

"You don't think what...that we should go to dinner?"

"No. I don't think you're a psychopath, or even a sociopath. You know, there's a big difference."

"Yes, I do...know the difference. And remember, I'm a graduate of the police academy. There are very few psychopaths or sociopaths allowed to graduate. If you're nice, I can show you my diploma to prove it."

"Okay."

"Okay, what? You want to see my diploma for proof?"

"No. Okay, we can have dinner."

Jeff was quiet for a second. He wanted to make sure Adam was answering him seriously before he showed any satisfaction. When Adam didn't add any caveats, any more jokes, he answered: "Great."

"Maybe Friday?"

"Great," Jeff said again as he shoved his hands back into his pockets, pushing them deeper than they were before, in a kind of inverted shrug that made him look like a boy again.

Fran, who stood by the table waiting to get the next game going, saved Adam and Jeff from having to talk about anything else. "Come on, Adam. You're up. I've already annihilated Dart and Veronica while you've been chattering."

"I think that's a challenge," Jeff said.

"I think you're right. Excuse me." And Adam hopped off his stool. He went around and grabbed the other cue. Jeff sat with Dart and Veronica to watch and occasionally comment on the game. This provided Dart an opportunity to query Jeff and learn what he could about the man who appeared to be making space for himself between him and his best friend.

"So, you live around here?" Dart asked.

"Not too far. Over on Fairther."

"Oh, one of Angelito's most eloquently named streets."

"I try not to say it more than once in a conversation," Jeff said. "Say it twice, and you really sound like an idiot."

"God bless the founding fathers and mothers of our great city," Dart declared, raising his glass of melted ice and watered-down soda. "Lived there long?"

"Ten years. Is that a long time?" Jeff answered, on guard against any trick questions.

"Hmmm," Dart said. "Ten years ago, eh? Let's see. Ten years ago, Adam and I were in the second grade."

"Well," Jeff said, "good thing I didn't meet you then."

"Yeah," Dart began, then he realized he was walking right into a trap.

"Good thing I didn't meet Adam then," Jeff said, "because he probably wasn't half as good-looking as he is now."

Now Dart was pissed, but mostly at himself. He'd set himself up for that one. Dart quickly tried to come up with a winner.

"You're right. He was pretty geeky back in the fourth grade." Then it came to him: "And he wasn't really into older guys yet either."

Jeff looked straight into Dart's eyes. He wasn't angry, but more curious. Was Dart jealous or mean?

Dart realized he had crossed a line and quickly tried to recover with a joke. "In fact, I don't even think he was into guys yet, period. For a few weeks there he even had a girlfriend. You'll have to ask him about Tiffany Brown, his first—and only, I think—girlfriend. But not that he would ever call it that."

But it was too late. Dart knew he'd blown the conversation, so he excused himself. "Pardon me. I've got to take a killer leak," he said, jumping down off his stool and walking away before Jeff could respond.

Jeff decided it was cute that Dart was jealous. He was glad because he thought that might show that Adam was interested in him, or at least interested enough to have let his friends know.

Adam won the match by default when Fran accidentally knocked in the eight ball.

"This must be my lucky night," Adam said to Jeff as he reached for the chalk.

"Well, I hope I don't have anything to do with it," Jeff said, "because I'm going to take off."

"Already?"

"Yeah, I've got an early shift tomorrow. Don't you guys have school?"

"Not really. My last exam was today. All I have to do is hand in a paper I already finished. So it's mostly just handing in books and stuff."

"When's graduation?"

"Thursday."

"That's soon," Jeff said.

"Yep, and real life starts on Friday."

"Oh, I'm sure you can put that off until at least the middle of next week," Jeff said, standing and checking for his keys and wallet. "Any word on the summer job situation?"

"No, but I got a lead about something at a publisher of outdoor lifestyle books—very second-class *Sunset* magazine kind of stuff. The pay's not great, but I really don't want to work in a restaurant."

"What's wrong with a restaurant?" Fran asked. She'd been preoccupied with Veronica, but whenever she sensed an insult, she paid attention.

"All that food, all those people, all those people touching food. I think I'm a little too OCD for that."

"That's true," Dart said, as he returned from the men's room and hopped up onto a stool. "Adam has a bit of a thing about cleanliness."

"Okay," Jeff said. "On that note I really should be going. It was nice meeting you all."

"Yeah, yeah," and "bye, bye" came from all sides until Adam walked Jeff away from the table toward the front door.

"Well," Jeff said, "can we go to a restaurant for dinner or does your OCD keep you from eating at them too?"

"No, I mean, yes, we can. I'm good at visiting restaurants. Just don't want to work at one."

"Cool."

"Cool," Adam echoed.

At the door, Jeff straightened up as if he was bracing himself for harsh weather outside. He twirled his key chain around his finger and caught his keys in the palm of his hand. "Should I call you Friday morning so we can decide where to eat?"

"Sounds good."

"Enjoy your graduation," Jeff said.

"I'll try."

"It's never as bad as you think it's going to be."

Adam reached out his hand for a shake. It felt like the right thing to do under the circumstances, with his friends watching and all. "Remember to call me at my dad's house.

They shook hands firmly, affectionately, and then let go reluctantly. Jeff waved good night to Dart, Fran, and Veronica, who were watching from across the room, and then left.

Adam tried to hide his excitement as he walked back to his friends.

WEDNESDAY, JUNE 16, 1999

After the last final exam was given and the last term paper handed in, the senior class of Angelito High School lined up on rickety layers of aluminum scaffolding to have their senior class picture taken. "An exercise in capitalism," Adam called it. The fact that each picture would cost $29.99 annoyed Adam to no end, and ever since the price had been posted on the window of the principal's office two weeks ago, he'd been threatening to boycott the shoot.

"Get off your fucking cheap-ass high horse and take the fucking picture," Dart said.

"Why?"

"Because maybe, just maybe, some dumb shit like me wants one of these pictures as a reminder of how stupid high school was. And if I'm going to buy one to remember that, then I need your dumb-ass face in the picture to remind me of how integral you've been to my stupid high school experience," Dart yelled. His end-of-the-year, end-of-high-school, end-of-life-as-he-knew-it anxiety was coming to a head.

"Fine, fine," Adam said, hopping off The Wall. "Let's get this shit over with."

The 1999 senior class of Angelito High School—all 423 of them—lined up and smiled. Adam refused to smile, but no one would know about his little act of rebellion until the middle of July, when the pictures arrived in mailboxes across the city in little cardboard tubes. Smiles fixed, flashes flashed—Angelito's principal yelled through a megaphone: "Be at the field tomorrow at 6 P.M. sharp. If you're late, you won't be in the graduation ceremony. And any of you in danger of not graduating—and unfortunately at last count there were 16 of you in this dire situation—you better see me tomorrow, starting at 10 A.M. to discuss whether or not you've passed your finals and whether or not you will be given the pleasure of accompanying your beautiful classmates down the aisle to adulthood. That's it. Go home. Bu-bye."

Students milled about in a daze of absolute purposelessness. Fran eventually went to work, and Adam and Dart piled into the truck to head home. On their way, Adam's oldies station failed to inspire revolt in Dart. He sat and listened, actually, to an old song about old songs. *"Those oldies, but goodies, remind me uh-uh-of you-ooh."* Neither of them paid close attention to the words, though they seeped into Adam and Dart's distracted heads and became part of them, whether they liked it or not. Years later, they will hear the song again—maybe while they're waiting in line at a grocery store, or on the soundtrack of some indie flick—and they won't remember where they heard it before. But they will feel something, some pang of queasy nostalgia. And they will reinhabit for a moment a long-past day—the last time they ever drove home together from Angelito High.

Thursday, June 17, 1999

"Could that have possibly been more boring?" Adam asked his family in the parking lot after graduation was over. "And to think they call that a ceremony. Do they think because there's music and robes it's a ceremony?"

Vivian, Marc, and even Sandra looked at Adam like he'd reached a new low, a level of cynicism even they couldn't understand. Why wasn't he happy, or at the very least, relieved to be done with high school? To Adam, it was just another exercise in pointlessness. "Stupid," he said. "A ceremony?" he asked again.

No one knew what to say.

"Ceremonies are for Catholics and Aztecs," Adam said as he pulled his gown up and over his head without rolling down the zipper."

"I kind of liked it," Sandra said. "It looked kind of fun."

"Liar."

"No. It looked fun," Sandra argued. "There was cheering, and I liked it when everyone threw their hats up in the air."

"I thought Jesse gave a very nice valedictory speech," Vivian said.

"Eew. Nobody likes Jesse, and I'm sure no one liked his speech. He's a total nerd…"

"Adam," Vivian said, interrupting him.

Adam looked at his mom, at her surprised and questioning face, and realized he was carrying on and they weren't buying it. "Whatever…It was a lame speech."

"It wasn't so bad," Marc said.

"What time is the reservation for dinner?" Adam asked, consciously trying to sound more positive.

"Not until nine. We're in no rush," Vivian said, looking at her watch and rubbing it against her wrist.

"Good."

"So go and say goodbye," Vivian said. "Make your plans for later…We've got how many cars?" she asked, looking at Marc.

"Three," Sandra said.

"Great," Vivian said, looking at Sandra. "Then we can just meet at the restaurant."

"Works for me," Adam said.

"Wonderful," Marc said, trying to wrap things up. "We'll see you there."

Adam cracked a quick smile before walking away from his family and back into the crowd. He found Dart and Fran still in their black robes. Veronica was snapping pictures right and left like she'd invented photography. Adam tried to have strange little chats with classmates he'd never been close to. He spoke with people that he didn't even know knew him, yet tonight were all of a sudden chatty. *Something in the air*, Adam thought, *like, "Hey let's be nice before it's too late."*

Some people weren't going to college, and this was the only graduation they'd ever know. Adam knew he should have felt sorry for them but didn't. Broad smiles must reflect their happiness, he told himself. Others, he thought—or imagined—looked sad or scared because they knew that high school had been their pinnacle of success and social connection. Never again would they have so many friends. Most of these people, Adam thought between flash-bulbs and yearbook signings, would go on to lead unexceptional lives. Maybe there would be a spouse, a kid or two, a big house. Or maybe there would be a dog, an addiction, a vacation home in Palm Springs, maybe a series of promotions leading to a higher-paying job in upper management but always at the same damn company.

So many different scenarios, so many faces, so many voices. Adam drove himself to the edge of feeling again, and he didn't like it. Wasn't this supposed to be fun, some kind of milestone in his life, some kind of mountaintop experience?

At 8:45, Adam left to meet his family. But before that, he found Fran and Dart and asked, "I'll call you after dinner?"

"Call me on my cell," Dart answered. "I'm sure my dinner will run longer than yours."

"I bet you're right. You're family speaks to each other while they eat. My family concentrates on the cuisine."

"Of course, we're having dinner at home," Fran said.

"What else did you expect?" Dart asked. "You have two mommies."

Now it was Veronica's turn to step in and wrap things up. "Okay," she said, taking Fran by the hand. "Call us at Fran's later…bye."

Vivian drove directly from one parking lot to the next. She arrived early and found a spot directly in front of the restaurant to wait in the car. Marc and Sandra, who rode together, did the same, but with half an hour before dinner, they decided to walk around the shopping center to kill time. Vivian saw them walk off. She stayed inside the safety of her Saab and listened to the radio. A sweet yet serious voice read the headlines on NPR.

"Experts say the nation's largest banks are closest to completing preparations for Y2K. But the smaller firms, they now believe, will not be finished reprogramming their computers in time. Temperatures will drop down to the mid 50s tonight. Currently, it's 67 and clear. Coming up next: Star Wars, Episode 1: The Phantom Menace. *Is it good for children? A professor at UC Berkeley is convinced otherwise. We'll have her story and speak with a psychologist who works with children, after this short break."*

The words, broken down into syllables, traveled through space from the speakers to Vivian's ears. She wasn't paying attention, though. She was back at graduation, thinking about how strange her son looked walking across the stage—how different, how grown-up. Vivian wasn't feeling pangs of regret; she felt a forward-moving déjà vu, a kind of anticipation of sadness at the growing distance between her and her only son. She was surprised and a little shocked to feel tears welling up and wanting to come out.

There must have been a time when a policeman's "beat" meant something, when cops paced sun-bleached sidewalks in hard-soled shoes. *Clip, little shuffle, clip, little shuffle, clip, little shuffle.* Today, Jeff and Sue's "beat"—although they never called it that—was rhythmless. They had been assigned to patrol Angelito's newest mall, Copernican Court, and their contemporary sneaker-esque police boots padded across the fake terrazzo floor in discrete pseudo-silence. Their beat's only discernable pattern consisted of the looping laps they made around the mall, floor by floor by floor.

Sue didn't mind the tedium of mall patrol. Copernican Court was only a few months old, and she was still discovering all the new shops and restaurants. Jeff hated shopping. He resented spending hours inside a room so tightly sealed that you couldn't tell the weather outside or even the time of day. Jeff felt like a better-paid security guard. Then again, police officers are simply better-paid security guards, and Jeff knew it.

Then there was Adam. He was with them too, in a way. He was lodged deep inside Jeff's head. Jeff wasn't obsessed, he told himself, just preoccupied. He wanted to call Adam and set up the dinner they agreed to—if only he could get away from Sue for five minutes. Then, finally, he saw an opening.

"I'm going to go get a smoothie," Sue said. "You want one?"

"It's barely 10 o'clock. Sure you won't ruin your lunch?"

Sue didn't always catch Jeff's humor. "I'm getting a small one...only a small. It's a new place, I want to try it out."

"I'll pass. But thank you."

Sue walked 50 yards into the COPERNICAN COURT FOOD COURT, as the sign above the entrance said in meteoric blue and white neon. She found the booth with a banner above it that read: FANCY FRUITS: FROZEN & FRESH & OUT OF THIS WORLD. When she joined a line five deep, Jeff saw his opportunity and called Adam.

Brrrrrrrng. Brrrrrrrrrng. From his comfortably horizontal position on Adam's couch, Dart reached over the arm to find the ringing phone. He located the button that said VOICE and punched it with his forefinger to stop the ringing.

"Hello," Dart chirped, wide-awake after only a few hours sleep, graduation "festivities" having ended only a few hours earlier.

After each friend had spent family time with their respective blood relatives, Dart, Fran, Veronica, and Adam met to drive together to *the* Angelito graduation blowout party of 1999, which was being thrown by some football player. Veronica was the one who actually knew him; he was in her otherwise-sophomore geometry class. Mr. Football Star told Veronica the reason he was in her geometry class was not because he'd failed, but because someone had lost his grade. "Sooo fucked up," he concluded.

Veronica said she didn't believe him, but that didn't stop them from becoming fast friends. It was Fran, actually, who explained it all by observing, "Lesbians and straight men have a lot in common— worldview kinds of things—not just that they both like girls a lot."

Adam never bought it. He said, "Straight guys like girls. Period. They like straight girls, dykes, trannies, bisexuals—which are their favorite by the way, because they're attainable *and* unattainable. And lesbians? Well, they only like straight men because lesbians like attention." At this point either Fran or Veronica would throw something relatively painless at Adam and everyone would sort of laugh.

But back to the party. They walked in and Mr. Quarterback Genius threw a big arm around Veronica. "Heyyyyyyy, Vern! I'm so glad you could make it." Then he turned away just as fast and left Veronica holding two blue plastic cups of beer, one in each hand.

"Oh, my God. That was so gross," Dart said to Adam.

"Oh, I don't know. I thought it was kind of hot," Adam said.

"You did not," Dart said, but Adam was already gone.

He was in the kitchen with Fran and Veronica. There, they jostled through the crowd to the sink, where various bottles of alcohol vied for space with bags of melting ice. The party turned out to be pretty fun, if not exactly exciting. There were people they knew and, more important, the people they didn't know were nice, or at least drunk enough to be acting nice. Over the next few hours, drinking was followed by more drinking, some dancing, and more drinking.

"There's another party just around the block," belched a mannish-looking boy with ANGELITO SUCKS written in magic marker across his forehead. The foursome stumbled around the otherwise quiet neighborhood until they heard Bob Marley coming from the backyard of a house with too many lights on.

"Bob Marley?" Dart asked. "My God!"

One more gin and tonic and Dart forgot about the music. Although later, he blamed the music for inspiring him to start making out with Veronica. It was all good and fine until Veronica pulled away and puked on Adam's shoes. Then it was downright hilarious. Adam laughed because he was too drunk to care about his shoes. He and Fran fell all over themselves because the idea that kissing Dart made Veronica puke was just too perfect. Only Fran remained relatively sober. By the time her blood-alcohol level was about to reach a point where Bob Marley began to sound like Melissa Etheridge, she saw her friends were trashed and remembered she needed to take her role as the designated driver more seriously. By 3 A.M., the party was so messy that even the completely inebriated Veronica said, "I think we should get outta here."

Fran obliged and dropped the boys off at Adam's house. Dart crashed on the couch within seconds of entering. It's a miracle Adam didn't join him in the living room due to his lack of motor skills and any sense of direction, but somehow he managed to make it to his bed, where he slept fully clothed.

Dart was awake by 8 A.M., as if it was a school day. He knew Adam would be passed out for a while, so he remained comfortably on the couch and watched television. Two hours later, as Matt and Katie signed off—*gay, not gay, or straight-gay?* Dart always wondered when Mr. Lauer was on—Adam's phone rang. That's when Dart picked it up and chirped, "Hello."

"Adam?" came a deep voice across fiber-optic cables. It was Jeff, and he was confused by the sound of Dart's voice on Adam's phone.

"No. He's still sleeping...I think."

"Oh," was all Jeff could think to say back.

"Who is this?" Dart asked.

"Jeff. Jeff Manfield." Momentary silence. "But don't worry about it. I can call back later. It's no big deal."

"Oh...Jeff," Dart slowly said, as if he was just learning to read. "It's Dart. Hi."

"Oh, hi," Jeff said, genuinely relieved. He wiped his sweaty palms on his cargo shorts one at a time.

"I'm just hanging out here waiting for Sleeping Beauty to arise from the dead," Dart said.

"Oh."

Sleeping Beauty? Jeff wondered. Was there something he didn't know? Did Adam and Dart have the kind of supercasual relationship that Jeff always wanted to have with another gay guy but had never had? To Dart it was nothing. His relationship with Adam was second nature. He wiggled back into the comfort of the couch like he was talking to an old friend.

"See now," Dart began, "with you being a cop, I mean, an officer of the peace and all, can this conversation be off the record?"

"Of course," Jeff said, beginning to relax. "It can be our little secret if you like."

"Well, now Jeff-y. I don't think we have to go that far."

"Okay, okay."

"So there we were last night—now remember, last night was a

pretty big night for us—you know, graduation and all. So because it was such an important, very important night for us, we, of course, had to go out and celebrate."

"As well you should have."

"I'm glad to hear you agree."

"Let me guess. Adam is a little hung over."

"Well…" Dart hesitated for dramatic effect, "the short answer is yes. Adam did have a couple of drinks. But not many. Nothing crazy."

"Okay."

"You sound bored," Dart said.

"No, no. It's early, I sound bored when it's early."

"Whatever. The long answer is that he's just sleeping in because, well, you know today is a little special. It's the first day of the rest of his life."

"You're right," Jeff said. He was getting into this now, enjoying Dart's sense of humor. "And here I thought it was just the first day of summer vacation. How could I have forgotten?"

"Well, it has been a while since you graduated from high school, hasn't it?"

"Hey, now…"

"No offense intended," Dart said, "just stating a fact, I think."

"Some facts can be left unstated, Dart."

"Are you telling me to lie, Officer?"

"No, I'm telling you to know when to keep your mouth shut because anything you do or say may be held against you in a court of law."

With that Dart started to understand what Adam liked about this Jeff guy. He was a mix of serious and not-so-serious, of mature and not-so-mature. Jeff wasn't youthful and cool one day, and old and mature the next. He was some kind of strange hybrid. Interesting. A challenge.

Dart wanted to see how far Jeff would carry their conversation. He swung his legs off the sofa with a plan and headed toward Adam's room.

"I hate to make you have to call back. Why don't I just take a little peeky-boo into Adam's room and see if he's still sleeping or just hiding from me. It was a rough night, but he should be reaching Level 2 consciousness soon."

"Level 2?"

"Didn't you ever watch *Aliens*?"

"Yes."

"When Sigourney Weaver woke up after sleeping for years, they called it Level 2."

"See how much has changed since I graduated from high school?"

Dart reached for Adam's doorknob and turned it slightly.

"Either way, I'm sure Adam would not want to miss your call, so I'll—"

"Oh, no, that's not..."

But it was too late. Dart was already inside Adam's room. He sat down on the bed, crossed his legs like a secretary and deepened his voice like a bossy boss.

"Yes, sir. It looks like he may be okay. We may not need the defibrillator after all."

Adam began to stir.

"Yes. It looks like he's rousing...yes, yes he is."

Adam turned over slowly and stared at Dart with an evil look that said, *You have two heads and deserve to have neither.*

"Oh, I think he's starting to speak. He's asking if you can hold on for just one more second while he gets a big piece of sleep out of his eye."

Then Dart covered the receiver with his palm.

"Who is that?" Adam said very slowly, still squirming under his covers and rubbing his eyes. "And what time is it?"

"It's Jeffy-poo...deary. And it's about 1:30 in the afternoon."

"No, way."

"Yes, way."

"Oh, God, you asshole. Give me that phone."

Dart handed him the phone, but he made no move to leave the

room and give Adam some privacy. In fact, Dart lay down right next to Adam on the bed.

"Hi," Adam said, staring at Dart and downgrading his evil look from angry to seriously annoyed. "Yeah, yeah…I'm awake…yeah, pretty late…yeah, well…yeah, you do. You only graduate once. Yeah, I think once is definitely enough."

With his free hand, Adam reached over and grabbed the alarm clock on his nightstand. When he realized it wasn't even 11 A.M., he reached out his leg and gave Dart a big kick.

"Ouch!" Dart yelled.

"That was Dart," Adam said into the phone. "He tripped on his way out…This weekend? Actually, I'm, um, completely un-booked…No, no job yet. Hopefully next week…Today? No, I've got nothing planned…Dinner? I guess. Yeah, a man does have to eat. Did your mom teach you that? Okay, fine…Tio Pepe's? Love it…Eight o'clock is fine. See you there…Okay. Bye. Okay, thanks… Bye."

Adam dropped the phone like a dead weight. Dart curled up next to his best friend like a newlywed. Adam turned away and Dart pulled closer. They spooned.

"You poor thing. Your new man is calling you so early and wak-ing you from your much-needed beauty sleep. Don't worry. As soon as he finds out what you look like in the morning, he'll never call you this early again."

"What the hell are you doing?" Adam groaned.

"I don't know, exactly. I woke up—with only the slightest hang-over around eight, found some Tylenol in your medicine chest, which when combined with your orange juice—which you're now out of, by the way—knocked my headache right out. And also, by the way, Aleve is much better than Tylenol. You should get some. Tylenol is so old-school. And you're almost out of that too. There is, I think, like, only two left or something. So you can try Aleve soon."

Dart had rolled away to deliver his pharmaceutical diatribe. When he finished, he swung back over and spooned Adam again. While hugging him he went on talking as if nothing had happened.

"Then I watched Matt and Katie. He looked good today; wore blue. Then I realized that as of last night it really is over. High school is finally, fucking, 100 percent, totally, absolutely over."

Adam still wasn't speaking.

"Do you realize what that means?" Dart asked.

"Um, yeah. It's over."

"There's more to it than that. Think about all the things we don't ever have to do ever again. We don't ever have to go into a locker room ever again…unless we want to. We don't ever have to share a hallway with girls in cheerleading uniforms."

Dart paused.

"Now, if we could only have had a few boys in cheerleading uniforms…"

"That you would have liked? I don't think so."

"But I would have liked the choice. Seriously, think about all the shit we don't ever have to do again. We don't have to follow a ringing bell to tell us when we're supposed to move. We don't have to eat on a wall."

Adam tried to extricate himself from Dart's spooning, but Dart wouldn't let him.

"Anyway. That's about the time my headache went away, and I noticed Regis and Kathie Lee had on that hot guy from *JAG*. I had to switch back and forth like a freak."

"You are a freak, get off of me!"

"Hello?" Dart sang, holding Adam tighter. "I really don't think you and yours should be throwing any stones when it comes to mental health issues. Especially not this morning. After last night, you are in no shape for stone-throwing."

"Oh, God," Adam whined. "What did I drink last night?"

He held his head in his hands.

"Not much…dude. Just a couple dozen beers."

"Feels like it."

Dart released Adam, rolled onto his back, and reached up to fiddle with Adam's headboard.

"So, what are you doing today?"

"I don't know. Probably staying very still until I feel better."

"Better not take too long, 'cause it sounds like you've got yourself a date tonight."

"It's not a date." Adam looked over at Dart. He looked so fresh, Adam thought. Had they really been at the same party last night?

"Then what is it?"

"Dinner. And where the hell did you get all this energy?"

"What energy? It's almost noon! The whole world is awake except you. People across the Western Hemisphere are up and at 'em, making money, finding themselves, doing things."

"Oh, God."

"You don't really think it's just dinner?"

"Of course it is." Adam was adamant.

"Honey, if it's 'just dinner' then I am 'just Dart.' There are so many layers to that lasagna—don't even pretend that you can't count them."

Adam didn't recognize Dart's last statement. Lasagna? What the hell was he talking about? Adam knew that anything defensive would only make him look like he cared—which he did, but he wasn't about to show Dart that.

"What am I doing today?" Adam asked. Through his hangover, he could see his post–high school life quickly becoming a reality. "Actually, I've got absolutely nothing I have to do today."

"I know. Isn't that amazing? And weird?"

"Yes, and yes."

For the moment, Adam and Dart were quite pleased with themselves and their place in the world. They stayed in Adam's bed, talking about nothing and everything. Adam's head continued to throb, and Dart's red hair stuck straight up and over like the droopy red skin on a rooster's head. Yet they were happy. It really didn't matter that Adam felt nauseated and Dart had to take a leak; they were free and they were together, talking. They really were two guys on the "precipice of manhood," as Dart liked to say. They spoke about Adam not having a summer job lined up yet and about

Dart starting his next week. They spoke about the night before, about who looked good, who didn't, and who could've looked better if only they hadn't started puking in front of everyone. In another reality, they didn't say much at all. They lay together like two adolescent walruses on a beach of blue cotton sheets. They tossed and turned, constantly shifting, adjusting, and rolling up against one another for companionship. Neither knew how to describe the way they felt, so they didn't even try to describe it. Life felt big, floating, and ambiguous.

Eventually they made it from the bedroom to the living room, with a brief stop in the kitchen. Dart found a box of Pop Tarts while Adam grabbed the entire Britta and an empty glass.

"I have no idea how old those are," Adam warned.

"They're Pop Tarts, Adam. I don't think they ever expire."

After mall duty, Jeff and Sue found their car in the attached, multi-level parking garage. Each floor was decorated with a six-foot-tall fruit or vegetable. ("Oh, Momma, don't you remember? We parked on Eggplant!" "Are you sure it wasn't Prune?") They drove down the spiraling ramp—from Carrot to Apple to Broccoli—until the reached the street level. If their descent had not been interrupted by an Isuzu Trooper holding up traffic while its driver backed into a parking spot, Jeff would have seen Adam in his truck driving Dart back home.

With his cap under his arm—they had to give the gowns back: they were only a rentals, which was kind of gross if you thought about it—Dart went into his parent's house through the back door. He hoped to get to his room without having to face any curious family members. He shut the door as quietly as possible and tiptoed down the hall. Success. He made it to his room unnoticed. But any triumphant feelings his elusiveness inspired passed quickly. Within moments of kicking off his shoes, he realized it was just him in his technology-filled bedroom—alone. And there was nothing Dart had to do; no homework to be done. No projects. Nothing. He turned on his computer and television to fill the void. Then he remembered that he'd spent most of the day in front of the TV, and seeing it again made him anxious. *TV is wicked,* he thought. *It sucks you in, hooks you with its electronic tendrils. It's fucking evil magic.*

Oprah was on.

Normally Dart would have been glad to watch *Oprah.* Her "very affirming yet basic psychology," as he labeled it, was right up his alley. But today Dr. Phil was on with her. Granted, sometimes he said something interesting, but today, after only a minute, Dart was sure it was not going to be one of those days. He was talking about straight people and their problems with monogamy—two things Dart had no interest in or experience with. He turned away to check his e-mail. Hello! Jackpot! A message from James.

"Hey, what's up? I think you're a graduate as of today too. Give me a call if you're free.

Dart reached for his phone.

Beep, Beep, Beep. Beep, Beep, Ba-Beep, Beep.

"This is James."

"Hello, James. This is Dart."

"Hi," James said, his pitch slightly higher, glad Dart had called.

"How are you? How was your graduation?"

"Lame."

"Yeah?"

"Gowns and speeches and rah-rah into the future. It's not my cup of tea," James said.

"I know what you mean."

"It's so stupid. It's so high school."

"*So* high school...Nice to be able to say that and mean it." Nervously, Dart realized he'd not asked a question; he'd left the conversation hanging. He quickly recovered, "What'd you do afterward?"

"Not much, went to a couple of small parties. Was home pretty early."

"We went to the worst party, some sort of jock nightmare. Guys were drinking beer through a funnel."

"Gross," James laughed.

"It was."

"So, what are you doing now?"

"Nothing. So much nothing that I just turned off *Oprah*."

"Oh, yeah?" James asked.

"Dr. Phil was on."

"Oh, I hate him."

"Me too."

The briefest of pauses while both silently pondered the possibilities hidden within a shared opinion.

"Hey, I don't know about you," James began, "but I've been inside all day."

"Me too."

"And I would really love to get out of the house. Wanna go catch a movie or something?"

Whoa! the little voice inside Dart's head yelled. Was Mr. Blue Eyes asking him out? *No time for delay,* the other voice inside Dart's head said: *Say yes.*

"Yeah, sure. What do you want to see?"

"I don't really care as long as Tom Cruise, Sandra Bullock, and Wesley Snipes are not in it," James said.

"Oh."

"They are on my can't-watch-on-the-big-screen list right now."

"I don't think that'll be a problem," Dart said. "None of them are in anything right now, are they?"

"I'm not sure, but let's not take any chances."

"Okay," Dart said, with mock gravity. "So where should we meet?"

"Let's go to that new super multiplex near you, the one with, like, 25 screens. I like to have a lot of choices."

"Copernican Court or some corny shit?"

"Yeah, love/hate that place…supercheesy. Can only go there for the movie theater."

"You've got a lot of rules," Dart said. Where he got the confidence to say that, Dart had no idea.

"Only a few. Don't worry."

"I'm not worried."

"Oh, yeah?" James asked. "Can you meet there in an hour?"

"Yeah. In front of the box office?"

"Cool," James said. "I'm looking forward to it."

He is looking forward to it? The little voice in Dart's head screamed. Then the other voice said, *No time for dawdling. Say yes and get going.*

"Me too," Dart said. "And I'm looking forward to hearing more about your do-not-watch list."

Dart spent the next 30 minutes worrying—in the shower, then dressing, driving, and parking. He worried while he waited at the box office, because he'd rushed and arrived 10 minutes early. Dart had nothing to worry about. James was on time and definitely interested in hanging out with him. They watched *The Matrix,* a film that massaged their science-geek hearts. Afterward, they grabbed a bite at the Copernican Court Food Court across the mezzanine. They discussed the movie over greasy food sold by people in brightly colored uniforms. James "loved it," but added, "one more hang-dog look from Keanu, and he's on my can't-watch-on-the-big-screen list."

Dart liked it too—it was his second time seeing it—and he said that this time he'd noticed "the parallel between the characters' technology-induced anxiety and our own Y2K drama."

While one half of Dart's brain was overanalyzing the movie, the other was overanalyzing the question of whether this trip to the movies was becoming a date. It felt like a date, looked like a date, but it hadn't been set up as a date date. Did that matter? Dart tried to squeeze such thoughts from his head, but it didn't work. At one point, James asked Dart if he "had a lot of friends" at Angelito that he would miss now that high school was over.

"No, not really," Dart said. "Adam and Fran are my only real friends, and I'm sure we'll stay somewhat close." But then Dart started wondering whether this was James's way of finding out whether Dart had a "friend" friend, like a boyfriend.

"What about you?" Dart asked, trying to keep the conversation going so he'd have a chance to clarify that he was definitely single.

"I don't know. There are layers. Like you, I've got a couple of friends that are close enough, and we've known each other since kindergarten, so I know I'll always know them. Then there's a whole group of people that I, well, I don't know if I'd say I *like* them, but I definitely don't mind them. It's kind of weird to imagine never seeing them again after seeing them basically every day for four years, which at this point is 25 percent of my life—30, if you don't count the first few memory-less years."

"Yeah," Dart agreed.

They each took bites of pizza, and sips of their drinks, and let the ideas float uneasily in the air-conditioned void around them for a moment.

"So, are there a lot of gay guys at Angelito?" James asked with confidence.

As soon as Dart could swallow without choking, he answered. "Well, not that I've slept with," he said with a nervous laugh. He was not prepared for that question, at least not yet. Then he realized James wasn't really laughing. "There are a few, but not many. And you? What about at your school?"

"I think there are three. Me, myself, and I."

"Oh, I doubt that."

"Me too. At my school, it's only cool to be a lesbian. Fags are still fags," James said.

"But you seem so…"

"Well-adjusted?" James asked.

"Yeah."

"That's what my shrink says. What choice do I have? Sit around and worry or whine?"

Not long after the last piece of crust was eaten, Dart and James walked back to the parking lot. They rode the elevator down together. James had parked on Turnip; Dart on Apple. For several moments, they were alone inside the industrial, dusty elevator. They looked at each other—looked closely, like they were each trying to figure out exactly what was going on. First stop was

Turnip. James stepped toward the door and then realized he was the only one getting off. He slid his arm in front of the sliding door's sensor.

"See…?" Dart blurted, trying to get the words out before the door shut. But he still didn't know what "this" was. Was it a date? Should we hug, kiss, French-double-air-kiss? Dart didn't know.

"Yeah?" James asked.

"No…"

"So," James began. "I'll give you a call…later?"

"Yeah," Dart replied. "That'd be cool."

James let go of the elevator door and disappeared behind it.

Blocks away, Tio Pepe's stood like a Mexican cantina dropped in the middle of Angelito. Two big arched windows flanked a small door painted bright green with Tio Pepe's spelled out in red neon script above.

Adam arrived first and waited off to the side of the host's stand. At the bar a half-dozen men drank beer near a television playing local news. On the other end—away from the television—a small group of ladies sipped daiquiris from plastic glasses through fluorescent-colored straws. Adam pondered the issue of gender-based drinking patterns while waiting for Jeff. *Nature or nurture?* He wondered.

Ten minutes later, the host asked Adam whether he wanted to sit down. She was older than most of the wait-staff, maybe late 30s. Her smile seemed less than forced, and it made Adam feel instantly more comfortable. They weren't supposed to seat anyone without the entire party present, but she—her name tag said Debbie— must have liked something about Adam, because she sat him prematurely. Adam probably looked nervous because he really didn't want to hang out by the bar where he couldn't order a drink. He hated the idea of ordering a Coke in front of so many people. He imagined they would assume he was a recovering alcoholic or something—and that, to Adam, seemed worse than being underage. Fifteen minutes later, Jeff was still not there, and neither were the butterflies in Adam's stomach. They'd been replaced by annoyance, which is only a half step away from angry.

Two glasses of water: down. Why did someone keep refilling them? He wasn't thirsty. One basket of tortilla chips on a paper napkin in a plastic basket: half gone. Two little dishes of salsa—one red and one green—gone except for a layer in the bottom, impossible to reach with a chip. Adam checked his cell. No messages. *Okay,* Adam decided, *I'm going to the bathroom, which could take a whole two minutes if I stretch it out, and if he's not here when I return, I'm outta here.*

Piss. Flush. Wash. Back out into the restaurant. Still no Jeff.

"Fuck this," he muttered on the way to his table.

He pulled out his wallet to find a few bucks to leave on the table when—

"Hey, Adam."

It was Jeff, through the front door, not stopping at the host's station and heading straight toward him. From the embarrassed look on Jeff's face, he (1) knew he was late, (2) hated being late, and (3) was quite insecure about the fact—maybe even insecure about having a date, er, dinner with Adam in the first place. Jeff looked humble despite his uniform—cuffs, gun, hat, the works—wrapped around him like a costume. Adam lifted his right hand to signal—*Hey, it's okay*—then dropped his arm to point to the table.

They met at the side of the table. Before they sat, each wondered whether they should shake hands, hug, or kiss each other. They both ran through all the possible scenarios before settling on nothing. They half-smiled and slid into the booth.

"I am so sorry I'm late."

"It's cool," Adam said, trying to mean it. "I hope you didn't get all dressed up on my account."

"Oh, God, I'm sorry. I got stuck dealing with an incident and had to come straight from work."

Adam slid his menu off the table and onto his lap. He'd long ago decided what he wanted to eat. "It works for you, this look. The uniform really butches you up."

Adam was unaware how much he was smiling. Something about

Jeff—about being with him across an expanse of Formica tabletop—
was so comfortable that his stabs at sarcasm were muted.

"I don't need accessories to be butch," Jeff said, pulling off his
radio and placing it on the seat next to him. From the number of
snaps and clicks he made, Adam thought Jeff must have pulled off
three or four other gadgets and placed them on the seat of the ban-
quette. When Jeff was done, he exhaled like a heavy load had finally
been lifted from his shoulders.

"An 'incident'?" Adam asked, "Sounds serious."

"It wasn't. Just annoying. Some bad behavior at a mall."

"Shoplifting? Ooh. Kids or grannies?"

"Huh?"

"Don't only kids or grannies shoplift?"

"Not really, although they are a high percentage of the cases.
Lewdness. But then the guy had a record and we had to take him in
and blah, blah, blah."

"There's lewdness in Angelito? Where? I need to go there."

"You need a little lewdness in your life?"

"Well, who doesn't?"

Adam lost track of the conversation. A patch of light-brown hair
peeking out the top of Jeff's shirt caught Adam's attention. What did
that signify? A chest obscured by hay-colored matting? Was
Jeff...hairy? Or maybe, were those little hairs just the beginning of
a thin coat of fuzz that accentuated a chest of well-defined muscles?
Adam had never seen Jeff without his shirt on, and he was taken
aback by how much he'd like to. He forced a new question to stop
his internal conversation about Jeff's chest. "You really like being a
cop, don't you?"

"Sometimes," Jeff said with a smile.

"Sometimes I like being a student. Sometimes I don't."

A goofball waiter with the personality of an old rag approached.
"You guys know what you want?"

"Um..." Adam began.

"Oh, take your time, man. Special tonight is chicken molé. It's
excellent." He turned to leave, then he turned back, like he'd for-

gotten something really important. "What can I get you guys to drink? Special margarita is prickly pear. It's pink. Some people really dig it."

"Sounds great," Jeff said.

"I'll have a coke," Adam said.

Jeff backtracked.

"You know what? I'll have a Coke too. Forget the margarita."

"Uh-okay, fine," the waiter said.

To avoid any further uncomfortable moments with the genius waiter, Adam decided he didn't need any more time to decide what to order. "I think I'm ready to order."

"Uh, okay."

"I'll have the chicken fajitas. Black beans. And can I get guacamole on the side?"

"Sure."

"Oh," Jeff muttered, realizing he was now on the spot. *What a drag,* he thought. *Why couldn't I have left work on time? I could've changed clothes, taken a shower, felt better, and not been so rushed. Now I'm rushing to order. Adam is going to think I'm a total flake.* "I'll have the fajitas too, but with steak. Black beans. Guacamole. No sour cream."

"Sure. Be right back with the Cokes."

"Sure," Adam mimicked to Jeff as soon as Mr. Genius was out of earshot.

"You're tough."

"Sometimes."

"Well, at least you admit it."

"I like to keep people a little off guard," Adam said. "You gotta keep people aware of you, or they'll run you over."

"Oh, that's a nice mantra, almost Jenny Holzer-esque."

"Well…"

"Well. Yes, well," Jeff settled back into his seat comfortably. "You've been a graduate for what, a day now?"

Adam looked at his watch. "Day? About 23 hours, actually."

"You are starting to look different."

"Really? How so?"

"Relaxed. You're looking more comfortable."

"The padding on this seat is quite nice and thick."

"Really?" Jeff asked.

"Yes, it is. I know your side isn't as comfortable. I sat there earlier, before you arrived, and that's why I'm over here. I like to get to places early so I can test out the seating and make sure I get the best."

Jeff tried not to smile, but he couldn't keep the corners of his mouth from hinting ever so slightly that he was enjoying himself.

"I'm sure we could get another table, if your side isn't comfortable enough. But I'm fine," Adam continued.

"Maybe I wasn't referring to physical comfort. More like, well…You look more comfortable with yourself, more confident."

Adam felt Jeff looking at him closely. "I think moving back home," he said, "to my dad's house, changed a lot."

"Oh, yeah. How's that going?"

"Fine, actually. I mean it was weird at first. Very weird."

"I bet."

"Weird because it looks the same—the same stuff is in it—but it feels different. And I haven't quite figured out exactly why."

"Don't you think maybe it's because the people in the house have changed? You're living alone now. The whole thing is different."

"Yeah, I know what you're saying, but what I mean is that as strange as it all sounds, I don't feel as different as the house, or everyone else, my mom or sister, or whatever."

"You're very independent. When I was—"

"When I was your age?" Adam said, interrupting him. "We barely know each other, and you're starting a when-I-was-your-age story?"

As soon as the words came out, Adam was embarrassed. He knew the comment showed he was thinking about the difference in their ages, and he wished he could take it back. Jeff understood; he could read the emotions on Adam's face clearly, so he forged ahead.

"Oh, give me a break, I'm doing no such thing. What I was trying to say was that at your age—18, or whatever you are—I would have liked to have had the wherewithal, the confidence, the whatever…to live on my own."

"Well, I don't know about the 'whatever' that got me here…maybe I am just 'mature for my age.' I think that's what my dad's shrink told him once."

"I always wondered about that phrase," Jeff said. "Like, who are they comparing you to when they say that? Some average level of maturity based on some kind of research? It's ridiculous."

"It's a cliché, mister," Adam said.

"I know. But clichés can be very revealing."

Mr. Genius Waiter interrupted them by sliding two Cokes onto the table. Straws stood out of them with an inch of paper left on to keep the ends clean.

"When I was really young," Jeff said, taking a sip, "like 10 or 11—I was very shy and didn't like to speak to anyone. It drove my parents crazy because they thought everyone would think I was rude. But I don't, and didn't, think anyone actually cared if I was speaking to them or not."

"It was a sign of their own insecurity," Adam said.

"Exactly, but my parents would never admit that."

A different guy in a matching white polo shirt and a green apron around his hips and looking no wiser than the waiter, delivered their plates. He didn't say anything, just dropped the hot plates of food in front of them and walked away. Adam and Jeff both said, "Thank you," but Mr. Server didn't hear them. They noticed though. Adam and Jeff each caught the fact that the other was courteous in the face of incompetence.

Cute and courteous? Jeff mused.

Does he do anything wrong? Adam asked himself.

Jeff reached for the hot sauce and sprinkled it all over the pile of grilled steak on his plate. Before putting the bottle down, he held it over Adam's Coke as if he was about to spike it. Almost 30 seconds went by before Adam noticed Jeff's hand holding steady above his glass. In silent retaliation, Adam scooped up guacamole in his spoon and bent his wrist back like a catapult. "Yeah?" Adam said.

"Okay, truce."

"Truce," Adam replied in his deepest I'm-a-man voice.

In the détente that followed, they began to eat. Adam dumped some meat and onions in the middle of a tortilla, threw in some avocado, and started eating with his hands. Jeff was more methodical. He laid out the meat in strips across his tortilla and then added small drops of guacamole.

"So, Mr. Mature," Jeff began after swallowing his first bite. "What do you do when you're tired of being all grown up?"

"Well," Adam began, "back when I was in high school, I used to loiter at the Sev and cruise strangers."

"Yeah, I seem to remember hearing about that," Jeff said, his mouth slightly full.

"Really?"

"Yeah, not sure where. Maybe someone around the office told me. I don't remember."

"Anyway." Adam rolled his eyes just barely—a half-sweep, really. "When I'm not there, well, school took up a lot of time. And, I, otherwise enjoyed a scintillating teenage life—playing pool, going to the movies—lots of movies. My dad always said I went to too many, but that's because he never cared for them."

"Movies are good."

"You think?" Adam asked, wondering if Jeff was being sarcastic.

"Yeah. Don't you?"

"Yeah, I do, but, well, anyway…Now that I'm a homeowner—or, well, actually a home-occupier—I'll probably have to start spending all my free time working around the house. You know, keeping it up, mowing the lawn, shit like that."

"You're right. A house is a lot of work."

"You have one? You mean you don't live in a shed or anything like the Unabomber guy?"

"I've got a little place over on Fairther, remember, just off Thurgood Marshall Parkway."

"You use the parkway's full name in conversation?"

"Sometimes. I like to pay tribute whenever I can."

"So valiant. You're such a good citizen," Adam said.

Now it was Jeff's turn to roll his eyes.

"As a homeowner," Adam said, changing the subject, "do you mow your own lawn or let it grow? You don't go for the I'm-the-crazy-man-on-the-block look, do you?"

"You have a thing about psychopaths," Jeff said.

"You think?"

Jeff took a bite and decided to leave that topic alone. *Too weird, too early,* he told himself. "No, I don't really have much of a yard. It's kind of a row-house thing."

"Oh. I didn't know there were any row houses in Angelito."

"There aren't really. It's, well, you know that block over on Fairther with the really skinny lots right next two each other? I live there."

"Oh, those are cute."

"Ooh, 'cute'? You say that like it's a bad word."

"Well, cute is cute."

"I'm not sure what that means."

"Some things you don't need to understand," Adam said. "So what do you do for fun, when you're not being a cop? What do you do around the house on Fairther for kicks?"

"I'm not really one for kicks. My life is not that exciting."

"Oh, come on. It can't be that boring."

"No, I didn't say it was boring."

"Well then?" Adam asked, taking a sip of Coke.

"Well, I guess when I'm not hanging around and working on my 'cute' house, well, for fun...I like to spend time at the beach."

"Sun worshipping? Are you a naturist?"

"No. Although I do consider myself a naturalist sometimes."

"Ooh. Sounds healthy."

"I surf."

"Unhuh. I get it. You're gay, you're a cop, a naturalist, and you surf? Is there anything else I should know about?"

"I can pick up small objects with my toes."

"T.M.I." Adam declared.

"What?"

"Too much information," he explained. "I don't need to know about your feet." With a huff, Adam feigned indignation. "We just met, you know."

"What do you mean? It's been almost two weeks. I thought toes and feet fell within the two-week rule."

"I think we have different copies of the rules."

"Oh, I have mine out in the car, I could go get them for you."

Dinner continued and so did the conversation. It flowed like they were old friends. It slowed periodically when someone would mention anything that hinted at Adam's dad. But neither of them pushed it. Adam wondered what other people in the restaurant were thinking about them. Did they think it was funny to see a cop—in uniform—eating fajitas with a much younger man? Then Adam realized that no one was watching them, so no one could be thinking such a thing.

At one point, they actually disagreed. Jeff thought *Toy Story* was proof that computer animation could be as charming as hand-drawn. Adam liked *Toy Story,* was genuinely moved by it, but did feel it was a bit cold. They talked about what they liked most about living in L.A. Jeff mentioned the snow-capped mountains being only a few hours from white-sand beaches. Adam said his favorite natural wonder was the few blocks in Angelito lined with jacaranda trees that exploded into lavender puffs twice a year, although Adam could never remember the proper name for them.

"I love that tree," Jeff said.

"It's the gayest tree."

"What, you think it only plays with other trees just like it?"

"Yep."

"If you like nature so much," Jeff said, "you'll probably like having to take care of your own lawn now."

"Maybe. But not having someone tell me to do it will be a good start."

"Will there be anything else for you?" Mr. Genius Waiter asked. Before they could even decide, he slipped the check between the salt and pepper shakers and walked away. Adam reached for it quickly.

"It's not so bad, $18 each," he said, doing the math as fast as he could, "with tip." He didn't want Jeff paying for dinner; he wanted everything on the up and up.

"Cool," Jeff said reassuringly.

He threw in a $20 bill. Adam added one of his own and slid them into the black, sticky folder. Adam searched for something to say that might wrap up the evening while it was still going well.

"Once I finish my first mow, you'll have to come over and check out my yard."

"I'd like that," Jeff said. He knew that Adam had subtly asked him to come over, maybe not tonight but someday. The bottom line was that he was being offered a chance at another meeting and that satisfied him. Jeff wanted to act cool, but he wasn't entirely successful. "Are you inviting me over to your place?" he asked.

"I guess so," Adam said with a slight hunch in his shoulders.

"Then I better not say no."

"No. I would advise against that."

"Okay then, yes."

"Good," Adam said, dropping his shoulders almost imperceptibly.

"When?"

"How about this weekend?"

"You don't think that's too soon for this?" Jeff asked.

"I don't know. What is 'this'? And what's 'too soon'?" Adam asked. He knew, but wanted to make Jeff answer the questions.

"This is…"

Jeff stopped, unsure, and fiddled with the refried beans on this plate.

Adam grinned, but didn't speak.

"I guess 'this" is our…burgeoning friendship."

"Is this too weird" Adam said.

"No. Well, sort of. But I think it's okay. It feels a little like it's happening somewhere else, and I can only see it from a distance." Jeff stopped. *Oh, shit,* he thought, *where am I going with this?*

"Yeah?" Adam asked, interested and concerned.

Jeff continued: "I'm sorry, sometimes I take things way off into…Oh, well, what do I have to lose? I feel like we're in a TV movie where everything happens so quickly and entire pieces of life get wrapped up in an hour."

"With commercials," Adam said sarcastically. "So it's less than 60 minutes."

Jeff panicked. *Where have I taken this conversation?*

Seeing room for a save, Adam said. "Sometimes I like TV movies. They're short, sweet, and cheesy as hell." And then Adam moved to get up. Jeff followed.

"Okay," Jeff said. "So maybe this weekend. You let me know when."

"Yep."

They walked outside together without speaking. They continued in silence till they reached the back parking lot. There were only two cars left.

"Well," Adam said. "That's my truck over there."

"And that's my car over there."

They pointed in opposite directions.

"So how about Sunday? My house. I'll barbecue."

"Barbecue?"

"Yeah. Nothing fancy. No ribs or anything. How about burgers?"

"I'll be there."

"Be there or be square," Adam said. "You know the address already."

"Yes, I do," Jeff said. After a moment, they shook hands and half-hugged, like rap stars and football players.

Saturday, June 19, 1999

Moments after waking, Marc pushed his way through paper-thin layers of cool cotton sheets to step out of bed.

"Where are you going?" Vivian asked, trying to sound surprised to see her husband get up so quickly.

"The gym."

"Now?"

Marc didn't stop until he reached the bathroom door, where he turned back toward Vivian and looked at the clock on the nightstand by her side of the bed. It was 8:30 A.M.—the same time he woke up every Saturday. "Yes," he said.

"What about Sandra?"

Marc did not respond immediately. He looked at Vivian and wondered what exactly she wanted to know about Sandra? "I think she's asleep, first of all," Marc finally said. He took hold of the bathroom door and continued speaking. "When she wakes up...have breakfast. She likes cereal." And then Marc proceeded into the bathroom, shut the door behind him, and ended the conversation.

The problem wasn't that Vivian didn't know how to be a mother—she'd been one for 18 years. It was that she'd become so used to being a mom for just a day or two per week; she could always cancel or reschedule if something more important came up. Today, as sunlight filtered through the blinds, reminding her it was morning whether she liked it or not, Vivian could not reschedule her family.

When Marc returned, Vivian was too angry to acknowledge his presence. She silently traded places with him in the bathroom, shutting the door with a decisive clack. She stayed inside until she knew Marc would be gone. When she came out, there was no sign of him. Vivian went downstairs and turned on the coffeemaker. She stood next to the machine, and waited until the first boiling drips dropped. From deep inside her spotless kitchen, she gazed upon the pieces of her domain that made her proud. *What a beautiful home,* she thought. *And I paid for it all with my very own money.* But satisfaction had a limited place in Vivian's emotional repertoire. Her eyes zoomed in on the superplush, superwhite carpeting just beyond the kitchen's boundaries and noticed how it was dotted with smudgy footprints. Vacuuming was the only solution. It offered instant gratification—immediate control of the chaos in the pile.

Upstairs she went, leaving the coffee to drip alone. Vivian pulled out the long, winding vacuum hose from the linen closet and shoved it firmly into one of the many Central Vac portals hidden low along the house's many bright white walls. She started in her own room, winding outward toward the door, erasing her steps along the way. *This is so great,* she thought. *With Marc gone, I can vacuum exactly how I like—from top to bottom, front to the back. I can make the whole house look like a freshly raked rock garden.* Through the hallways she made long strokes from beginning to end, left to right...

"What time is it?" Sandra asked from her open doorway, dangling Jacqueline toward the now-smooth carpeting.

Vivian quickly turned off the vacuum. "Good morning, honey. Did I wake you?"

Sandra didn't answer. She was too tired to unravel the passive-aggressive layers in her mother's speech and smart enough to know there was too much to get into at the moment. She descended the stairs gingerly, lifting her nightgown up so as not to trip. When she was halfway down the stairs, Vivian yelled to her, "Honey, why don't you turn on the TV for a little while in the den until I'm finished? I'm just going to finish vacuuming upstairs, do the front room and dining room, then we can have something to eat."

Sandra heard her mother but didn't pay attention. She settled into the couch and turned on the television. Cartoons bored her, so she quickly flipped through the major networks, the secondary wannabe networks, and the news channels until she reached the minor leagues—the cable channels dedicated to gardening, shopping, books, etc. Something on *Animal Planet* caught her attention: a man traipsing through a mossy marsh and ripping away bark from fallen trees to reveal an assortment of insects, worms, and various bug-like things underneath. Sandra hiked up her nightgown and nestled Jacqueline in the basket of cotton that formed between her legs. The screaming whine of Vivian's vacuum continued and grew louder as Vivian worked her way from the front door to the back den. Sandra turned the volume up until it was unbearably loud. *Headache warning*, she thought. The louder the vacuum became, the louder she made the TV. Okay, major ear pain, head pain—*click!* Off went the television. Goodbye, Mr. Bug Man.

Sandra stood up and went into the kitchen, where it was a fraction quieter. She poured herself a bowl of cereal and sat down at the small white table to eat and wonder, again, how something called riboflavin could possibly be essential to life as she understood it.

A large woman with too-tight denim shorts, white sneakers, and little white bootie socks—the kind with mini puffballs the size of a gumball on the back of the ankles—ran a groaning industrial vacuum across the floor at Limonetta. Busboys set white napkins down on all the tables, along with silverware, glasses, and decanters of jam. Fran organized the menus, making sure the freshly printed brunch listings were on page one. Brunch wasn't Fran's favorite shift, but since it was shorter than most, she didn't mind it. Because Limonetta was all about fresh, fresh, fresh, customers came expecting fruit only hours from being picked; eggs laid that morning; bacon and sausage no more than a day away from…well, best not to go there. Not that the customers consciously thought about these things as they munched egg-white omelets and blueberry pancakes with lemon butter from lemons grown on the carefully manicured lemon tree right in front of the restaurant.

Eating requires a suspension of disbelief not too different from fiction, from the kind Mr. Dryden liked to talk about in English class. Fran pondered this and similar issues—food "subversions and perversions," she once called them during a particularly intellectual moment—while holding court at Limonetta's sleek host's pedestal. But, there was seldom time for musing during brunch. The shift did offer plenty of distractions, most importantly the hip gay waiters—Ed, Matt, and Julian—whom Fran considered cooler than cool. They always had great stories to tell her about their adventures the night before.

Sometimes they came straight to work after not sleeping at all. The guys would sit at the bar and drink double shots of espresso while regaling Fran with stories about fancy benefits, pool parties that turned into sex parties, and nights spent dancing until it was time to come to work. "Sometimes with 'eel-legal substances'," as Matt from Texas would say. Fran liked the way these actor/model/waiters told stories. They had ways of making the search for fun sound like it was the most important thing in the world.

On the edge of Vivian's nose sat her brand-new sunglasses—orange-tinted because the lenses were "infused with melanin, the same pigment found in human skin," the salesman had pointed out. Questionable biochemistry aside, the glasses looked good, and Vivian knew it. Looking more chic than one should on a Saturday morning in June, she pulled into the parking lot at Costco with Sandra in the passenger's seat next to her—buckled-in safely. Jacqueline was comfortably ensconced in the pocket of Sandra's windbreaker.

There were hundreds of parking spaces in Costco's lot. About halfway down the seemingly mile-long aisle, the spaces began to randomly fill up with cars until they were solidly packed in the last quarter mile. As someone who might be labeled risk-averse, except at work, Vivian approached parking like a strategy game—like Battleship or Mastermind. She was defensive and would be happier to grab a space farther out than risk going too close to the store and not finding a space. She didn't want to have to turn around and go up the next aisle, thus moving away from the store. For her, the goal was never to have to move away from a goal, which in this case was the warehouse-turned-supershop Costco. This neurotic tic left Vivian in the unfortunate situation, however, of always parking farther away from wherever she was heading. *What-ever!* Vivian told herself when she heard her inner voice telling her she needed to stop being so obsessive. *Everyone has the right to set their own limits and no one should judge anyone else because they set their limits differently.*

Vivian's other problem, according to Adam—who was never afraid to share his opinion with his mother—was that she didn't need to shop at discount warehouses in the first place. Vivian was not exactly hurting for cash.

If she was going to be a mom again, she might as well go all the way. Vivian was going to make dinner. She clicked her wooden sandals up and down several aisles, adding random items to her double-wide shopping cart. When Vivian became bogged down in the refrigerated section, Sandra slipped away to warmer climes. It could be argued that Vivian was the one who wandered off. She left the dairy/cheese/eggs aisle without wondering where Sandra was. She was so used to shopping alone that she simply left the cart— with Sandra standing next to it.

"I should pick up a case of Diet Coke from the back, shouldn't I?" Vivian asked the empty space surrounding her.

If she was asking Sandra her opinion, why didn't she wait to hear Sandra's answer? *Whatever,* Sandra thought as she wandered off to find a place to sit until her mom was finished. From where she stood, Sandra could see dozens of sealed boxes at just the right height for sitting in the center of the enormous steel-shelving units that displayed the food. Sandra left the cart and went inside. She easily walked under the seven-foot-high shelf and sat down on a case of Campbell's soup.

"I think we could stay in here forever," Sandra said to Jacqueline after pulling her out of her pocket and placing her on a case of Cream of Mushroom. "We could live here. There's food and clothes and TV—and bathrooms."

Sandra didn't always speak out loud to Jacqueline. She was well aware of the opinion adults held toward children with imaginary friends. She knew they judged them to be significantly off-kilter. Mostly, she carried on conversations with Jacqueline inside her head. When Sandra thought about that, she decided it wasn't as weird as talking out loud. At her age, she knew there was no point in arguing with adults—yet. Those arguments she would have to save until she was on a more equal footing.

Just when she and Jacqueline were getting into a good conversation, Sandra heard what sounded like a crazy woman calling her name at what can only be described as a cross between a yell and whisper.

"Saaaaaaaaandra? Saaaaaaannnnnnndra."

Oh, yeah, Sandra telepathically whined to Jacqueline. *Now that she's good and ready, it's time to go. When I'm tired or ready to leave, no one ever lets me decide it's time to go.*

"Saaaandra?" Vivian yell-whispered again.

Vivian almost sounded concerned, Sandra thought, so she crawled out. She walked over to her mom and said, "I'm right here," as if she'd been in plain sight all along.

Sue's and Jeff's shift began at 9 A.M. Today they were "floaters," which meant they had to drive around certain parts of Angelito and hang out for periods of time at certain strategic locations to give the populace the impression that there were police everywhere, even if there weren't. By early afternoon, they'd already had breakfast and lunch together, read the *L.A. Times,* the *LA Weekly,* the *Daily News* and *New Times L.A.* For Jeff, reading was a way to avoid having to talk to Sue all day. But today Sue was having a problem with her sister in San Diego, and in between calls to family members on her cell, she needed to talk to Jeff about it. He listened because when you're trapped in a car only two feet away from someone, you don't have much choice. Then again, that's not a completely fair assessment. Jeff listened because he cared and Sue was apparently quite distressed by the situation. He was also glad for the distraction; his mind was otherwise stuck replaying his dinner with Adam—*ad infinitum.*

Sue went on and on about whether she and her sister should both fly to Minnesota to see their dad for his 65th birthday party next month. Or would it be okay to wait to see him in the fall when the family gathered for either Thanksgiving or Christmas. Sue wanted to go sooner. She liked her dad and felt that because of his poor health—he had diabetes which led to bad eyes, bad feet, and some recently diagnosed liver problems—they should "definitely be there for his birthday" and see him again during the holidays.

"Who knows how many more birthdays he's going to have?" she said to Jeff.

"What does your mom say?"

"She says she doesn't care. She doesn't think dad cares much either way, but I know they must."

"How do you know?"

"I just do."

"But if your mom says she doesn't care, shouldn't you listen to her? Maybe she doesn't want you to come and she's telling you that on purpose."

Vivian was glad to find Marc home when she pulled into the driveway with Sandra and a carload of groceries. "There's a ton more in the car," she said to him after carrying the first load in.

"Hello, Sandra," Marc said. "Do you want some help with that, honey?"

He found Sandra struggling up the driveway with a case of Diet Coke that was obviously too heavy for her.

"No," she said.

From which parent Sandra and Adam had inherited their masochistically self-reliant disposition was unclear.

Once all the food was inside and the three of them were almost finished putting everything away, Vivian announced that she would be cooking tonight. But before that, she would be going upstairs to take a bath.

Feeling generous and not knowing why, Marc said, "Great. Why don't you go ahead? Sandra and I can finish this."

Vivian easily agreed and went upstairs. She plugged up the tub and turned the faucets on full speed. Vivian slid into the tub before it was half full. She left the water running and enjoyed the burning sensation of hot water surrounding her, reaching in between her toes, her legs, under her arms and finding its way inside every nook and cranny. It felt so good that she reached down to encourage the tingling sensations running around and through her. She opened herself up to let the hot water find an easier route inside. Vivian began rubbing herself until she was trembling quietly and experiencing a low-level orgasm. Then more, more, and more she rubbed until she was out of her body and vibrating with little aftershocks.

Adam didn't know about Vivian's big cooking plans. He showed up at the house unannounced because he didn't want to cook for himself and because he knew he should hang out there as often as possible to reassure his mom that he was okay. He wanted to see Sandra too, and he was a bit lonely, although he'd never admit that.

Vivian's idea of cooking was making a special salad—something a little different, using things like arugula, asparagus, pieces of pink grapefruit, and roasted Roma tomatoes with a smattering of super-thin sheets of dry, hard cheese—and serving it with something good, but already prepared, like a roast chicken, the kind that glistened under the heat lamps in the deli section of Costco.

After dinner, Adam drove back to his dad's house, or his house, or whatever he was calling it. A meal he could handle; spending time with his family afterward was another issue entirely. Alone in his truck, he played a Beach Boys' tape he'd found while going through a few boxes of his dad's stuff in the garage. They weren't as good as Jan and Dean. Too peppy, too happy. But to Adam, tonight, there was something he could not explain in the twangy optimism of the music and the slightly off-kilter singing that drew him in. He had the stereo cranked up so loudly to "Little Deuce Coup" that he barely heard his cell phone ring on the seat next to him.

"Where are you?" Dart yelled upon hearing the sound of Brian Wilson drowning out Adam's voice.

"In the car."

"Going where? And what the fuck are you listening to now?"

"You ask too many questions," Adam said, turning down the music, but only slightly.

"No, I don't."

"Yes, you do."

"*No*...I don't."

Adam tried to change the subject: "I'm on my way home from my mom's house."

"Oh, how was that?"

"Fine. What're you doing?"

"Nothing. I'm at home."

"Sounds exciting."

"Exciting doesn't do justice to the ennui of youth I feel," Dart declared.

"The ennui of youth? Do you even know what ennui is?"

"Of course I do. It's boredom, listlessness," Dart explained. "It's the state we're both in, which is a symptom of the late stage of capitalism Western culture is currently in."

"Dart, are you reading *Lingua Franca* again?"

"Yeah, have I told you how amazing it is? Why doesn't everyone read it?"

"Dart...have I told you what an idiot you sound like after reading that thing?"

"Yes. You have," Dart answered. "Have I told you how much I don't care what you think?"

"Oh, my" Adam said. "I'm almost home."

"No problem, no need to chatter with me," Dart said. "I just called to make sure we're still on for tomorrow."

"Of course. Did I call and cancel? Did I call and say something that might lead you to believe otherwise?"

"No," Dart admitted

"Then why don't you just chill out and show up here tomorrow after 10, and it'll all be okay."

"Do you think I advance-worry?"

"No, Dart, I would never think something as crazy as that."

"I don't."

"Of course you don't," Adam said. "I never said you did. Okay, I'm really home now."

"Hey, but you never told me about last night. How was your dinner/date/whatever. . . ?"

"Interesting. I'll tell you about it tomorrow."

"Promise?"

"Of course."

"Liar."

"Oh, no, going inside. I'm sure we're going to get cut off. B-b-bye." And Adam clicked off.

Sunday, June 20, 1999

An undersea canyon runs beneath the Pacific Ocean along L.A.'s west coast. The whole city—hell, the whole state—is supposed to face west, but doesn't. Los Angeles begins where the coast swoops down to the east, then south, and then east again, like an upside-down staircase. The two main south-facing beaches are calm and family-friendly. The west-facing beaches have the best waves for riding. The waves begin way out in the middle of the ocean, as wind rushes against the surface of the sea. Surface water molecules bump into each other, pushing forward, creating thrust below the surface, building energy that will push slowly toward the coast. The movement is slow and steady until it nears land. The ocean floor rises up into the coastal plain. Then it ends. The bottom of the sea drops out and the water becomes ever deeper, which causes peaking swells to curl in on themselves and crash.

An area near Manhattan Beach called El Porto is popular with serious surfers because even if the waves aren't the biggest, they are consistently surfable. Wave after wave rolls in and breaks. El Porto is Jeff's favorite spot, and he arrived early as usual this morning—around a quarter to eight. His was the second car in the lot. Jeff was always early because he liked being alone on the water. He thought it made the sea feel even bigger, more massive, and more unknowable, which in turn made him feel safe in a strange way.

By 8:30, the rest of the serious surfers had arrived. They wiggled into their wet suits in the parking lot and zipped themselves up with the rubber-covered ropes that hung down their backs. One guy Jeff had admired often in the past—for his lean, muscular body, toothy smile, and the tight electric-blue trunks he wore under his wet suit—waved to him from across the sea. Jeff lifted his hand in return and smiled. Beyond them, a ripple was growing into a swell and would soon become a wave. They turned from each other to notice it. They each began to paddle toward it. Jeff must have been out too far; he couldn't get on top of it. Electric Blue was faster; he caught it, stood up, and rode it till it was little more than foam. Jeff didn't wait for Electric Blue to paddle back out—as he would have any other day. Such ambivalence surprised him. But Jeff was thinking about Adam—their plans for tonight, and what Adam might look like in a pair of swimming trunks. Would there be hair between his navel and the top of his trunks? What about his chest? Jeff paddled back out to sea knowing that Electric Blue would likely be back next Sunday. Opportunities with Adam were much less assured.

Dart showed up at Adam's house around 10 A.M. wearing a green T-shirt over a white T-shirt that hung lower, creating a band of white cotton around his waist. Below that, his jeans ran down until they fell in casual clumps on top of old sneakers.

"Hello…Adam?" Dart asked, pushing the front door open.

"Hello, Dart…" Adam yelled. "I'm in here."

Adam was sitting at the kitchen table with the *L.A. Times* spread out in front of him and dirty dishes pushed to the periphery.

Dart closed the front door and walked to the kitchen.

"Is there a reason why you don't believe in locking the door? Like, oh, I don't know…maybe because you're stupid?"

Adam looked up just in time to see Dart around the corner. "Yeah, that's exactly it."

"Whatever."

Dart sat down opposite Adam and declared, "I think I'm having an identity crisis."

"Why don't you grab a seat? Make yourself comfortable."

Dart exhaled dramatically. "School is over and college isn't for three months."

"I know. I'm on the same schedule."

Dart glared at Adam for a just a moment, then continued. "Well, it's a problem. I don't think I know what to do in the meantime."

"Huh…?"

"Yesterday, I worked my first day at Unitek"—the computer store where Dart had lined up a summer job—"and it was awful. I mean, awful. It was only my second day as part of the proletariat—that means the working class."

"I know."

"Well, I think I hate it." Dart exhaled again. "I just don't think I'm cut out for this real-life shit."

"Oh, God."

"No, really. It's bad. I can feel myself getting depressed. I'm not sure who I am without school to go to, without a goal—assignments, grades, whatnot. Without a goal, it all feels so, so…meaningless."

Okay, Adam thought, *Dart is seriously freaking out.* He'd felt the same apprehension lately, but had been able, at least so far, to keep it from overwhelming him. So he kind of understood. But Adam wasn't feeling that way this morning. He didn't want to get into it. He knew there was no easy answer to Dart's questions—he'd asked them himself too many times in the last week. Adam tried to change the subject. "Are we going to the movies or not?"

Dart looked like he hadn't heard a word Adam said.

"There's a new homo-flick at Sunset 5, which you know isn't coming to Angelito anytime soon. I saw something about it online—*Edge of Seventeen* or something like that."

"Great, they're already making gay movies about people who are younger than us."

"You don't want to see it?"

"Yeah, yeah, but…"

"But what?"

"You don't understand the implications of this," Dart said, his face twisting into a knot. "How can there be movies about people younger than us? We're still young!"

"Goddamn, Dart. Did you skip your Zoloft this morning?"

"I don't take Zoloft."

"I know, but you should."

"No, *you* should."

Adam raised his hand and showed Dart his palm. "Please, talk to the hand."

"Oh, God, I hate when you do that. This is serious. Can't you see I'm upset?"

"Dart, calm down. What about kids' movies? Disney and shit. They've always been about and for people who are a lot younger than we are."

"It's not just this movie. Every high school movie will now be different. It won't be about us. It will be about other people, about our pasts."

"Dart...shut up!" Adam stood up to clear his dishes. There was no talking sense into Dart when his mood was this off. Adam knew he had to take charge of their morning before it careened completely out of control. "If we leave now, we can get to the first screening."

Dart looked helpless. "Okay," he said with all the confidence he could muster. "Let's go quickly, because if I don't get out of this funk soon, well, I might just be lost forever."

Adam walked into the living room to grab his sneakers. He slipped them on, pulled on his zip-up sweatshirt, and grabbed his wallet and car keys from the little table by the front door. Dart was still in the kitchen.

"Hello, Sylvia Plath...would you pull your ass out of that chair? Let's go."

On the way to the theater, with the truck's engine rumbling along, Dart began to relax. For the moment, he and Adam both realized how good they had it. Whatever was in their past, well, it was in the past, and that was fine. It was safely behind them. Today, they were just two guys—free, in a way—and they were doing whatever they wanted. Dart needed to remember that while he didn't have any immediate goals, he also didn't have any immediate responsibilities. And that was a good thing.

Adam found a parking space under the theater, right near the elevator. The ticket seller was either very hungover or seriously stoned. He gave them both $17 back instead of $12, which they each took without comment and gave to the concession guy for tubs of popcorn larger than they would have regularly ordered. The movie had just opened, so there were quite a few people in the theater for a Sunday morning—most of them men.

"Homos are out *en masse* today," Dart said, not quietly enough.

Some were youngish, most were older—who else is up this early on a Sunday morning? Only the usual group of old ladies who saw every film the Sunset played. These ladies always sat near the back and kept their jackets on and their handbags placed squarely in their laps. During every film, at least one of the ladies would dig into her handbag and pull out a roll of Certs or a handful of butterscotch candies to share.

Two blocks from Sue's house, a big park had recently been renovated from '70s cheap to '90s chic. Part of the upgrade included a new running track around the periphery, which she used whenever she could. Every quarter mile, a little exercise station had been installed for runners to add intensity to their workout. Sue thought this was an "awesome" feature and utilized the equipment whenever she ran there. Today Sue finished three laps—almost three miles—before getting so tired she decided to cut across the park to jog home. There she peeled off her sweaty T-shirt in a hurry, revealing her pale frame, which was bisected twice: once by her black shorts and again by her shiny black sports bra. Sue considered the sports bra one of Western civilization's better inventions—so snug, so supportive, and so comfortable. She downed a big glass of water like she was a champion athlete in a Gatorade commercial. Then she refilled her glass, reached for her phone, and walked outside. She plopped down on her porch to cool down and dialed Jeff's cell.

With his beach towel wrapped awkwardly high around his waist,

Jeff slid off his trunks. Just then his phone rang. He grabbed his shorts, skipped the underwear, and pulled them on before looking to see who was calling. Once he found his phone on the front seat, he checked the number on the little screen to see who was calling. It was Sue. *Why not?* he thought. So he stood up straight, settled a bent arm on the hood of his car, and gazed out toward the beach. "Hello there, Sue."

"Hello there, Jeff. Where are you?"

"At the beach. Just leaving the beach, actually. Just packing up."

"Great," she said with a bit of urgency in her voice, although mostly she was just out of breath from her run.

"Are you all right?"

"Yeah, I just finished 40 minutes of running over at the park. It was great."

"Great."

"I'm glad to hear you're done at the beach."

"You are?" Jeff was suspicious.

"That means you can meet me for lunch. I'm famished."

"Sorry. No can do."

"Why not?"

"Got some stuff to do."

"Figured as much, so get your stuff done and come with me tonight."

"Huh? "

"I'm invited to this dinner over in the Valley. A birthday party for some chef friend of my friend Monica. She says he's a bit stiff, so the crowd may be, too, but the food should be top-notch and she'll be there. She's great. Did I ever tell you about her? We used to take judo together."

"No, sorry. And no, sorry, I don't think I've ever heard about her. And no, sorry, I can't make it."

"Whoa…" Sue said, frustrated and hurt.

"I've got plans."

"What kind of plans, and with whom?"

Should he come clean and tell her about his date with Adam?

No, he decided. Way too soon. "Nothing special," he said.

"Oh, come on. You never tell me anything," she said, disappointed. She took Jeff's reticence personally.

When Sue first joined the Angelito Police Department, she developed an instant crush on Jeff. She thought she was really in love with him. Dating a fellow cop is so obviously inappropriate, however, so she repressed her desire and turned it into a kind of intense adoration. To Sue, Jeff was perfect, not macho: a strong and silent type who did everything right and never got into any trouble. A year later, when they were assigned together as partners, Sue had the chance to get to know Jeff more personally, and she liked him even more. She quickly discovered he was gay, which one might assume would dampen her crush, but it didn't. Sue figured it out after they started driving around on patrols. Every man she'd ever met was unable *not* to look at women, whether they were women driving by, sitting nearby in a restaurant, or walking across the street in front of the car. With Jeff, she noticed, the most buxom babe could saunter right in front of him and he wouldn't even notice.

"Okay. I guess I'll have to go alone," Sue whined.

"Have a good time and remember everything they serve so you can tell me all about it on Tuesday."

Adam and Dart both thought *Edge of Seventeen* was only "pretty good."

"I learned something," Dart said.

"What? That the Midwest sucks?"

"Yeah, and…"

"And what?"

"And that some guys dress worse than you do," Adam said as he pushed open the exit.

"You are so bitter for your age."

"What does my age have to do with it?" Adam asked.

"Nothing, nothing, sweetie."

On the way back to the truck, they squinted in the bright afternoon sun.

"I did like the music," Adam said. "Wonder if they'll put out a soundtrack."

"You would," Dart said. "Is '80s New Wave going to replace Surfer Pop now?"

Adam easily ignored Dart's bitchiness. Movies did that for him: They chilled him out, reminded him that everything was going to be okay, in some little way. "What do you want to do now?" he asked.

"I don't know."

"Me neither."

"How weird is that?" Dart asked, looking at Adam for help.

"Very."

They cruised out of the parking lot at a moderate speed. As they drove faster, the open windows traded warm air for cool until it was the same temperature inside as out. They drove and turned, slowed and stopped, and drove again until they were back at Adam's house.

"We're on the verge of becoming aimless," Dart said as Adam turned off the engine.

"You think?" Adam asked, wondering whether there wasn't some truth to Dart's conclusion. After all, he'd never experienced such a profound transitional period in his life.

Dart turned and stared out the window toward Adam's house and front yard. He was so anxious, couldn't stop feeling guilty for being so unproductive. "I know what you should do," Dart finally said.

"What?"

"Mow this lawn. It looks like shit."

"Um. Hello? When did you become Martha-fucking-Stewart?"

"Well. Your dad used to tell you when it looked like shit. I guess that's my job now."

Adam opened his door and got out. Dart followed. Adam's first instinct was to tell Dart to fuck off. Who did he think he was? Then he looked at the lawn and couldn't deny that is was more than a bit overgrown. And, yes, Jeff was coming over later, but God, how he hated to admit Dart was ever right. "It's not exactly at the 'shit' stage," Adam said.

Before Dart could respond, Adam walked over to the garage and swung open the heavy door. He pulled the lawn mower out and checked the gas: still full. He pulled the ignition cord again and again until the machine finally rumbled to life. *Why,* he thought, *has no one invented an easier way to start a lawn mower? Really. This pulling shit sucked.* Adam rolled the mower down the driveway to the edge of the front lawn and began. He went back and forth, forth and back until the front was covered with clean, green stripes. He pushed the mower through a small side gate and created the same back and forth pattern in the backyard, except where a few trees and shrubs around the edges forced him out of his decidedly logical path. When he finished as much of the lawn as he could with the mower, he maneuvered an orange Weed Wacker around the edges of the aforementioned trees and shrubs, around the sidewalk, and across the skinny front strip of lawn between the sidewalk and the street.

The two hours he spent working weren't more time than he usually spent, but Adam was very aware of a major difference: Today his mood was lighter. Usually, when he mowed the lawn, seeds of bitterness were sowed. Adam spent the time wondering why he had to do this. Why wasn't it his dad's job to take care of the yard? After all, he hadn't chosen to live in a house with a big, boring lawn in the front and back. Today Adam didn't think about these things. So what if his dad hadn't been able to find the energy to take care of the yard. Hadn't he always found enough energy to basically take care of him and Sandra? Wasn't that enough? Adam wondered whether he was the most selfish person in the world for having thought otherwise.

Dart passed the time reading magazines inside Adam's house. When he couldn't read another story about Meg Ryan's divorce, he stood up and looked outside. He stuck his head through the sliding door and yelled, "Mr. Man...you are sweating bullets."

"Yeah, well, it's a million fucking degrees out here."

"Why don't I make you something cold to drink?"

"Yeah, why don't you?"

Dart liked the way "something cold to drink" rolled off his

tongue. It reminded him of his grandmother, who always called anything with ice a "cold drink."

"Think you know how to make lemonade?" Adam asked.

"Of course I do."

"Well use the pile of limes on the table. I had to pick them up from that stupid tree over there."

"Where?"

"Right there. On the table."

"Let me guess: limeade?"

"You think you can make it?"

"Of course. I am the Martha-fucking-Stewart of limeade," Dart declared.

"Well, then, Martha, go get busy before I have heat stroke."

Dart grabbed as many limes from the picnic table as he could carry and went back inside. Fifteen minutes later, he returned, wearing a white apron wrapped around his waist and carrying two tall glasses of something slightly greenish and icy-looking.

"Oh, what a good little wifey you will be," Adam said, one hand on the Weed Whacker and the other on his hip. What a man Adam *almost* was, Dart thought. His muscles were clearly developing. His posture was ever so slightly becoming that of a man trying to take up the most amount of space in the world that he could.

Dart sauntered over like a slutty waitress. "This one is yours," he said, handing Adam a glass. "This one's mine. It's got an extra splash of bourbon in it."

"Yeah?"

"Yours has one splash. Mine has two."

"That doesn't sound fair."

"Well," Dart said, drawing the word out into at least three syllables. "I don't have a date tonight, Buttercup. I don't have to keep my wits about me."

"Oh, please. Not this again." Adam looked a little closer at the glass, brought it to his lips and tasted it. "Limes. Sugar. Bourbon. By George, er, Martha, I think you've got it."

"And you questioned me..."

"One lime drink does not a domestic doyenne make," Adam said. "And my dinner is not a date."

"Oh, yeah? Then what do you call a gentleman caller coming over for dinner?"

"Dinner. A barbecue, actually."

"Adam. No matter how you spell it, fry it, or grill it…it's a date." Dart took another sip. "The yard looks great, by the way. If he doesn't like you after tonight, you can't blame it on the ugly yard. It'll have to be something about your personality that turns him off."

Adam walked over to the small brick back porch. He grabbed a plastic banana chair that was folded up and resting against the wall, unfolded it and sat down.

"It is *sooo* not a date. We are just friends. I wish you'd quit calling it that."

Dart grabbed the other chair, opened it, and sat down next to Adam. "You and I are friends," Dart said. "And you never made me dinner."

"I bought you dinner just the other night. Pizza. Nobody called that a date."

On the way home from the beach, Jeff ran a few errands, drove through the post office, and picked up a 100-pound bag of dog food. He spent the late afternoon at home, cleaned up the house a bit, played with Chops, and washed a load of laundry. By early evening, he took a long hot shower, spending a little extra time with a scratchy loofah sponge trying to get as clean as possible, just in case. *Loofah? What a racket,* he thought. *It's bristly and it hurts.* No wonder he hadn't used it since his mom gave it to him as part of a Christmas gift years ago. Jeff washed his hair twice and even used conditioner, a bottle of which had been sitting in his shower longer than the loofah. Jeff always thought hair didn't feel as clean after conditioner, as if it was a little greasy or something. Tonight, Jeff used it anyway. He figured having softer hair couldn't hurt in the short run. But after he rinsed it out, Jeff started worrying that the fragrance in the conditioner was too strong, and the shy side of him came rushing to the surface. Adam might think he was some kind of a product fiend, so Jeff tried to shampoo it out with another round of fragrance-free Neutrogena shampoo.

When Jeff was finally satisfied with his level of cleanliness and fragrance, he turned off the water and began to dry off. Before he was completely dry, he wrapped the towel around his waist and moved toward the sink. Because he'd left the window open, the mirror was unfogged and offered an enticing view of Jeff's broad chest—its angularity, its bulk—and especially the hair that descended evenly across his chest before it tapered into a line that ran down the center of his abdomen, around his navel, and below. Jeff rubbed shaving cream on his face and then removed it stroke by stroke. Jeff followed this exercise with a splash of cold water instead of after-shave—another way he'd found to avoid fragrances while still closing the pores. He leaned toward the mirror to get a closer look, stretched his skin to see whether he'd gotten every little hair. His face, he thought, looked sturdy, only slightly worn—a state Jeff hoped Adam would find attractive.

Jeff unwrapped the towel from his waist. He wiped the few remaining wet areas in his crotch and under his arms until he was completely dry. He walked down the hallway to his bedroom, naked. He pulled open the top drawer of his dresser and picked out his favorite pair of underwear: faded blue boxers. They were soft from wear without being worn-out. More importantly, Jeff thought, they looked good on him. They weren't too long in the leg or too baggy. They were snug in the butt and loose in the waist, making him look slightly leaner than his 194 pounds. He looked at his reflection in the full-length mirror inside his closet door. What was he thinking? Why was he spending more than two seconds thinking about his underwear? He looked fine. *Same as yesterday,* he told himself.

Chops was looking at him too, the real him, not his reflection, as if he knew the difference. How did dogs know the difference? Jeff wondered as he bent down to rub Chops on the head. His favorite boxers stretched and wrapped around his ass in a way that made his behind look like a baseball player's. Chops wiggled his head beneath Jeff's hand. He stared up at Jeff in that desperate-for-attention way that makes people fall madly in love with their pets. Was this the look of a dog that knows another man is temporarily displacing him from the pecking order of love and affection?

What the hell am I thinking? Jeff wondered. Why was this dinner making him even crazier than the one two days earlier? Was it because it was taking place at Adam's house, the scene of the incident, accident, or crime?

Jeff knew the facts. Well, at least, he knew some of them. Jeff didn't have any proof that Adam knew more about his father's death than he'd already told him. Why then was Jeff still a little suspicious? Why was he still nervous there was more to the story? Because in his gut he knew there *was* more to the story. There always was, wasn't there? That's life...isn't it? You never know the half of it.

At the exact same spot along life's space-time continuum, Adam stood in his kitchen dressed in his favorite clothes, the ones he felt most comfortable in, the ones that made him feel most like the Adam he wanted to be. He wore a year-old pair of khaki cargo shorts with enough pockets to survive in the wilderness of Los Angeles for, oh, years at a time, if one had to. On top he wore a plain but bright white T-shirt, also one of his favorites because it was just snug enough to make him look bigger than he felt and long enough to hang over his waist without needing to be tucked in. Over the T-shirt, he wore a vintage gas station attendant's shirt, which he left unbuttoned. "Derek" was sewn with red thread into the fabric over his heart. Adam wore his Birkenstocks Southern California style with short white socks. They made scruffy shuffling sounds as he moved about the kitchen with determination. He'd already picked out the essentials—plates, glasses, place mats, forks, knives, and napkins—and was now working on the toppings. He had a question, so he pulled his phone out of one of his many pockets.

"Dart, it's Adam."

"What's wrong?"

"Nothing's wrong."

"Then why are you calling me only minutes before your date?"

Dart asked. "Can't get the barbecue started or something?"

"Helloooo," Adam said until the "o" was almost broken. "He's not coming over for 45 minutes."

"Details, details," Dart said dismissively.

"And it is not a date."

"Whatever."

"I need your advice."

"Of course you do."

Dart was sprawled out on his bedroom floor in front of his laptop chatting with Baby Blue.

"I'm making burgers, right?"

"That's what you said."

"Which is fine, I think: very low-maintenance, doesn't mean a lot, low investment personally."

"And this is not a date?"

"Dart."

"Fine, fine."

"But I don't know if I have the right toppings. Burgers can be complicated."

"Not really, Adam, but hold on for just a second."

Dart quickly sent Baby Blue an I.M.

"BRB in 5—phone."

"No prob," James sent back.

Dart rolled over onto his back, stared up at his ceiling, and decided that he really did hate Adam. How could he be so cute, so cool—sometimes—and yet so fucking insecure?

"Okay, shoot. And start at the beginning. You mean condiments, not toppings. Toppings are for sundaes."

"Details, details," Adam said as he stood in front of his refrigerator with the door wide open. "I've got ketchup, mustard, and mayonnaise. The hot dog relish looks a little old, but it's for hot dogs, so I'm probably okay without it, right?"

"Probably."

"I've also got Thousand Island dressing. Some people like that on hamburgers, right?"

"Nobody I know. But then again, I'm not as popular as you are—don't know as many people—so you shouldn't ask me questions like that."

"Dart, please! This is not about you."

"Go on," Dart said, exhaling deeply and dramatically.

"Lettuce, tomato, pickles, and cheese—both yellow and Swiss."

Adam started to calm down as he recited various condiments and realized he had pretty much everything anyone could possibly want on a hamburger.

"Why do you call it yellow cheese?" Dart asked. "It's not even yellow; it's orange. And it's probably some kind of cheddar, so why not call it cheddar?

"Dart!" Adam snapped.

"Lighten up, man. It's a joke. Don't be such a fucking freak."

"Sorry. I'm almost done. Bear with me. I've got an avocado that I was going to make into guacamole, but maybe it would be better just sliced onto the burgers. What do you think?"

"Hmm. Good idea. What do you have for pre-barbecue nibbling?"

"Chips and salsa. Fresh salsa. That's cool, right?"

"It's pretty generic, don't you think? Fresh salsa was new and cool like two years ago. Make the guacamole anyway. It's better than salsa and if he's really into avocados—like say he turns out to have an avocado fetish or something…"

"Dart."

"Okay, okay. Well, let's just say that if he is really into avocados, he can put guacamole on his burger as well as dip his pre-dinner chips into it."

"Good idea. You don't think I'm preparing too much, do you? It's supposed to be a simple barbecue. "

"No, no. You're fine." Dart thought Adam had certainly lost his mind, but as a best friend he knew when to keep his thoughts to himself. Tonight was the rare instance when he followed through and didn't say what he really thought.

"Okay. That's it, I guess," Adam said with a sigh.

"Good luck," Dart said reluctantly. "And call me later."

"Okay, okay. Bye."

Adam finished his preparations by straightening up the house, refolding the afghan on the back of the couch, fluffing the pillows, straightening the magazines Dart had spread across the coffee table, and picking up the dirty clothes lying around his room. While he worked, he felt strange inklings of guilt mixed with loneliness and wondered what his dad would have thought of his having a 38-year-old man over for dinner. Technically, Jeff was old enough to be his dad. And there was only a 13-year difference in age between Jeff and his dad. Maybe they would have gotten along in some weird brotherly way. Or maybe not. Maybe Greg would have completely disapproved. Maybe he would've worried his son had a serious father-figure issue or something. Adam wondered whether he would ever have had the courage to bring home a date—or even, someday, a boyfriend. There was little point in wondering about such things, Adam decided. They just didn't matter. Then again, if they really didn't matter, why did he keep obsessing about them?

"Back," Dart typed into his computer.

"Cool."

"Friend in culinary crisis."

"RU a culinary crisis counselor?" Mr. Blue Eyes asked.

"Only when called upon."

"Good 2 know. I've been without one for a while…it's good to know I've met someone I can call on in times of culinary need."

Dart knew sarcasm when he saw it, but didn't care. *Good 2 know. Someone to call. Times of Need.* These were phrases that made Dart very happy—happy in ways he didn't yet know how to explain.

Jeff drove by the Sev on his way to Adam's. It was only one of 5,700 7-Elevens in the world, and he was one of six million individuals to visit one today. He pulled into the lot and went inside. He grabbed a six-pack of Dr. Pepper from the bank of refrigerators that lined an entire wall filled with more kinds of juice, beer, water, and soda than anyone could ever drink in a lifetime. Each 7-Eleven carries up to 2,500 different products—a number Jeff had no time to fathom. He traded money for the soda at the counter and left. On his way back to the car, he glanced over at the short dividing wall where Adam and his friends hung out. He could see shoe marks and scuffs along the beige stucco, something he'd never noticed before. Jeff decided he liked the wall, scuffs and all. It had become, for him, a significant place in his own personal pantheon of Southern California historic sites.

Jeff parked his Bronco in front of Adam's house and hopped out like a kid on the way to buy new shoes. While locking the door, he checked himself out in the window's reflection. *Not too much effort with the outfit? No.* Jeans and a clean T-shirt are about as casual as you can get, he had to admit.

Ding, ding, ding...dong rang the synthetic bell. Very medieval-techno. Jeff stepped back.

Only minutes before, Adam finished preparing the house and had settled into the couch to kill time in front of the television. His channel surfing lead him to an episode of *Conan,* which to Adam was the best and most homoerotic of all cheesy action-adventure movies—a veritable classic of the genre. When Adam heard Jeff drive up he switched from *Conan* to MTV and lowered the volume to an atmospheric level. Even though he could argue the semiotic significance of a hot guy in a loincloth on mainstream television so early in the '80s was a cultural milestone, Adam had absolutely no desire to let Jeff know he enjoyed such lowbrow pop culture. Adam also figured leaving MTV on was less stressful than having to pick out the perfect CD. Adam let a few more seconds pass—he didn't want Jeff thinking he was waiting by the door. Then he opened it.

"Hyello," Adam said strangely. *Yikes.* What realm of insecurity had caused such a stupid inflection? But before Adam could correct himself, Jeff replied.

"Hyello to you too."

Adam looked Jeff up and down. His teeth were so white. His chin so ruggedly chiseled. His arms the perfect length. Even though he was built, his torso was slightly V-shaped. The effect was accentuated by the way Jeff tucked a dark-blue T-shirt into his jeans. *Nice,* Adam thought. *Maybe too nice.*

Jeff reached out his hand to shake. Adam reciprocated.

"Nice to meet you...again," Jeff mocked.

It may have sounded stupid to anyone else, but it sounded perfect to Adam. Any ice between them was broken, melted down, and washed away.

"Come on in," Adam said.

Jeff stepped inside, and Adam shut the door behind him.

"Welcome back to the scene of..."

Jeff spun around on the slippery parquet floor and raised one of his big, strong policeman's hands into the air, as if he was a traffic cop signaling Adam to stop.

"Kidding, kidding...relax," Adam said.

"You know there are no such things as jokes," Jeff said with a smile.

"Yeah, that's what Dart tells me."

"Well, he's right."

"Don't tell me, you're into Freud, too?"

"Only the good parts."

That is it, Adam said to himself. *He's gorgeous, smart, and can talk about Freud without sounding pretentious.* "Come on into the kitchen," Adam said. "Can I get you something to drink?"

"Here, this is for you." Jeff handed him the bag.

Adam pulled out the six-pack of Dr. Pepper. "Right on, thanks. You can't ever have too much Dr. P."

"I was going to bring beer, but figured it might not be—"

"Appropriate?"

"Legal."

"You are so conscientious."

There was something else in the bag. Adam reached in and pulled out a bag of marshmallows. He gave Jeff a confused look.

"I didn't think it would be a barbecue without them," Jeff explained.

"But it's a barbecue, not a campfire."

"Details, details," Jeff said, curling his boyish grin into a devastating smile.

Adam had to look away for fear of appearing turned on. He looked down at Jeff's arms, noticed how the blond hairs twisted around his wrists. Adam put the Dr. P in the fridge. He found a beer left over from God-knows-when and showed it to Jeff. "Don't worry," Adam said. "I won't tell your boss."

"Thanks. I appreciate your thoughtfulness, but..."

"You're not comfortable getting all liquored up in front of me? Well, um, Dart made some killer limeade this afternoon. It's very seasonal," Adam said with his eyes wide open enough to show how not-serious he was.

"Sounds great."

Adam put the beer back in the refrigerator door and poured them both a glass of limeade. For a moment, no one spoke. Adam wanted to ask Jeff how his day was, but that's what housewives ask their husbands. Jeff stood conscientiously on the other side of the kitchen, wanting to ask Adam how his day was, but that was what dads ask their kids.

"Chin, ching," Adam said, closing the space between them and clinking his glass to Jeff's.

"Chin, ching to you too."

"I never know if it's 'chin, chin' or 'ching, ching,'" Adam said

"Me neither."

"That's why I say one of each."

"To cover all the bases."

"Exactly," Adam said. Pregnant pause. This was going to be okay. "Well, I think you've already had a tour of the inside. Want to check outside? See what I've done with the lawn?"

"Give me the grand tour."

To the north, past Angelito and beyond Los Angeles proper, past Santa Barbara even, on the grounds of Vandenberg Air Force Base, the countdown reached zero and the engines beneath a Titan II rocket began to rumble. Shooting flames became explosive thrust; smoke and steam billowed out from beneath the rocket perched on Space Launch Complex 4 West. Slowly and steadily, the rocket lifted up and away from its steel trappings, carrying NASA's latest satellite, the Quick Scatterometer (QuikSCAT). Its reported singular goal: to measure wind speeds across the world's oceans.

The rocket and its cargo lifted off at exactly 7:15 P.M. and moved in a south-southwesterly direction, quickly leaving Southern California for the sky above the Pacific on its way into orbit, completely bypassing the airspace above Adam and Jeff. The rocket chased the setting sun for two and a half minutes before veering more south than southwest over Mexico's Baja California coast. One minute later, the nose cone separated into two parts and fell away. Two minutes later, the second-stage engine dropped. And 16 seconds later, the rocket named Titan turned itself about like a parent shielding his child from the scene of a violent crime: The rocket rotated away from the sun's harsh rays to protect its cargo—in this case, QuikSCAT—until it was completely through the Earth's atmosphere.

Through the sliding door, Adam led Jeff into the small fenced-in backyard. The sun had already slipped below the house next door, casting a long shadow over everything. The green lawn looked darker, blue-green, like a lagoon. The smell of cut grass hung in the air. The plastic banana chairs were still unfolded, their finger-like stretchers long ago returned to shape after Adam and Dart had left them. Adam pointed to the neighbor's lime tree that hung over the wooden fence, its limbs weighed down by abundance, and said, "The source of the limeade."

Jeff kicked a few pieces of sliced lime splayed by the lawn mower. "Looks like you ran over a few."

"God. If you only knew how frickin' many I picked up before I could even start to mow."

Jeff turned, headed for the banana chairs, and sat down. He bent the back down toward the middle—*clickity-clickity-click*—until it reset itself, then he opened it up again until the back was at an angle he felt comfortable with.

"It's a nice yard," Jeff said. "Everything seems very alive."

"I don't know about nice. But it's definitely alive."

"It's nice and it's bigger than mine."

"I didn't know bigger was—"

"Sometimes. Not always, but sometimes," Jeff said.

Adam clicked the other chair into place and sat down. They were both facing the wooden fence, the neighbor's house, and the blue-turning-to-black sky. They didn't turn their heads; they just spoke with the understanding that the other was listening.

"I guess it's nice enough. It's only been my complete responsibility for a week. But at least there isn't a rusty swing set or crap all over place. It could be worse."

"You're right about that. It could be worse."

Adam didn't respond right away.

"No," Jeff added. "You're doing a fine job."

"Whatever," Adam said.

"You got a thing about compliments?"

Adam coughed. "Yeah, I'm allergic to them." Then he coughed again harder and started sniffling like he was having an allergy attack. "Oh, God, I am so…"

Now it was Jeff's turn to roll his eyes. "You are a piece of work. You know that?"

"Believe it or not, I have heard that line before—from my dad, actually. He used to call me a 'piece of work' when he really wanted to call me something he felt was probably inappropriate."

"Well, he was right."

"Yeah?"

Adam stood up and went over to the barbecue.

"Yeah."

To Jeff, Adam was hands-down, plain-and-simple, spot-on adorable. His khaki shorts hung past his knees like he was the coolest kid in school. Below them, Adam's calves were slightly hairy and bulged with muscles. Inside Jeff's head, an argument: *Sexy? Too young. Adorable? Off-limits. So frickin' cute—18. Smart? Wise ass.*

Adam was unaware of such important interior conversations. He said, "Once I start this up, it should only take 20 minutes or so. How hungry are you?"

"I'm hungry. But I can wait a little bit. I'm not going to pass out or anything."

"That's good. I'd hate to have to call the paramedics to come and pick you up here."

"Well, at least they should know how to get here."

"Are you allowed to make jokes like that?" Adam asked.

Jeff was slightly embarrassed. Where the confidence to make such a crack came from, he had no idea. "I don't think so, actually."

"That's cool," Adam said, wanting to show he didn't care. "Well, I'm starved. Yard work is very hard, you know."

Adam took the lid off the barbecue. The coals he stacked earlier were still in their slightly pyramidal shape. He reached down and grabbed the bottle of lighter fluid he'd set out along with a box of wooden matches. He popped open the cap and started soaking the coals. He kept squirting till the bottle was half empty.

"Easy Firestarter," Jeff yelled from his banana chair. "You trying to blow up the neighborhood?"

"Relax, I just want to make sure it lights the first time. Nothing like finding out 30 minutes later that the coals never took because you didn't make the fire hot enough."

Adam put down the fluid. "Stand back," he said, which wasn't necessary since Jeff was 20 feet away.

Whahawhahawhooosh!

Flames shot up, up and away—burned with fury—and then retreated back down to just above the edge of the grill.

"Hmmm," Adam began, "Don't see any fatalities."

Jeff stood up and walked over. He leaned in close, as if inspecting something on Adam's nose. Adam pulled back.

"What?" he asked.

"Just checking to see if you've still got your eyebrows. Looks like you do."

In Studio City—which doesn't host a major Hollywood studio or have a downtown that resembles a "city" in any pre- or post-modern sense of the word—Sue held a glass of white wine, something German, a Gurtzweimer-something she'd never heard of before but was enjoying nonetheless. Sue knew only two people at the party: Monica and her friend Bruce, who was throwing the shindig in Monica's honor. Everyone in attendance seemed either to own a restaurant, cook in a restaurant, or write about restaurants. More wine, she decided, so she excused herself from a small group that hadn't yet noticed she was standing near them. On the way to the kitchen, she emptied her glass in one big chug without even considering the 120-plus calories she was imbibing. Her recklessness made her almost happy. In the kitchen, she poured herself another glass. Actually, she held out her arm with glass in hand while an actor/model/waiter filled her glass with, oh, whatever it was called.

Sue ambled outside along a huge deck surrounding a very light-blue pool. A few men in colored sport coats with polo shirts underneath stood around smoking cigars. By the edge of the pool, Sue found a bench made of some oily wood and sat down. She framed her view to include a certain man who was handsome enough to compete with the view. He stood out from the crowd in a lavender shirt starched within an inch of its life.

With the wine sending her inhibitions on sabbatical, Sue decided to flirt. She fixed the slightest pout on her face and waited to catch Mr. Starchy's eye. Like most men who know they are handsome, Mr. Starchy noticed Sue watching him. He slid his hand into the pocket of his crisply pressed pants and posed like a man in control—if not of his destiny, then at least of his appearance. Sue closed her eyes just the teensiest bit, as if she was doing a very challenging crossword puzzle. It worked. He took that look of consternation as a look of interest and smiled to show how pleased he was with the attention.

Sue imagined Starch-n-Stuff becoming obsessed with her, buying her expensive gifts and sexy lingerie in perfectly gift-wrapped boxes. She swore she could hear him trying to finish his conversation and come over to talk to her. He spoke in shorter and shorter answers—

"yes" and "no"—with building impatience. She knew once he did get away, he'd walk over directly and at the very last moment, he'd take his hand out of his pocket to meet hers. Still warm, his hand would wrap around her palm, and he would say, "Hi. My name is…and you are the most beautiful woman I have ever seen."

In the kitchen, Adam pulled a chipped Pyrex bowl of hamburger meat covered in Saran wrap out of the fridge. He pulled back the covering and scooped out a handful of red meat and started beating it into shape.

"You know the secret to a superior hamburger, don't you?"

"Which secret?"

"This one," Adam said, reaching up into the cupboard and returning with a package of Lipton onion soup mix.

"That is no secret," Jeff said.

"I know. And it hasn't been since Lipton ran ads suggesting it way back in 1960-something."

"They teach you that in school these days?"

"No, actually. The history of domestic advertising is a hobby of mine."

"Please."

"You don't believe me?"

"Oh, no, no, no…" Jeff surrendered. He wasn't about to question Adam's hobbies or his sense of humor. He was enjoying Adam's company too much. He didn't want to admit it, but he was just a little thrown by the fact that he was standing in this kitchen with Adam, a 6-foot-tall 18-year-old boy built like a man yet still so obviously a work-in-progress. He was too excited, on the inside, because their conversation was flowing effortlessly. Jeff wondered why this didn't happen with other guys. With Adam, Jeff felt like he could talk about anything. He even asked Adam whether he'd ever seen a dog look at himself in a mirror. He hadn't. Adam told Jeff about seeing *Edge of Seventeen* earlier and Jeff said, "What, no *Austin Powers* for you? I thought that was the movie to see this weekend."

"It might have been, for the rest of the world…"

"Oh, right…but you are not the rest of the world."

"You're learning fast," Adam said, smacking the meat into a patty. "So, do you like 'em flat and wide, or small and thick?"

"Excuse me," Jeff said, "this is only our second…meeting. I don't know if that's an appropriate question."

"You got a hang up about what is 'appropriate'?"

"I don't think so."

"Let me guess, you like 'em thick and wide."

Little sparks of seduction, flirtation, and inspiration crackled in the kitchen air, invisible but tangible to both of them.

"Actually, mister, thick and wide isn't all it's cracked up to be," Jeff said. "For starters, we are a country of overeaters; no one needs to eat the big, fat hamburgers this country seems to specialize in. And secondly, thick and wide can be very unwieldy."

Jeff walked over to the bag of hamburger buns sealed with a twist tie. He untwisted the tie and pulled one out. Then he moved real close to Adam and his bowl of burger meat and held the bun in his two hands like a little pillow.

Ooh, ooh, too close—too intimately close—he is in my space, Adam thought. Alarms started sounding inside his head. Jeff looked straight into Adam's eyes and said, "I prefer my patties just a little bit bigger than the bun and of medium thickness. That way, while they're cooking, they can shrink down to the exact size of the bun and not become a mess."

The words went into Adam's ears and through the tiny vibrating bones of his middle ear, but he didn't hear them. He was looking at Jeff's eyes and noticing the little crows' feet that spread evenly on the side of each eye. Instead of listening, Adam was looking at the blue inside Jeff's eyes and thinking it was too blue, too open, and too damn sexy for words. Jeff noticed Adam's silence and wondered whether he'd taken the joke too far. "Is it so bad that I don't like a messy burger?"

"No, no." Adam pulled himself together.

"Because I can do messy, if that's easier. Don't let me become a problem guest."

"Please. I'm just a little thrown off by the specificity of your burger rules. I'll get over it. I'm cool. Very adaptable. So you like a burger that is under control. Ain't nothing wrong with that." Adam finished patting one into shape. "And don't ever let anyone tell you otherwise."

Adam's inflection confirmed that he was kidding and Jeff continued. "Like most things—" he began, "under control is under control and out of control is, well, out of control. And under control is almost always better than out of control."

"You saved yourself with 'almost' because I can think of at least two times when out of control is optimum," Adam said with a squeeze and a slap against the fleshy meat.

"Touché, but only sometimes."

Jeff laughed a tiny, embarrassed laugh. "So tell me your ways. When do you think out of control is better than under control?"

"How about art? What kind of an artist creates when he is under control? To create, you've got to let it all out, just let it all go."

Jeff paused. Adam was right. "Okay. Give me another one," Jeff said.

"Later, Teach. These gotta get on the grill." Adam started walking back outside. "You coming? Bring the spatula."

Adam dropped the burgers onto the rack with a thump and a sizzle.

"You may have a point there," Jeff said, watching him. "My problem is that I'm a cop. And being a cop makes you think about being in control all the time. Everything is about control. It's the only option for keeping the peace."

"Maybe control is right for that, but does it have to be? Is it really the 'only' option?"

"No. We just act like it is."

"Yeah, and why? Because you're taught that's the only way."

"I think I was taught that as a kid, way before I went into police work." Jeff's voice was beginning to sound softer, a bit reflective. "My life is so much about my job, and because my job is so much about control, I forget about other things."

"Like having a life?" Adam said.

The flames rose higher as the burgers began dripping fat onto the coals.

"Well, let's not get too personal," Jeff said with a smile. "I do have a life. It's just different from yours. It's not very exciting all the time, and it's not influential in any sense. But I wouldn't say it's insignificant."

"My job should be OK, eventually," Dart typed into his laptop. *"Selling computers is pretty easy."*

"Yeah? My job sucks," James—a.k.a. Baby Blue—typed back.

"What R you doing, again?"

"St. Luke's. Admitting office."

"Right. You should call it 'hospital administration.' Sounds better and I hear the pay can be good."

"If you're the director or something."

"You're not?" Dart asked, slightly worried that his sarcasm would be lost through the ether of instant messaging.

"LOL. Do you know how many moronic white-haired ladies work at St. Luke's?"

"No, I don't."

"A lot. If you need surgery, go anywhere but St. Luke's."

Dart dug his toes into the plush—but beige—carpeting that stretched from wall to wall in his bedroom. He was pretty excited to still be chatting with Baby Blue an hour after they'd begun. Did this mean they were becoming friends?

"I do remember a particularly high ratio of white-haired ladies to young bucks the last time I was there," Dart wrote, *"about 8 or 9 years ago…when my grandma died."*

"Nothing has changed."

"Did I just say young bucks?"

"Yes, but you wrote it, so that's only half-sick," James wrote back quickly.

Looking for a quick save, Dart typed: *"Am I on crack?"*

"Not sure. R U?

"No, but I need a good excuse for using such a corny phrase."

"No, you don't."

He is flirting with me? Dart wondered. *I think he is, and I am turning to mush. How gu-ross!* Lucky for Dart, all this nonsense stayed inside his head and did not make it through his arms to his fingers to his computer and to Baby Blue across town. *"What are you doing tomorrow?"* Dart wrote instead. *"It's my day off from computer-land."*

"Nothing planned. No work either."

"Hmm. Wanna catch a movie, or something?" Oh, shit! Dart thought. *Did I just ask James out?* But before Dart could panic too much, his computer sang, *Bli-bling,* and Baby Blue's answer arrived.

"Yes."

He answered too quickly, Dart thought. Was this guy desperate, a loner, not half as cool as he thought? *Chill out,* he told himself. *We're online. You can't read too much into anything.*

"Still there... young buck?" James wrote in a second message.

Oh, fuck it, Dart thought. *Go with it, go with it.*

"Yeah. Sorry. Parental intrusion at portal three (a.k.a. bedroom door)."

"LOL."

"You LOL too much."

"You think?" James asked.

"Not really."

"So a movie or something?"

"What's the something?"

"I don't know... maybe some young buck activities."

Too much, too much, Dart thought reading James suggestion. *Way too much. He's being way too cute.*

"So?" James asked again.

Oh, fuck it, Dart thought, and he typed back his answer. *"How about all of the above."*

More grease dripped from the burgers onto the hot coals—*sizzle, crackle, phwoosh.* Small flames burst forth until the next drip dropped and the flame sizzled higher. Jeff stood back and off to the side as dozens of little fires joined together to create a conflagration. Adam looked over before Jeff could speak.

"Relax. It's fine," Adam said.

Jeff's brow was furrowed. The light from the flames shined yellow and orange on his face, making him look, Adam thought, like the Marlboro man.

"I think these flames are about to become officially out of control," Jeff said. "I'm not concerned about this little bonfire you've created jumping from the grill to any adjacent structures…but I am concerned that dinner may be burning as we speak."

"I think the word you are looking for is charbroiled. 'Burning up' is so pejorative."

"Oh, right. I did see a Burger King sign out front. How could I forget?"

"You know that pile of stuff I put out all together on the counter, the plates and stuff?"

"Yes."

"Why don't you grab the last of it and put it on the picnic table with the rest—eating outside is fine, right?"

"Yeah, yeah."

"Meanwhile, I'll just give these puppies two more minutes, and then we'll be ready."

Jeff went inside, leaving Adam to fight the flames. He took two trips and set the table much more formally than Adam would have. On his last trip, he carried a handful of silverware and napkins in one hand and a big glass of water in the other. He put the utensils down and carried the glass over to Adam. Then, just when Adam had the last burger off the grill, he poured the water over the glowing coals, raising whistling plumes of grayish-white steam.

"Hey!" Adam protested.

"Pretend I'm Smokey the Bear," Jeff said. "Playing with fire is dangerous."

Adam lifted his hand and turned his palm toward Jeff dismissively. "Danger my ass. What about the marshmallows?"

"Something tells me that won't be a problem. One glass of water appears to have barely tamed these flames, not extinguished them."

The way Jeff said the word "tamed" Adam couldn't resist. *Well, well,* he thought, *there is a gay boy underneath that policeman's body after all.*

"I guess we could always steam them," Adam suggested, sitting down at the table. "Just because I've never heard of such a thing doesn't mean it doesn't exist."

Jeff pulled out his napkin and spread it on his lap. "You definitely didn't get your sense of humor from your mother."

"No?"

"Well, from my brief interactions with her, she's no, um, comedienne." Jeff searched his brain for an erudite-yet-brutally-frank comedienne. "She's no Whoopi Goldberg, that's for sure."

"No, she's not," Adam laughed. "Although with the dreadlocks, she does come close."

"Maybe you got it from your dad."

Adam was surprised to hear his dad brought up. He'd secretly assumed it would come up eventually, but so soon? They'd just sat down.

"My sense of humor, you mean? Some of it's from my dad, but I like to say I earned it rather than learned it."

Jeff knew by the way Adam spoke to stop. This conversation isn't going anywhere. He'd asked the wrong question, led the conversation in the wrong direction.

"Hey, I'm sorry, I didn't mean to bring up your dad."

"Forget it," Adam said, trying to act nonchalant. "It's no big deal. You can bring up anything you want." Adam took a bite, gave himself time to regain his composure.

"But how can you be over it when it's only been a couple of weeks?"

"I don't know, just am."

"Well, I guess that's cool. Maybe you're stronger than I am, or than I would be if I were in your shoes."

"You know," Adam began. "All losses aren't the same. Everyone isn't equal."

"Oh?"

"He was not exactly a poster child for good fathers."

"Not many are," Jeff said.

Adam put down his hamburger. He needed his hands free to concentrate on what he was about to say. "Another thing...when people die, I just don't get it. I mean, there's this thing that happens that is really fucking stupid. People die, and all of a sudden everyone pretends they were really great, perfect, and that they never did anything wrong, like it was all wonderful all of a sudden." Without slowing the words tumbling out of his mouth, Adam wiped a finger across his forehead. "Have you ever been to a funeral where you heard someone bitching about what a jerk so and so was, or what a cheap lying bastard so and so was? How about even a little bit? Like 'Oh, my sister was such a sweet, kind person I can't believe she's gone. It's terrible—but remember what a stubborn, old cow she could be about her house? She made everyone take off their shoes, kept rolls of plastic all over the carpet, and kept some rooms, literally, off limits because she didn't want them to get messed up. And if you ever tried to talk to her about her OCD weirdness—Forget about it!—she would have nothing of the conversation. You were the one who was crazy.' It's that kind of shit that I can't fucking stand. It's so phony."

Adam stopped for a second before continuing. "Things were pretty shitty with my dad most of the time and my sister and I had to deal with a lot of shit and take care of him, and we had to take care of ourselves at the same time too."

"I understand."

"Come on. How could you?" Adam looked at Jeff's sympathetic face, then down at his hamburger, and then back at Jeff again. Suddenly, it all seemed so clear to him. No matter how organized it begins, a hamburger always gets messy once you start to eat it. The less of it there is, the more it starts to fall apart, until all you're left with are crumbs and drips on a plate. *Whoa,* Adam thought.

He was seriously loosing it. Life in a crumbing burger? Way too symbolic.

"Adam? Is everything cool?"

"Yeah, I'm fine. Except for the fact that people always say they understand when they don't...they can't."

"You're absolutely right. I'm sorry. It's just habit. People say that because they want to comfort someone, and they think that by telling that person that they understand, it will just maybe, somehow help." Where such coherent sentences were coming from at a time like this, Jeff did not know.

"But it's not true, so people shouldn't say it."

"But the intentions are good. Doesn't that count for anything?"

"No," Adam snapped, revealing a level of anger he didn't want to show.

"Easy, buddy. I'm not the enemy here, remember?"

Easy, buddy? Adam heard the words, but wasn't sure what they meant. He played them back inside his head several times. By about the sixth time, he had to admit they sounded nice, almost sweet, like a really nice pediatrician would say to calm a child after scaring him with a tetanus shot. *Easy, buddy. Easy...buddy.* The words were friendly and casual, and rolled together like they'd been friends for ages, instead of just two single sets of letters always separated by a comma and a lonely strike of the space bar.

Jeff looked at Adam, tried to discern what was going on inside his handsome head. On the outside, he looked so displeased...with him, with dinner, the conversation, life? He couldn't tell. One thing was for sure: In between all the gestures and question marks on Adam's face was a sign that asked, *Whose side are you on?*

"I guess what I wanted to say is that from what I can see and hear, I think I can tell a little bit about how you might be feeling." *Urgh, this is getting so cheesy,* Jeff thought. *I must change the subject...quickly.* "And then I was going to suggest that maybe because you grew up the way that you did, well, maybe that is why you're so mature and independent."

"Maybe."

"And both of those are good things." The conversation's temperature dropped a notch. "And I'm not trying to give you some look-at-the-silver-lining bullshit either. You know that," Jeff said.

"I know, but that's not what I was trying to say. I wasn't trying to complain."

"Okay, then what were you trying to say?"

"Oh, I don't know. Forget it," Adam said.

"You sure like to say 'forget it' a lot."

Adam tried to go back to eating. Maybe he could forget about everything except the food in his mouth. Not a chance.

"Do you have any idea who my dad was?"

"No."

"Exactly," Adam snapped, but less aggressively than before. He sounded more hurt than angry.

"So why don't you tell me about him then?"

"Because what good would that do? What purpose would that serve? Remember: He's gone."

"I don't know—I mean, I know, but..." Jeff was grasping but knew there was something he wanted to say. "Maybe it's as simple as sharing something with a...sometimes just talking is cool."

"Do you have any idea how long he'd been depressed? Do you know that's why my mom left him years ago? Do you have any idea how many times I tried to get him to do something instead of hanging around the house feeling depressed all the time, complaining about his life?"

"No, I don't know about that."

"Well, it just wasn't something he could snap out of. And kids can't exactly divorce their parents."

"And you would've liked to?"

"Hell, yeah."

"So that's why you..."

Jeff stopped. What the hell was he saying?

"Why I what?" Adam asked, spitting out his words. His temper flared back up, just as it was coming back down. *If he thinks I know something more about how my fucking father died, why doesn't he just ask me?*

Jeff regretted the words almost before they made their way out of his mouth. Suddenly, he regretted the whole evening; regretted coming over at all. Adam was so handsome and charming and warm and unbearably attractive. What was he thinking—that they could become friends? Why did he allow himself to get his hopes up at all? Adam looked so angry, confused, and terribly hurt. Jeff was a little afraid, and worse, felt guilty because he knew he was responsible for not turning off the inquisitive cop in him for one fucking evening. Jeff knew he needed to make things right, and quickly, or the whole evening would be lost. He reached back to one of his oldest defense mechanisms—pretending that nothing was wrong. He reached for his glass of limeade and took a drink.

"Let's just forget I ever said anything, okay?"

"Forget it? Just like that?" Adam asked.

"Yeah. We'll talk about something else. This isn't important."

"You tell me I say 'forget it' too much…now you're using it?" Adam didn't sound as angry as he sounded confused

"Why don't we talk about…oh, I don't know…limes?" Jeff suggested. "They're underappreciated. How did lemons reach beverage hegemony?"

"You don't need to change the subject. I am a grown-up here," Adam said.

"Okay."

"What do you want to know?"

Clearly changing the subject wasn't going to work. "Nothing, Adam, really," Jeff said, and he looked down at his plate, feeling very humbled. He was apparently not going to be able to salvage the evening and that disappointed him greatly. He'd had such hope.

"I'm sorry. I really didn't mean to bring any of this up. I just wanted to hang out and have dinner. I'm really sorry."

Adam could not and would not accept Jeff's apology.

"Why don't you quit this nicey-nice bullshit and just say whatever it is you want to say and get it over with?

Once the words were out, it was Adam's turn to feel regret. Something deeper within him had taken over, not just his mind, but apparently his mouth. The little ball of anger that was always inside of him was now much bigger and lodged in his throat.

Jeff put his hands on his legs, felt his jeans and his warm legs. "Adam, I don't have to ask you anything."

"Not anymore? You obviously thought you needed to ask me something a second ago. What are you afraid of?"

"I am not afraid of anything," Jeff said, rubbing his hands against his legs in fidgety frustration out of Adam's view.

"Well, I'm not either." Adam cocked his head. "You want to know something about what happened with my dad that you don't already know? You think there's some secret that I haven't told you?"

Jeff stayed quiet.

"Well, there isn't. There's nothing to say. Some things just don't make sense."

Neither of them moved. The only sign of life in this small backyard in the middle of Angelito, in the center of Los Angeles, on a planet located on the periphery of the Milky Way—but in the dead center of Adam's universe—was the dusty crackle and intermittent pop emanating from the smoldering coals. Adam and Jeff stared at each other as if they were having a staring contest. Adam broke first. He hated games like this because he could never win them.

"Nothing happened that anybody would ever understand except me because I was there. Nobody else was there...remember? Nobody. So actually, I don't think it's anyone's fucking business what happened to my dad. And it's pretty fucked up that people only start caring about me, about what I've been doing, after my dad dies. Whatever, man.

"The facts are the facts no matter how few there are. He's dead. That's it. Any new story that gets told isn't going to change the facts. It's just a story, just what someone imagined or remembered, and we all know that's bullshit. It's faulty and filled with holes. It doesn't matter—does it?—what gets said or unsaid, who talks about what for however long. Yeah, yeah, I know…whoever talks most controls the story, controls history. But dead is fucking dead, you know? And no one else can talk about that night except my dad or me. And he can't talk."

"I know that," Jeff said calmly, trying to be a friend, trying to push his policeman side far away from him.

Adam wasn't done. "And no one—no one—will ever really know anything. It's impossible, really, even if you were there, like I was, 'cause sometimes shit just doesn't make any sense. Just like no one will ever really know what it was like to live here in this house for 18 years, just like no one will ever know how you ended up here tonight. Don't you think some things just happen for no fucking reason?

"Adam, I don't care what happened that night." And Jeff meant it. "I'm here as a friend. Can't you—"

"A friend with a lot of fucking questions!" Adam scrunched his eyes, shuddering with annoyance.

"Adam," Jeff said, his voice shifting down a notch. "I'm sorry."

The word "sorry" jolted Adam back down to earth, back into the present.

"Look," Adam said, and then paused to exhale.

Meanwhile, Jeff thought Adam was about to cry. And a shooting, painful sensation ran from Jeff's chest through his mind and back again. What had he done? *I am such an asshole,* he told himself.

"My dad died," Adam said. "He wanted to die, and that is all there is to it." Rocking back and forth, partly out of tension, partly to lull himself, he continued: "If you really care so much about my dad, then you should talk to my mother about how miserable she was. If you or anyone else really wants to know what he was like—why he might have fucking offed himself—ask Sandra or even Marc. Call his sister, Patricia. People know—they knew—even if they didn't do anything about it. They'll tell you."

Jeff didn't respond. He was waiting to make sure Adam was finished. He wasn't.

"But you know what? They won't tell you the whole story—my

story," Adam said, "because they weren't here. They didn't have to deal with him every single day."

The longer Adam spoke, the calmer he became. Something had clicked off and every sentence relieved him of a piece of feeling; the angry fireball inside him subsided with every sentence that came out. Finally, as he began reaching the end, he focused, looked at Jeff, and spoke as calmly as a ghost.

"Jeff—Officer Manfield—whatever," Adam wanted it known that he knew that it wasn't just Jeff asking the questions, "You already know what happened that night."

After the briefest of pauses, Jeff exhaled quickly and said, "I know…"

Adam kept staring anyway, as if to see whether Jeff was telling the truth, the whole truth, and nothing but the truth, so help him somebody.

"Really," Jeff said. "And look, it doesn't matter."

Stillness followed. But not really. Earth continued to rotate on its invisible axis and the universe continued to expand imperceptibly. A few more bites were taken, small ones—insignificant little morsels picked up and eaten out of habit.

"Finished?" Adam asked, reaching for Jeff's plate. He stood up before Jeff could answer, picked up as much as he could carry, and headed inside.

"Sure," Jeff said, but Adam was already gone.

At the sink, Adam dumped the pile of dishes down against the stainless steel. He put the ketchup and mustard back into the door of the refrigerator. He was moving slowly; he was pouting, and he knew it. He inhaled and turned to head back outside.

"Hey," Jeff said, stepping inside the sliding glass door with his hands full.

Adam tried to form sounds into words to say something but couldn't. When he returned, Jeff had turned on the sink and started rinsing the plates, washing crumbs and bloody-looking burger drips off of them.

"You don't have to do that. We can throw them all into the dishwasher."

"Sure?"

Is he blowing me off? Jeff wondered. *Doesn't he need or want my help? Should I just leave and write the whole night off as a bad experiment, a miscalculation, a missed opportunity?*

"Okay, then. I guess, maybe, I suppose I should be going." Jeff stammered like a schoolboy. They were words he didn't want to say. He let the sentences drift from his mouth anyway, as if they were balloons released into the atmosphere to gauge the weather where the eye cannot see.

"Before marshmallows?" Adam asked, his voice rising toward the question mark.

Jeff didn't lift his outstretched hands from the countertop. He leaned against it as if it was strong enough to brace him against all the forces of the world, or at least against the withering blows of this warm evening in a simple house. He shrugged his shoulders affirmatively.

"Cool," Adam said. Then he reached for the jars of pickle relish, mayonnaise, and Thousand Island dressing with its paper label—crusty and greasy at the same time—and put them back in the fridge.

"Hey," Jeff said, in a way that got Adam's attention.

Adam shut the fridge and turned to look at Jeff. They faced each other across the kitchen, 10 feet of linoleum—and 20 years—between them.

"I'm sorry," Jeff said, sincerely, as if he knew what mattered and it wasn't the linoleum or the 20 years between them.

"Okay."

"I'm sorry I brought any of this up."

"Forget it," Adam said, finally sounding like he meant it, like he truly wanted to move past it. "It's okay."

Damn, Adam said to himself. *Jeff was cool.* He stood there across the room and looked like a man, but he wasn't acting like any man Adam knew. He was kinder; his feelings were so much closer to the surface. He was easier to read, and that was thrilling. All his life he knew he liked men, thought they had unappreciated potential for kindness and strength, greatness, and surprise. It's not like he knew or saw or even heard about cool, understanding, sexy men, but he always believed they were there.

"Why don't you pick out some marshmallow-roasting music?" Adam suggested. "The stereo is inside the cupboard down the hall, first door on the right."

Yes, Jeff thought. *I think this means the score is tied and we are going into extra innings.*

He moved toward the stereo and over his shoulder yelled, "What, may I ask, is marshmallow-roasting music?"

"If you don't know, I don't think I can explain it to you."

While Adam filled the dishwasher, Jeff flipped through books of CDs, looking for the perfect disc. He wanted something clever, but cool, not too old—no Dire Straits or something that might seriously date him—and nothing too distracting. He breathed a sigh of relief when he found Air's *Moon Safari,* a CD he had too. The whole CD was great—moody, ambient, and seductive—yet as musical foreplay, it kept the bumping and grinding just below the surface. Track 2 was called "Sexy Boy," and it was one of Jeff's favorites. After sliding in the disc and hitting play, Jeff hit forward to skip track 1. On his way back to the kitchen, he wondered whether Adam would notice. As Jeff's shoes went from hallway carpeting to the sticky linoleum, the sexy synth-pop began vibrating through the speakers and out into the house.

"Nice," Adam said, closing the dishwasher. "You may be allowed to play DJ again someday."

From the back of the drawer filled with spatulas and eggbeaters, Adam grabbed a handful of wooden shish kebab skewers that had to be as old as he was, because he couldn't remember ever having shish kebabs of any kind growing up. They would work for marshmallows, Adam thought...then he stopped, as if he was trying to remember something on the tip of his tongue. Adam realized what track was playing. Jeff had not only chosen a good CD but he'd also skipped to track 2. His eyes closed almost imperceptibly as he processed the information.

"What?" Jeff said, noticing Adam's stillness.

Nah, too cute—way too cute—I'm not giving him this one, Adam thought. "Nothing," he said, moving toward the sliding door. "Let's see if you put the coals out completely with your water-brigade idea, or if there's still some hope for this barbecue-slash-campfire."

"Oh, buddy," Jeff said. "There is always hope."

"Give me a break. When did you become such a fucking sap?"

A few coals still glowed in the bottom of the barbecue—enough to emit a steady, roasting heat. Adam motioned to Jeff to help him lift the picnic table and move it across the porch until the end was right in front of the grill. Once it was in place, they sat on the end of the table shoulder to shoulder, with their feet dangling off, as if they were sitting on the end of a long dock overlooking a wide lake. Adam and Jeff skewered marshmallows onto the wooden sticks like worms onto hooks—only the marshmallows didn't put up a fight. The glowing coals were like fish, smart enough not to bite as the bait hovered inches above them. Instead, they stayed down low, nestled up against each other, and breathed steadily through their ashy gills. Each time they inhaled and exhaled with the breeze, the coals turned from gray to red and back again. While they waited for the marshmallow's white skin to turn gold, an easy quiet overtook Jeff and Adam—as if they knew they would be floating in this boat for hours and there was no urgency to chatter. They sat quietly until Adam decided to break the silence.

"Do you think I killed my dad?" he asked simply, not too loudly, like it was an ordinary question.

Jeff answered quickly, but spoke slowly, letting each word carry as much, and as little, weight as possible.

"I don't know."

"Really?"

"Yeah, really. What do I know?"

"I don't know, you haven't said, or asked anything…specific. You've just sort of asked vague, roundabout questions."

Jeff took a moment to think of the right response. He didn't want to let Adam off the hook by saying he didn't care, when he did care. But he also didn't want Adam to shrink back, and not share something if he wanted to. "Maybe I never said anything because I really don't care."

Adam took it all in. *What did that mean—don't care? Fuck, fuck, fuck. What the hell did anything mean?* Adam reached behind him and pulled two graham crackers from their wax paper wrapping. He gave one to Jeff and kept one for himself. He broke off two pieces of chocolate and showed Jeff how to use the cracker to pull the molten marshmallow from the fishing-pole skewer by pinching the goo between the two pieces.

"You have perfect parents?" Adam asked.

"No. My father is, or, well, he can be a real asshole."

"Yeah?"

"He never dealt with the whole gay thing very well. In high school, I was really into doing school plays and stuff, thought I was going to be an actor, a *real* actor like William Hurt or Peter Fonda."

"They are both skinnier than you," Adam said.

"Are you saying I'm fat?"

"No, no, go ahead. Just can't imagine you aspiring to be Peter Fonda. Maybe Warren Beatty without the schmaltz, maybe a little Robert Redford—you've got the face—but both of them are a little too soft. Don't you think? Anyway…I'm sorry for interrupting, go ahead."

"Yeah, anyway," Jeff said, picking at his marshmallow. "My dad was an ink salesman. He sold ink to newspapers. Sounds boring, I know, but you'd be surprised how much money there is in it. To him, all my stuff was too 'artistic,' which I thought was code for gay. So I figured if I kept playing sports, maybe that would balance it out for him. So I played baseball, sat in right field for hours on end waiting for a ball to come my way. I could hit the ball out of the park, so they kept me in the rotation. But tell me: Is baseball not the most boring game ever? Every game takes forever. All those tight uniforms and guys playing with themselves while they're supposedly adjusting their cups—it's so gay. And so macho at the same time."

"You say 'gay' like it's a bad thing."

"Oh, no," Jeff said, looking over at Adam and smiling. "I definitely don't think it's a 'bad thing.'"

"That's good," Adam said with a slight laugh. "But I think volleyball might be slightly more gay. All that jumping around, and have you ever seen the guys who play volleyball at the Olympics? Two words. Karch Karai."

"He is pretty hot," Jeff said. "And he looks gay. But I don't think he is."

"I don't know. I never slept with him."

"Oh, is that your basis if someone is gay or not?" Jeff asked.

"Well…"

"Don't answer that." Jeff said. "Please."

Adam wobbled back and forth on the end of the bench, easily pleased by his ability to tease Jeff. "Okay," Adam began, trying to get the conversation back on track. "So you're in right field and…"

"Yeah, so later on, during college, I decided I wanted to become a teacher. I thought I'd be a good one—sort of intellectual, sort of creative, sort of socially conscious. But then my dad talked me out of that too, and I majored in political science. Can I tell you…there is nothing scientific about political science."

"You must have been very different then. I can't imagine you being that easily persuaded by anyone."

"I guess I was flexible. My personality was…versatile," Jeff said with a smile.

"Versatile can be good," Adam said, nodding slowly.

Jeff continued, "After the teaching thing passed, or was pushed away, I got really depressed and angry and sort of had a 22-year-old's version of a midlife crisis after graduation. I was so bitter, so angry. At myself, mostly, because I realized I was such a wimp, a pushover for letting someone else control my life. And that only made me feel worse. I decided I was a weakling. Not physically, but emotionally. I was a mess."

"What did your mom ever say about this stuff?" Adam asked.

"Nothing. She's a smart woman. A head nurse at an old folks' home. But she was a wuss at home. Always deferred to my dad."

"That sucks."

"Tell me about it," Jeff said, poking his empty skewer among the coals. "So I decided I would do something really tough, something that would harden me up. The military was a little extreme, I figured, but becoming a police officer had some appeal."

"Like what? Other than the uniform, guys in the locker room…" Jeff scowled.

"Kidding, kidding," Adam said.

"I don't know. I thought I could become a detective or something. That takes a bit more brains, you know. Also, being a police officer is pretty respectable in some places. And respect was something I was always looking for from my dad."

"I wonder what my dad thinks," Adam said.

"About me becoming a cop?" Jeff asked, turning away from the barbecue to wink at Adam.

"I mean," Adam said, "I wonder if he regrets anything."

"That's not fair."

"Why not?"

"Because there's no answer," Jeff said. "You'll never know. You can't know."

Adam tossed his skewer onto the coals and watched it catch fire, curl up, and become ash. He leaned against Jeff, just a little nudge, something to tell him that he knew what he was trying to say and appreciated it.

"If he's thinking about anything right now," Jeff said, "it's probably that he never taught you how to light a barbecue without using half a bottle of lighter fluid."

Adam looked Jeff straight in the face. "You're not ever going to bring up this conversation again, are you?"

"No," Jeff said plainly.

"Good. Because I'd like to leave this conversation right here, tonight, and then forget about it."

Jeff lifted his right hand and put three fingers up and held two down like a Boy Scout. "Promise," Jeff said.

"Scout's honor my ass," Adam said. "I got my first blow job in the Boy Scouts."

After dinner, Sandra joined her mom in front of the television while Marc cleaned up. Vivian watched *The Practice*, a show Sandra found particularly unbelievable. But she wanted to be with her mom tonight, so she took her book—Madeleine L'Engle's *A Wrinkle In Time*—to the couch with her. Sandra snuggled up against her mom's warm body. Vivian hardly noticed. But she did wrap her arm around Sandra affectionately, if subconsciously.

As the coals burned lower, the lights in neighboring backyards slowly blinked off one by one until Adam and Jeff were together, alone. Their arms touched casually. They leaned against each other, enjoying the sense of someone else in such close proximity. Jeff's body was reassuring: Adam couldn't explain why, but he knew he liked the feeling and needed more of it. He leaned against Jeff a little harder, and didn't pull back, stayed in tight. Jeff looked over and tried to translate the exact meaning of Adam's gesture. Their eyes met again; if they had been actors in a movie, cheesy music should've kicked in. Instead, the hum of suburbia filled the air and they looked away from each other.

Adam turned back first. He started with his eyes on Jeff's hands. He read the skin on Jeff's right arm closest to him. He wondered where else Jeff might be as hairy. Up to his face. He looked at the pores on Jeff's nose, the sun-made freckles on his cheekbones, and in the corner of his mouth, he studied a tiny patch of stubble Jeff must have missed while shaving. Adam saw lips that were pink and a little dry. He found a small crack in the bottom lip and thought it was the most adorable thing in the world. *This is crazy,* Adam thought. But he couldn't stop himself. He leaned over farther, until he reached Jeff's lips.

Their mouths stayed connected for only seconds. It was the gentlest of attachments, followed by a slight exertion of pressure, followed by a slow release, a steady pull away. Once they parted, their eyes slowly reopened to face the fact that, yes, they were kissing each other.

And it was a good thing.

Adam began to turn his shoulders back toward the fading embers of their barbecue. Jeff stopped him, reached around, and put his hand on the back of Adam's head. He pulled Adam toward him until their lips met again. This time they kissed longer and harder, and only separated when they needed to catch their breath. *Never has breathing felt so necessary,* Adam thought, *and so unnecessary.*

Then again. Longer. With their mouths open. They kissed and pulled apart and then breathed each other's breath. Back again and their tongues met, wrestled each other, and took turns winning. Sweet marshmallow, dry crackers, loneliness, and anticipation.

They were making out. Full-on. The uncomfortable wooden table beneath them didn't matter. The exhausted barbecue didn't matter. The difference in their ages didn't matter. The different places they were each at in life did not matter. What mattered was that their arms reached around to embrace, hold, and absorb each other's warmth. Neither of them could remember what it felt like not to be holding each other. Neither could imagine ever letting go. So they didn't.

"I'm sorry," Jeff said finally pulling away. He sounding almost embarrassed.

"Sorry about what?"

"I don't know. It's just that I've wanted to do that since I walked in the door, and, well, it feels really good. Too good, maybe. I hope it's okay."

"Oh, I don't know. Has it been that long?" Adam asked. "You only got here a couple of hours ago."

"Details, details," Jeff said. "Okay, so I've really wanted to do that since I first saw you hanging at the 7-Eleven, and what was that…two weeks ago?"

"It's probably a good idea that you waited until tonight. You never know what they might have done at the Sev if they saw us making out."

"I hope, I think…" Jeff couldn't get the words out. "I'm hoping that you're feeling what I'm feeling."

"Didn't you learn anything earlier?"

Jeff looked confused.

"Don't ask questions you already know the answer to," Adam said.

"Uhhnyhhoo," Jeff moaned, stretching his arms up in exasperation. "You are such a piece of work. You know?" His arms stayed above his head, moving higher until they couldn't reach any further. Jeff looked at the sky, at how peaceful, deep, and almost black it was. He leaned back, pulled his arms beneath him, first resting on his elbows, and then flat on his back, like he needed a rest. Adam tracked Jeff's every move. Once he was lying down, Adam scanned from Jeff's jeans to his face and back again to the center, where Jeff's T-shirt had been perfectly tucked in. Now there was an opening, a wrinkle in time, a space between cotton and denim where Jeff's skin was revealed, tan and pink, marked by lines of darker hair marching down into the top of his jeans, the silver button an ineffectual stop sign.

This region, this erogenous zone, was now the sexiest thing Adam had ever seen—replacing Jeff's cracked lip from a moment earlier. Adam's hand lifted itself up and settled on the magic carpet of small hairs. Jeff flinched and grabbed for Adam's hand, but didn't push it away. He pressed it down against his stomach, held it. Everything was warm and hard, skin and muscle, soft and sturdy. Adam's hand tried to break free of Jeff's grasp to explore more, but Jeff held tight. Adam gave in and lay down next to Jeff, his free arm making a triangle to hold up his head. Their faces were back in each other's space, and Jeff let go of Adam's hand. He moved to take hold of Adam's head, gently pulling it toward his own until they kissed again. Adam kept his hand on Jeff's stomach, spread his fingers out, felt as much of Jeff's stomach as he could without being too aggressive. He slipped his pinky under the waistband of Jeff's favorite blue boxer shorts.

Bing, Bing, Bing, Bing, Whooooaaa, Whooooaaa, Whooooaaa, Whooooaaa, Reewruuu, Reewruuu, Reewruuuu… A car alarm started

going off—maybe out in the street or maybe inside Adam's head—
he couldn't tell. Adam pulled his lips away, rubbed his nose against
Jeff's cheek to show he wasn't really pulling away, and lay flat on
his back next to Jeff. They were two men on a picnic table in the
middle of the night. The alarm became a horn from a ship miles
upstream. The table was now a raft and they were two boys floating down a river. Their feet dangled in cool water; their bodies
were warm and dry.

Deep into a repeat of *thirtysomething* on Lifetime, Dart's computer
beeped next to his bed. *Bli-bling.* Having seen the episode six times,
the one where Hope has a miscarriage, he rolled over to see if it was
a friend or foe IM-ing him. It was Mr. Baby Blue.

"*Still up?*" flashed across his screen in a little white box.

With a flash of excitement, Dart responded. "*Yeah, of course.
What's up?*"

"*Nothing.*"

"*Boy, we're exciting,*" Dart wrote.

"*How was dinner with the P's?*" Baby Blue asked.

"*Palatable.*"

"*That good, eh?*"

"*They're my parents,*" Dart typed. "*We've been eating together for
years. Why aren't they as bored of it as I am?*"

"*I have no idea,*" Baby Blue wrote back. "*My parents still like each
other too. Strange world.*"

Dart settled into his desk chair and sat up straight. *Boy,* he
thought, *this is way better than Lifetime.*

"*Did we decide what to see tmrow?*" he typed.

"*No.*"

"*Seen* Star Wars: Episode I *yet?*"

"*Twice,*" Baby Blue answered.

"*Thumbs up or down?*"

"*Neither. Love* Star Wars, *so can't hate it.*"

"*Me, too.*" Dart wrote, "*But didn't love it. Hated Jar Jar.*"

"*Totally,*" Baby Blue's message began. "*When I saw* Star Wars *for*

*the first time, during the rerelease, I thought it was amazing, definitely
worth all the legend and hype."*

"Yeah. For once, the public was right."

"But the original makes Episode I *look stupid."*

"Totally," Dart wrote. Inside, he pondered the implications of
such a crucial cultural agreement. He pulled down his bookmark for
local movie times and started checking to see what was playing until
another message popped up. *Bli-bling. "We were basically born in the
wrong time...for* Star Wars *at least,"* it said.

"Yep again," Dart typed back. *"Hey...shit for sci-fi playing now.
I'm checking the listings. What about* Election *w/ Reese Witherspoon?
She's very funny/cool."*

"Have not seen it yet," Baby Blue wrote back.

"Okay then?"

"Great."

"Matinee?"

"Yes," Baby Blue's message began. *"Theaters are empty...no obnox-
ious talkers, etc.."*

"Exactly," Dart wrote, deciding it best not to point out that they'd
now agreed on everything.

"And that leaves the rest of the afternoon for young buck activities,"
James wrote.

To say that Dart was excited and scared by James would be true,
but not the whole story. Thrilled and terrified would be more accu-
rate adjectives. The more Dart liked James, the more frightened he
became. And vice versa. Dart knew there were too many possibilities
for failure; something could go wrong, and it could all end. He had
to push those ideas out of his head, Dart told himself, at least for the
time being. Because hey, there were "young buck activities" being
talked about...

"Call you in the morning?" Dart typed.

"Great."

"Thanks for the chat."

"U too," responded Baby Blue. *"U give good chat."*

"Blushing now. :)" And Dart really was.

"Note to self," Baby Blue's last message began. *"Get a webcam!"*

"I can prove to you what a city boy I am," Jeff said from his place on the table/raft. He lifted Adam's hand off his stomach—loved the feeling, but was getting a little too turned. Jeff kept Adam's hand in his and lay both down between their bodies. "I am such the city boy that I can't even remember how to find the North Star. I know it's like, find the Big Dipper and then something, but that's all I know."

"Good thing you live in Angelito."

"Yeah?"

"Because there isn't a lot of need for navigation by starlight."

"You're right."

"Of course I am," Adam said.

"You're cocky too."

Adam ignored the comment.

"I'll tell you a secret," Jeff said.

"Another secret?"

Jeff turned his head against the table till he was facing Adam. "Shut up," he said. "It's not that kind of secret." Then he turned back to look at the few—very few—little stars in the sky. "When I was little, I thought every time I saw a plane flying at night it was a UFO."

"You weren't the brightest kid in the class."

"I was inquisitive."

"Dart's really into the stars. He's got a big, fancy telescope and even did his science-fair project this year on light pollution in the city."

"Really?"

"Well," Adam said, "it was about how light pollution might harm people's sleep patterns. But it didn't really work."

"Oh."

"It's a long story. Don't ask."

"I have a lot of respect for people like that, guys who can remember all the constellations. It always seemed like such a cool idea, finding shapes out of nothing, people and crabs and heroes. Every time I look up there—which, granted, isn't all that often—everything looks completely different and the same."

"Don't forget, the whole plan was made up by a bunch of drunken shepherds."

Jeff turned again toward Adam and looked at his profile. "I'm not the first man you ever kissed?" Jeff asked with curious insecurity.

"That's quite a question. Are you authorized to ask it?" Then Adam paused to see whether Jeff would retract it. When he didn't, Adam answered plainly: "No. But there have only been a handful."

"You kiss like you've had a lot of practice," Jeff said.

"And like you're some kind of rookie?"

"Well…"

"Well, nothing." Adam changed his tone. "Successful kissing—I have learned—has nothing to do with experience and more to do with intelligence."

"Oh, God."

"No, really," Adam said. "I don't mean book smart. I mean, intelligent in that you have to know what the other person is thinking. You have to anticipate where their moving parts are moving to next, and more importantly, I guess, where the other person's thinking is going. Does this make any sense?"

"Yes, but you still need some experience to have figured that out."

"Yeah, yeah, yeah," Adam said. "Well, I'm 18 and this is L.A. There isn't exactly a shortage of guys looking to lock lips with other guys."

"Ai-yai-yai…all I asked was a simple question, yes or no. I don't need details, names, or telephone numbers."

Adam moved to kiss Jeff out of sheer…happiness? It wasn't a word, or even an idea, Adam was ready to consider, but it came the closest to describing his current state of mind. Then the phone rang, interrupting them.

Budabrrrng, brrng, brrng, brrng.

"Huh?" Adam said, lifting his head to make sure it was his phone that was actually ringing and not just another noise inside his head. "I'm not expecting anyone."

"Can't be for me," Jeff said.

"I would hope not."

Adam sat up, hopped off the table, and went inside. "What time is it?"

"About 10:50," Jeff said, but by the time he read his watch in the dark Adam was already inside with the phone in his hand saying, "Hello?"

"What the hell is going on? Why haven't you called?"

Dart was barking into his phone while sitting on his deck under the same night sky as Adam and Jeff.

"Dart?"

"Yeah?"

"What are you doing?" Adam asked.

"I told you to call me after ten, didn't I? And it's 11 P.M. You're lucky I've been chatting with James from the science fair. We're going to the movies tomorrow—not that you care, now that you're all preoccupied with whatever—but anyway, I was chatting with him, and so that's why I didn't have a chance to notice you hadn't called until now. What's wrong?"

"Dart, there is nothing wrong," Adam said. He turned to watch Jeff slide the screen door shut behind him as he came inside. "I've just been busy."

"Busy? Busy with what? Is he still there?"

"Yes, actually."

"What is he doing there this late? What are you guys doing?" Dart's sarcasm revealed equal parts envy and curiosity.

"We're just hanging out."

"Oh, right."

"No, really."

"You are so lying. Is he putting some illegal moves on you?"

"Please, Dart. You are losing it."

Jeff walked through the kitchen into the living room and fell into the cushions of the couch.

"Is he standing right there? Can you not talk because he's right there?" Dart was getting his sense of humor back, but his mock horror was bordering on annoying. "Should I come over?"

Adam tried to think of some way to get back at him. "Actually, he's right here and says, 'Hello.'"

"Hello," Jeff yelled from the living room.

"Hear that? I'm not making this up."

"Let me talk to him," Dart said. "I'd like to ask him a few questions."

"I'm so glad you called too," Adam replied. "I guess we're not on for the movies tomorrow afternoon now that you have a date."

"Oh, Adam, don't play that…"

"How nice for you. No, really, I'm so happy for you. I'll call you tomorrow and get the scoop."

"Oh, my God, Adam. This is serious. You are playing the I-can't-talk-in-front-of-my-new-boyfriend-game. You never play that game with me!"

"No…"

"And you're admitting it!"

"It was great talking to you too…no, thank you. Thanks for calling."

"Adam! You are not going to hang up on—"

Click. Adam knew he was probably throwing Dart into a death spiral of romantic rivalry, and for that, he felt slightly guilty. But he made himself feel better by remembering that he had promised to call Dart tomorrow. Then he would reassure Dart that everything really was fine, and not just tonight, but in general and in the future.

Adam laughed. There was something particularly exhilarating on a microcosmic scale about knowing you have at least one really good friend in the world who likes you, even cares about you. Adam rode the feeling into the living room, where he found Jeff sitting in the half-darkness. Some light from the kitchen spilled into the room and mixed with hazy blue light from the window facing the front yard. The CD player had long since moved on from Air. Who knew how many discs had played while they were outside? Looking at Jeff, Adam wanted to laugh again at the ridiculousness of what was playing: "Love Comes Quickly" from the Pet Shop Boys' *Discography*. He seriously hoped Jeff hadn't noticed.

"Sorry about that," Adam said. "Dart can get a little crazy sometimes. He means well, but he's still crazy."

Jeff reached his hand out as if to say, No problem, buddy. Don't worry about it. Adam answered his gesture by plopping himself down on the couch right next to him. Together, they sunk further into the cushions.

"This couch is a piece of shit," Adam said.

"Shshsh," Jeff said as he reached around and nestled his face between Adam's neck and shoulder. Jeff's nose and mouth found where Adam's shirt met his neck and he began tickling his neck with his lips. Adam cringed and squeezed Jeff's face between his head and shoulders. Adam reached a hand behind Jeff's head, felt his thick, sunburned hair.

The house was empty, all the beds unoccupied. The possibilities for how the evening might yet unfold were endless, and Adam and Jeff both knew it. Their actions became more tentative than they were outside. Jeff wasn't sure how far Adam wanted to go, and Adam wasn't sure how far Jeff would let him go. But two guys can't kiss forever before hands end up beneath shirts and belts start getting unbuckled. Crotches get rubbed and the contents get aroused. Unstated wishes, desires, and hopes are revealed. Adam explored the hot and slightly sticky area where the elastic of Jeff's boxers kept him out. Jeff found Adam's nipples and rubbed them between his finger and thumb. They found ways to rub their bodies against each other until they were horizontal. Adam pulled up and took off "Derek" and then his T-shirt. Jeff thought Adam's chest gleamed something crazy in the shadowy light.

"Take off yours too," Adam whispered.

And Jeff did. He pulled his T-shirt up and over his head in one quick move, revealing a slight eagerness. The short hairs on Jeff's stomach were shiny like silk. The hair on Jeff's chest was evenly distributed, only barely hiding the muscles that held him together.

"Hold on," Adam whispered. "Let me get some water."

Both men thought, *Holy shit! What is going on?* And both men thought, *Whatever it is—it's more than okay.*

Adam returned with a cold bottle of water from the refrigerator. He unscrewed the cap and began drinking while he walked back into the living room. Jeff admired Adam's silhouette as the kitchen light shined behind him. How well-defined he was, how irresistibly sexy. Adam stopped in front of Jeff and held out the bottle. With Adam's crotch directly at eye level, Jeff couldn't help but notice Adam's state of arousal. This turned Jeff on even more. The idea that he was turning someone on always felt like finding the solution to one of the world's greatest mysteries.

"Thanks," Jeff said, taking the wet bottle from Adam's hand. He lifted it up to his mouth and drank without ever taking his eyes away from Adam, who stood silently in front of him. Jeff put the bottle down between his legs and exhaled. Adam held out the cap and Jeff screwed it on with a smile, glad that Adam had anticipated his need, even one as simple as a bottle cap. Jeff reached out, grabbed the top of Adam's shorts to pull him nearer. But no. Adam grabbed Jeff's hand and held it in place.

"Come on. Let's go to my room."

Adam leaned back and pulled Jeff up from the couch. They met face-to-face. Their chests touched, their torsos connected, their crotches met again and shared not-so-secret information.

"Uhmhmm," Jeff mumbled, the pleasure too much to keep inside.

Adam wasn't as comfortable expressing his feelings. There were too many of them, and they were coming too quickly. He didn't know how to express them. Adam diverted Jeff's face from his neck and kissed him on the mouth, immunizing himself from the need to speak. Then Adam pulled back, turned away, and led Jeff by the hand down the hall.

Adam sat down first. His weight pushed into the mattress and he kicked off his Birks. Adam pulled Jeff down with him and they lay back together. Their combined weight collapsed into a pile of limbs and sheets, ideas and past disappointments, immediate desires and future plans.

And that was it, really. There were no more hesitations or questions or interruptions. Adam and Jeff went at each other like children finally released onto the playground for recess. They wrestled and rolled, turned and grinded, kissed and smelled, looked and tasted. When Jeff rubbed Adam's hard-on through his pants—squeezed down intensely—Adam followed suit. He began in the back, reached inside Jeff's shorts, and felt the fuzzy, warm softness of his butt. Adam ran his hand around and over and down, and he felt the little hairs in Jeff's crack. He squeezed his hand past Jeff's hip to the front and found his penis. His balls were hot and loose, sweaty. Adam wrapped his hand around Jeff and moved his hand from scrotum to shaft to head until he discovered a drip of something wet at the top.

This sent little electric shocks through Jeff. He pushed Adam away and onto his back so they were side by side. Jeff slid his hand across Adam's smooth chest, down his belly, and below. His eyes followed his hand as it moved further down and slid between Adam's shorts and skin. Jeff pushed his hand past the waistband of Adam's underwear, through his warm hair, until he found Adam's very hard penis. It was larger than Jeff had imagined, thicker too. Jeff held it tightly inside his fist while he leaned down to kiss Adam hard on the mouth.

Adam reciprocated, letting his tongue enter Jeff's mouth before pulling it back and taking Jeff's with him. Adam rubbed his hand across Jeff's chest until he found each nipple, grabbed each pec, and squeezed like he needed to make sure Jeff was real. He grabbed at Jeff's shoulder and kneaded the taut muscles just beneath the skin.

With a grunt, Jeff sat up and pulled off Adam's shorts. He threw them onto the floor and looked at Adam's naked body on the bed. Unraveled, Adam reminded Jeff how long a man can be without clothing to divide his body. Jeff lay down right on top of Adam's naked body and released his weight. "Grrrrrr," Jeff mumbled, wanting to devour Adam.

"Take your pants off," Adam said.

Jeff pushed himself up and stood. He kicked off his jeans quickly but left his favorite boxers on. Adam sat up, opened his mind and his eyes wide enough to take in Jeff's almost naked body. *This is it,* Adam thought. *This is what adolescence is for. You go through all that shit so you can grow up and become a man and play with other men who are naked and beautiful and want to play with you.*

In his baby-blue boxers, Jeff looked like a boy at a sleepover—which is exactly what Adam now hoped this would become. Adam reached out and grabbed Jeff by his hips, pulled him closer, and pushed Jeff's boxers down for him. He had to pull the front out to get it over Jeff's hard-on, which was pointing right up to the stars. Adam put his mouth around it. Dry, a little salty. Downward he moved until the slightest scent of shampoo mixed with sweat.

Jeff wanted back down on the bed—not because it didn't feel amazing—but because he wanted to feel Adam's whole body and not just his mouth. Again they became a tangle of parts: pushing and pulling, rubbing and squeezing, tasting, nibbling, sucking, licking, and breathing.

At some point—it's unclear exactly when—Adam and Jeff stopped being Adam and Jeff and became two men, two bodies, two centers of gravity drawing closer together. As people, personalities, as individuals, they drifted out of their bodies and became observers of their own actions.

Adam looked down on himself and wondered why he was feeling so good. Was it Jeff? Was it sex? Was it merely a chemical reaction in his brain triggered by the stimulation of certain parts of his body? Or was it psychological, a consequence of being with someone without clothes, words, attitudes, or jokes? Jeff saw himself in comparison to Adam. Their bodies were similar in height but not in width. Jeff was hairier and blonder. Flecks of gray edged various patches. Adam seemed to have more skin, more surface area. But underneath, they were very alike. Both were strong and weak and hid that fact as much as possible. Both were afraid and boldly confident at the same time. Tonight their insecurities were not on display, their vulnerabilities not so vividly apparent.

For each of them, being touched and kissed in places usually hidden from view felt like someone, somewhere, was trying to make contact. A message was being sent from somewhere in the universe that said that everything, somehow, was going to be okay. Both men knew there were many meanings—and repercussions—for what they were doing, yet they didn't care. That was for tomorrow, or the day after that. For now, everything was perfect.

Back on earth, on the bed in the middle of Adam's bedroom, Adam pulled on Jeff's balls and licked his dick—down and up and down and up—until Jeff said, "Uhh, I'm…"

And Adam let go. Jeff clenched his teeth and started to cum. He exhaled and inhaled like he couldn't get enough oxygen, like he'd been holding his breath for hours, and then he grabbed hold of himself. Adam grabbed on too, and Jeff wrapped his hand around Adam's. Together they held onto Jeff. They moved up and down, up and down—together—until Jeff sputtered and shook and vibrated until any further stimulation caused him to squirm and giggle. Adam jumped to his knees and started beating off. He came quickly—almost instantly. Then, Adam collapsed onto the twisted sheets. Jeff reached his arm out and across Adam's chest. He pulled Adam closer and they lay in close contact with as many parts touching each other as possible.

When their breathing returned to normal, Adam was the first to speak. "Come with me," he said, getting up slowly. Jeff followed Adam to the bathroom down the hall. Adam handed Jeff a towel and turned on the faucet.

"Gay sex can be so messy," Jeff said with the sleepiest eyes Adam had ever seen.

"But in a good way," Adam said.

"The best possible way."

Adam moved away from the sink to let Jeff have a turn. They looked at each other's reflections in the mirror as they dried themselves off. Each of them looked more handsome and grown-up than he had ever looked before.

"Hey. Do you want to take a shower?" Adam asked.

"No, actually. I'd like to stay smelling like you for as long as possible."

"You're disgusting…" Adam said, turning to leave.

Jeff grabbed Adam's hand before he could leave. They walked back together, their hands fitting together quite perfectly. On the bed, they held each other. Their bodies warm and relaxed. Slowly, their skin began sticking less and less as the water and sweat on their bodies evaporated. Nobody spoke. There was nothing left to say.

Jeff wondered whether he should get up and leave, although he secretly hoped he wouldn't have to. Adam wondered whether it was okay for Jeff to stay over. Or would that be rushing things? It was their first time together, which usually means no sleeping over, Adam knew. But how could that rule apply in a situation like this?

"You can stay over," Adam said, rolling just far enough away to see Jeff's face, "if you like."

"What time is it?"

Adam looked at the alarm clock on the side of the bed. "Almost two."

"Good."

"Good?"

"Yeah, that means it's too late to go home, so I should stay over." Jeff waited for Adam. When he didn't respond, he added, "If that's okay with you."

"Yeah. I offered, didn't I?"

"Cool."

"Although I hope that isn't saying too much," Adam said. "I mean…I could pretend not to want you to stay over, if that would make you want to stay more. I know how guys work."

Jeff grinned, and Adam watched a slight dimple form in the left side of Jeff's face. Jeff felt Adam's eyes on him. He leaned over and rubbed his nose against Adam's cheek, behind his ear, and down his neck. Now there was really nothing else to say, and Adam and Jeff fell asleep. They drifted off easily, knowing at least one thing was for certain: Tomorrow they would wake up right next to each other. With that in mind, they slept with their limbs intertwined, like the roots of two very old trees planted very close together.

Monday, June 21, 1999

Against the dark of early morning, the fluorescent bulbs across the ceiling of Angelito's 7-Eleven make it brighter than day. The night shift ends at 4 A.M. That is when a departing employee must empty the garbage can stationed outside the front door on his way out. It is the employee's last task of the night/morning. Lift the bag, tie it off, set it down, reach inside, pull up a new bag, close the lid, carry the full bag around to the dumpster in the back, and toss the garbage inside.

This morning, everything went as planned. The departing employee dropped the garbage off in the back, as the just-arrived employee emptied bags of ground coffee into six oversize coffee-makers. The timers were set so that a new pot would brew every 30 minutes. By seven o'clock, there would be as much coffee ready as this one Sev could provide.

Two blocks to the east, a teenage boy of 17—maybe 18, judging by the softness of his scruff—wore a T-shirt that said No Fear. He sat on a bench in front of Pavilions. Open 24 Hours the sign above him read. Mr. No Fear didn't smoke; he simply told his boss he did, so he could get a 10-minute break every hour or so throughout his overnight shift, which he spent restocking the store's shelves. At 4:30 A.M., the sun was not yet above the façades of the buildings across the street, yet the first glimmer of dawn mixed with the lights from the parking lot to make the asphalt spread before him look silvery gray.

Two hours later and two blocks east along the same street, the big hand on wristwatches and clocks slipped past the number six on the bottom of the dial. It was 6:30 A.M. The ramp to the 110—the oldest freeway in L.A.—wedged off from the right lane. Even at this hour, the curved ramp was already clogged. A year ago, someone in charge of screwing with the city's transportation put in a stoplight where the ramp met the freeway—five seconds green, five seconds red—hoping to ease the congestion. The plan didn't work. Instead, it backed up traffic out onto the surface street. Five seconds green, one car goes. Five seconds red, everyone moves up. Every five seconds each car moves only a few feet closer to the flow of commuters on the highway. Every five seconds, a different car leaves the ramp for the freeway. Each car is different, holds a different driver, a different passenger. Each car began its life with a different sticker price, and now has a personal history of collisions and traffic violations, dings and scratches that are uniquely its own.

First in line at 6:31 A.M. is a green Chevy truck with a bearded man behind the wheel. He's wearing a ruddy canvas jacket, drinking a Diet Snapple Raspberry Tea, and listening to morning radio. Behind him, in a dingy white Corolla, is a young woman driving alone. She's using the rearview mirror to apply mascara with her right hand while holding the wheel with her left. Behind her is a Cadillac. A white-haired gentleman, a senior citizen he might be called, sits confidently behind the leather-covered steering wheel. He's wearing a crisp, white shirt, fresh from the dry cleaner's plastic bag, and yellow and white checked suspenders. He's listening to the news—politics, world headlines, and stock reports from New York and places where the day has long ago begun. He's on his way to an office where he has earned a lot of money. He looks, acts, and drives like he did when he first struck it rich in 1963. The success and security that his good fortune has brought, has also held him frozen in time. And why not?

The look and feel of the day he made his first $500,000 on a real estate deal gone wonderfully right are still with him as if it was yesterday.

His wife doesn't complain about his conservative attire. She was with him before that day. She knows the difference his success has made in their lives—what it enabled them to give their kids. She doesn't complain about his style or his schedule, his long hours or his resistance to change. She doesn't care that strangers see him, that new business contacts meet him, and think he's old-fashioned, maybe even an old fogy. As his wife of 54 years, she likes him. A lot. She thinks he's wonderful. She thinks he was a good father to their two sons. She thinks he is handsome in his white shirt, yellow suspenders, and black pants because they are, by now, as much a part of him as his crusted pinky toenails that won't grow straight. She loves him, actually. She thinks he is the most wonderful man in the world.